HOME

Print ISBN 978-1-63409-955-4

eBook Editions:
Adobe Digital Edition (.epub) 978-1-63409-957-8
Kindle and MobiPocket Edition (.prc) 978-1-63409-956-1

Scripture taken from the HOLY BIBLE, NEW INTERNATIONAL VERSION®. NIV®. Copyright © 1973, 1978, 1984, 2011 by Biblica, Inc.™ Used by permission. All rights reserved worldwide.

This book is a work of fiction. Names, characters, places, and incidents are either products of the author's imagination or used fictitiously. Any similarity to actual people, organizations, and/or events is purely coincidental.

Cover design: Kirk DouPonce, DogEared Design

Published by Shiloh Run Press, an imprint of Barbour Publishing, Inc., P.O. Box 719, Uhrichsville, Ohio 44683, www.shilohrunpress.com.

Our mission is to publish and distribute inspirational products offering exceptional value and biblical encouragement to the masses.

Member of the
Evangelical Christian
Publishers Association

Printed in the United States of America.

HOME

A Novel

GINNY L. YTTRUP

SHILOH RUN PRESS

An Imprint of Barbour Publishing, Inc.

For my dear friend Sharol
Thank you for so often asking the questions
I most need to answer. . .

God is at home, it's we who have gone out for a walk.
Meister Eckhart

He has also set eternity in the human heart...
Ecclesiastes 3:11

You can't depend on your eyes when your imagination is out of focus.
Mark Twain

If you do not tell the truth about yourself
you cannot tell it about other people.
Virginia Woolf

Chapter 1

MELANIE

I run away.
From conflict. From pain. From reality.

At least, that's Craig's assertion—one he's maintained through twenty-three years of marriage. Why do the odd-numbered years feel less certain? But I don't run away. I'm present. I live in the moment. It just happens that sometimes the moment takes place in an alternate reality.

Alternate reality? Mel, it's fiction.

Exactly.

The conversation is on a loop, set to repeat at least once a year. It came around again last night over seared sturgeon at Ella, where we dined to mark an odd year of marriage.

Fingertips poised on the keyboard, I squint at the computer display on my desk and read the last scene I wrote. It doesn't work. Something's off. My forehead furrows in a way I've noticed is leaving a crevice between my eyebrows—a mocking cleft that suggests Botox is my singular hope for redemption from the evils of age. I let the muscles in my face go lax and open my eyes wide. *Run away*, my foot. Wrinkles are real. They're right now. And I'll deal with them. I move the cursor from my document to the Safari icon and do a search for *Wrinkle Creams*. After several clicks, I end up on Amazon, where I pay $29.95 for one fluid ounce of "the most potent serum available," guaranteed to restore my skin to its once smooth and youthful appearance.

$29.95? That's almost four dollars more than my last royalty check.

Note to self: destroy the receipt.

I click back to my WIP—*Work in Progress*—or in this case, *Worst Imaginable Project*. But rather than read the scene again, my gaze lands on the Apple insignia on the bottom of my display, and my stomach rumbles. I push away from my desk, slide bare feet into slippers, and pad down the hallway to the kitchen, where I set a fresh pot of coffee to brew. I munch on a tart Gravenstein while I wait. In a moment of pure delusion, I bought the Gravs thinking I'd bake a pie for Craig. But who was I kidding? I don't have time to bake. I'm on deadline. After tossing the core into the compactor, I reach for a mug, but the cabinet is empty. My cell phone vibrates in the pocket of my robe as I begin unloading the dishwasher. "Hi there."

Craig raises his voice against the nail gun popping in the background. "How's your afternoon going? Words flowing?"

Afternoon? I glance at the clock on the microwave. "Dribbling. The words are dribbling. You're on-site?"

"Yep, remember? I have a meeting with the homeowners."

"Right, I know." Did he tell me that?

"Mel, I'm sorry about last night—I wanted to celebrate, not argue."

With the phone propped between my ear and shoulder, I set a stack of plates down and lean against the quartz countertop. "Yeah, me too. I'd hoped to make it up to you when we got home, but—"

"I fell asleep. I know. This job's taking a toll."

"You missed the big reveal—lingerie purchased just for the occasion."

"My loss. Rain check?"

Not even a chuckle? "Sure. See you for dinner?"

"Probably not. I need to get back to the office and get caught up. Late night."

"Okay. Well, hang in there."

I slip the phone back into my pocket and rub at the knot that's formed in my neck, a result of either cradling the phone or hearing the tension in Craig's tone—I'm not sure which. *Sorry I'm late. Sorry I'm tired. Sorry I yelled.* He's apologized a lot in recent months. Fallout from the job, he says—pressure as he adjusts to building high-end custom homes for wealthy clients, those who still enjoy liquid assets in this ongoing recession. The tract developments he built for so long are a thing of the past, at least until the economy recovers.

"Building sixty tract homes was so much easier than building one custom for entitled clients who think they own me." Craig's oft-stated complaint plays again. After reaping the benefits of a booming housing market in the Sacramento area and calling his own shots, Craig's frustration is palpable. Daily. However, his current clients, Serena Buchanan and her daughter—*the homeowners*—do sound like the epitome of entitlement, according to Craig's descriptions. Although, it seems his attitude toward Serena has softened in recent weeks. He said something about her being widowed last year, didn't he?

Widowed or divorced? I finish unloading the dishwasher as I attempt to recall details, but my memory of the conversation is fuzzy. What's clear is the feeling the conversation evoked—a feeling I didn't care to explore. That's it. Serena Buchanan was widowed.

Menopause is rodent-like in the way it nibbles holes in one's memory. Or maybe Craig is right—my mind is always somewhere else. *"Are you listening, Mel?"* How often has that question punctuated our conversations? Too many times to consider.

The back door scrapes open, conveniently scattering my thoughts. "Melanie?"

"In here."

"Is Craig ever going to fix that door?" Jill walks into the kitchen, grabs a mug out of the cabinet, and pours herself a cup of coffee.

"Make yourself at home."

She laughs and then turns to me, looks me over, and, still smiling, raises one perfectly plucked auburn eyebrow. "Nice outfit."

I glance down at the black satin peeking from under my robe and the plaid cotton PJ bottoms I pulled on with my nightgown this morning. I pull the robe tight. "I'm working."

"Clearly."

"And I need to get back to it."

Jill holds up one hand. "Hold on." She takes a sip of her coffee. "Why is your coffee always better than mine?"

"Because I made it. Anything we don't make ourselves is always better, remember?"

"Right. Listen, this is your afternoon reminder—we have group tonight, and you're leading. 7:00 p.m."

My shoulders droop.

"You'd forgotten, right? Or, better stated, you put it out of your mind."

"No." I pour myself a cup of the fresh French roast. "You know, this thing you do"—I motion between the two of us—"it's called codependency."

"It's called accountability."

"It's just. . .Craig is working late, so I thought I would, too. This story"—I shake my head—"isn't going anywhere."

"He's working late again?"

I wave off her question.

"So come and brainstorm. We're the Deep Inkers. We'll energize you, stimulate your creativity. . . . We'll work our writers' group magic. You know when you isolate yourself it dulls your vision. Anyway, you're leading—you have to come."

"Facilitating." I look at my neighbor and, next to Craig, the closest thing I have to a best friend, and I wish, as I often do, that I had just half her energy. Not only is she a sought-after freelance editor, but she also has three little ones to chase after. Somehow she accomplishes more in one day than I do in a week. Of course, I remind myself again, she's also twelve years younger. "Since you're reminding me, remind me where we're meeting."

"My place."

"Where are the kidlets?"

She takes a deep breath. "The kids are with Marcos's parents for the afternoon and evening. Marcos took the afternoon off and is there with them." She glances at her watch. "I have a cobbler in the oven." She goes to the sink, dumps the rest of her coffee, and then rinses her cup. After she rinses it, she reaches under my sink for the dish soap, thoroughly washes the mug, and then opens the dishwasher and sets the overturned mug on the top rack. Then she goes back to the sink and washes her hands, using the same antibacterial dish soap. She puts the soap back under the sink.

I watch her routine, mentally calling her plays like a sportscaster, but I know better than to say anything. We all have our quirks.

She turns to go. "See you at seven?"

I follow her through the laundry room to the back door. "What kind of cobbler?"

"Peach."

"I'll be there."

———————◆———————

I toss my robe on the bathroom counter, peel off my black satin night-gown and pajama bottoms, and then reach into the shower to test the water. Shivering, I wait for the hot water to make its way to the upstairs master bath. Where's a hot flash when you need one? I turn toward the mirror and startle at the image reflected back to me. I run my fingers across the pooch of my abdomen mapped with stretch marks. Having had children might make the marks worthwhile, but mine only remind me of the multiple pounds gained and lost over the last few decades. I turn to the side to view my profile and then lift my sagging breasts. It's evident I need more than wrinkle cream or Botox can offer. A silver landing strip has appeared atop my head since just yesterday, highlighting my once-natural, now bottled, ash-blond tone. Who am I kidding? My ash-blond is almost platinum now. Every time I've seen my stylist in the last year, she's dyed my hair a shade lighter so the gray roots show less, but they only hide for so long.

Is it any wonder Craig doesn't want to come home or falls asleep on me when he is here?

With steam collecting on the mirror and obscuring my reflection, I turn away and step into the retreat of the warm shower, grateful for an excuse to take a break from my manuscript. With hot water pelting my back, the tension in my neck and shoulders eases. But just as I begin to relax, an annoying question poses itself: *What does Serena Buchanan look like?*

I close my eyes and turn my face to the spray of water, considering the question for a moment. Then I file it in a thick folder titled *Things to Think About Later* and stuff it into a dusty cabinet somewhere in the back of my mind.

———————◆———————

I was five years old the first time I lost myself in a maze of words printed on a page. Or maybe I found myself there. As I sounded out the words, a new world came to life. The beat of my heart quickened as I ran with Dick and Jane. The sweet scent of freshly cut grass swirled as we yelled, "Go, Spot, go." Jane and Sally became the sisters I never had, and Spot was the dog I'd longed for. With head bent over that first book, my imagination filled in the details between the lines. Or maybe the lines blurred the details of my reality. Either way, as a child, books became my savior.

Books filled the empty space.

Stories set the stage for something more.

And later, writing became my religion.

I began writing during the years we were working to conceive. And it was *work*. I charted my basal body temperature each morning and wooed Craig home from the jobsite each time I ovulated. And every month, the cramping of my uterus reminded me of my failure. After two years of trying, we succumbed to testing and discovered I was the problem. I was unable to conceive.

Craig said he didn't blame me, but I blamed myself. What was wrong with me that I couldn't fulfill the most primal act of womanhood? I straddled the chasm of grief and self-loathing.

Then I buried my failure under a pile of words.

In a way, books saved me. Again.

A year after I gave up on pregnancy, my debut novel was born.

Now we're godparents to Jill and Marcos's brood. If anything ever happened to them. . . I shudder at the thought. Those tykes would run us into the ground.

After showering and dressing, I return to my desk and take stock. My word count for the day thus far is a paltry 453 words. This, my sixteenth novel, may be my undoing. I click my calendar icon and count the number of days between now, August 8, and October 1, my deadline. I divide the number of words still needed for the manuscript, approximately 78,000, by the number of days, and come up with the daily average I need to write: 1,472 words. That's doable. Although, I didn't account for weekends, unforeseen circumstances, or days like today, when the words refuse to show themselves on the screen.

I have three hours until our meeting. "All right, time to buckle down." I take a deep breath and read the last scene again. It's bad— so bad. I have no choice. I highlight the scene—approximately 2,000 words, including the 453 I wrote earlier—and press DELETE. For the next sixty minutes, I write and delete, write and delete, write and delete. By 6:00 p.m., I still have a negative word count for the day.

I get up from my desk, lift my arms to the ceiling, and bend at the waist, stretching my back. I grab my mug, go to the kitchen, and pour the last of the cold coffee from the pot, popping my mug into the microwave. In the forty-five seconds it takes my coffee to heat, it occurs to me what's wrong with the scene I'm trying to write. It needs to be told from another character's viewpoint. But whose? A male character's, maybe?

I wander back to my office and settle in my desk chair. If I add a male character, he could ask Chloe, my protagonist, pertinent questions and offer a different perspective. I lift the mug of hot coffee to my lips. He could give the reader the understanding they need of Chloe's struggle. My fingers twitch, anxious for their place on the keyboard. Once there, my pulse pounds. Caffeine? No. "It's creative energy, ol' girl, remember?" I open a new document and begin typing notes, considering plot points a new character might facilitate. I bullet point several ideas—just enough to remind me of the thoughts as they form. After several minutes, I lean back in my chair, read my notes, and smile.

I drop down a few spaces in my document, ready to create a persona. I stare at the monitor for a moment. "So, who are you?" I ask my unknown character, half expecting to hear him answer. Again, I bullet point information:

- Stature: 6'2"—195 pounds—fit
- Hair: dark brown, cropped short

I think of Craig's hair—the way it's grayed at the temples this past year, giving him a distinguished, okay, even sexy George Cloony-ish look. Why is age so much kinder to men? I go back and add "graying at the temples" to my description.

- Eyes: hazel
- Age: 50-ish

I spend the next hour imagining, developing, creating Dr. Elliot Hammond, psychologist. After I have a solid physical composite, I make notes about his personality and emotions. I even go as far as assigning him a personality type based on the Meyers-Briggs Type Indicator. Once that work is done, I open my Internet browser and do a search for the actor I had in mind when I listed Elliot's physical features—there are hundreds of pictures to choose from. I pick a close-up and print it. When I hear the printer stop, I get up, grab the photo, and pin it next to the pictures of the other characters gracing the bulletin board that hangs above my computer.

I stand back and stare at the photo. He seems almost familiar—like someone I've met or known. Something stirs within me, but I don't ponder the feeling long enough to name it. Instead, I smile.

It seems the new man in my life has inspired my creativity.

———————◆◆———————

"How many words have you written?" Valerie, a nonfiction writer and the newest member of the Deep Inkers, asks.

I glance at Jill, the freelance editor whom the publisher has hired for my last three books—and for this one. I swallow. "Seventeen thousand-ish."

Quinn, a young blogger who never has to write more than five hundred words to complete a post, taps on her phone, pulling up what I fear is her beloved calculator app. "And your deadline is—"

I hold up one hand. "I know, I know, I know." I fire my declarations in rapid succession. Then I take a deep breath. "You don't need to remind me. I'm behind. I know."

"You haven't missed a deadline yet," Jill encourages. "We'll brainstorm with you."

"Okay"—I glance at my watch—"Quinn, keep track of the time for me, will you?"

Quinn nods and looks at the phone still in her hand. "And three, two, one, go." She points at me.

Because our group is small tonight, I have a full thirty minutes rather than the standard twenty minutes to discuss my project. "Okay, so the good news is that I created a new character this afternoon. A therapist—someone Chloe can talk to."

Valerie leans forward. "Why did she seek out a therapist? What's she working through?"

"Oh. . ." I'd forgotten that Valerie *is* a therapist—a marriage and family counselor is what I think Jill told me when she mentioned

Valerie joining the group. "Well, she's. . .you know. . ." I slump in my seat. "She's. . .struggling. But Dr. Hammond—this character—he's good. He's going to be important."

"Mel. . ."

Jill and Craig got together at some point, I'm certain, and designated my nickname as code for "confront her." I square my shoulders.

"Does this story line, a struggling protagonist seeing a therapist, fit your brand?"

I stare at Jill.

"It's a little deeper than—"

"She can make it humorous," Quinn interrupts.

"Or maybe you're ready to write something deeper?" Valerie sits, pen poised above a notepad, her reading glasses low on her nose.

"Quinn's right. I can inject humor."

Jill smiles. "You're a great writer. You can write whatever you set your mind to as long as it fits your brand. But if you find yourself going off-brand, let your agent know ASAP. He'll need to work through the change with the publisher. And let me read a few chapters so I can ease the way with the publisher, too." Jill, always the mom, makes sure all the bases are covered.

"Okay, great, but that doesn't answer Valerie's question. What's Chloe working through? Maybe she's just. . .struggling with life. You know? She's discontent." I slap my hands on my legs. "That's it. She's disgruntled. Discontent. And doesn't know why. Just because Elliot's—"

"Elliot?" Quinn squints at me.

"Dr. Hammond. Just because he's a therapist doesn't mean I have to dredge the depths, right, Val?"

"It's Valerie, and you're right. Maybe Chloe is lonely, needs someone to talk to, someone to process life with." She sets her pen on the notepad on her lap. "I know I don't write fiction, so I'm not the expert, but don't you need tension in the story—something to keep the reader turning pages?"

"Tension. Right." I glance at my watch again.

Quinn holds up her phone. "Keep talking. You have lots of time yet."

I look over to Jill. "Where's that cobbler you mentioned this afternoon?" I've had enough tension for one evening.

Our yard is dark as I cross the strip of lawn between Marcos and Jill's house and ours. Craig must have set the yard lights to come on later. Looking up, I see the house is still dark, too, which means he's still at the office. Either that or he's working by candlelight in the house to save utility expenses. The man gets loony about lights left on, at least lately. I make my way to the side garage door, feel for the switch, and then turn it on. Craig's empty garage stall confirms that he's still working. Once I reach the door adjoining the house, I'm sure to switch the garage light off again.

I drop my bag on the counter in the laundry room and then shuffle through the darkened kitchen and down the hallway. I stop outside my office door. *"Maybe Chloe is lonely."* Valerie's right: there's no tension in that plot. Maybe Jill is right, too: I'm in over my head with this story line. I know that's not what she said, but isn't it what she meant? I write fluff. Jill would never say that either, but maybe it's true.

And this new story is deeper. Maybe?

Who am I kidding? I'm just not all that deep. I laugh—a staccato burst of air that echoes in the empty house.

"Time for bed," I tell myself as I head for the stairs, but I pause before I get there. I put one hand on my chest. My heart has taken off round the track and is racing toward the finish line. The caffeine that was my friend earlier in the day has betrayed me now. The prospect of staring at the ceiling until Craig gets home doesn't appeal. Instead, I two-step back to my office and drop into the chair at my desk, where I sit enveloped in darkness.

And silence.

I'm used to a silent house. No children. An absent husband. Not even a pet. I shift in my chair. Nothing to distract me as I write.

I reach for the lamp on my desk and switch it on. The light illuminates the bulletin board hanging above, where Elliot smiles down at me.

I lean back in my chair, my shoulders relaxing. "Well, hello there, handsome. And here I thought I was all alone."

Then I wink at the picture of the actor, now known as Dr. Elliot Hammond. "Elliot, you're not only going to make this story more interesting, you're going to make my life more interesting."

What'll we do with ourselves this afternoon?
And the day after that, and the next thirty years?
F. Scott Fitzgerald

Chapter 2

CRAIG

A developer married to a tree hugger. That's me and Mel. Polar opposites. I used to poke fun, telling her the pages of her books murdered more trees than the homes I built, but then came the e-book. Her books are still available in print, but a lot of her sales are electronic now. And the houses I once framed with Douglas fir I now build with steel framing systems. Long live the tree.

Our differences never bothered me. At twenty-six, my attraction to Melanie hit like a hammer to the head. It still does, when I'm not too beat to notice. Mel's a looker. Long slender legs and big, round—I smile—eyes. A man could drown in those pools. And yeah, I fell asleep on her last night. But. . . I stick my phone into the back pocket of my jeans and look up at the newly hung Sheetrock on the twelve-foot walls of Serena Buchanan's butler's pantry. I shake my head. "Yo, Dan!"

"What?" He yells from the kitchen, where he and his guys are hanging rock now.

"Come here." But physical attraction isn't enough, you know? It's great. But it's not all. Our differences used to keep it interesting, but now—

"Whaddaya want?"

"Look." I point to the gaps in the Sheetrock above the header. "There's not enough tape and mud anywhere to cover that mess." Dan takes off his baseball cap and wipes the August heat from his forehead. He looks down, shakes his head, then puts the cap back on. "I'll take care of it."

"Thanks, man. The homeowner will appreciate that."

Dan chuckles. "If Serena ain't happy—"

"Ain't nobody happy." I shrug. "She's our paycheck, pal."

Last night, last year, the last two decades, Melanie has checked out. Not out of the marriage. Just out of the moment. I get that she's introverted—she lives in her head. But it's more than that. I glance at my watch. Serena and her daughter are late for our meeting, so I continue my walk through without them. When did Melanie change? Or was she always this way? Nah, it's gotten worse through the years. The woman is an emotional Houdini, able to escape any hardship. Which means the hardships fall on me. I tried to explain it again last night, but we ended up on the well-worn *alternate reality* path—she lives the *realities* she writes. So then I tried to get specific. "Mel, we're not making it. We're going in the hole every month."

"How much in the hole?"

Her question had surprised me—the fact that she'd engaged enough to ask. But I was already geared for a fight. "How much? The answer will dish more reality than you'll find appetizing."

"What?" She'd laughed. "What did you say? Will dish more reality than I'll find appetizing? That's such a clever line!" She'd pulled a notebook out of her purse and wrote it down. "I can use that."

I leaned back in my seat. "Mel, I'm serious."

"So am I. You're providing great material." She'd laughed again.

"Just forget it." That's when the waiter showed up with our sturgeon, which we ate in silence. Or I ate in silence. Mel apologized and tried to get the conversation back on track, but I was ticked. I have to give her credit though—

"Craig?"

"Back here."

"Did you see the Sheetrock in the butler's pantry?"

"Hello, Serena, Ashley. Dan's taking care of it."

"Good." Serena smiles and puts out her hand. "Hi, Craig." Under her other arm is a set of blueprints.

I shake her hand.

"Sorry we're late. Wow. . .look at this, Ash." She does a slow turn in the middle of the master bedroom, head tilted up. "I love the way the tray ceiling turned out. Sheetrock changes everything. This is always my favorite stage of a project."

"Yeah, mine, too. Glad you like it."

Serena looks back at me. "Great shirt, Craig. It brings out the green flecks in your eyes." She takes a step forward and brushes Sheetrock dust off the right shoulder of the sage-colored oxford Melanie bought for me.

"Thanks. I guess that's the type of thing an interior designer notices."

"She notices *everything*."

I shift my attention to Ashley. "So you must not get away with much?"

"I wouldn't say that." She smiles.

She's a beautiful girl. Eighteen years old. When I met her, I couldn't help but think that if Mel had gotten pregnant, we'd have a child about the same age now. A college student. I'd have taken a boy, a girl, or three of each, for that matter. But I accept that this wasn't God's plan for us. Doesn't mean it didn't hurt, though. I respect Serena's choice to stay in the area for Ashley's sake. *"You know, Cow Town is a bit passé for this city girl, but it's home for Ashley, and she needs stability now that her father's gone,"* Serena had told me during our initial consultation on the house. I knew after researching Serena that she could live anywhere she chose. Her clients hail from places like London, Paris, New York, and Beverly Hills. *Architectural Digest* did a spread on her last year. Sacramento might be the state capital, but it's still Hicksville in her world. But it was home for her family—her husband was California's attorney general before a heart attack took his life.

Ashley turns away from us. "I'm going to check out my room."

I follow Serena into the master bath, which she gives a cursory once-over.

"Listen, Craig, I found a gorgeous vintage claw-foot tub for Ashley."

"A tub?"

"I know. I know. We only spec'd a shower for her bathroom, but I'd like to surprise her."

"It's a little late in the game—"

"It just means moving the wall between her bedroom and bath— say, five feet? There's that nook in her room on the other side of the bathroom. We can use that space."

"It's a load-bearing wall. That means engineering, permits—"

"I know. I have a friend at the county—I'll take care of the red tape."

One of the advantages—or disadvantages, maybe—of building for an interior designer is that she gets how it's done. I feared she'd be a diva about the whole thing, but I was wrong.

"It will cost me, too, I know."

"You're the boss. I'll work up a change order."

"Thanks." She steps back, looks at me, and tilts her head to one side. "You seem a little down, Craig. You okay?"

The thing I've always liked about building houses is the clear beginning, middle, and end. You start with a slab or subfloor, frame the beast, let the electrician and plumber do their thing, rock and mud it, and then do the finish work—flooring, cabinets, trim, appliances. Maybe a little landscaping. Whether it's one house or thirty, the process is the same. Sure, plans differ, but the beginning always leads to the end.

Marriage, on the other hand, gets stuck somewhere in the middle. You're never aiming for that moment when you turn the house key over to someone else.

You're never aiming for the end.

Not that I'm looking for the end. It's just that the middle is feeling. . .long. The problems we began with are, for the most part, the same problems we are facing twenty-three years later. Somewhere along the way, we lost sight of the goal. The dream. Or whatever it was we were working toward.

It's late when I pull into our driveway. I stare at the four carriage-style garage doors with forged iron hardware. I built spaces for both our cars, a bay for our boat, and an extra space for my workbench and tools. I reach for the garage door opener but then change my mind. Opening it would wake Melanie who, at this hour, is asleep in the master bedroom above the garage. I put my truck in PARK, look around the neighborhood—a gated community of large custom homes—and then rest my forehead on the steering wheel. Unless the economy does a fast turnaround, we need to put the house on the market. We can't hang on to it. I sigh and rake my hair with my fingers. I need to man up and tell Mel.

Hey, maybe failure will add a new dynamic to our relationship.

I open the door of the truck but don't move. C'mon buddy, go into the house. Climb into bed with your wife. Again. Twenty-three years? That's a lot of time spent with the same person. I'll go to bed, get up tomorrow, drink a cup of coffee with her, and give her a peck on the cheek before I leave for work. I swing one leg out the door and then stop. I'll call her sometime during the afternoon to check in and then come home for dinner, go to bed, and get up and do the same thing all over again. There was a time when the routine represented comfort. But lately. . .

I pull my leg back into the cab.

Nah, not again. Not tonight. Something's gotta give.

I close the door and shift the truck into REVERSE.

A ruffled mind makes a restless pillow.
Charlotte Brontë

Chapter 3
MELANIE

I've just turned off the lamp in my office when two orbs of light shine through the sheer drapes and then bounce across the walls of the room. Craig's home. I turn to leave the office and meet him when he comes in, but I pause. Instead, I turn back to the window, pull the drapes aside, and watch—waiting for him to open the garage door and pull the truck inside. Only the silhouette of his form is visible in the cab of his truck. It appears he's resting his head on the steering wheel. It's well past midnight—he must be exhausted.

When I see him lift his head and open the driver's side door, I realize he assumed I was asleep and didn't want to wake me by opening the garage door. He's thoughtful that way. I leave the window, make my way down the dark hallway, and flip the light on in the laundry room. I open the door that leads out to the garage and tap the garage door opener—I know he doesn't like leaving his truck in the driveway overnight. As the door lifts, I see the wheels of his truck backing out of the driveway. "Craig?" I dash down the steps and through the garage. "Wait!"

When I reach the driveway, I track his taillights to the exit of our gated community. I stand motionless for several minutes, a warm delta breeze swirling, carrying the sweet scent of honeysuckle from Jill and Mark's front yard as stars wink through the branches of the giant oak that shelters me. I wait for the knot in my stomach to unbind itself. "He probably just forgot something at the office," I whisper to the sultry night.

As I go back inside, it occurs to me that my cell phone is still in my purse in the laundry room where I left it when I came home from Jill's. I'm sure Craig called and I just didn't hear the phone ring. He'll have left a message. I rummage through my purse, find the phone, and then go to the kitchen for a glass of water to moisten my dry mouth before looking to see if Craig called.

After a few swallows of water, I set the glass in the sink and punch in the code to unlock my phone, but there are no messages. Not even a missed call. I never was the popular girl.

I lean against the counter and call Craig's number. Will I tell him I saw him arrive and then leave? Will he tell me he came and went?

His tone is casual when he answers. "Hey, you're still awake?"

"I am. You're still working?"

"Nah. . ." He hesitates. "I left the office twenty minutes ago. I pulled into the driveway, assumed you were asleep, and knew I was too keyed up to go to bed."

I shift my weight from one foot to the other. "So. . . ?"

"Yeah, so. . .listen, Mel, I just need some time. Go to sleep. I'll be home soon."

"It's almost 1:00 a.m.—where are you going? Can't you just come home?" There's more bite in my tone than I intend. "Sorry." I take a deep breath. "Are you okay?"

"Yeah, I'm okay. Just keyed up, like I said. I'll come home when I'm ready."

"Fine." I end the call and toss the phone onto the countertop.

<hr />

As children, when the dust on the playground settled and we went to our respective homes, I opened the front door of an apartment with the key I wore on a chain around my neck. Craig walked through the front door of a four-bedroom, three-bath, Tudor-style home that smelled of freshly baked pies. His mom poured him a glass of milk, while my mom received other people's soiled clothing at the neighborhood dry cleaner.

Home is either the sturdy foundation or the crumbling underpinnings a child is built upon. Leave it to a builder's wife to come up with that line. My underpinnings crumbled early. I was eight years old when my father left on a warm summer night. I stood outside and watched the taillights of his Buick until they turned the corner away from our apartment building.

Away from me.

He never came home again.

———————◆———————

I tug the chain on the bedside lamp, pull the sheet over me, and fluff my pillow. Then I stare into the dark. I roll over, kick the sheet off, and will myself to sleep. I must have dozed, because I wake with a start and sit up. I'm drenched. A glance to my left tells me Craig hasn't returned. The digital clock reads 2:23 a.m. "Shoot!" I swing my legs over the side of the bed and push my damp bangs off my slick forehead. I'm not sure which has me more frustrated, the night sweat or Craig's disappearing act. My nightgown is soaked through, and the sheets on my side of the bed are damp. I get up, turn the overhead fan to high, and stand under its breeze, arms outstretched, until my body, my betrayer, cools.

After taking a tepid shower, donning a fresh nightgown, and changing the sheets on our king-sized bed, I'm wide awake. I was certain by the time I got out of the shower he'd be back. I stare at the clean, crisp sheets on the bed and debate. If I don't get some sleep, I won't be able to write later today. Instead, I'll stare, glassy-eyed, at the computer screen all day while consuming enough caffeine to restart the heart of a mummy. Yet I know sleep won't come again soon—especially with Craig still absent. I grab my robe and stomp my way downstairs to my office. I might as well use the time now to eke out as many words as I can.

Anyway, writing will keep me from dwelling on negativity.

At my computer, I open the scene I worked on after our writers' group meeting. Why my single, on-the-verge-of-turning-thirty, shopping-obsessed protagonist needed a therapist still wasn't clear to me when I came home, but I decided not to worry about it. The story will come, just as it always does. Jill was right—I haven't missed a deadline yet.

But there's always a first time.

I shake my head and focus on the scene:

> Michael Bublé's voice, smooth as melted chocolate, interrupted Chloe's reverie. The lyrics of the song reminded her of all she'd left behind. "I have to

change that ringtone." She reached for her phone and recognized the number she'd called just an hour ago. Recalling the message she left, her tongue threatened to stick to the roof of her mouth as she answered, "Hello?"

"May I speak to Chloe?"

"This is Chloe."

"Chloe, this is Dr. Hammond. I received your message and understand you have a few questions about the therapy process. And likely about me as a therapist, which is very common. If you have a few minutes now, I'd be happy to answer any questions you may have."

The timbre of his voice was solid, deep, and sure. It resonated somewhere in the cavern of her soul. "Yes, now's fine."

The cavern of her soul. I like the sound of that. Who says I can't write a deep, meaningful scene? Okay, no one has ever actually said that, but Jill's right, cavernous souls aren't exactly my style. But Quinn was right, too—I can bend this to fit my brand. I think. Aren't unfulfilled longings the core issue for each of my protagonists? I just don't often choose to focus on the state of my characters' souls. I usually write more about the deficiencies of their wardrobes and love lives. Shopping cures all, or something like that. Well, at least until the bank account is empty. Then chocolate usually does the trick.

Clearly, I'm overthinking this. I return to the scene:

After getting the answers to her questions and listening as Dr. Hammond described the therapy process, she hung up, leaned back against the sofa, and inhaled the damp, warm air. The rhythm of her heart beat strong and steady as one word played in her mind over and over: *safe*. Dr. Hammond was safe. The resonance of his voice—the way it burrowed into the depth of her being in those first moments of conversation—told her all she needed to know.

Burrowed into the depth of her being? "Who am I kidding?" I stretch my right pinky toward the DELETE key, but with the realization that my word count for yesterday—I glance at the time displayed in the upper corner of my monitor—and for today is still in the negative zone, I stop myself and leave the sentence as written. It's only a draft.

Leaning back in my chair, I twist my robe tie around my index finger then untwist it, lift my fingers back to the keyboard, and rest them there. "So, Chloe, what's your deal? What is it you've left behind? And why do you need a shrink?" Is *shrink* a derogatory term? I'll have to ask Valerie.

In fact, there's a lot I'll have to ask Valerie. She's a great resource. Glad she joined the Deep Inkers when she did. What a boon. I'd hate to have to make an appointment with a therapist just for the sake of research.

I press RETURN, center the cursor, and type the POUND key, indicating a scene break and a POV shift. It's time to see things from Dr. Hammond's point of view. But just as my fingers begin flying over the keys, the sound of the garage door going up pulls me from the new scene. Craig obviously saw my light on and parked inside. I exhale, drop my hands to my lap, and wait until his steps echo in the hallway.

He stops at my office and leans against the door frame. "Why are you still up?"

"I'm working. What's your excuse?" I keep my tone light.

"Good question." He shrugs. "How about we both call it a night?"

"Go ahead, I'll be up in a few minutes."

Craig nods. His eyes are bloodshot and his frame is stooped. "You look beat."

He runs his hand through his thick hair. "Yeah, I am." He turns to go then stops. "Mel. . . I love you. You know that, right?"

I nod. But do I know it?

"Good night." He turns back to the hallway.

"Night."

I love you, too. The words drifted through my mind but were hijacked somewhere between there and my mouth. Where did he go tonight? I save my document and shut down the computer. Why didn't I ask him where he went? My breathing becomes shallow and my shoulders tighten. I didn't ask because I'm not sure I want to know. I get up from my desk, turn off the light, and follow Craig. But when I reach the bottom of the stairs, the question I filed away hours and hours ago returns. *What does Serena Buchanan look like?*

Was Craig with her tonight?

Why did he tell me he loved me? Did the declaration come from a guilty conscience?

"Where's Dr. Hammond when I need him?" I mumble. The irony isn't lost on me: the idea of me walking into a therapist's office is laughable. It makes for an interesting story line, but I'm all about looking forward, not back.

"Did you say something?" Craig calls down from the bedroom.

"No, nothing. I'm coming."

As I climb up the stairs, I drag leaden legs. Five steps up, I stop, sit on the step, and rest my head against the wall.

I'm just tired.

Really tired.

But as hard as I try to convince myself of that, dread tunnels like a mole into my carefully preserved sense of well-being.

Very few of us are what we seem.
Agatha Christie

Chapter 4

Jill

Dessert plates stand at attention and coffee cups sit ordered in a row on the upper shelf of the dishwasher. I close it, start it, and wipe the countertop. Then I spray it with disinfectant and wipe it again.

"I should have bought stock in paper towels before I married you—we'd be millionaires by now."

I drop the clump of towels into the trash can under the sink and then turn toward Marcos, who stands in the entry of the kitchen watching me. His dark hair is mussed and his faded Cal-Poly gym shorts, left over from his college days, ride low on his hips. "A million isn't what it used to be."

"True." He moves into the kitchen and settles onto one of the stools at the counter. "So, did the Deep Inkers resolve the issues of the literary world?"

I smile. "All the issues except Melanie's."

"Melanie? I thought she cranked out manuscripts like a machine." He leans his elbows on the countertop.

"Usually, but this one is challenging her, which is good. I think the only thing she'd allow to challenge her *is* a manuscript."

He nods. He's heard my concerns about Melanie before. And he's likely heard some of the same concerns from Craig, though Marcos would never tell me what Craig shares in confidence.

"How was dinner with your folks?"

"The kids were *muy bueno.* . . ."

"Your mom's words?"

"Yeah." He smiles. "She made enchiladas with *mole poblano.*"

29

"They love her *mole*."

"Me too."

"I know. I'll get her recipe someday." Though I know that isn't true. Why would I attempt to duplicate what his mother has already perfected? I glance at the clock on the microwave. "Thank you for slipping in and putting the kids to bed. I thought you'd gone to bed, too."

"Couldn't sleep." He runs his hand over his chin. "I dozed, but. . ."

"Were we too loud? We had fun afterward, but they stayed late."

"Laughter is the sweetest lullaby, no?"

I come around behind him and put my arms around his smooth bare back and chest. I drop a light kiss on the nape of his neck and whisper in his ear, "*You* are the sweetest."

He doesn't respond. Instead, he seems to stare at something I can't see.

I pull back and look around at his face. "You okay?"

He shrugs. "*Mi padre*. . ." He shakes his head. "I think his memory is going."

"No. Your dad? He's sharp." I pull out the barstool next to his and sit down.

He shakes his head. "After we had dessert tonight—Mom's sopapillas, his favorite, right?—I got up and helped her clear the table. She took my dad's plate first and then grabbed a few other things and took them to the kitchen. I took the kids' plates and followed her. She was rinsing dishes when he yells from the dining room, 'Gabriella, what about the sopapillas?'"

I cock my head. "Was that his way of asking for more?"

"I thought so. I went back into the dining room, laughed, and accused him of trying to pull one over on us. But his expression"—he turns and looks at me—"was blank. Nothing registered in his eyes, you know? Then it was like he tried to cover his blunder. He smiled and said there was always room for more. But before that? Nothing."

"Did you ask your mom about it?"

"Yeah, later. But she blew it off. 'Marcos, you know your padre—always teasing.'"

"It was probably nothing."

"I don't know, Jill. Something wasn't right. He looked so bewildered."

I reach over and rub his shoulder.

He leans his cheek against my hand. "You coming to bed?"

"Yes, soon. Go ahead, I'm just going to finish cleaning up."

Marcos looks around the kitchen. "It's already perfect."

"Just a few more minutes."

He leans over, kisses my forehead, and then gets up. "Don't use all the paper towels."

I swivel the barstool I'm sitting on and watch him walk down the hallway to the master bedroom. When I think he's gone back to bed, I get up, straighten both barstools under the counter, and then tear a few more paper towels from the roll. I reach for the disinfectant and go back to the bar top where Marcos had leaned his elbows. I spray not only that area but the entire slab of granite and begin wiping it clean again.

Marcos was waiting tables in SLO—San Luis Obispo—when we met. I'd just graduated from UC Berkeley with an MA in English and was taking a trip along the coast with a couple of girlfriends before beginning my dream career as an editor for a New York publishing house. It was an opportunity I'd like to think my GPA and reputation garnered for me, but I also suspected the offer came through one of my father's connections.

Marcos would graduate the following week with a BS in engineering and would begin graduate studies in the fall.

"Congratulations." I offered him my hand over the bar top.

He wiped his hand on the apron tied around his waist before shaking mine. "You too. An MA is an accomplishment."

"As is a bachelor's." The warmth of his hand seeped into mine, and I didn't want to let go. Heat scaled its way up my neck and into my cheeks. Was he the cause, or was it the hot coffee he'd served me a few minutes earlier? I would soon learn Marcos was the one with the power to ignite me.

My girlfriends told me later they could almost see the current arcing between us, so they gave us some space to talk. Fortunately, it was also a drizzly afternoon during finals week—most of the tables in the restaurant were unoccupied.

As we chatted across the bar, I learned Marcos was working to put himself through school. My parents, on the other hand, had opened a tax-advantaged ESA when I was a child to save for my college expenses. Marcos and I were the same age, but I'd sailed ahead of him in school on the ship of privilege.

His work ethic earned my respect. And the roped muscles I noticed in his forearm when he shook my hand earned that first heated blush.

Two years later, following too many long-distance phone conversations to count and numerous flights between the East Coast and the West Coast, I was promoted to senior editor of fiction and told I could work remotely. I packed a few boxes, shipped them to Marcos's apartment, and then went home and stayed with my parents until Marcos and I married under a perfect harvest moon just a month later.

I'd had the idyllic childhood—parents who loved and supported me, the trappings of money and ease, which included getting straight A's from the time I was in kindergarten, not because I studied and worked hard, but rather because I didn't have to. I had a career I loved, and I married a man who exceeded everything I'd hoped for in a partner. As the years progressed, three babies were born, all with ten fingers, ten toes, and stellar APGAR scores.

It all came so easily.

It was all so perfect.

But somewhere along the way, the whispered warnings from my personal antagonist began. *Be careful, Jill. Perfection isn't sustainable. You'll lose it all.*

I sweep the paper towels across the counter again. And again.

So is Marcos's dad it? Is he the beginning? Will he be the first?

I continue wiping the counter.

And wiping.

Until there's nothing left in my hand but shredded ribbons of paper.

On my way to bed, I stop and check on the kids, and then, knowing I won't yet sleep, I wander into the den, pick up my laptop off the desk, and sink onto the sofa. The walls are lined with library shelves, which hold hundreds of books—new, classic, even several rare first editions. I breathe in the scent of the books, which usually calms me, but tonight the effect is lost on me.

I open the laptop and click on the photo app, where years of family pictures are stored. I search for a photo of Marcos's parents taken when they were here a few weeks ago for Sunday dinner. They're sitting on this very sofa, each with one of the twins on their lap. Gabriella is looking at Luis, Marcos's father, her smile radiating happiness. Luis is looking down at Thomas, who is snuggled against him and smiling for the camera. Luis's eyes look clear, his expression engaged. There can't be anything wrong with him. Yet as that thought attempts to take up residence, a more daunting thought evicts it.

He's going to die.

I click through other images until I find one of my parents taken this spring. My father is older than Marcos's father but is still fit and active. The photo was taken on their sailboat. My dad's smile gleams against his tanned face, and my mother's auburn hair blows in the wind. *"You look just like her, Jilly. God drew from the right gene pool for you,"* my dad has always said, and as I examine the photo, I know he's right. I see my future in her gently aging features.

She's going to die.

I work to ignore the thoughts as I look through photos of the kids as babies, Marcos holding Gaby as a newborn, Gaby just after she learned to walk, the twins in their matching bassinets.

It's going to happen.

I click through the photos, one after another, each a reminder of a joyful moment.

Yet only darkness permeates my mind and soul.

Because I know, as hard as I work to push the thoughts away, I can't.

They're all going to die.

It's going to happen.

The novel is just fine: It's novelists who aren't doing so well.
Russell Smith

Chapter 5

MELANIE

Who comes up with these names? *Chai Latte, French Roast, Biscotti?* They sound like breakfast fare, not hair colors.

As I sidestep for a woman who pushes her cart past me, I dip my head so my hair falls over one side of my face—just in case I know her. Maybe I should don a pair of dark shades and a hat, too. Why does buying hair color in a grocery store feel like a covert mission when color is applauded in the salon? I glance back at the boxes lining the shelves and look for the Safeway Club Member price on the box of *Biscotti*: $4.97. Ah, there's my answer. The $180 I pay my stylist for color and a cut makes me elite. $4.97 says I can't afford the salon.

At least Craig can't say I'm not helping, not paying attention to the financial burden *he's* carrying. Don't I carry it, too?

I grab the box of *Biscotti*—a sort of toasted platinum color. Toasted platinum? That would never fly in one of my books. Who toasts platinum? Well, it looks good on the model whose locks grace the front of the box. On me, I fear it may look more like *Pasty Oatmeal*. But at this price, who cares? I can try *Whipped Caramel* next week and still be ahead.

I maneuver my cart to an aisle a few rows down and toss a pound of French roast into my cart. Coffee—the reason I'm here in the first place. After so few hours sleep last night, waking to a near empty bag of coffee beans was traumatic. I grab a second bag, a backup pound, and toss it into the cart, too. I turn around and there, in the same aisle as the coffee, are the cookies. Coffee and cookies—smart marketing. I roll the cart a few feet until I find what I'm looking for:

chocolate-dipped, almond—wait for it—*biscotti*. I toss the package into my cart. Then I grab a second package—

"Melanie?"

I spin around, evidence of my debauchery in my hand. "Val..."—I force a smile. Then I remember—"...erie. Hello." I shoot a sideways glance at my cart and place the second package of biscotti in the basket so it covers the box of hair color. Then I look back at Valerie's bouncy, shiny, bob—a golden blond with both highlights and lowlights. A definite salon job. Though I'd guess her to be several years older than me, her fair skin glows and her expression is marked by enthusiasm. Maybe she actually sleeps at night.

"It's fun to see you here. Is this where you usually shop? I'm still getting used to the area."

Note to self: the hat and sunglasses are a necessity whenever I leave the house. "That's right. You haven't lived here long." I grab the handle of my cart. "What brought you to this area?" Shoot. First rule of introversion: don't ask questions. They prolong conversations. Oh well, I missed the meeting where Jill introduced Valerie and she told the group about herself. Valerie and Jill have been friends since Jill was her editor a few years ago. I suppose I can spare a few minutes and a few ounces of emotional energy. Despite her perkiness, she is likable.

"Glen, my husband, died."

"Oh, I'm so sorry." And I really am.

"Thank you. He'd suffered a long time, so although I miss him terribly, it's good to know he's no longer in pain."

"I can imagine. Well, actually, I can't imagine." I don't want to imagine.

"I sold our home in the Bay Area and came inland. It's more affordable, and I have a daughter who lives here." The corners of her eyes crinkle with her smile. "And grandchildren. And"—she lowers her voice—"believe it or not, I was able to pay cash for a new home in Roseville. I'm still in awe."

There's no trace of pride in her tone, only what seems like genuine gratitude. "Wasn't it hard to leave your home? How long had you lived there?"

"Almost thirty years. Our children were born and raised in that house. But it was just that: a house. Home is in here." She puts her hand over her heart. "It's where those we love reside, and our true home is beyond here. This is all temporary. So while I have a lot of good memories from the years we spent in that house, selling it didn't mean selling my home."

"Right. . . Well, I'm glad you found a house here. The recession helps. Home prices are ridiculously low right now."

Valerie's brow creases. "Your husband is a builder, isn't he? How has this market affected his business?"

"He's building custom homes now." I hope my response will suffice. No need to get into the ugly details. "By the way, thank you for your input on my manuscript last night."

"Oh, anytime. In fact, if I can help you with research—"

"Great minds. . . I was just going to ask if you'd have time. I don't know any other therapists."

"I hope to set up a practice here, just part-time so I can pursue my writing, too, and, of course, spend time with the grandbabies, but until I start seeing clients on a regular basis"—she raises her hands, palms up—"I have time. Maybe we can meet for coffee, or tea if you'd prefer."

I point to the bags of coffee beans in my cart. "Coffee."

"Oh, good. Me too. Coffee and writers seem to go together, don't they?" She eyes the coffee and biscotti. "I see you buy things in twos."

My shoulders tighten, and then I cross my arms. "I guess so." I swallow. "What does that say about me?"

She looks back to me and lifts one shoulder. "I have no idea. I just wondered if there was a two-for-one special I'd missed."

"Ah, no. Just the old adage: if one is good. . ."

"Two are better." Valerie reaches over and places her hand on my arm. "That also goes for friends. So, shall we set a coffee date?"

"Well. . . I need to get into the story a little more before I'll know what I need to know. You know?"

She laughs. "No, not really, which is probably why I don't write fiction. Just let me know when you're ready. I'd love to get together. I haven't met a lot of people here yet."

"I'll e-mail you."

"I'll look forward to it."

"I better run. I have a word count to make. Good to see you, Valerie."

I reach for my cart and race down the aisle toward the registers.

In the parking lot, I drop my bag of loot on the passenger seat of my car, buckle myself in the driver's seat, and then put one hand on my chest, where my heart is threatening to burst through my ribs. "What is this about?" I look out the front window toward the heavens and wait for a response. When nothing comes, I shrug.

Racing pulse? Probably just another sign of menopause. I lean forward, put the key into the ignition, and then shift into REVERSE. I glance at the rearview mirror, and just before backing out of the parking space, I spy Valerie walking out of the store. My pulse revs like the engine of the car as it lurches backward. I slam on the brakes before I take out the car parked behind me. Then I take a deep breath, avert my gaze, and focus instead on maneuvering out of the lot. When I reach the exit, I stop for the light, which is red, of course. I fumble with the radio dial while I wait, searching for something to listen to. Anything to listen to. But all I get is static.

A lot like my prayer life.

Then I remember that the radio hasn't worked in eons.

◆

So was it the widow thing that got to me? Valerie *and* Serena What's-Her-Name. Two widows in the same week make it hard to ignore the reality that husbands do sometimes die, leaving their wives alone. Okay, maybe not totally alone, but if you don't have children or a husband. . . That's more alone than I care to consider.

As I pull into the driveway and then the garage, I'm grateful that Jill and the kids aren't in their front yard, as they often are. Not that I don't love them, but the gurgling in my stomach doesn't lend itself to more conversation. The upset stomach isn't a result of the widow thing, I'm pretty sure.

Was it something else about Valerie?

The open package of cookies on the passenger seat woos. *One more and you'll successfully stuff all thoughts of Val.*

"Who am I kidding? The three cookies I ate on the way home are the likely cause of the stomachache. One more of those and my word count for the day will slide right into oblivion along with me." I set the parking brake and then push the package of biscotti back into the grocery bag. My splurge is over; it's time to work. Time to enter my alternate reality.

Alternate reality. Boy, Craig gets riled up about that term. I stop just before reaching the steps that lead into the house from the garage. He won't die on me. But he might...

I take the last step up and then pause on the landing.

...leave me.

My stomach somersaults and then burbles like rain in a down-spout. I reach inside the grocery bag and feel for another piece of biscotti. It isn't thoughts of Valerie I need to stuff. I bite off half the cookie, no longer tasting what I'm eating. When I swallow, the dry crumbs go down like a mouthful of sand.

Would Craig ever consider divorce? It's a question I've refused to ask in our twenty-three years of marriage. But lately...

Once inside, I set the grocery bag on the counter, dig out one of the bags of coffee beans, grind some, and then set the pot to brew. I lean against the counter, the scent of coffee enveloping me, the rich aroma comforting like a favorite sweater.

The anxiety following my encounter with Valerie and the intrusive thoughts about Craig are just lunacy. "Pure lunacy, Melanie." The deadline's getting to me. Stories have always come so easily, but not this one. I close my eyes and rub my temples as I vow to push the crazy away.

"Focus." That's how I can help Craig—by getting this book done and collecting the remainder of my advance. Then starting the next book... "Just focus on Chloe."

And Elliot...

As the photo of Elliot Hammond comes to mind, my stomach settles, the only gurgling coming from the coffeemaker. I turn and grab my favorite mug out of the cabinet. I smile as I fill it. "So, Dr. Hammond..." I wander down the hall toward my office. "Elliot... How about we linger over a cup of French roast and chat the afternoon away? Maybe you can tell me what's going on with Chloe."

This counselor I can trust.

He won't ask personal questions.

He won't analyze my habits.

He won't uncover anything I don't want to know about.

Life's under no obligation to give us what we expect.
Margaret Mitchell

Chapter 6

CRAIG

C'mon, how many loans have I steered your way? Work with me here." My tone is gruff even after trying to temper it. The phone is hot against my ear as I listen, again, to all the reasons Melanie and I don't qualify to refinance the house: two delinquencies on our mortgage payment in the last six months, a few ninety-days-past-due notations on various accounts, and a credit score that's plummeted from the high sevens to the mid-fives in the past eighteen months. Not to mention the out-of-whack debt-to-income ratio. "Okay, okay. I get it. Thanks anyway."

I hang up the office line. Piles of paper clutter my desktop, and rolled blueprints for the last subdivision I built stand in the corner, mocking me.

When we built our home, I assured Melanie it would provide a nice retirement nest egg when the time came. Now we're upside down on the loan with no apparent hope of righting ourselves.

I pound my fist on the desk, making the piles of paper jump.

"Craig?"

I spin around to find Serena standing in the doorway of my office. "What—"

"I'm sorry. You obviously didn't hear me come in. Where's your receptionist?"

The one I had to lay off last week? I stand up and wave her over to the chair across from my desk. How long has she been standing there? I clear my throat. "She's taking some time off. Did we have a meeting scheduled?"

I wait for her to get seated before dropping back into my chair. The scent of her perfume follows her into the office, reminding me of plumeria and tropical islands. Makes me want to hop a plane to some-place exotic. Maybe I'm starting to get the method of Mel's madness. An escape is exactly what I need.

"No, we hadn't scheduled a meeting. I just hoped I'd catch you. I'm sorry if it's a bad time, but I have your check for that change order and"—she pulls something out of a leather portfolio—"the approval from the county."

"Wow. Record time."

"I told you I had connections."

"Know anyone in B of A's mortgage department?"

"Probably."

I read kindness in her eyes as she smiles. Her long dark hair, usu-ally in a tight knot of some sort on top of her head, now hangs over her shoulders and shines under the commercial florescent lights.

"Why? What do you need? If there's anything I can do to help. . ."

"Nah. . ." I look from her to the piles on my desk. "Just one of those weeks. Thanks for this." I hold up the check and look back to her. "We'll get the wall moved, get it rocked, and then schedule the nailing inspection."

"Inspection by week's end, you think?"

I look at the calendar on my desk. "Yeah, Friday, if all goes well."

"Perfect."

I lean forward, ready to stand, expecting her to get up to go, but she stays put. "Something else?"

She tilts her head to one side and seems to study me. "Well. . ."

I sit back. "Another change?"

"Oh, no. Nothing like that. I love how the house is coming together. Really, Craig, you're doing a fabulous job. I've appreciated having a man. . ."

She looks down at her lap for what feels like an awkward amount of time then looks back at me. Please tell me those aren't tears in her eyes.

She takes a deep breath. "I appreciate working with someone I can depend on. Since Charles died. . ." She hesitates. "What I'm trying to say is, thank you. I am quite capable, you know, but it's nice to know I don't have to worry about too many details right now."

I've no doubt she's more capable than me and all my subs put together. "You're welcome. It's great to work with someone who understands the process and wants to create a quality product." I chuckle. "And someone who doesn't complain when they have to write a check for a change order."

She seems to get her emotions under control. "I've presented many change orders to my own clients through the years. I know they're often received with something less than enthusiasm."

She sets her portfolio on my desk and seems to relax in the chair. "Craig, I was serious. If there's anything I can do to help you, I'm willing. Not only do I understand change orders, I'm also aware of the impact this recession is having on builders, especially in this area. You know, they're now calling it the Great Recession. It's by choice that I'm not working right now. I want to be available for Ashley, but I have friends in the industry who are really struggling. This economy is hurting a lot of people."

Her green silk blouse is the same color as her eyes, which isn't the type of thing I need to be noticing. I mentally checkmark the moment so I can smack myself later.

"I have funds available for investment, or"—she waves her hand—"whatever."

Funds available? She's offering to loan me money? Or invest in my business? I swallow and then open my mouth before I realize I don't know what to say.

"Craig?"

Of course I won't take her money, but. . . "Serena, I'm. . ." Emotion, like a wad of insulation, has lodged itself in my throat.

She holds up her hands. "Listen, we don't have to talk about it now. I just wanted to let you know there are options—should you ever need an option, that is."

"Thank you. I mean it. I really appreciate—"

"Enough said, all right?" She picks up her portfolio and gets to her feet. Then she holds out her hand.

I hesitate for just a second then take her hand in mine, shake it, and quickly let it go.

But the feel of her hand in mine lingers.

When we were children, we used to think that when
we were grown-up we would no longer be vulnerable.
Madeleine L'Engle

Chapter 7

MELANIE

Craig drinks the last of his juice and then sets his glass on the table. "What's on your schedule today? Writing, I assume?"

"Always. But it's a busy day. I'm having coffee with"—I sigh—"Valerie Griffin this morning. And I'm watching Gaby for Jill this afternoon."

"Who's Valerie Griffin, and why don't you want to have coffee with her?"

"I didn't say I didn't want to."

"Right. And she's. . . ?"

"Oh, she's a new gal in our writers' group. I thought I'd told you about her. I ran into her at the grocery store last week, and she offered to help me do some research for the book. She's a counselor."

Craig's expression is blank, and then he combs his fingers through his hair—a sure sign that he's perplexed. "A counselor? As in therapist?"

"I know. I know. This story is going somewhere other than I'd planned. You know how that happens sometimes."

"If you say so."

I shrug. "I was supposed to e-mail her to get together, but she beat me to it—said she had an idea for me. We'll see. . ."

He gets up from the table, clips his phone onto his belt, grabs his briefcase off the kitchen counter, and then plants a kiss on my forehead. "There's a BIA reception downtown this evening. I'll go straight there from the office and then come home." He stops at the laundry room door. "Unless you want to join me?"

I fold the newspaper I read during breakfast. "Hobnob with members of the Building Industry Association or stay home and scour toilets? Yeah, I'd have to choose the toilets, unless it's important to you that I go?" I plaster on a faux smile. "Then I'd *love* to attend."

He laughs. "Stay here."

"Do you really need to go?"

"Honestly, I'd rather come home and help you with those toilets, but I can't bypass any opportunity to network right now. You never know what'll come of it. I won't be late."

"Enjoy."

After Craig leaves, I clear the table of our breakfast dishes—two mugs and a plate with a piece of leftover crust from the slice of toast I made for Craig. I pop the crust into my mouth on my way to the sink.

Craig's mood this morning puts me at ease. I can't believe I'd even entertained the idea yesterday that he might consider divorce. That thought was a rude intruder and one I won't welcome again.

I glance at the clock on the microwave. I have almost an hour and a half to work before I leave to meet Valerie.

Valerie. . .

I pull my robe tight across my torso and then cinch the tie at my waist.

———————————◆-◆———————————

When I get out of my air-conditioned car in the small parking lot of the French bakery I'd suggested to Valerie, I slam into a wall of dry, oppressive heat that feels as though it will scorch my lungs when I inhale. Great, both the economy and the ozone layer have crashed.

I take quick strides across the blistering asphalt, open the door of the café, and push my bangs off my already damp forehead. But I stop cold and wrap my arms around myself when I spot Valerie seated at a corner bistro table.

Smiling, she waves at me. But as I remain rooted, her smile fades and her eyebrows rise. She's made the dash from welcoming to quizzical in record time. When I regain my equilibrium, or my marbles, or whatever it was I lost when I saw her, I wave back and point to the counter, where I go and dally over the bakery case.

Again, I cross my arms and wish I could pull something over myself. A pillowcase over my head, maybe? What *is* my problem?

"What can I get for you?"

My problem? I'm better off not knowing.

"Ma'am?"

"Oh, sorry." I offer the barista a weak smile. "I'll have a cruller—chocolate—and. . ." I stare at the menu artfully lettered with colored chalk on a board hanging behind the registers. A menu I know by heart, mind you. "Um. . . How about a latte—whole milk—iced—extra ice."

"For here or to go?"

Valerie's seen me; I can't bolt now. I turn back to the barista. "Here."

She puts the cruller on a plate and hands it to me. "I'll bring your latte to you when it's ready."

I glance over my shoulder at Valerie and then look back to the barista. "I'm happy to wait for it."

—————————◆◆—————————

"So, how's Chloe?" Valerie's blue eyes twinkle. "These characters become very real to you, don't they?"

"Too real. And this one may be the death of me. Either that or the deadline will kill me."

"Oh dear, that's a little melodramatic, don't you think?"

"According to my agent, the word *dead* is in *deadline* for a reason. 'Miss it and you're dead,' he says. You're an author, so you know. A missed deadline can set a publishing schedule on its head, costing the publisher a mint." It will also set Jill's schedule on its head, and *flexibility* isn't in Jill's vocabulary. Just the thought causes heat to embrace me in a sticky hug.

"Are you okay?" Valerie leans close.

"Hot flash." I pick up the napkin in my lap and fan myself with it.

"This valley heat can't help. It sure takes some getting used to, doesn't it? I'm accustomed to fog in the summer, and when the sun did break through, we'd get a cool breeze off the bay. I'd have hated to go through the change in this heat."

"Sadly, our delta breezes seem to have gone into hiding this week."

Valerie nods as I drop the napkin back into my lap and instead pick up my iced latte. I'm tempted to rub the cold glass over my hot brow, but I resist and take several sips instead.

"Have you made *any* progress on the book?"

"No progress. Nada." I shake my head. "I've got nothing. I'm dead. Have you ever missed a deadline?"

"No, but it happens. As much as we'd like to believe we're in control, we're not." She lifts her hands in what I take as a gesture of relinquishment.

What, so I can blame a missed deadline on God? I'm sure that will go over well with my publishing company. I sit back in my chair, more relaxed than when I came in. Valerie's delightful. Really. I put my earlier angst out of my mind.

"Melanie, have you considered getting away? Taking a retreat of sorts? Time alone. A place to write without interruption?"

"Oh sure. I've also considered winning the lottery."

"No, really. I'm serious."

"So am I. Unfortunately, I can't afford to rent a place right now. That's definitely not in the budget."

"Who said anything about renting?" Valerie leans across the table like she's about to share a secret. "I have a place. It's the perfect get-away. In fact, before my husband got ill, I spent a lot of time there— wrote most of my last manuscript overlooking the lake."

"Lake?"

"There's a breeze—a cool breeze off the lake. It's perfect."

"A breeze?"

"Yes. And the place is yours. You can use it if you'd like. When I e-mailed you and said I had an idea for you—the lake house was the idea. I know how productive it can be to get away from the distractions at home and just focus on work for a time. Maybe it's just what you need."

Maybe it is. "Wow, thank you. So this is your. . . ?"

"Vacation home. My grandparents built it and lived there until they died. My mother was an only child and passed the home to my sister and myself. When my sister died, it became mine. I'll hang on to it for our kids. They've grown up spending summers there. But now that they're grown and have jobs and families, well, it doesn't get used as much as it once did. So it's just sitting there."

"Your sister. . . ?" And her husband? How is she still standing?

Valerie's brow creases as she nods. "Breast cancer. She fought long and hard. She went home three years ago."

Home? She speaks of heaven as though it were a cozy three-bed, two-bath in the suburbs. "I'm so sorry. You've been through a lot."

The twinkle returns to her eyes. "I couldn't have done it without God's support—His strength through my weakness."

I nod like I've had the same experience. I get it in theory, but. . . "So, where is this place?"

"Lake County. Not quite three hours from here—an easy drive. The best part is there are so few distractions. The area is depressed, economically speaking, so there's not a lot to do. Although, in recent years a lot of vineyards have gone in and wineries have popped up all around the lake. But other than wine tasting and bass fishing, your options are limited. Will your husband mind you running off?"

"He'd tell you he's used to it," I quip.

Valerie doesn't say anything. Instead, she looks at me likes she's waiting for me to expound or confess or something.

"It's nothing. Just a joke." I pick up my glass and take another sip as Valerie watches me.

Then she fills the gap. "My husband used to drive up on week-ends when I'd spend time there writing. We'd sit out on the dock in the evenings and watch the fish jump and the birds swoop low over the water. Oh, the birds—so many varieties! The sun sets behind the house rather than over the lake, but the colors reflected on the lake look like paint on a palette. When it got dark, we'd go inside and cook a simple supper together or hop in the car and drive over to the Saw Shop in Kelseyville or the Blue Wing in Lower Lake for dinner. He'd tell me what he'd done during the week, and I'd talk through my manuscript with him. Later, we'd go to bed and"—her cheeks turn a deeper shade of pink—"we'd catch up there too. . ." Her voice trails off. She's no longer looking at me but just beyond me. "I miss those times—everything about them."

"I'm sorry." I shift in my seat.

She looks back to me. "I'm not. I have so much to be grateful for. We had a good marriage. It took work, but it was well worth the investment. We're created for connection, for intimacy. It's natural to miss it."

I nod as I stare at the table.

"Oh, I hope I haven't made you uncomfortable, Melanie."

"No!" I look at her then back at the table then back to her. "Nope. Not at all."

"So, tell me about you."

"Me?" I pick up my glass again. Now would be a good time for a refill. "There's not a lot to tell."

"Everyone has a story, don't you think? I'd imagine that's why readers love fiction. It's someone's story, even if the character is fictional."

"Oh, I never thought about it that way. I guess I haven't given my own story much thought either. Would you like more coffee? I think I'm going to order another latte or maybe get some water." I get up out of my seat. "You?"

"No, thank you. But you go ahead."

Again the desire to pull something over myself, to pull a sweater or jacket tight, to cover up, to hide, accosts me.

Why is it that spending time with Valerie feels like spending time naked?

In public.

With everyone pointing at me.

There is a condition worse than blindness,
and that is, seeing something that isn't there.
Thomas Hardy

Chapter 8

MELANIE

The doorbell rings, followed by a light knock, rousing me from my lethargy in front of the computer. I stand, stretch, and head to the front door. When I open it, Marcos is there with Gaby.

"Hey, you two."

Marcos smiles, and Gaby reaches up for a hug, her long, dark curls bouncing. I bend down, put my arms around her, and give her a squeeze. "I hear we get to spend the rest of the afternoon together." I pull back and smile at her gap-toothed grin. Gaby is always a welcome interruption.

"Thanks so much, Melanie. The twins are a handful at the pediatrician's office, so I took a few hours off. I'll follow Jill over there then go back to work. No reason for Gaby to have to sit through the appointment, too."

"The boys hate the shots." Gaby's expression is serious now. "They'll cry." Her lower lip protrudes at the thought.

I look back to Marcos. "Shots? Didn't they have their physicals a few months ago?"

"They've had their physicals. They're fine." He looks down at Gaby then pats her shoulder. "No shots today." Then he looks back to me. "Jill just wants to have them checked again. You know."

I do know, though I don't say as much to Marcos in front of Gaby. "Well, Miss Gaby is one of my favorite people on the planet, so it's my pleasure to spend time with her."

Marcos hands Gaby her pink backpack and then bends and kisses the top of her head. He turns to leave then says over his shoulder, "Jill will text you when she's back home with the boys. Thanks, Melanie."

Gaby reaches up to hold my hand as we go into the house. "What's in your backpack?" I already know the answer, but I can't resist asking.

She looks up at me, her eyes as dark as Marcos's. "My books and my bacteria wipes."

"Bacteria wipes?" I suppress a smile.

"They kill germs." She follows me into the family room, where she sets her backpack on the sofa.

"I see. And what book are you reading now?"

"*Harriet the Spy*. Did you read that one?"

"I don't think so. You'll have to tell me all about it."

"It's for third and fourth graders, but my mom said I read beyond a third-grade level already."

"Your mom's a good teacher."

"Yep."

For the next hour, Gaby regales me with details of the stories she's read this summer and the seven-year-old gossip from a birthday party she attended over the weekend. When I asked if the party was a sleepover, she told me it was, but that her mom thought she'd sleep better in her own bed, so her dad picked her up early.

"Were you disappointed you didn't get to stay?"

She looks at her lap.

"It's okay, Gabs—there will be lots of other sleepovers."

She looks back up at me. "I know. I get to have one for my birthday. It's safe at my house."

I smile at Gaby. I hope that's always true for her.

And for Jill.

———————◆◆———————

"Who are those people?" Gaby asks from the big upholstered chair in my office, where she settled to read after we made a batch of cookies together. When I turn in my chair, she's pointing at the photos on my bulletin board.

"Those characters? They're characters. For the book I'm writing."

Gaby's brow creases, my play on words lost on her.

"They're not really the characters in my book. They're real people, but I use their pictures as inspiration for the characters I'm creating. Make sense?"

"I guess so." She points again. "I've seen that man on TV."

"Him?" I reach up and tap the photo of Elliot.

She nods.

"He's an actor. But in my story, he's Dr. Elliot Hammond."

"Oh." Her gaze drops back to the pages of her book.

I return to my manuscript, fingers flying across the keys for the first time in over a week—until I run out of words. Stumped, I look back at the photos, hoping one of those characters will whisper a plot point I haven't considered.

Elliot smiles down at me.

Could he and Chloe have a romantic relationship? I cock my head to one side as I stare at Elliot. Probably not. There must be some ethical rule against that kind of thing in counseling relationships.

Valerie's words about her husband and the time they spent together come back to me now. There was such certainty in her tone as she spoke of their love, such confidence as she recalled not only their conversations but their private moments. It was so obvious she knew she was loved. What must that feel like?

But who talks about that kind of thing? I mean, Valerie hardly knows me. Jill and I don't talk about the intimate details of our lives, and we've been friends for years.

But then, Jill and I don't talk about much of anything beyond the day-to-day activities and writing.

Maybe I could create a romantic subplot using Elliot and someone else. Another character, maybe? What do you think of that idea, Dr. Hammond?

I mean, look at you. That dark hair, those hazel eyes. . .

His expression, even his body language when I've seen him in films or on one of the talk shows on TV—everything about him exudes empathy and tenderness.

I can easily imagine him having long conversations with a woman, delving into those sacred spaces she's never shared with anyone.

"Aunt Melanie?"

Obviously, he's a sensitive man, yet strong emotionally and physically. My gaze wanders over his physique in the photo.

Sacred spaces? Who am I kidding?

"Aunt Melanie?"

"Hmm?"

"You stopped."

His shoulders are so broad, and his lips look so—

"Aunt Melanie?"

"What?" I struggle to pull myself from my thoughts. My gaze lingers on the photo a moment longer, and then I turn around and look at Gaby, hoping she doesn't read impatience in my expression.

"You stopped. Your fingernails aren't clicking on the keys anymore."

"Oh." I steal one more glance at Elliot.

"Why'd you stop?" Gaby's eyebrows are raised in the same way Jill raises hers.

"Well, I was. . ." As I struggle to form an answer, heat climbs up my neck to my cheeks.

"You're turning red."

I put my hands on my cheeks. "Oh. . ." I shake my head. "I'm just"—I cough—"warm." I stand up. "Aren't you warm? I'm going to turn on the air conditioner." I rush from the office and down the hallway to the thermostat. I fan myself with my hands until my heartbeat slows and my temperature cools.

My goodness, my hormones must be raging.

I lean back against the wall, my body burning.

It's a good thing, a very good thing, that Gaby couldn't read my mind.

"Stay" is a charming word in a friend's vocabulary.
Louisa May Alcott

Chapter 9

CRAIG

I pull up in front of the job site, Serena's house, putting the truck in gear and and turning off the ignition. I'm later than I'd hoped, but maybe I beat the inspector here.

I hop out of the cab of the truck and make my way into the house. Once Sheetrock is hung, a nailing inspection follows. As I'd told Serena, I scheduled the inspection for this afternoon. Problem is, you never know exactly when the inspector will show.

I find the inspection card and see that it's already been signed. I missed the guy. I kick at a few loose nails on the floor—I like to get the site cleaned up before an inspection, but I got hung up at the office this afternoon.

Well, we passed—that's the important thing. Though my jobs are rarely flagged. I have a good crew, and I keep a close eye on things. A quick look at my watch tells me I still have time to do what I came to do, so I go back to the truck and grab a push broom out of the back. I lean the broom against the outhouse, and then I walk the perimeter of the house, picking up scraps of wood, paper coffee cups, and miscellaneous debris and tossing it all into the Dumpster.

I used to pay a kid to clean up my sites, but now I do the work myself. Instead of paying someone else minimum wage, I need to drop those coins into my own pocket. Plus, I like the physical work.

When I'm done outside, I grab the broom and go inside the house. At almost four thirty on a Friday afternoon, the subs have laid off for the day. The place is quiet—no blaring music, no roaring generators, none of the yelling back and forth or other constant noises that characterize a construction site.

I'll do a quick cleanup inside then go back to the office to change my clothes before heading downtown for the BIA reception. Those receptions definitely aren't my kind of thing, but as I told Melanie this morning, I can't afford not to go. And I was straight with her when I said I'd rather help her clean toilets—or whatever it is she'll do this evening.

The broom slows in my hand and the cloud of Sheetrock dust settles. I sigh. Some part of me knows that isn't all true.

When did I stop wanting to go home?

I lean on the broom and look around the house. Mel and I were so happy when we built our home. We were still planning for a family then. Still had hope that we'd fill the rooms with kids.

It's a family that makes a house a home.

But the kids never came. That's old news, but it comes to mind repeatedly about this time every year.

That's when things began to change—when we learned we'd never conceive. Was it just Melanie who changed? Is that when she left? Not physically, but—

"Hello there."

I turn toward the entry of the house, where Serena stands holding what looks like an ice chest.

"So, I assume it passed inspection?" She smiles as she walks toward me.

"Of course." I chuckle. "It's easy to sound confident after the fact. What are you doing here?"

"I was supposed to meet Ashley, but she stood me up. She called just as I pulled into the neighborhood, so I thought I'd come by anyway and walk around."

I point at the ice chest. "Bring your dinner?"

She laughs then holds up the chest. "Sushi. Ashley and I were supposed to celebrate." The laughter is gone and her expression turns serious. "Or maybe *commemorate* is the more appropriate term."

I walk over to a wall, lean the broom against it, and then walk back and take the ice chest from Serena, setting it on the floor. "Commemorate?"

She takes a deep breath and seems to struggle with what to say.

"It's... Today is the one-year anniversary of..."—she looks down at the floor then back to me—"Charles's death."

"I'm sorry. I didn't realize..."

"It's all right. We're all right. So in a way, it was meant to be a celebration—a celebration of our survival." She looks around the house. "Of new beginnings." Her voice drops to a whisper. "And a time to remember..."

I can't think of anything to say, so I just nod.

"I think it was too much for Ash. She apologized profusely then told me she's getting together with friends. That'll be good for her, actually. Anyway, I saw your truck, so I brought the ice chest and"—she lifts one shoulder then lets it drop—"thought I'd see if you had time to celebrate with me? It's a shame to let the food go to waste. We can toast to passing another inspection."

Everything in me, every good sense I have, tells me to go. I'll tell her I have a meeting. The BIA thing. I made a commitment. Have to be there...

"If you can't stay, I certainly under—"

"Nope. I mean, I can't stay long, but sure, let's celebrate."

"Really?"

I nod. "You bet."

"Great. I'll be right back."

As Serena goes to get whatever she's gone to get, I pull my phone out of my back pocket—I'll text Melanie and tell her what I'm doing. Then I hesitate. What *am* I doing? I put the phone back into my pocket and comb my fingers through my hair.

I'm meeting with a client. That's all.

———————————— ◆ ————————————

We sit on the veranda—which is nothing but a poured slab and concrete balustrades at this point—in two folding beach chairs Serena had in her trunk for the occasion. Two giant heritage oaks shade the area from the late afternoon sun.

Serena looks around. "This will be lovely when the stone is laid, don't you think?"

"You bet."

She opens the ice chest and pulls out two champagne flutes, a bottle, and an assortment of sushi rolls and sauces. She takes a couple of paper plates, some napkins, and two pairs of chopsticks out of a bag and sets them with the food on a blanket she's tossed on the ground between the low chairs.

She hands me the bottle. "Will you do the honors?"

I look at the label and smile. "Sparkling cider?"

"Of course, you didn't expect that I'd serve my underage daughter champagne, did you?"

"Nah, I guess not." I pull the foil off the top of the bottle then unscrew the cap and fill both glasses. I put the cider back into her ice chest, hand her a glass, and lift mine. "To Charles and to new beginnings."

Her features soften. "Thank you," she whispers. "Cheers." She clinks her glass against mine and then takes a sip of her cider. "Help yourself." She points to the spread.

"This looks great. Mikuni's?"

"Best sushi in the area."

"Agreed."

Once I've served myself, she does the same, and, with plates balanced on our laps, we fall into easy conversation.

I stretch my legs out in front of me. "So how'd you get into the design business?"

"Oh goodness. . . My mother said I started decorating things about the same time I started walking. Some things are just in our blood, I suppose. My last year of college, I applied for a design internship in Paris, and, by some miracle, I was chosen for the position. I spent the first semester of my senior year living, studying, and working in France. After graduation, I was offered a job there. That's how my international career"—she rolls her eyes, poking fun at herself—"took off."

"What's it like? That kind of success?"

"I used to think success was important, but I've learned otherwise. It doesn't define you. It can't make you happy—not really, anyway. Yes, money makes life easier in some ways, but it also complicates things. I'm good at what I do—I enjoy using the talents I've been given. But my definition of success has changed over the years."

I chuckle. "I have a confession to make."

"Uh-oh."

"I was afraid you'd be a diva—demanding, entitled, that kind of thing."

She laughs. "Oh, I can be, believe me. But only when necessary. The last project I completed—just before Charles passed—was a Beverly Hills mansion owned by a young starlet, who shall remain nameless. It didn't take me long to figure out that I'd have to out-diva her if anything was going to get done. And believe me"—she raises one eyebrow—"I did."

I laugh with her.

"So what about you, Craig? I know you're married. Tell me about your family."

"Yep, married. Melanie, my wife, is a novelist—she's working on her sixteenth book."

"Ah, another creative woman."

We just celebrated twenty-three years. No children. In fact. . ."— I hesitate—"I was thinking about that when you walked in this afternoon."

"About not having children?"

"Yeah. Eighteen years ago this month a doctor told us we'd never have kids—at least not our own biological children. I always wanted a house full of kids. We talked about adoption, but in the long run, Melanie. . ." I shake my head. "Anyway, I guess this time each year I revisit that news for some reason."

"I'm sorry. That must have been difficult for both of you. Maybe revisiting that news, as you say, is your way of grieving. Of acknowledging the pain."

I focus on the balustrades surrounding the veranda. "Maybe."

"Grief is powerful. Either we own it and experience it, or it owns us."

I turn and look at her. "What do you mean?"

She inhales as though she has to muster the energy for what she's about to say. "I'm not an expert, but after Charles died"—she looks out over the veranda at the canyon below, the American River snaking through it—"I just wanted to push the pain aside. I didn't want to deal with it. But then I recognized Ashley doing the same thing. Her activity level became frenetic, and she was making some poor choices. I felt myself changing, too." She looks back to me. "It's difficult to explain, but I felt like I was becoming a lesser version of myself. I knew for Ashley's sake, and for my own, that we needed to deal with the loss rather than try to move on as if it had never happened. So I did some research, found some books on grief, got Ashley connected with a good counselor." She shrugs. "Now, we're moving through the pain. There are days when it's still quite. . .hard. But I let myself feel the pain, let the emotions come." Her lips curve into a slight smile. "Well, I do try to control them when tears aren't appropriate, like during a meeting with my contractor." She winks at me.

I chuckle then grow serious as I consider what she's said. "You're a smart lady."

"I don't know how smart I am, but I am committed to dealing with what life hands me. It's the only way to live, really. Simply existing isn't worth the effort. We were created to live life to the full, and we can only do that if we're willing to fully participate."

My heart rate kicks up a notch as I listen to her. And watch her. . . Her green eyes spark with conviction.

"So there's your life lesson for the evening, not that you asked."

"Actually, I did ask." My gaze locks with hers, and we stare at each other for a moment.

Then she blushes and looks away from me, suddenly seeming self-conscious. She stands and walks to the edge of the veranda. With her back to me, she raises her hands to her head and pulls out a few pins that held her hair in its usual knot. She tucks them into the pocket of her jeans, a casual look for her, and then runs her hands through her long hair. Her back rises and falls with each breath she takes.

She glances at me over her shoulder then looks back. "This view is therapeutic."

I look at my watch. Either I leave right now and go straight to the BIA gig. . .

Or. . .

I don't.

I get up, go to where she stands, and watch her. I can't take my eyes off her. "It is a beautiful view."

———◆———

When I pull into the driveway, the house is dark except for the reflection of the moon on the windows. At my insistence, Melanie even turns the porch light off when she goes to bed now.

I leave the truck parked outside and sneak into the house, careful not to wake her. I'd like to tell myself I'm being thoughtful, but I know the truth.

I don't want to wake her, because. . .

I don't want her to ask about the reception.

Hesitation increases in relation to risk in equal proportion to age.
Ernest Hemingway

Chapter 10

JILL

Shh. . . Sleep now." I rub Luis's back until I think he's gone to sleep. He is named after Marcos's father. Thomas is named after my dad. Thomas fell asleep in the car and thankfully stayed asleep as I carried him into the house, which, at almost three years old, is a feat on my part. I tiptoe out of the twins' room. *Please God, let them stay asleep.* The twins' energy never seems to wane. I check the baby monitor in their room to ensure it's working then gently close their bedroom door.

Praying for the twins' sleep is my second-most oft-uttered prayer. I tiptoe down the hallway into the family room. *What happened here?* Several magazines peek out from the spot between a wingback chair and a Longaberger basket, I use to hold magazines. The boys strike again, no doubt. Before straightening up the mess, I go to the kitchen and grab a dust rag. When I return, I dust the handle and the sides of the basket then pick up the magazines from the floor and dust each one before placing them back into the basket.

The last magazine catches my eye—*Architectural Digest.* It's an edition from last year, which I normally wouldn't have kept, but there was a spread on a local interior designer who did gorgeous work. If we're ever going to remodel, I want to work with a good designer. I'd kept the magazine as a reference.

I straighten the basket, swipe the dust rag across the handle once more, and then take the *Architectural Digest* with me back to the kitchen and set it on the bar. After dropping the dust rag into the washing machine in the laundry room, I wash my hands with the antibacterial soap I keep by the kitchen sink. I pour myself a glass of iced tea and then sit at the bar to thumb through the magazine.

I settle on the stool, set my glass on the counter, and take a deep breath, hoping to ease the constriction between my shoulder blades. *It's okay to relax for a moment. Nothing will happen. Gaby is with Melanie. The twins are fine. They're asleep, aren't they?* I turn my head toward the monitor plugged in at the end of the bar and listen for the steady rhythm of their breathing. Then I get up, go to the monitor, and switch it off and on several times to make sure it's working. Then I return to the glossy pages of the magazine.

The rooms depicted are lovely. Every accessory placed just so. Woods oiled to a sheen. Glass tables and windows shined to perfection.

But where's the article I was looking for? I turn back to the table of contents and find it: "High Design in River City." I turn to the page number noted. The interior designer is pictured, but it's the featured room where she stands that I stare at. The clean, contemporary lines of the furnishings and the monochromatic color scheme make for a serene environment. It's exactly the type of peaceful backdrop I'd like our home to provide.

As I begin rereading the article about the designer, the front door opens. I swivel the stool toward the entry, where Melanie and Gaby tiptoe across the threshold—a precaution both have practiced since the twins' birth, whether it's nap time or not. I've schooled everyone to tiptoe. . .just in case. The moments when both boys are asleep at the same time are precious.

I wave them both into the kitchen, but Gaby holds up her book and points to the den. I nod my approval to Gaby and pat the barstool next to me for Melanie. I'm up to make her a cup of coffee before she even crosses the family room.

As her coffee brews, I stand across the bar from her. "Thanks for walking her home." I keep my tone low, just above a whisper.

"Sure. But you know, she is almost eight years old. She could probably cross the driveway without being kidnapped by hooligans, attacked by zombies, or sustaining life-threatening injuries."

"You sound like Marcos."

"Exactly. And guess what? Marcos and I share equally outrageous IQ scores." She looks expectant, like she has just imparted ground-breaking research stats and is waiting for my awed response.

"If you were. . ." I stop when I realize what I was about to say.

"If I were a mother?"

"That's not what I meant. I'm sorry. It's just that. . ."

"Never mind. I know. If I were a mother, I'd understand."

"Maybe. . ." I lift my hands, palms up. "Maybe I worry too much."

"And *maybe* the sun will rise tomorrow."

I smile at Melanie's sarcasm, though the smile doesn't still the ever-present voice of warning in my head. "I really am sorry."

Her expression reassures. "I know you are, but Jill, you're wasting your life worrying about things you can't control."

"But these are things I can control, at least as much as any of us controls anything. It's my responsibility to protect my children. You can't argue with that, and neither can Marcos."

"I know, but—"

"So I worry a little. You escape a little. No one's perfect."

"I don't. . . Oh, never mind. Truce?"

"Truce." I reach for a mug. "Cream today or black?"

"Cream. I'll go back to black after the deadline." She looks down at the open magazine on the counter. "They say fat is necessary for optimum brain function, right? Although. . . Maybe I should reconsider."

"Why?"

She picks up the magazine and studies it. "Wow, look at those slacks she's wearing. So classy. Her legs must be a mile long. Her waist, too." She shakes her head. "I could never pull off that look."

I come around the bar with Melanie's coffee and set it in front of her, looking over her shoulder at the photo she's examining. "Of course you could. Your legs are just as long as hers—you could wear those pants."

She shakes her head. "No, I need a WIDE LOAD warning on my back end these days. Deadline spread."

I swat her shoulder as I sit down next to her. "Forget the designer—look at her work. That room is pure perfection."

She flips the magazine closed, keeping a finger in place to mark the article. "*Architectural Digest*? You're not thinking of her for your remodel, are you? I hate to break it to you, but if she's featured in *Architectural Digest*, you can't afford her."

"Wishful thinking, I guess."

Melanie opens the magazine to the article again. "But you're right, her work is beautiful." She sets the magazine down and reaches for her coffee, lifting the mug to her lips.

"She's a local designer, though the article says she's worked all over the world. Serena Buchanan. Why does her name sound familiar?"

Melanie sputters then coughs and coughs again. I give her a couple of gentle pats on the back. "Are you okay? Want some water?"

She shakes her head, coughs a few more times, and then catches her breath. "That. . ." She picks up the magazine again. "That's *her*?" She shakes her head. "Well, that answers *that* question." Eyes wide, she stares at the photo of the interior designer.

"What question? Do you know her?"

"No. But Craig does. The custom he's building. . ." She points, tapping the photo with her index finger. "It's for her."

"Craig's building for *her*?" I take the magazine out of Melanie's hands to get a closer look at Serena Buchanan. "I knew her name sounded familiar. Wow, she's—"

"A knockout."

"I was going to say *talented*. I'd imagine she could be a demanding client, though."

"Actually, I think he said the job's going well—evidently she isn't as entitled as he feared. He said it's nice to work with someone who. . ."

"Who what?"

She sighs. "I don't remember." She continues staring at the photo. "I just remember that the last time he talked about the job he seemed more—I don't know—settled, maybe?" She glances at me. "Less stressed. Not less stressed overall—just about that job."

"Well, that's positive, isn't it?"

She shrugs. "Has Craig said anything to Marcos about her?"

"What do you mean?"

"What do you mean, 'what do I mean'? You know. Has he mentioned Serena Buchanan? Talked about her?"

"I don't know, why? You're not concerned he's. . ." I hesitate as I recall the long hours Craig's worked recently. The many nights we've heard his truck pull into the driveway well after midnight.

"What? No. No, of course not. Craig would never. . ." She shakes her head, shuts the magazine, sets it down, and then picks up her mug, takes a sip of her coffee, and swallows. Then she looks back to me. "Did I tell you I ran into Valerie at Safeway?"

"No. . ."—I hesitate a moment as I try to track with her—"you didn't mention seeing her."

Melanie has just closed and padlocked the subject of Craig and Serena Buchanan.

————————◆————————

"Good appointment with the doctor today, no?" Marcos climbs into bed next to me.

"I think so. Do you think her assessment of the boys' development is accurate?"

"Absolutely. She said they're right on target. So you can stop worrying."

"Maybe. I'm not sure about her though. I wonder if we should get another opinion."

"Another opinion isn't necessary, Jill. The boys are fine. They're doing well. And Dr. Mikkelsen is one of the most sought-after pediatricians in our area. You told me that yourself." He leans over and kisses me on the cheek then points to the magazine on my lap. "*Architectural Digest*? Dreaming of remodeling again?"

"Actually, no. I mean, I was, but not tonight. I wanted to show you something." I open the magazine to the article about Serena Buchanan and then hand it to Marcos.

"Okay, what am I looking at?"

"Her—the designer. The house Craig is building, the custom home? It's for her."

"Impressive." He moves to hand the magazine back to me.

"No, wait. Really look at her."

He holds the magazine up and studies the picture of the designer. "What am I supposed to see?"

"She's beautiful, don't you think?"

He looks at me and smiles. "Not nearly as beautiful as you."

"Marcos, I'm serious."

"So am I. What's your point?"

I take the magazine back from him, close it, and set it on my nightstand. "When Melanie brought Gaby home this afternoon, she saw that photo, and it really seemed to rattle her. She asked me if Craig had mentioned Serena to you."

Marcos shrugs. "No, but I haven't seen Craig much lately. Why did she ask?"

"She seemed worried that maybe Craig would—I don't know—find her attractive or something. You don't think he'd ever get involved or have an affair, do you?"

Marcos seems thoughtful as he considers my question. "Yes, Craig may find her attractive, but that doesn't mean he'd act on the attraction. Men can appreciate an attractive woman without it going any further. Craig is trustworthy."

"But you know the late hours he's working."

He nods. "He has to, Jill. They're struggling financially; he told us both that. But if you're concerned, I'll give him a call—connect with him. I need to do that anyway."

It's my turn to lean over and kiss Marcos. Then I pull the sheet back and climb out of bed. "I'm going to check on the kids."

Marcos sighs. "Again?"

"I'll be right back."

I go down the hallway to Gaby's room, open her door, and go in. I don't tiptoe. It would take an earthquake with a magnitude of 6.0 to wake this one. I lean over her, brush her bangs off her damp forehead, and then pull the light blanket covering her down to the bottom of the bed. I straighten the sheet over her and then watch her for a moment. *Father, please protect her from any harm. Watch over her.* Before heading for the twins' room, I check the monitor I still keep in Gaby's room—the one Marcos chides me about.

I stop outside the twins' closed bedroom door and listen. Do I dare risk waking them by checking on them again? I'd heard steady breathing through the monitor on my nightstand. But were they both breathing? I reach for the handle on the door and crack it open. It's silent in the room—neither boy stirs. Are they okay? *Oh, Lord. . .*

"They're fine, Jill," Marcos whispers behind me. Then he reaches for the door and closes it, the movement gentle, soundless.

I turn and look into Marcos's eyes. "Are you sure?"

"I'm sure."

"But—"

"No buts. Come to bed." His tone is patient but firm.

Protect them, Father. Watch over them. I follow Marcos back to our bedroom and climb back into bed.

He stands by his side of the bed, his gaze cast at the floor. When he looks back to me, tears shine in his eyes. "It's time, Jill."

"Time?" I can't look him in the eye, so I turn away and busy myself with my phone, pretending I don't know what he's talking about.

"Yes."

Heat rises to my face.

"Jill."

I set the phone aside, take a deep breath, and then turn back to Marcos.

His broad shoulders lift then drop with his sigh. "It's time to get help. I love you. I will always love you." His Adam's apple bobs as he swallows. "And you need help. For your sake, Jill. It's getting worse." He wipes his eyes with the back of his hand. "I don't know what it's like—I don't know what you feel. But I know something's wrong. Maybe you could talk to Valerie, get a referral, and—"

"Nothing's wrong. There's nothing wrong with me. Just because I care about our children, just because I care about their well-being, you think I need help? What's wrong with caring, Marcos? Tell me, what's wrong with that?" My voice quivers.

He lowers his gaze to the floor again. When he looks back at me this time, he looks weary. He shakes his head. "We'll talk more tomorrow." He climbs into bed, turns off the lamp on his nightstand, and then rolls over, his back to me.

When was the last time I saw tears in my husband's eyes? The last time was the night the twins were born, and those were tears of joy. Not tears of pain or grief or whatever it is I've made him feel.

I bite my bottom lip. I bite it so hard, I hope it will bleed. I deserve to hurt for hurting him. But even as I take responsibility for my actions and vow, again, to change, I know I'm powerless to do so. All I can do is hope and pray that tomorrow never comes—the follow-up conversation he mentioned. Will he let it go? Will he forget?

Maybe tomorrow my behavior will resemble that of a normal wife and mother.

Maybe tomorrow the obsessive thoughts will wane.

Maybe tomorrow I won't give in to the compulsions that drive me.

Maybe I'll start now. . . . I turn toward my nightstand, where the baby monitors are plugged in. *They're on. They're working*, I tell myself.

I reach to turn off the lamp but hesitate.

The monitors are working. They're fine. No need to check them. The monitors are working. The room is still, quiet, the only sound coming from one of the monitors as one of the twins sighs then rustles his bedding. *See, it's working. You just heard one of the boys move.*

I take a deep breath, switch the lamp off, and lie down. I can do this. *They're working. The monitors are working.* I turn my head toward the monitors; a red light glows on each, indicating the monitors are on. *They're on. They're working.*

But. . .

I have to check.

I can't *not* check.

I sit back up, reach for one of the monitors, and flip the switch off. Then I turn it back on. Then I turn it off. Then back on. Then off and on one last time. Then I check the other monitor. . .

Off, on, off, on, off, on.

That's the pattern.

Every. Single. Time.

Writing a novel is a terrible experience,
during which the hair often falls out and the teeth decay.
Flannery O'Connor

Chapter 11

MELANIE

My phone vibrates and skitters toward the edge of the desk. I sigh at the interruption—it's been a day of them. I grab the phone before it falls. Even as I'm telling myself to ignore the call, I glance at the screen of the phone, where I see Craig's name. I hesitate then answer. "Hey..."

"Hi. You working?"

"Actually, I was lounging on the sofa nibbling bonbons."

He chuckles. "You know, we should try that sometime."

"You're on. What's up?" I lean back in my desk chair and swivel away from the display, which, if I didn't know better, I'd swear was glaring at me.

"I thought I'd do something different this evening and actually leave the office on time and come home."

"Ah, tossing in the towel on work?"

"Sort of. It doesn't seem to be getting me anywhere."

"I know the feeling. I suppose you thought I might cook dinner?"

"If you have time. Otherwise I can build a couple of sandwiches for us."

I swivel back toward the display and glance at my lagging word count. Who has time to cook?

"Mel?"

Guilt presses against my chest, eliciting another sigh, but I don't let Craig hear it. "You've probably done enough building for one day. I'll go take something out of the freezer."

"Great, thanks. I'll see you about five thirty."

After hitting END, I toss the phone back onto the desk and stand up. I stretch, feeling as though my back end has molded itself into the shape of my desk chair. Then I stomp my way to the kitchen—and not in a Broadway-musical kind of way. I don't know why I'm angry with Craig. I told myself to ignore the call and instead ignored my own advice.

I reach the freezer, swing the door open, and stare at the contents.

If I hadn't answered, Craig would have left a message, and I could have pled ignorance when he showed up for dinner. He knows I rarely remember to listen to my messages.

Anyway, why'd he pick tonight to come home? He hasn't been home for dinner in weeks. He got home late again last night and was gone before I woke this morning.

I shove a bag of corn aside, hoping there are a few chicken breasts behind it. Instead, I find a pint of fudge brownie ice cream. I pull it out of the freezer and go to a drawer for a spoon.

I only knew he'd come home last night because I woke briefly when he slid into bed.

I scoop a spoonful of ice cream out of the carton and into my mouth. I let it melt on my tongue until I'm left with just chewy bits of brownie—the best part.

His call was an interruption just now, but I've never wanted to ignore Craig's calls before. In fact, I've always looked forward to a call from him during the day. Why the change?

I shovel one more loaded spoonful into my mouth.

It's the *D* word, no doubt.

Can I blame everything on this deadline, including my bad attitude? I nod as I eat. Yes, yes I can. It's all the deadline's fault.

I put the ice cream back into the freezer and dig until I find a package of pork chops. I set them on the counter to thaw then check the pantry for a can of cream of mushroom soup and a few other ingredients. Upon finding what I need, I determine I can throw together a simple dinner with minimal effort.

While I'm in the kitchen, I load our breakfast dishes into the dishwasher, make a fresh pot of coffee, and then swing into the laundry room, where I put a load of clothes into the washing machine. Then I take a load of towels out of the dryer, fold them, clean the lint out of the trap, and carry the towels to both the guest and master bathrooms, where I put them away. While I'm in the master bathroom, I also clean the bathroom mirror and sinks because, well, they need it.

My phone vibrates again. I pull it out of my pocket to see Valerie's name lighting up the screen. Really? This time I do ignore the call and put the phone back into my pocket.

Thirty minutes later, I'm back at my desk where, when I look at the scene I was writing, I have no idea of the direction I was headed. I do, however, recall the now-rare sense of inspiration I'd felt just before the phone rang.

Even more rare is the irritation I feel with Craig. I shake my head, trying to clear it of the negative thoughts, and work to refocus my attention on the scene.

Who am I kidding? It's more than negative thoughts I can't get out of my mind. It's that spread in *Architectural Digest*. The photo of Serena Buchanan.

A sense of foreboding weasels its way into my psyche. "Get over it, Melanie."

And determined to do just that, I focus again on the display on my desk and reread what I'd written. I place my fingers on the keyboard, and then the doorbell rings.

I slump in my chair and lift my eyes to the bulletin board. "Elliot, Valerie's right. We need to get away."

Instead of answering the front door, I pick up my phone and return Valerie's call.

I need a few details.

And a key.

Painful as it may be, a significant emotional event can be the catalyst for choosing a direction that serves us—and those around us—more effectively. Look for the learning.
Louisa May Alcott

Chapter 12

CRAIG

The laundry-room door from the garage scrapes against the hardwood floor as I open it, grating on my conscience. How many times has Melanie asked me to fix it? The door scrapes closed behind me as I drop my briefcase—a black leather messenger bag Melanie gave me several birthdays ago when money was still plentiful and life was still predictable—on the laundry-room counter.

I stand in the dark laundry room for a minute, muscles in my neck tense. This isn't going to be an easy conversation. . . .

Jaw set, I allow the scent coming from the kitchen to pull me into the nook where Melanie's set the table. "Wow, that smells good. Pork chops?" I cross the nook and come up behind Mel, who's uncorking a bottle, and I put my arms around her waist.

"Pork chops it is. Not the perfect summer meal, but it's what I found in the freezer."

"Sounds good."

"Thanks for coming home," she says over her shoulder as she pours.

Is there an edge to her tone? My shoulders stiffen, and I pull away from her. "I know I haven't been around much, but—"

"Craig, that wasn't a jab." She turns toward me and hands me a glass. "I meant it. I'm glad you're here. When you called earlier, I wasn't thrilled with the idea of quitting work early, but"—she shrugs—"I'm glad you're here."

I look at my feet then back to her. "I'm sorry."

She picks up her glass and lifts it toward mine. "To an evening at home together."

"Cheers." As I say the word, I hear Serena's voice, see her lifting her glass to mine. I clear my throat. "How long until dinner?"

"Ten minutes or so."

"Okay. I'm going to get cleaned up."

I take the stairs two at a time, go into our bedroom, and head for the walk-in closet off the bathroom. But in order to get into the closet, I have to dodge a suitcase sitting open on the upholstered seat from Mel's vanity. She's moved the seat in front of the closet door and put the suitcase on top of it—her habit when she's packing for a trip. The suitcase is filled with folded clothes. Her cosmetics bag sits on the counter next to her sink.

The muscle in my jaw twitches. I push the seat and suitcase aside then go into the closet and change my shirt. She didn't mention going anywhere, did she? As I pass the suitcase again on my way back to the bathroom, my chest tightens, and acid burns my throat.

I splash cold water on my face, dry it off, and then reach for an antacid tablet. As I chew the chalky disk, I look into the mirror. The lines around my mouth are deeper than they were just a few months ago, and there's more gray in my hair. My eyes are bloodshot. With palms flat on the bathroom counter, I look away from the mirror and down at the sink.

"Craig?"

I don't move. "What?" My tone is flat.

"I just remembered. . . I meant to. . ."

I take a deep breath and then blow it out. I turn toward Melanie and point at the suitcase. "Something you need to tell me?"

"I was going to tell to you about it over dinner. Why don't you come down—"

"Where are you going? Why didn't you tell me you were going somewhere?" Although, to be fair, when would she have told me?

"It's a writing retreat. I *have* to get that book written. Come downstairs. We'll eat and. . .talk."

Fatigue weighs on me like an anvil. It isn't like Mel to issue an invitation to talk, and we do need to talk. I don't know what she has to say, but what I need to say will take more energy than I have. But it has to be done. She deserves the truth. "Go ahead. I'll be right there."

After she's gone, when I look back into the mirror, I barely recognize the reflection staring back at me.

I am not the man I used to be.

——————◆◆——————

If only I could cut the tension between us with the same ease that I cut through the tender pork chop on my plate. It doesn't seem possible, though I try again. "So, when did you make this decision to go away to finish the book?"

"Today. I said that, didn't I? Valerie offered her place last week, and I didn't think much about it. But it's become evident that if I'm going to make the deadline, I need uninterrupted time." Melanie pushes her plate away.

"You spend all day home alone. How many interruptions can there be?" She looks away from me, and I know I've gone too far. "I'm sorry. I know there are interruptions. It's just. . . I need you, Mel."

"You'll have to help me understand what exactly it is you need from me."

"Fine." I swallow the last bite of my dinner along with the last of my. . . What? Patience? Something. "You want to understand? I haven't wanted to tell you this, but here it is in black and white." I ball the napkin in my lap and toss it onto the table. "I don't see any way out of our financial mess other than. . .putting the house on the market. And if we're going to do that then I need you here." This isn't the way I wanted to tell her this, and I know there's more to it than that, but. . . I can't tell her everything.

Her eyes reveal nothing. She straightens the knife and spoon at her setting.

"Did you hear what I said?"

"Yes. That's all the more reason for me to go."

"Excuse me?"

She reaches for her cell phone and stares at the screen.

"Melanie?"

She punches a few keys on the phone and seems to scroll through something. E-mail? Facebook?

I take a deep breath. "Please listen to me."

She sets the phone down and stares across the table at me, but I've lost her. Her expression is blank, vacant.

"How does putting our house on the market equate to a stronger reason for you to leave? I can't. . .I can't do it all, Mel. I need your help."

"Finishing the manuscript means I'll receive the second portion of my advance. Which is money that, as I understand it, we need very much. Finishing the manuscript means I'm free to begin the next book, which also comes with an advance. More money." Her tone is tight. "Do you see where this is going?"

"You've always written at home. Why do you have to take off now?"

She leans back in her chair and stares at something beyond me. "I'm not taking off. I'm working."

"I'm sorry. I didn't mean it that way. It's just. . ."

Or did I mean it the way it sounded? How many times has she run from a situation when I needed her? If not physically then emotionally. Ever since—

"Just what?"

Ever since she started writing—ever since she started losing herself in her fictional worlds. "I need you to be present, Melanie. Not just physically, but emotionally." I put my hands on the table, palms down, and work to keep my tone steady, but I fail and raise my voice. "I need your support." My jaw clenches.

A flame I've rarely seen ignites in Mel's blue eyes, and she stands up quickly, rattling the dishes on the table. "I am not the one who has checked out!"

She picks up her water glass, and for a second I consider ducking. But instead of throwing the glass at me, she goes and sets the glass in the sink.

I take a deep breath. "Don't walk away. Come back so we can—"

"You're the only one who has walked away." She turns back from the sink and faces me. "Do you have any idea how many nights I've gone to bed alone? Only to wake up hours later, still alone? Where are you spending your time? It certainly isn't here. Am I truly supposed to believe you're sitting alone at your desk all those hours?" She spits her questions at me.

"What are you implying? You know exactly where I am."

"No, I don't! I just know you aren't here. And now you're

complaining because I'm leaving for a few weeks? Why the double standard? Why?!"

She's yelling at me now, something she's never done. Never. In all our years together. I stand to meet her gaze. My surprise at her raised voice is squelched by a burning in my chest that explodes out my mouth. "How dare you accuse me. Stop! Stop it!" I roar.

The fire in her eyes is doused with tears. "Defensive, aren't you?" she whispers as she swipes at a tear on her cheek. Then she turns and walks into the kitchen, stopping in front of the freezer.

I can count on one hand the number of times I've seen my wife cry. I know this means something—her tears. I know I should let her pain impact me, soften me. I should apologize. I should take Mel in my arms and assure her of my love. I should.

But I can't seem to bring myself to put my own pain aside.

My heart pounds against my rib cage, and I ball my fists at my side. What is she thinking? I can't believe. . . I shake my head. Yeah, there are a lot of things I *should* do, but right now, I'm not doing any of them.

She opens the freezer and rummages around for something. When she turns back and looks at me, there's doubt in her eyes. "You don't need me. You won't even miss me." She shakes her head. "Forget I said that—forget everything I said. I'm. . . It's this deadline. That's all. The stress. . ." She holds the freezer door open. "This is why I'm going. If you needed a reason, there it is. I'm crazed. I'm not thinking clearly." She turns back to the freezer and stares inside. "How about dessert? Ice cream?"

"Wait. Please." I take a deep breath, my tone measured now. "Since we're talking about this, since you asked, I need to tell you something. I want to tell you—"

"I don't need to hear anything. I don't, Craig. Really, everything is fine. It'll be fine."

She doesn't put her hands over her ears, but she may as well. The moment of honesty is gone. She's gone. I try again. "Can we just talk? Can you come back, sit down, and just listen to me for a minute? Please."

"Fudge brownie or. . ." She moves a few things around inside the freezer. "Vanilla." She doesn't look at me. "Which would you prefer?"

"Melanie."

"The fudge brownie is good, but then, you're not really a brownie guy. So, vanilla?"

"Please."

She stands with the freezer door open, the carton of vanilla ice cream in her shaking hand. If she could, I've no doubt she'd climb inside the freezer and close the door just to get away.

"Mel. . ."

She shoves the ice cream back into the freezer, slams the door, and then heads for the stairs. I get up out of my chair and step in front of her, blocking her exit. "Melanie!"

She stands still.

"Please. Can we just talk?" I keep my tone even.

She keeps her eyes focused on the floor and says nothing.

"Okay, if this is how you want to do it. Late yesterday afternoon, I was cleaning up the job site and Serena came by. I wasn't expecting her—she just dropped in."

Melanie looks up at me. Is that fear in her eyes? I take a step back and clear my throat. "Anyway, I. . .never made it to the BIA thing last night. But—"

She skirts around me, running down the hallway and up the stairs. "Melanie!"

Do I follow her? I comb my fingers through my hair. Or do I give her space? I need to tell her. Need to explain. She needs to understand. I walk to the stairs, climb the first few, and then stop. Does she need to understand, or do I just need to unburden myself? Am I doing this for her? For myself? Or for us?

Maybe Melanie isn't the one I should be talking to.

I sit down on the step and put my head in my hands. Sounds of her rustling around drift down the stairs. What's she doing?

In less than a minute, she comes down the stairs, stopping when she gets to me. "Please move."

I get up and turn toward her. "Wait. You're not leaving now, are you? Please, Melanie. It isn't—"

She tries to step around me, but she can't maneuver past me with the suitcase in her hand.

"Melanie, I love you." I swallow the lump forming in my throat. "Please. . . This isn't how I wanted to tell you any of this."

She doesn't look at me. Just stands there, suitcase in hand, purse flung over her shoulder.

I step aside, making room for her to pass me on the stairs. She goes down the rest of the stairs and then stops at her office, where she sets the suitcase down in the hallway, goes in, and comes out with her laptop bag and a stuffed backpack. She tries to pick up the suitcase, but she can't carry it all.

"Here"—in a few quick strides I'm by her side—"let me help you." I pick up the suitcase, take the backpack out of her hand, and then follow her to the garage, where I load her suitcase into the trunk of her car.

She puts her purse and laptop bag in the backseat then gets in the driver's seat.

I go and stand at the open car door and bend down so I can see her. "Mel, I don't even know where this house is—I don't know where you're going."

"Lake County. I'll text you the address."

I sigh. "Please call me when you get there so I know you're safe. Or at least text me."

She nods.

And then. . .

She's gone.

It takes several minutes before I work up the energy to walk back into the empty house. I climb the steps in the garage to the landing, press the button to close the garage door, flip off the light, and then open the door into the laundry room. The door scrapes as I push it open and scrapes again as it closes.

I stop and examine the floor. For the first time I notice the groove the sagging door has worn into the hardwood. The finish on the pine floor is scratched, and there's a deep arc-shaped dent in the wood.

I shake my head then smack my fist against the wall.

The damage appears permanent.

How could I have been so stupid?

She generally gave herself very good advice,
(though she very seldom followed it).
Lewis Carroll

Chapter 13

JILL

When I get out of my car in front of Valerie's house just before 7:00 p.m., heat assaults me as it rises off the asphalt. I click my key fob to lock the car then make my way up the front walkway to her door. Before I ring the doorbell, I pull my phone out of the pocket of my shorts and check it for messages or texts.

I want to call Marcos to check in, but based on our conversation the other night—one we haven't yet revisited—I don't want to do anything that he may interpret as odd. And calling home to check on my husband and children ten minutes after leaving them is odd. I know that. Regardless of how much I want to call.

This evening, for whatever reason, resisting the urge to check in seems, if not an easy choice, at least a choice I'm able to make.

Maybe Marcos is wrong. Maybe I am just protective. Okay, overly protective, but a lot of parents can claim that title.

I click the phone off and on a few times, check the volume to make sure I'll hear it ring if Marcos calls, and then tuck it into my purse and ring Valerie's doorbell. As I wait for her to answer, I turn and look at the cars in her driveway and in front of her house. With the exception of Melanie, it looks like I'm the last one here. When I called Mel this afternoon to see if she wanted to ride together tonight, both her home phone and her cell went to voice mail. Where is she?

———————————◆————————————

Quinn's long dark hair hangs down her back in a tight braid, and her reading glasses are perched on the end of her nose. While the rest of us hold glasses of water or iced tea and chat before the meeting begins, Quinn's nose is buried in the pages of the latest dystopian novel.

I take the last seat between Quinn and Valerie and then lean toward Valerie. "Thank you for hosting us this evening. Your house looks great."

"You're so welcome. I love filling it with friends. I'm finally feeling like I'm settling in here."

"I'm so glad. I know the move wasn't—"

"*Shh. . .*"

I turn to Quinn, who has her finger to her lips. "I'm sorry, are we bothering you?"

"I'm facilitating tonight, and I'm going to recite this passage to the group. I have it almost completely memorized. So if you don't mind. . ." Her gaze never leaves the pages of the book.

Valerie and I share a giggle at Quinn's expense, though there's no malice intended.

As we wait for Quinn to prepare, I pull my cell phone out of my purse and check it for texts or messages from Marcos. After assuring myself that I haven't missed anything, I click the phone off and wait for it to power down. Then I click it back on, wait again, turn it back off, and then—

"Having trouble with your phone?" Valerie whispers.

I turn the phone back on and check to make sure—again—that the volume is set at a level I'll hear if a text or call comes through. "No, I think it's fine. Just. . .checking it." I set the phone in my lap. Mouth dry and palms damp, I pick up the glass of iced tea I'd set on a coaster on the small side table between my chair and Valerie's and take a sip. Will she believe my explanation, or will she know something's wrong with me?

"*It's time to get help, Jill.*"

"*Maybe you could talk to Valerie. . . .*"

No. Marcos is right—he doesn't understand. He doesn't know what I feel. If I tell Valerie, she might think I'm unfit. An unfit. . .mother. She might turn me in. And then what? Then we lose the kids? Oh no. That's not a risk I'm willing to take. Who would protect our children—

"Jill." Valerie's hand is on my forearm.

"I'm sorry, what did you say?"

"Quinn's ready—we're ready to begin. You usually open the meetings, don't you?"

"Right. Yes. But where's Melanie?"

"I thought you'd know—she's at my vacation house. She left last night, I believe. She's taking some time away to work on her book."

"Oh. She. . ." I shake my head. "No, I didn't know. Okay, let's get started." I glance at the phone in my lap. Is it on? Is the volume set loud enough? Yes, I just checked it. But what if the battery died? What if. . . "Let me put this away." I pick up the phone, click it so the screen lights up, check the battery icon to confirm it's charged, and then click the volume setting one time, just to be sure. *Drop it in your purse, Jill. Just put it away. It's working. You can't let Valerie see you checking it again. Just put it in your purse. If Valerie sees you checking again, she'll wonder. And if she wonders, you could. . .lose everything.*

But. . .what if something happens to one of the kids and Marcos needs me? Anything could happen. The twins are so rambunctious. . .

Just put the phone away.

Put it away.

But it's no use.

I have to know it's working. I have to check it again.

I click the phone off, then on, then off, then on. I take a deep breath, and then I drop the phone into my purse.

When I glance back at Valerie, her eyes meet mine. What is it I read in her expression? Compassion? Or judgment?

She knows. *Oh, Lord. . .*

She knows.

Everyone thinks of changing the world,
but no one thinks of changing himself.
Leo Tolstoy

Chapter 14

Melanie

The first time I left home, I had just turned eighteen years old. While my friends were leaving for college, I'd touted my hundred-words-per-minute typing skills—learned in a high school typing class, the only class in which I'd received an A—and secured my first full-time job as a secretary. We weren't called admins back then. The salary was just enough to cover rent and utilities for a studio apartment in a converted Victorian downtown. The "apartment" was a bedroom with a hot plate and small refrigerator—the shared bathroom was down the hall.

For an average student and child of a single parent, college wasn't affordable. But at that point, I didn't care. At that age, home represented something one left. It represented adulthood, and that came with freedom. And free is exactly how I felt when I slammed the hatchback of my 1974 Pinto after unloading the last of my belongings in front of my new place.

The second time I left home was ninety minutes ago as a forty-nine-year-old, menopausal, midlist author and wife. And freedom isn't what I'm seeking. Well, not exactly, anyway. Though, as I round another bend on the winding road to Clear Lake—suitcase in the back, windows down, warm wind whipping my hair, and my phone connected to a portable speaker sitting in the passenger seat blaring classic rock tunes—*free*, I tell myself, is exactly how I feel.

Why is it that not much has changed in thirty-one years?

Flames of color lick the wheat-colored hillsides as the sun makes its descent. Within moments the palette changes from hot corals and oranges to the deep lavenders and blues of twilight.

Who am I kidding? A lot has changed physically in thirty-one years. But with the exception of additional wrinkles and pounds, I'm the same as I was at eighteen. That's something to take pride in, isn't it?

I knew who I was then—I know who I am now.

Well, sort of. . .

As the sun slips behind the coastal range, my sense of freedom slips with it and, like an albatross nesting on my head, guilt nests in my soul.

I shouldn't have run.

Why am I such a ninny?

But—I square my shoulders and sit straighter in my seat—guilt is no match for my well-developed skills. I can deny an albatross sitting on my head, if I so choose. Although I suppose I'd never admit that to Craig.

Maybe I've never admitted it to myself.

Dry grass covers the oak and manzanita-studded hills, and the wind carries the musky scent of summer into the car. And if I were to close my eyes for just a moment, I could even imagine Elliot sitting in the seat next to me. Though I don't dare close my eyes on this winding road.

As I round another bend, the darkening landscape changes to moonscape as the charred remains of a wildfire set a desolate scene and the scent on the wind changes from life to death.

My mood follows suit as images from earlier this evening play against the somber backdrop. Though it isn't the images that bother me—it's the words spoken.

"*Serena came by. . . .*"

"*I never made it to the BIA thing. . . .*"

"*You're not leaving now. . . .*"

I shake my head and then glance over at the passenger seat, the interior of the car almost dark now except for the lights on the dash.

"Elliot, let's ditch the downer thoughts, shall we?"

I reach over and turn up the speaker, and, although it takes enormous effort to push the words past the ache in my throat, I sing along with the lyrics reverberating in the car.

I sing so loud I'm certain that the annoying albatross will wing its way back to wherever it came from.

I sing so loud that I'm certain it will quell the flood of tears that blur the road ahead.

———————————◆———————————

When I open my eyes, diffused light bathes the room. I sit up, my head heavy, and look around. *Where am I?* The answer to the question presents itself almost in tandem with the question itself—Valerie's lake house. I sweep my hair out of my eyes and give the master bedroom a quick once-over—shades cover French doors facing the lake, I assume, and the side windows are draped. I'd guess the pink cotton chenille bedspread is circa 1950's, as is the rest of the decor. The pale pink paint on the walls is likely called *Shrimp* or something equally inane. I could ask Serena if I wanted to know for sure. As if... I roll my eyes and push the sheets and blanket back, drop my legs over the side of the bed, slip my feet into the slippers I placed bedside last night, and then pad my way to the bathroom.

One look in the mirror and I'm reminded of my unraveling. My eyes are puffy and circled—my nose is chapped and stuffed. When was the last time I cried? "Wait, don't go there. You know when it was," I mumble. As the memory threatens to make an appearance, I squint my eyes and give my reflection an *I dare you* glare. I point my finger at the mirror. "I said no."

What caused that upheaval anyway? Hormones, I assume. But the truth, uninvited, barges in and challenges my excuse. My tears had nothing to do with hormones and everything to do with Craig—and the way we left things.

Okay, the way *I* left things.

I know I've disappointed him. Again.

No longer able to look myself in the eye, I drop my gaze to the sink, where an infantry of ants are marching up the wall of the basin. "Well, hello there." At least I'm not totally alone.

I leave my new friends to their endeavor and meander down a short hallway that leads out to the living room, where vertical blinds cover the floor-to-ceiling windows. As I pull the shades back, the room is awash in sunlight. I squint against the bright light as I look out—lawn, trees, lake. Lovely. But not nearly as lovely as coffee.

When I arrived last night, I alternately blew my nose and unloaded the necessities—my suitcase, a pound of coffee, and the pint of half-and-half that I'd packed in a gallon-sized zippered plastic bag. I'd thrown some ice cubes in the bag with the small carton and hoped for the best.

I set the coffeepot to brew, took off my makeup and brushed my teeth, pulled on my pajamas, and climbed into bed with my phone. I texted Craig both the address and notification of my safe arrival. It was after sending the text that I realized I'd failed to pack my phone charger. Of course. So I turned the phone off to save the battery in case of an emergency.

Great. Here all of twenty minutes, and I already had one interruption on the calendar. Are scheduled interruptions better than unscheduled? Only slightly. But I'd have to leave the house in the morning to find somewhere to buy a phone charger. That was my last thought before falling into a fitful sleep.

I head for the kitchen, slowing my pace as I pass a wall of books on my way. After filling my mug, I go back and stand in front of the bookshelves. Classic titles, many appearing to be first editions, line the shelves. With the exception of a few newer bird-watching books stacked near a set of binoculars, the shelves hold an antiquarian's delight. The books must have belonged to Valerie's grandparents. Jill would go nuts over this collection.

After a few more sips of coffee, I turn away from the bookshelves and take in the furnishings—they're as old as the books. Worn with age. Comfortable.

A clock over the fireplace tells me that Craig is likely at the office or on the job site already. Is Serena there?

What was he going to tell me last night?

I turn and look back at the view. Boy, it's quiet here. Too quiet. A person might have to listen to the dialogue in their head. The hairs on the back of my neck stand at attention. I shiver and wrap my arms around myself, though the sun shining in the windows has already warmed the room.

It's time to stop this nonsense and get to work. "No more lollygagging, ol' girl. You have a job to do." My voice reverberates in the empty room. The empty house.

I spend the next forty-five minutes unpacking, getting settled, familiarizing myself with the place, and showering and dressing. Who has time to shower and dress when there's a word count to make? Not me. But my scheduled interruption demands that I clothe myself rather than spend the day in my robe.

Then my stomach growls.

Make that two scheduled interruptions. I need to find a grocery store, too.

I go back to the kitchen and pour myself another cup of coffee—my meal for the morning. I want to knock out at least a thousand words before running my errands.

Coffee mug in one hand, laptop bag over my shoulder, I go back out to the living room, choose the most comfortable chair—a leather recliner facing the windows—and then pull a small side table over to the chair. I set the mug on the table, pull my laptop out of the bag, and set it next to the mug. Then I settle into the recliner. Perfect. My new office.

As the laptop powers up I raise my gaze above the screen and stare at the view. Vivid hues of green, every shade imaginable, dot the landscape, and trees, lots of them, protrude from the lawn. Birds dart and swoop between the trees. Beyond it all, sunlight shimmers on the lake.

I set the laptop back down, get out of the recliner, and go to the windows, where I close the blinds against any distractions.

I have work to do.

Just one thing left to do before I dive into my manuscript. I pull a notebook out of my laptop bag, open it, and retrieve the printed photograph I'd pressed between its pages.

Elliot.

I left my other characters hanging at home.

I smile at the photo then look around for a place to put it. Hmm. . . I get up and tuck the photo into the edge of a framed painting. The only problem is that my inspiration now hangs behind the recliner. I cock my head as I look at the photo, and an idea comes to me.

I go back and drop into the recliner again, connect my laptop to the house's Wi-Fi, and then do an Internet search for photos of Elliot, looking for the one I'd printed. I want to use it as the backdrop for my desktop, where it's more easily viewed.

There are literally hundreds of photos of him in every pose imaginable. Shots from movie sets, in character, in costume, and—heat rises to my cheeks—out of costume, bare chested. Wow. There are shots of him taken all over the world, including several with him standing in vineyards. Italy or France? Or Napa, maybe?

I lean back in the recliner so the footrest rises.

There are action shots and photos from award ceremonies, including one where he's holding an Oscar. His black tux—Armani, according to the caption—hugs his broad frame.

That same sense of familiarity breezes through my mind again, though I still can't pinpoint why.

I reach for my mug and take another sip of my now lukewarm coffee.

I skim photos of him with costars—gorgeous, young actresses hanging on him, looking into his eyes, their yearning unabashed. Who do you women think you are?

When I come across a spread of Elliot on a recent trip to St. Croix, where it's said he owns a home, I linger. Craig and I spent our fifth anniversary on St. Croix. The photos are obviously taken by paparazzi, but they show the real man in a real setting. I study each picture as I try to read his expressions, his body language. Island life seems to suit him—his dark hair bleached to a deep golden, his skin bronzed, his smile easy.

One image shows him walking a beach alone at sunset—his body silhouetted against the breaking waves. What is he thinking? Feeling? Why is he alone?

Is someone waiting for him at home?

———————————◆———————————

Warm rain pelts my bare shoulders. I hood my eyes with one hand and lift my face to the sky, where a pregnant cloud births its gift. I let my hand drop, close my eyes, and, with arms stretched in welcome, sway to the lilting rhythm of steel drums drifting from somewhere up the beach. A breeze, barely more than a breath, stirs the thick tropical air.

Laughter bubbles from my core and burbles like a wave meeting the shore as it comes out my mouth. I let my arms drop to my sides.

He calls to me from the shore. "What're you laughing at, silly girl?"

How long has it been since he's called me that?

I open my eyes, the smile still playing on my lips—the lips of a woman, not a girl—as his long strides cover the distance between us. "I'm laughing because I'm happy. You, this"—I do a slow spin—"all of this makes me happy." I yell over the sound of the rain, pounding the sand now.

His lips curve into a smile as he moves close, his cotton shirt soaked through, clinging to his chest. He puts his arms around me and pulls me to himself. "You're the one I've always wanted."

His whisper tickles my ear, and I close my eyes as I fold into his embrace. Overhead the sky rumbles a deep, resonant tone.

And then it rumbles again.

Or does it growl?

I open my eyes, and my stomach gurgles. What time is it? I glance at the time in the upper corner of the screen of my laptop. 12:42 p.m. What?! I turn in the recliner and look at the clock over the fireplace. How can that be?

I've spent the entire morning. . .

I just wanted one picture.

I click the back arrow on my browser, quickly find the photo I was looking for, and set it as my desktop. Now Elliot, my inspiration, stares at me from the screen.

His smile, like a Caribbean breeze, ruffles my equilibrium. His gaze pierces my soul. I wipe a tear from the corner of my eye and take a deep breath. I shake my head, a slow, deliberate movement meant to bring me back to the moment, to the present.

The here and now.

I close the lid of the laptop, another deliberate movement, and then pull myself out of the recliner. I stand still a moment until I gain my footing, inhaling again. Then I go in search of my car keys and my phone—it's time to get a charger and some food. It's time to get to work.

I find my phone on the nightstand where I left it last night. When I turn it on, I discover Craig's response to my text last night, along with a few more texts from him asking me to respond. And missed calls from Valerie and Jill. And two voice messages from Craig. His last message conveys his concern. *Mel, we need to talk. We can't leave things this way. I'm sorry—I didn't mean to. . . Where are you? Are you okay?* Emotion was woven in his tone.

Of course he would have responded to my text last night. And called. It's not like Craig to just let things go. He's a man who apologizes. Who takes responsibility. He's a man who. . .cares.

Why didn't I wait before turning off my phone? How could I have forgotten to check for a text or voice mail from him first thing this morning? Why can't I ever get it right?

The albatross lands again, but with it comes desire.

Longing.

For something. . .

Undefined.

Life is easy to chronicle, but bewildering to practice.
E. M. Forster

Chapter 15

MELANIE

After finding the local Kmart, the only place that sold a phone charger, I return Valerie's call on my way to the only grocery store in town: Safeway. Valerie and Safeway seem to go together.

Valerie's phone rings through the Bluetooth speaker in my car, and I tap my hands on the steering wheel as I wait for her to answer or for the call to go to voice mail. Just when I'm certain we'll just trade messages, she picks up.

"Good afternoon. I hope you're having a wonderful day."

Who answers the phone like that? "Valerie, it's Melanie. Are you always so chipper?"

She laughs. "Chipper? Don't you just love that word? It's so much fun. I'm calling that one an onomatopoeia."

I laugh. Only a writer. . . "Well, *chipper* fits you."

"Why, thank you. So how's the house? Are you settled in?"

"It's really wonderful. Thank you again. It's quiet and will be the perfect place to focus. And I'll fully settle in after I pick up a few groceries."

"Good. Well, if you have any questions about the place, just call. In the meantime, I had an idea for your main character."

"Chloe? Spill it. I'm short on ideas."

"Is she single or married?"

"Single. My protagonists are typically single so there can be a romantic thread or, more likely, dating drama."

"Is a single protagonist a rule for the genre?"

"Well, no. . . The hallmarks of the genre are modern women and some humor. It's usually a lighthearted read."

"Sorry, I typically have my nose in a nonfiction work or a research book of some sort."

"That's okay. When you're ready to lighten up—I mean branch out—I can recommend a few titles by an author we both know and love."

Valerie giggles. Really, there's no need for the woman to lighten up—she's a great audience.

"Actually, I ordered one of your books yesterday. I can't wait for it to arrive."

"Thank you, but I'd have given you a book."

"Oh, no. I was happy to order it."

"So, what were your thoughts about Chloe?" I pull into a parking spot in front of Safeway.

"What if she decides to run away?"

"Have you been talking to my husband?"

"What?"

"Never mind."

"You mentioned she's lonely. Some of the loneliest women I know are married women—I've counseled quite a few. Maybe Chloe leaves her husband—that creates a purpose for the counselor, right? Chloe can be talking to him about her marriage."

"A crumbling marriage is pretty serious stuff."

"Struggling and crumbling are two different things, don't you think?"

"I suppose. I'll give it some thought. Thank you. Again. I just keep thanking you."

"No need. I'm happy to help."

Valerie's idea isn't bad. It gives Chloe a purpose for seeing Dr. Hammond, and a struggling marriage would add tension. But humor? No. I get out of the car, push the lock button on my key fob, and head inside the store.

One thing is certain: I won't need to do much research for that story line.

———————◆◆———————

I wander the aisles of Safeway, picking foods that I read stimulate brain function. Spinach. Sweet potatoes. Strawberries. I need all the help I can get. As I wheel the cart into the meat department, I pick up a package of filet mignon. I don't recall the article mentioning specific proteins, but surely a tender filet can only boost my creativity. I check the price. Yikes. But a couple of small steaks won't break the bank, will they? I toss the package into the cart. Maybe I'll make a béarnaise sauce to go with the filet.

I could spend my spare time developing gourmet cooking skills. Spare time? But I can't write around the clock, can I? Suddenly everything, even cooking, holds great appeal. Everything but writing. I sigh. Why is that?

I make my way to the seafood case, and as I stand staring at fresh tiger prawns, my long lost friend Inspiration taps me on the shoulder with another idea. Of course! Why didn't I think of it before? Coupled with Valerie's idea, I may now have both a plot and a setting for Chloe.

By the time I'm carrying the bags of groceries into the house, I'm anxious to get back to work. I set the bags on the counter, unload them, throw together a spinach, chicken, and strawberry salad, cut a slice of bread from an artisan loaf I purchased, slather it with butter, and then pour myself a glass of iced tea. I put the rest of the food items in the fridge and pantry then carry my lunch to the kitchen table. As I eat, I stare, unseeing, out the window toward the lake, letting my mind wander away from the story for a few minutes.

I called Craig and left him a message before I left for my errands, but he hasn't returned my call. I thought I'd hear from him. He's not a turnabout-is-fair-play kind of guy—he wouldn't not call me because I'd forgotten to call him. Though he has reason to be angry.

Or hurt.

I take a bite of the bread, but it doesn't go down easily.

But then, don't I also have reason to feel angry? Or at least confused? Why did he spend time with Serena instead of going to the BIA reception as he'd planned?

That is what happened, right? He didn't go because of Serena? I guess I didn't hang around long enough to hear the whole story.

Fear spins its web. Maybe I don't want to hear the whole story.

Why didn't he just do what he said he was going to do?

I pick my phone up off the kitchen table and check again for texts or voice messages. But Craig hasn't called. He's probably just busy.

That's the excuse I land on—it's the one I can swallow. A call from him now would only distract me anyway.

After my quick lunch, I return to the recliner and my laptop, anxious to flesh out Chloe's story. I place my fingers on the keyboard and let them run with the new ideas.

> She hadn't planned on staying. . .
>
> Chloe made this trip several times each year. San Francisco to St. Croix. The Virgin Islands were a destination she often suggested to companies seeking venues for events, especially team-building events. This one she'd planned for a group of techies from a Silicon Valley start-up. Sure, it required a long day of travel from the West Coast, but it offered warmth, beauty, and a vast menu of activities. Plus, the Caribbean fed egos.
>
> *Stayed at the Buccaneer. . . Pig roast at the Mermaid Friday night. . . St. Croix—the Caribbean, of course. . .* All good lines to drop at the water cooler. Or the juice bar, as was more often the case in the valley.
>
> A quick island getaway didn't do her any harm either.
>
> She'd planned a four-day turnaround. Carry-on only. She'd supervise the setup, greet the attendees as they arrived, and then leave the event in the hands of her capable team, who'd arrive on Wednesday.
>
> Her return ticket would have her back in the city Friday evening in time for Brats and Brew at AT&T Park. Chad's favorite meal. It was the Giants versus. . . Who knew? Chad knew. The Giants were his first love. But she'd known that when she married him last year.
>
> That *was* the plan.
>
> But when she walked out of the Henry E. Rohlsen terminal pulling her Louis Vuitton carry-on behind her, the trade winds had stilled, and the thick island air felt like a sultry kiss on her bare neck.

And there were far too few kisses these days for her to ignore this one.

Chloe's in St. Croix. That's where she was when she made the call to Dr. Hammond. I hadn't known where she was when I wrote that scene. I search for the scene and then add a few setting details. I'll put the scenes in order later.

I click back to the scene I've just written and read it again. *Far too few kisses these days. . .* I put my hand over my heart where the same ache, the sense of longing, stirred this morning. Is this what Chloe feels? Valerie's words come back to me. *Some of the loneliest women I know are married women. . . .* I close my eyes for a moment then open them and take a deep breath.

I put my fingers back on the keyboard. They're heavy now, and the words come slower. . .

She'd checked into the hotel then decided that if she had to endure bratwurst on Friday, she'd savor shrimp saltimbocca with its tender artichokes, sun-dried tomatoes, and lemon and capers at the Terrace overlooking the palm-studded grounds of the resort and the Caribbean Sea in the distance. She'd changed out of her travel clothes, slipped on a turquoise linen sheath, and spent the evening dining under the stars. Alone.

On Friday, rather than catch the shuttle back to the airport, she'd called Chad and told him she'd been detained and to give her ticket to the game to one of his buddies.

Was that disappointment she heard in his voice? Or was that only what she'd hoped to hear?

On Sunday morning, she sat on her balcony clad in a soft white terry robe courtesy of the Buccaneer, sipping a cup of coffee, the *New York Times* draped across her lap. Her stomach roiled at the thought of returning home.

She set her cup on the small table next to her and

took a deep breath. Then another. When the nausea passed, she made her decision and pulled her phone from the pocket of her robe.

It was time to tell Chad she didn't know when she was coming home.

Or was it that she didn't know *if* she was coming home?

Memories of our anniversary spent on St. Croix flood my mind. I'd sat on the beach as Craig snorkeled. I was careful to keep track of the tip of his snorkel poking out of the water. When he'd dive under the water, I'd count the seconds until I saw him resurface. Once, after counting to 160, my heart sank. I knew he'd drowned or, maybe worse, had become shark bait. But wouldn't I have seen flailing and blood? By the time I spotted his snorkel in another area, I'd composed his eulogy in my mind and my tears had dotted the sand around me.

We spent seven glorious days on the twenty-two-mile island. We walked the beaches, sipped drinks arrayed with colorful little umbrellas, gorged on fresh fruit and fish. I'd also spent much of the time trying to avoid running headlong into the iguanas that roamed the island. I smile at the memory of Craig trying not to laugh at me dodging a large lizard that had crept into my path when I'd let my guard down.

Those were the days before. . . When we still hoped for a family. When I let myself think about it, I can mark our marriage like the calendar. BT—Before Trying. AF—After Failure.

BT life was still easy and our relationship sweet. Now it would be a very different trip.

My phone vibrates next to the laptop. Craig's name flashes on the screen.

I pick up the call. "Hey. . ."

"Sorry I missed you earlier. Thanks for the message."

"I'm the one who is sorry. Sorry for the way I left. I do need to finish the book, and this is a great place to do that, but I wish I'd discussed it with you first. Anyway, I'm sorry. . .for everything. . . ." Will he know that *everything* includes everything for the last twenty-three years?

He hesitates before responding. "Yeah, I know. Me too. I got angry and said things I shouldn't have—or at least said things in a way I wish I hadn't. So, are you okay? Are *we*. . .okay?"

"We're fine, right? It was a fight. Maybe we rarely fight because we're not very good at it."

He chuckles. "Well, let's keep it that way. So how's the place?"

"Great. Quiet. Very, very quiet."

"Well, that's what you need, right?"

"Right."

"So, Mel. . ."—he clears his throat—"I do need you to know that the reason I didn't make it to the BIA reception was because I was—"

"You don't need to explain."

"I want to explain. Hear me out, please?"

I get out of the recliner and wander into the kitchen where I stare, again, out the only window I've left uncovered. "Okay."

"Serena dropped by the job site, and then it got late, and I was running behind, and. . .I just wasn't in the mood to go. I should have gone, but I didn't. Life is just hard these days, and occasionally it gets to me."

"Where did you go?" I let the question slip out of my mouth before I think it through. Do I really want to know where he was? Do I believe he wasn't with Serena? "Craig?"

"Yeah, I heard you. Mel, have I ever given you reason to distrust me?" I turn my back on the view and look at the floor. "No." Not that I know of.

"Can you trust me now? Trust that I love you?"

I close my eyes. "Sure." But do I believe he didn't spend the evening with Serena? Why doesn't he want to tell me where he was if he wasn't with her? These are questions a wife might ask. Questions I likely should ask. But I guess it's just easier to keep my doubts—if that's what they are—to myself.

"Thank you. So how long are you staying?"

I open my eyes. "As long as it takes."

"You're not coming home until after your deadline? That's still weeks away." His tone is stiff, brittle, like if he spoke the question too loud he might shatter into little pieces.

"I have to finish." That's all I can tell him, because the truth is, I don't know when I'm going home.

The proper function of man is to live, not to exist.
Jack London

Chapter 16

CRAIG

I circle the block once, as has become my habit since the first time I came here. The bugs of summer swarm under the streetlights, and tonight a group of kids spread out across the lawn of the closed library, the bass of the music thumping from their car parked nearby.

They're probably around the same age I was the first time I circled this block.

I'd followed my mother here, though she didn't know it—or at least, I didn't think she'd noticed my battered GMC truck, my first car, tailing her. My mom was a quiet, private woman. She didn't speak much, but when she did, we listened. She was also a woman who regularly disappeared for a few hours each week without ever telling my brother or myself where she was going.

As kids, she'd leave us in the care of a babysitter, or on weekends our dad would take over.

Not long after I got my driver's license, I asked my mom where she spent those hours. A Mona Lisa–like smile was her only response—a smile that conveyed both peace and mystery.

A mystery I had to crack.

I turn into the parking lot of the library, pull around back, and park in the same place I always park—under the only light in this part of the lot. I turn off the ignition, climb out of the cab of the truck, and lock it. I cross the parking lot and follow the fence that runs between the library property and the property next to it.

The last time I came here I'd just left Serena. Two nights ago. I had some things I needed to straighten out in my head. Along with some things I needed to confess. This was the place to do both—has been the place for those types of things since I discovered it. It probably offered my mom the same kind of solace, but we never talked about it. We weren't ashamed of it. Instead, it was private. Intimate. Something we shared, but each of us on our own terms. At least, that's what I choose to believe.

Tonight, as I walk along the fence line, a dark grove of trees on the other side, loneliness swoops down like an owl—its talons digging deep.

When I reach the place where the fence ends between the two properties, there's a gate. A heavy chain and padlock are loosely hung around the gate and the post it's attached to. So loose, in fact, that if I pull on the gate, it opens about three feet—just enough for me to slide through to the adjacent property.

I turn, look around, and then turn back and slip through the opening, ducking under the chain and padlock.

Trespassing? Sort of. But I got permission a long time ago, so long ago that I'm not sure anyone remembers giving it to me. The front gate is locked well before dark, so this is the only way in. But I'm known here during the daylight hours when I volunteer to fix things or build things—whatever they need. So I'm not too worried.

Twigs and dry leaves crunch underfoot as I amble through the thicket of trees. The sweet scent of dry grass, leaves, and dust welcome me. When the ground turns loamy, I stop. Tall pines and oaks block any light coming from the library parking lot.

I feel my way for a few more steps and then stop again. I wait for my eyes to adjust, but the inky night reveals nothing. Cars sound on the busy streets surrounding the property, and a siren wails in the distance.

I pull my cell phone out of the back pocket of my jeans and click it so the screen lights up. It shines just brightly enough that, if I hold it with the screen pointing at the ground in front of my feet, I can take another step, sure not to trip over anything. Though, truth be told, I could probably make this walk with my eyes closed—I've done it so many times.

I make my way through the trees leaving the sounds from the outside world behind. When the thicket gives way to a clearing, I turn my phone off and push it back into my pocket. I stand on the edge of a grassy knoll and survey the area. The first night I snuck in here, the night after following my mom to the front gate, when I got to this exact spot it was like I'd just walked through the wardrobe into Narnia or a similar magical place. The memory pulls a smile out of me, maybe the first one since Melanie left.

Landscape lighting reveals the pathway around the lawn area. On the other side of the knoll are buildings, mostly dark except for the glow of a few interior lights.

I step across the pathway onto the lawn so the crunching of decomposed granite doesn't give me away. I don't want company tonight. I follow alongside the path until it veers from the grass. Then I walk through an area of bedded plants, stepping as softly as my weight allows, until I reach the place where landscape lights are set in a large semicircle. Above the first of the landscape lights, a placard reads, STATIONS OF THE CROSS.

I didn't fully get the significance of the Stations until I met Marcos. Though I'd walked through the fourteen stations many times, it was Marcos who explained the meaning of each one. He was raised Catholic. Me? We were Protestant. So how'd my mom end up at a Catholic retreat center?

I won't get that answer this side of eternity.

I lift my eyes heavenward. "Thanks for the legacy, Mom," I whisper. Though she's been gone for several years, I think she knows, maybe even knew, I'd followed her here and then kept coming back. It wasn't the kind of thing I had words for as a kid. Then as a man, well, it was—it is—just between me and God.

Tonight, I go sit on a familiar bench near the Stations, its wood worn smooth. I settle on the bench because I have nowhere else to be and no one waiting for me. I settle here because I know I still have some things to work through. It's the same place I sat two nights ago when I spilled my guts with God, even though He already knew everything I thought and felt.

I lean forward, put my head in my hands, and close my eyes. Although I made my confession two nights ago, it seems that understanding what I felt—feel—will be a process.

My conversation with Serena has replayed over and over. At first, I tried to ignore it, but the way it's repeated in my mind? I need to deal with it.

Show me, Lord. . .

Eyes still closed, I recall the scene, careful not to let my mind run away with the details. Serena's gorgeous. Period. Anyone can see that. I don't need to dwell on her looks. Instead, I let the words she spoke play again, and this time, rather than working to ignore them, I pay attention.

"I am committed to dealing with what life hands me."

"Simply existing isn't worth the effort."

"We were created to live life to the full, and we can only do that if we're willing to fully participate."

I open my eyes and lift my head. I stare at the landscaping, the shadows that the low lights cast across the beds and lawn.

Willing to fully participate. . .

I lower my head again and take a deep breath as the owl's talons dig deep, causing an ache like I've never known.

———————◆————————

"Hey, thanks for coming." I shake Marcos's hand and then slap him on the back.

"That's what friends are for, no? We played phone tag long enough. I was happy to get your message asking to meet."

We walk together into the Granite Rock Café, our standby when we get together for breakfast. Best biscuits anywhere. We're greeted by the scents of maple syrup and bacon. Once we're seated, we glance at our menus as a waitress fills our glasses with water and offers us coffee.

When she's gone, Marcos looks at me. "So what's up? You sounded pretty tense in your messages."

I sigh, set my menu down, and then lean back in the booth. "I don't know, man. I'm just. . ." I lift my hands, palms up. Where do I start?

"Might as well put it all out there."

"Yeah. Okay, bottom line, I probably need some accountability." I watch Marcos's reaction to gauge how much to tell him. But then, if I don't tell him everything, what's the point of this?

"I don't know a guy who doesn't."

"Yeah, I guess. I could probably use some words of wisdom, too."

"I'm happy to hear you out, amigo."

"Thanks. So, Melanie left a few nights ago."

"What do you mean by 'left'?"

"Not the marriage. I mean, I don't think that's what she's doing. She's taking some time away to finish her book. But she was upset when she left—or angry, maybe. It's hard to know what she was thinking or feeling."

"Why don't you start from the beginning and tell me what's been going on."

"Yeah, okay." I clear my throat. "I'm in a vulnerable spot with Melanie. Things are just tough, you know?"

"I do know."

"Yeah, I know you do. How's Jill?"

The shake of Marcos's head is slight, but it tells me all I need to know. "She's struggling. But this morning, it's your turn to talk."

"Okay, but know I'm available when you need a turn again."

"I know it."

"Anyway"—I take a deep breath—"this client I'm building for. . ."

"Serena Buchanan? She's a beautiful woman."

"You know her?"

"No, Jill showed me a picture of her in a magazine. She told me that Melanie didn't say as much, but Jill thought she might be concerned about your relationship with Serena."

I nod, not too surprised after Melanie's interrogation.

The waitress reappears to take our orders. As Marcos is placing his order, I consider what I told Melanie when we talked on the phone—I clarified things, didn't I? She has to know there's nothing between me and Serena.

After I've placed my order, Marcos leans forward, his gaze intent. "So, does Melanie have reason to be concerned?"

I pick up my coffee cup, take a sip, and then swallow the coffee—along with my pride. "Listen, Marcos, I'm going to be straight with you."

"I expect nothing less."

I nod. "Yeah, she has reason, or had reason, to be concerned. But"—I hope what I'm about to say is true—"I caught myself before I let anything happen."

"You know as well as I do that what takes place in the mind can be as powerful as what happens in the physical realm. So what do you mean by 'nothing happened'?"

Marcos is hard on me, as he should be. It's what I appreciate most about him as a friend. He's got my back. He won't let me get away with anything. And it's why I have to tell him everything. I scoot forward. "I'm going to lay it out for you. Everything was fine: the job was going well, I appreciated Serena's professionalism, and that was it. Is she a looker? Yeah, and I noticed, but I didn't dwell on it. The world is full of beautiful women. Then, last week, she dropped by my office and overheard me talking to a mortgage broker. At least, I think she overheard the conversation." I shake my head. "I'd applied to refinance the house, but. . .we didn't qualify. My credit's shot."

"Things are getting pretty bad?"

"Worse than bad. Anyway, long story short, she offered to invest in my business or loan me money. She didn't say that in so many words, but it was clear. It just. . ."—I look down at the table then back to Marcos—"hit me."

"Gotcha. You haven't been able to get Melanie to really engage, yet here's a beautiful woman not only willing to engage but also offer solutions."

"Maybe not solutions, but options. And yeah, that's what got to me. But I gotta tell you, I think Mel's trying in her own way, but I just haven't had the energy lately to talk to her." I shrug. "I'm not placing blame. It takes two."

"Yep. So then what?"

"Two nights ago, I was supposed to go to a BIA reception downtown. I'd told Melanie about it. I went to the job site late in the afternoon to clean up the place, and Serena showed up. She was supposed to meet her daughter there, but Ashley cancelled." I go on to tell him about her husband's death and the reason she and Ashley were planning on meeting at the house. "Anyway, I ended up staying, toasting her late husband, and just getting to know her better. Letting her get to know me. She's easy, you know? She's the real deal."

"Did you go to the reception?"

I meet Marcos's stare and then shake my head. "No, I didn't make it."

"You spent the whole evening with her?"

"No. But. . .I wanted to. There was one moment when. . ." I run one finger through the condensation on the outside of my water glass as I recall what I felt. "Man, everything in me wanted to stay, to be with her. That's when I knew I had to get out of there."

Marcos nods but doesn't say anything.

"I can't do that. It's not an option. What kind of husband would I be? What kind of man? I can't do that to Mel. Or Serena, for that matter. I can't lead her into that type of relationship. Most importantly, I won't do that to God. I won't let what I desire in the moment derail what He intends for me long-term."

"You got that right. So you left?"

"I left. I told her I'd committed to attending the BIA reception and that I had to go. That was it. You have my word on it."

"I believe you. So what's your plan?"

"Keep my mind in check. Focus on my wife. Although that's a little harder now that she's away."

"And financially? Because that's the real vulnerability right now, isn't it?"

I roll my shoulders back. "Yeah." I exhale. "I'm going to have to put the house on the market. I've exhausted my options."

"Move?"

"I don't know what else to do."

"Does Melanie know?"

"Yeah, I finally told her. I feel like such a failure."

Marcos leans forward. "Hey, you don't control the economy. In fact, you don't control much of anything, do you?"

"No, I guess not."

"So, let me ask you again. What's your plan?"

"Okay, I hear you. My plan is to trust. One day—one dollar—at a time."

"That's a solid plan. And let's keep talking, deal?"

"Deal. Thanks."

"One more thing. . . Jill and I've noticed the long hours you're keeping. We hear your truck pull into your driveway at night."

"Yeah, sorry about that. I've pulled some late nights recently."

"You always at the office that late?"

I shake my head. "Nah, not always."

"Where you spending your time, amigo?"

"I was being straight with you when I said nothing's happened with Serena."

"I don't doubt you. I'm just asking what you are doing."

I look down at the table then pick up a spoon and roll it back and forth between my index finger and thumb. I set the spoon back on the table and look at Marcos. "I'm wrestling, man. Just wrestling."

Illusion is an anodyne, bred by the gap between wish and reality.
Herman Wouk

Chapter 17

CRAIG

I pull the sheet up and roll onto my side, the sheet twisting with me. I refuse the thoughts knocking on my mind. "Just sleep," I mumble to no one but myself. Still unsettled, I stretch across the king-sized mattress into the void Melanie left. I will myself to sleep. But numbers loiter at the corners of my mind, and as soon as I close my eyes, they take center stage.

The numbers that make up our mortgage payment.

Health insurance for both of us.

Our homeowner's insurance.

I roll over again, the sheet following me.

Auto insurance.

And the dwindling number of dollars in our bank accounts.

I roll to my other side then to my back, the sheet now tightly wound around my legs. I open my eyes and stare into the dark. My heart races, my shoulders and neck ache, and acid burns the back of my throat.

"We were created to live life to the full, and we can only do that if we're willing to fully participate."

Not again.

I throw the sheet back as far as it will go then sit up and unwind it from my legs. I reach over, turn on the bedside lamp, and then open the drawer of my nightstand, pulling out a bottle of antacids. I pop two chalky tablets into my mouth then lean up against the headboard.

I don't know what's worse: having the bills I can't pay keep me awake or that phrase Serena tossed at me repeating in my mind.

"We can only do that if we're willing to fully participate."

What does that even mean?

Aren't I fully participating in life? C'mon. Like I have a choice?

I reach for the remote and flip on the TV that hangs over the fireplace in our room. But as I surf through the channels and my mind begins to go blank, I know I'm checking out. So Melanie can check out—but not me? I glance over at the digital clock on the nightstand. 3:18 a.m.? So what? At this hour, I don't care if I am escaping.

Or not *fully participating.*

I stare at a late-night talk show host on the screen laughing with the latest young hot pop singer. Her laughter is an annoying squeal, so I turn the volume down and continue staring through the commercials and the next guest, whoever he is.

But the whole time I'm watching the screen, my mind is adding and subtracting. I calculate when I'll receive the next draw on Serena's house, subtract what I'll owe my subs, add the remaining amount to what's already in our bank account, and add in the remainder of Melanie's advance, which—if she finishes the book on time—we'll see this quarter. Then I begin subtracting the bills we have due for the next few months. By the time I'm halfway through the bills, not including our mortgage payments, I'm in the red.

I make a mental list of my options, which takes all of one second. I've run out of options.

Well, except for one. . .

Serena.

And, for obvious reasons, her offer's not really an option. Or is it?

Maybe Serena is God's provision.

I've followed every other lead, talked to every potential investor in the last year, and no one else has stepped forward. My contacts are all in the building industry, and this recession hit us all hard. Everyone is leery.

I adjust the pillow behind my back. Maybe what happened with Serena—or rather what I felt or thought I felt—maybe that was God testing me. And now that I've gone through that test, I know the importance of staying focused. I swing my legs over the side of the bed, stand, and walk the length of the bedroom and back as my mind spins.

It's not like I can avoid Serena completely anyway. I have to finish her house, and that will take months yet. We'll stick to business. Keep it all on the up and up, of course. I shrug. Why wouldn't that work?

"I have funds available for investment." Isn't that what she said?

If she'd invest money for land, plans, permits, construction costs. . . Maybe we could put together a development. We'd start small. Twenty homes? It's worth a shot, isn't it? Would the market in this area support a tract development yet? There is talk of recovery.

Adrenaline pumps. It might just work, depending on how much Serena is willing to invest. But it could be a great return on her money if we buy the land right. Of course, I'd have to ask for an advance, too—enough to cover our expenses until we've made a profit. It's a risk, but what business venture isn't? The question is, exactly how much is Serena willing to invest?

The TV casts blue light across the dark room. I continue my pacing until I can't think of any good reason why partnering with Serena isn't a great idea.

But as I fall back into bed, one reason occurs to me. No, make that two.

Melanie.

And Marcos.

Maybe I jumped the gun talking to Marcos this morning.

But if God intends to provide through Serena, then they'll both have to understand, right?

And yet to every bad there is a worse.
Thomas Hardy

Chapter 18

JILL

The sprays, four of them, are white. Roses and carnations. The scent of the flowers, like noxious fumes, curl around my head. I lift the linen handkerchief to my face—my mother's handkerchief, the one with the delicate blue crocheted edge—and cover my nose and mouth.

I gag and then cough, and tears blur my vision.

Mommy! Mommy!

I whip around. Who called me?

Or was it me who cried out?

My mother is there, dressed in black, a veil covering her face. But she doesn't respond to my cries.

Mommy!

Or am I the one not responding?

"Mommy! Mom—" My tongue is thick in my mouth.

"Jill, wake up. Jill. It's a nightmare."

"Wha. . . What?" Marcos shakes me.

"It's a nightmare."

My heart pounds, and my face is damp with tears. He turns on his bedside lamp then fumbles for a tissue and hands it to me. I pull myself up, still groggy, and wipe my eyes and cheeks.

He rubs my arm until I calm. His voice is heavy with sleep. "Was it the same?"

I nod.

It is always the same.

Call.

Make the call.

It's going to happen.

You need to be prepared.

Call.

The vegetable drawer from the refrigerator fills with hot water as I hold it under the kitchen faucet. I add a few drops of dish soap then reach for a sponge which I've soaked in a mixture of bleach and water to kill germs. I scrub the interior and exterior of the drawer.

Make the call.

It's going to happen.

You need to be prepared.

The warnings have repeated in my mind over and over and over this morning, as they always do the morning after a nightmare, and for days, sometimes weeks, afterward. The thoughts persisted as I worked on a manuscript. As I homeschooled Gaby. As I played with the twins.

As I clean the refrigerator.

When my phone rings and Melanie's name appears on the screen, I turn off the faucet and dry my hands. I'm grateful for the call—a possible reprieve from the obsessions of my mind. "Hello."

"I left."

Melanie? "What? Left where?"

"Home. I'm at Valerie's lake house. I'm writing. It's a retreat. A writing retreat. It's good—it's going to be good."

Call.

"Valerie told me. Why didn't you tell me you were going?"

Make the call.

"Valerie offered her place last week, and a few days ago I decided it was a good idea. Kind of spur of the moment. But I wanted you to know in case, you know, you decided to walk over for a cup of my superior coffee or something. You talked to Valerie?"

It's going to happen.

"Jill?"

"What?"

"Did you hear me?"

I set the sponge I'm holding in the kitchen sink and turn on the faucet again. "Yes, I heard you. I talked to her during group. The Deep Inkers, remember? We had a meeting earlier this week? We missed you."

"I'd forgotten, but I left anyway, so I couldn't be there. Well, I just wanted you to know where I am."

"Thanks."

"So, I guess I'll talk to you later."

"Melanie, wait." *You need to be prepared.*

"What?"

I tuck the phone between my ear and my shoulder, pump some soap from the dispenser onto my hands, and then rub them together. "Why. . . Why are you there?"

"I'm writing. It's a writing retreat."

Call.

"Right. A few days or. . . ?"

"Until I'm done with the manuscript."

I rinse my hands under the hot water.

"Done. Okay."

"I'll make my deadline."

Make the call.

"Of course you will. Enjoy the process. Anything I can do for you while you're gone?" I know she doesn't need me to water houseplants, which she equates with pets. I tear a couple of paper towels off the roll and dry my hands.

Call.

"Just. . ."

I open the cabinet under the sink and toss the paper towels into the trash. "Just what?"

"Check on Craig. Have Marcos call him, okay?"

"Call?" I close my eyes, take a deep breath, and work to focus on Melanie. "Yes, I'll have him call." I dry my hands again. "Oh, wait. Marcos had breakfast with Craig this morning."

"Good. That's good. Okay, I'm off to write."

"You're a great writer. Don't forget that."

"Thanks. I'll talk to you in a few weeks."

"Wait. Melanie, are you okay?"

She laughs, but her laughter sounds forced. "Of course. But I was just about to ask you the same thing. Are *you* okay?"

"Yes, of course. Yes. Just. . .distracted. Sorry. Lot's going on. So, I'll talk to you later. Keep in touch."

I'm already walking toward my laptop plugged in on the kitchen bar when I hang up my phone. I lift the lid, wait for the Wi-Fi to connect, and then click on my Internet icon and type what I'm looking for into the search bar. When the list loads, I jot down a phone number.

After I put the boys down for their naps, I'll make the call.

I have to make the call.

———————◆◆———————

Phone at my ear, I listen as the line rings. Once. Twice. My heart pounds, and my palms are damp. Then I pull the phone away from my ear and press END, fingers trembling.

What am I doing?

What is wrong with me?

I set the phone on the desk in the den, turn my back on it, and walk away. I go to the kitchen, where I left my laptop, sit at the bar and open the computer. I stare at the screen. *Work, Jill. Just work.* I click on a file on my desktop—a manuscript I'm editing.

Make the call.

I ignore the thought. I find where I left off in the document, turn track changes on, and begin working through the next chapter of the manuscript. I make minor grammatical and punctuation changes and insert comments for the author that appear in the margin.

It's going to happen.

I stop. *Please, Lord, make them go away—make the thoughts go away.* But then images accost. Gaby—a gash in her small chest, blood spurting. The twins. . .

"No!" I cry. No more. I get up from the bar and stumble into the living room, where I collapse in the wingback chair. I put my head in my hands, no longer strong enough to stop the flow of tears that has threatened all day.

Make the call.

You need to be prepared.

I know that making the call will only feed the obsessive thoughts but will never satiate them. The more I feed them, the hungrier they become, and the more of me they'll devour.

It's going to happen.

I put my hands over my ears, wanting to block out the voice, but it plays in my mind, repeating what I know is true—only it isn't. It can't be. I shake my head until my neck aches and my head throbs.

"Please, please make it stop," I sob.

It isn't true.

It isn't true.

But, what if. . . ?

What if this is a warning, and I ignore it? How will I deal with all the details afterward? I have to prepare. Yes, I have to. I jump to my feet and rush to the den. I grab a tissue from a box on my desk and wipe my eyes and nose, though I can't dam the flow of tears.

I pick up my phone and punch in the number I've now memorized, and then I wait for someone to answer. As I listen to the line ring, knowing this time I won't hang up, my shoulders relax. My breathing slows.

"East Lawn Cemetery."

When I hear the gentleman's voice, for just a moment my mind quiets. I've made the call.

"Yes, I need to talk with someone about plots and arrangements."

"I'm happy to assist you. Has there been a loss, or are you planning ahead?"

"Planning ahead."

"Wise, very wise. You mentioned plots. So you're considering in-ground burial?"

"Yes. I'd like five plots—together. I'm wondering about. . ." My voice catches, and I clear my throat. "Excuse me. I'm wondering about pricing for the plots, the cost of burial, and. . .all that entails. I need to make funeral arrangements as well."

My mother drops the rose onto a shiny black casket with brass hardware. Then she nudges me forward, a white carnation in my hand. Not tall enough to lean over the rope surrounding the plot as my mother did, I throw the flower up and over the rope and watch as it flutters and lands on top of the casket. I look up at my mother to see if I've done it right, but she's staring beyond the grave, tears wetting her cheeks.

"Mommy?"

Who's calling me? Or did I just say that?

"Ma'am?" A man's voice.

"Mommy?"

"What?! I'm here." I whip around. Just as I do in the nightmare.

"Mommy?"

My heart batters my rib cage, and my breath catches again. I gasp. Gaby stands in the doorway of the den—fear etched in her delicate features. "Who. . .died, Mommy?" She whispers. Her eyes wide.

I pull the phone away from my ear. "Gabs. . ." I choke back a sob as I shake my head. "No. . ." I see myself, wild-eyed, crazed, reflected in Gaby's eyes. Her face crumples as she watches me, and her tears spill.

"No. Oh, no." I grip the phone. "No one. No. . ."

"Ma'am? Are you all right?"

Gaby takes a step toward me then stops. She doesn't know what to do.

I don't know what to do.

She steps back, away from me, her voice tiny. "Is it Daddy? Did he. . ." Her sobs match my own. "Did he. . .die?" She ends on a wail and then drops to her knees, her hands covering her ears as though she can't bear to hear the answer.

It may be the part of a friend to rebuke a friend's folly.
J. R. R. Tolkien

Chapter 19

CRAIG

I pick a piece of lint off my navy slacks. *"Business meeting attire,"* as Mel would say. Then I give the proposal I've put together for Serena another cursory glance.

When I called her to set the meeting, she said she'd look forward to discussing my ideas and would meet me at my office this afternoon.

With the proposal ready and the meeting set, shouldn't I feel a sense of relief? This partnership, if Serena agrees, offers the potential to get my business back on track and, hopefully, for us to keep our home. Instead, my palms are sweating and my shoulders are knotted, which, I'm beginning to think, is a chronic condition.

I crack the knuckles on one hand and then the other. I lean back in my desk chair and exhale. If God is in this, then there's nothing to worry about. But even as I tell myself that, my chest and throat tighten.

When I hear the outer office door open, I stand, wipe my palms on my slacks, and go to greet Serena.

"Hello, Craig." Her emerald eyes sparkle as she smiles. She puts out her hand to shake mine.

"Hot out there?" I give her hand a quick, firm shake. This is business. That's all.

"It's another scorcher. I must say, I miss traveling this time of year. We used to spend the month of August in the Northwest. I had an apartment in Seattle for a while—I did quite a few projects in the area. Ashley loved it. She and her father loved early mornings at Pike's Market. And I loved the fog."

"Fog doesn't sound too bad about now, does it?" I follow her into my office and point to the two upholstered club chairs in the corner.

"Have a seat." The chairs seem to make us equals rather than me sitting behind my desk and her on the other side. That works when I'm the builder and she's the client. But if we're going to form a partnership, I want to set a stage of equality now.

Sure, she has the money, so she has the upper hand.

But I offer expertise, experience, and the desire to do the hard work. "Can I get you anything? Ice water, tea. . . ?"

"No, thank you." She sets her portfolio on the small table between the chairs and takes a seat in the corner chair. The red bottom of her black pump flashes as she crosses one long leg over her other knee. Her fitted skirt cuts just above her knees. Noticing that doesn't help me in any way.

I turn away from her, reach for the two copies of the proposal I prepared, and then take my seat. But the way the chairs are situated, kitty-corner from one another, causes my knees to bump her legs as I sit. "Oh, I'm sorry." I stand back up, push my chair back at an awkward angle, and then sit again.

"Take a deep, cleansing breath, Craig."

"What?"

"You're tight as a drum. Breathe."

Is it that obvious? I take a deep breath, lean back in the chair, and work to relax my shoulders. "There. Better?"

She tilts her head to one side and studies me for a moment. "I don't know, is it?"

"Sure. I'm fine. Busy day, that's all." It's time to dive in to avoid any more of her astute observations. "Thanks for agreeing to meet."

"You piqued my curiosity."

"Good. That was my intent. Once a business woman, always a business woman."

"Maybe so. I am missing work. But, as you know, I'm not quite ready to go back. Locally, maybe. But"—she waves her left hand, a large diamond and band still on her ring finger—"I can't travel like I did. I'm not ready to leave Ashley on her own."

"Well, maybe this proposal will interest you, then." I hand her a copy of the packet I've prepared.

"Tell me what you have in mind, and then I'll look at this." She holds up the proposal.

"Well, I thought we might partner on a small development of homes.

I've included three plans I designed with an architect a few years ago—the plans are unique, attractive, yet still affordable. I'd love your input on the designs, of course. There are also plot plans for two pieces of property. The property out toward Lincoln is especially desirable, as improvements have already been made—streets are in, utility lines run, etc. Another builder pulled out when the market tanked." I'm talking too fast. I don't want to sound desperate. I lean back in my chair and shrug. "I think the timing is good. By the time we have models built, the market will, I believe, support a project like this. Economic recovery has begun; interest rates are the lowest they've been in years. It's a buyer's market."

She opens the folder and starts flipping pages. "Interesting. So, I'm the bank?" She looks up from the page she'd landed on back to me. She's making it easy on me.

I take a deep breath. "Well, if that appeals to you. Of course, I'd pay interest on the funds, and we'd split the profits based on a percentage agreeable to both of us. And, though this isn't the type of work you're used to doing, I thought you could handle the models—finishes, decor, furnishings."

She nods and looks through a few more pages until she seems to find what she's looking for. "This is the bottom line? What you foresee the project costing?"

I clear my throat. "Yes. As you'll see, the figure includes a monthly salary for me as we're working through permits, construction, etc. Of course, it's actually an advance and would be deducted from my portion of the profits as they come in."

"And if they don't come in? If the homes don't sell?"

"They'll sell."

"You sound pretty confident."

"I've done my homework. If you look at the projected cost for each home—including the land—versus the sale price, you'll see a wide profit margin."

"What if I don't like the plans? You know I'll have suggestions." She raises an arched brow and laughs.

"Well, we can make changes. I'm open to suggestions. Any major changes will hold up the project and cost money, of course."

"Isn't that always the way?" She smiles and then closes the proposal, tapping her fingernails on its cover. "I like the idea, Craig. I'd enjoy the design work on the models, and I agree, I think there will be a market for homes this size and at this price point. The money is available." Her expression grows serious, and she stares at me a moment. "I just have one question."

"What's that?"

She glances away, takes a breath, and then looks back at me. "How does your wife feel about us partnering on a project like this—continuing to work together?"

That wasn't a question I'd anticipated. "Oh... Well, she... I mean..." I comb my fingers through my hair. "There's no reason for her to object." I swallow.

Serena leans forward, her tone gentle. "Isn't there?"

◆

"I'd love to partner with you, Craig. I think we'd make a fabulous team. But..." She'd hesitated and then looked away. *"I'm not sure it's a wise choice for either of us."* When she'd looked back at me, what was in her expression? In her eyes? Leaning back in my desk chair, lights still off in the office even though the sun set hours ago, I ignore the alarm dinging on my phone—likely a reminder of something I no longer care to remember. At least not tonight. What was in Serena's expression?

Resolve.

She'd made up her mind before ever walking into my office.

Smart lady.

I sit forward and put my hands on my desk.

Smart. Beautiful. Resolved. Lady.

I pound the desk with my fists.

Now what am I going to do?

I never intended for her to see anything or to sense anything I was feeling. I didn't say anything inappropriate. I didn't do anything inappropriate. Did I? Yet somehow she knew. A muscle in my jaw twitches. Way to blow it, man. Way to blow it.

Or did she only suspect because she was feeling the same way? Was the attraction—*is* the attraction—mutual?

It's a question I can't let myself ponder.

The answer doesn't matter either way.

The answer doesn't get me any closer to solving my problems—financial or otherwise.

Life—how curious is that habit that makes us
think it is not here, but elsewhere.
V. S. Pritchett

Chapter 20

MELANIE

When I get to heaven, if I get to heaven, I plan on asking God how many hours I wasted standing in line at the grocery store. Of course, watching the young mother in the line next to me—her toddler screaming like someone's assaulting him as she pries a candy bar out of his chubby little fingers, one he swiped off the display next to the cart—I decide my quiet moments in line aren't so bad.

Maybe infertility wasn't so bad either.

Who am I kidding? I'd scream too if someone took my candy bar. Poor baby.

As I unload my items onto the conveyer belt and then push my cart forward, my home Safeway beckons. I know just which cashiers aren't too chatty, which ones check items at the speed of light, and which ones will bag the groceries for you when the bagger has run out to the parking lot to retrieve the carts.

I also know where to find each item I'm shopping for. No wandering around lost like I did this morning. Although, if I'm telling the truth, even a strange grocery store holds great appeal when I'm on deadline.

Everything becomes fascinating when I'm on deadline.

As the checker runs my items over the scanner, I dig through my purse for my wallet then pull my debit card out of its slot. Once my total appears on the register's screen, I slide my debit card then, with finger poised, wait for the prompt asking for my PIN. But once I've entered the number, I'm met with a rude statement telling me my card was declined.

The cashier pushes a few keys on the register. "Try sliding it again."

I go through the motions again. And again, the card is declined.

Heat rushes up my neck as the cashier asks if I'd like to try another card.

I fumble through my wallet until I find my Visa. "Huh, I don't know what could have gone wrong. Let's try this." I hold my breath until the transaction is approved.

When Craig and I married, I thought I had close to a thousand dollars in my checking account. When we returned from our honeymoon, there was a notice from my bank waiting in our mailbox telling me I was $9.39 overdrawn. That's when we decided Craig would handle the finances.

So once I've unloaded the groceries and I'm sitting in the car, I pull my phone out of my purse to call Craig and discover there's a message from him I haven't listened to. But rather than listen now, I push his number into the phone.

He answers on the first ring. "Melanie?"

"As opposed to?"

He doesn't laugh. "I'm just surprised you're calling."

"Well, I have a little problem." Is that the only reason I'd call him? Is that what he'll think?

"What's that?"

"I. . . You sound exhausted."

"Yeah, it's been a long couple of days. So what's wrong?"

I want to say more. To ask why the days were long. To console or encourage him, but I don't know what to say, how to go beyond the lines it seems we've drawn. "I tried to use my debit card at the grocery store a few minutes ago, and it was declined. Twice. Thought I'd better check in and make sure our account wasn't hacked or whatever it is they do these days."

"I guess you didn't listen to the message I left this morning. There's just over thirty dollars in the account until I get my next draw. So if your total was more than—"

"Craig, thirty dollars is nothing."

"I know." The fatigue is evident in his tone again, along with a fair amount of tension. "But that's the reality."

"When's the next draw due?"

"It's a couple of weeks out. You can use the credit card, but let's try and save it for emergencies. In the meantime, I'll see what I can do."

"See what you can do?" The phone is hot against my ear, and the interior of the car is stifling. I put the key in the ignition, roll down the two front windows, and turn on the air conditioner.

"Yeah."

"What do you mean?"

His sigh sounds like one of exasperation. "I mean I'll see what I can do to come up with some money."

"So things are really that bad?"

"Yeah, they're that bad. I'm sorry, Mel. I don't know what else to do. I really am sorry."

"Craig, this isn't your fault. It's not your responsibility to apologize for the state of the country's economy. I bought enough groceries to get by on for the next week at least. Do you have enough food there?"

"Sure. You keep the freezer stocked. I'll get by."

"How did we get to the point where we're talking about whether or not we have enough food? This is crazy. I need to get this book finished and get another one going. Maybe I can—"

His tone softens. "Mel, this isn't your responsibility either. We're both working as hard as we can. We're in this together, and neither of us is in control. God is in control, and He is trustworthy."

"Oh sure, He's entrusted us with a whole thirty dollars. What's the date? When's the mortgage due?"

"Today is the tenth—it was due on the fifth."

"Was due? You paid it, right?"

His silence doesn't incite confidence. "Craig?"

"Not yet. I haven't paid it yet. I hope to catch up when I get paid again. Mel, I should have told you about selling the house months ago. I should have laid it out for you—let you know the severity of the situation. Instead, I got angry and just dumped it on you the other night. I'm sorry. Maybe things will still change. Maybe something will come up."

"Who are you kidding? Putting the house on the market is definitely not information I would have entertained. I don't believe I care to entertain it now, either."

"I should have given you the chance to make that choice."

"Okay, we'll let you take the blame this time." I laugh, because what else is there to do? "I guess I better get back to work."

"Yeah, me too."

"Don't spend our wad all in one place."

He chuckles. "You either."

"Talk to you later."

"Mel, wait. . . . I miss you."

I hesitate. "This will all be over before we know it."

I end the call. Why can't I tell Craig I miss him, too? Why don't I reciprocate when he tells me he loves me? It's as though there's a padlock on both my heart and my mouth, and I can't seem to find the key.

Do I miss Craig?

I put my hand over my heart like it might soothe the ache nestled there. Then I roll up the windows against the oppressive heat. I guess the answer to that question is one more thing I don't care to entertain. Martha Stewart, I'm not.

I toss my phone back into my purse and then stare out the front window of the car. Across the street that borders the parking lot, a couple of old bungalows sit on small lots—houses that look like they're losing their stuffing. Battered toys, a pile of tires, yard tools, a few dead plants, and other miscellaneous items of debris spot the yards. A shutter on one of the houses hangs lopsided, and both roofs look like they've weathered one too many storms.

Valerie was right; the economy in this area is as depressed as anywhere. A drive down Main Street, like I made this morning, tells the story. Businesses dark, CLOSED signs on the doors, a woman pushing a shopping cart filled with the remains of her life.

Trust God?

Heat swelters across the black asphalt of the parking lot, and dead, dry plants and trees pock the landscape. A cerulean sky hangs low over the lake in the distance. "No offense, Big Guy, but I'm not sure You're trustworthy." I glance up, expecting a bolt of lightning, but the only thing that stirs is a gaggle of geese coming in for a landing on a strip of brown grass at the edge of the parking lot. I point. "The lake is thataway, gang."

I put the car in gear. It's time to go back and put my meager rations away before returning to the trade winds, the surf, and the man of my dreams.

Sell the house? Craig designed and built our house.

Selling it will devastate him.

It's the first time since our argument the other night that I've let myself consider that possibility.

Or is it a reality?

The difference between fiction and reality?
Fiction has to make sense.
Tom Clancy

Chapter 21

JILL

Is she okay?" I hang my head, unable to face Marcos.

"She's okay. She fell asleep. She was exhausted. I sat next to her and rubbed her back until I was sure she was asleep." He drops onto the sofa next to me then leans his elbows on his knees and puts his head in his hands. "Explain to me exactly what happened. I need to understand, Jill."

The tension in Marcos's tone causes my already knotted stomach to clinch tighter. I wrap my arms around my abdomen and lean over. I slowly rock back and forth. "I. . .I'm sorry. I thought if I just called you, if. . .if Gaby could just talk to you, hear your voice over the phone, she'd be okay. I didn't mean for you to come. . .home."

"Jill, she was hysterical. She thought I'd died. What in the world happened?"

"I know you're angry. I'm. . .sorry." My head weighs on my neck, heavy from my own tears.

Marcos lifts his head from his hands. "I'm not angry. I'm frustrated. I need answers. Now, Jill."

"Okay. I know." I reach for the glass of water on the coffee table—the glass Marcos brought to me earlier. I take a couple of sips then set it back down. Marcos watches me, his knee bouncing. "Um, okay, so. . . I'd made a phone call, and Gaby must have come into the den at some point and overheard my end of the conversation. She just. . .misunderstood." I raise my palms. "She thought. . ." I shrug and look at Marcos.

"Who were you talking to?"

I look away from him. I have to tell him. There's no way out of this except the truth. But where will that truth lead? What will happen when he knows just how. . .sick I am?

"Jill. Talk to me. Who was on the phone?"

Tears prick my eyes again. "I called. . .East Lawn."

"The cemetery?"

For just a moment I consider bending the truth—lying to Marcos. Telling him I was doing research for an edit I'm doing. Checking facts. But what's the point? If this episode doesn't out me—expose just how far I've slipped—something else will. There will be a next time.

I sit up straighter, hoping that maybe Marcos will understand. "Yes, the cemetery. I was just checking on costs for plots and. . .arrangements. It's wise to plan ahead. It saves money and—"

"Jill, we've never even discussed this."

"No, I know. I was just going to get the information so we could discuss it. Make an informed decision."

"Gaby said you were crying when you were on the phone. Why were you crying? If this was just a business call, why"—confusion marks his features—"were you crying?"

I rub my temples. "It's just. . .just the thought of losing you. . .and the kids. It just got to me."

He shakes his head. "There's more. There's something you're not telling me. What was going through your mind? What prompted the call? What were you hearing?"

"I don't hear voices, Marcos."

"You know what I mean. What thoughts were running amok in your mind that made you pick up the phone?"

He knows? Does he understand?

"How. . .how do you know what happens in my mind?"

"Research."

Marcos has done what I've feared doing. He's looked up my symptoms—those I couldn't hide. Is this it then? Is this what I've known would come? A sob, unbidden, escapes. I cover my face with my hands as my shoulders shake.

"Jill, honey." He scoots closer and puts his arms around me. "I love you. Always. No matter what," he whispers. "I just need to understand.

Help me understand so I can help you. Please. What are you afraid of—what do you think will happen?"

How can I tell him what goes through my mind? Then he'll know just how. . .sick I really am.

"Talk to me," he whispers again.

I pull away and face him. "It's the. . .nightmare."

He nods.

"It's gotten worse."

"Worse how?"

Talking about the nightmare seems safe—it's not something I can control. Though it's not like I can control my thoughts either. Not anymore. "It's not just at night anymore."

"What do you mean?"

"I. . .I see the images during the day, when I'm awake. They're not exactly the same, but. . ." I look down at my hands resting in my lap and see my mother's hands. "She—my mom—she's wearing the black dress and the veil. She's standing by an open grave, and she drops a white rose into the grave—onto a casket. That part isn't in the dream. It's more like. . . It's like I remember it happening. But"—I shake my head—"whose grave is it?"

Marcos reaches for my shoulder and rubs it. "What else?"

"My grandparents, my mom's parents, are both there, standing behind her. My grandma is wearing a dress and a black wool coat. It was cold—winter, I think."

"Are your grandparents in the dream?"

"No."

I hope telling Marcos this will appease him, but he pushes me further.

"Jill, what are you afraid of? What makes you so anxious? Obviously, you're concerned about the kids and germs and other things. But why are you afraid to talk about it with someone?"

I lift one shoulder and stare at my lap. After what happened with Gaby—her seeing me come unglued—I know I can't go on like this. For the kids' sake. For Marcos's sake. I have to do something. But. . .

Marcos leans over and nudges me with his shoulder. "You can talk to me. You know that."

Tears fall and my throat aches. "But...what if..." I pull at a thread on the hem of my shirt.

"What if what?"

I tilt my head up and look him in the eyes. "Marcos, I can't...I don't want to...do this."

"I know you don't. But you have to. You have to talk to me. I'm concerned. Very concerned. It's time, Jill. As I said the other night, it's time to talk. To me. And to a professional. I still don't understand what happened today, but whatever it was, it scared Gaby. I had to leave work. And you were crying. I don't even know what you were feeling—what you were going through. It's time to get help."

I get up from the sofa, my back to Marcos now. "You don't understand. You just don't."

"How can I understand if you won't explain?" Frustration marks his tone again.

I turn on my heel. "Fine! Fine, you want to know? I'll tell you." I choke back a sob. "What if I talk to someone, you or a therapist or whoever, and you all think I'm crazy and..." I wipe tears off my cheeks. "And..." I can't say it. I can't get the words to come out of my mouth. If I say it, it might happen.

"And...?"

I shake my head. "Nothing. Just forget it. Forget all of it!" I cross the room toward the French doors that enclose the den, but as I reach for the handle on one of the doors, Marcos, who must have gotten up and lunged across the room, grabs me from behind—his arms around my waist.

"No, Jill. No! We have to finish this. Tell me. What are you afraid will happen?"

I flail against him, and he loosens his grip. Then I spin around, sobbing again. "You'll think I'm unfit! An unfit mother! And I'll...I'll lose..." I collapse against him, no longer able to hold myself up. I sob into his chest. Then I whisper, "I'll lose my babies..."

———————◆———————

By the time Marcos and I fell into bed last night, I'd agreed to get a referral from Valerie for a therapist or to find one through another means. Agreeing to take that step was the only way to end the conversation, and I desperately needed to end it.

But this morning, even with my head throbbing and my body exhausted from yesterday's upheaval, I wonder if the conversation with Marcos didn't unlock something in me. I have just enough courage to pick up the phone. But not to find a therapist. Instead, I dial my parents' number. As active as they are, I expect to leave a message, so I'm surprised when my mother answers.

"Hi, I didn't expect you to be home."

She laughs. "You got lucky, darling. We're home. But only for a bit longer—we're meeting friends at the harbor. Sailing and lunch on the boat."

"Sounds wonderful. And cool." I can almost feel the relief of the wind in my hair and the spray coming off Mission Bay.

"So what's up with you? Is everyone well?"

"Yes, everyone is well. I just wanted to"—I take a deep breath—"ask you something."

"Anything, of course."

"Did we go to a. . ." I drop onto one of the stools at the counter. "When I was little, did someone we know die? Was there a funeral?"

My mother is silent.

"Mom?"

"No. Why do you ask?"

I rest one elbow on the counter and lean my head on my hand. "Are you sure? I mean, I remember a funeral. You were there, and Grandma and Grandpa. And there was another older couple, about the same age as Grandma and Grandpa, but. . .I don't know who they were. The woman was crying. You were wearing a small black hat with a veil. And you were crying, too. There were flowers. White." I lift my head and stare across the kitchen.

"I would think I'd remember that. The only funerals we attended were for your grandparents, and surely you do remember those. You were a teenager when your grandfather passed. And in your twenties when my mother went. You must have dreamed up the other scenario. Really, Jill, can you picture me in a hat with a veil?" She laughs a sharp note.

And yes, I can picture her in a hat with a veil. So well, in fact, that I'm sure it's a memory. Or. . .I was sure. "Maybe it was a dream, but it doesn't feel like one." It feels like a nightmare.

"Honey, your father is calling. I need to run. We don't want to keep Bob and Mitzi waiting. Just put all that nonsense out of your mind. Focusing on funerals certainly isn't healthy. Love you. Talk soon."

And with that, she's gone.

"Focusing on funerals certainly isn't healthy." If she only knew. But if I'm not remembering, then what is happening?

What *is* wrong with me?

Courage is found in unlikely places.
J. R. R. Tolkien

Chapter 22

JILL

"Mind if I join you for a few minutes?"

Gaby looks up from the page of the book she's reading. "Okay."

I sit down next to her on the sofa and put my arm around her. When she leans into me, I pull her close and kiss the top of her head. "I'm sorry about what happened yesterday."

"I know. You already said that."

"Yes, I did. I just wanted to explain a little bit more. I haven't been feeling quite right. And—"

Eyes wide, she looks up at me. "Are you sick? Is something wrong with you?"

I read the fear in Gaby's expression. How many of my own fears, my worries, my obsessions, am I passing on to my kids? It's the first time that question has struck me, and it strikes right at my heart. Is that why Gaby reacted the way she did yesterday? Does she fear losing one of us as much as I fear losing her or her brothers? *Oh, Lord, what am I doing?*

"No, honey, I'm not sick. I'm fine, really. It's just my mind. My head. I worry too much. I love you and your dad and your brothers so much, and I just worry about things that don't even make sense. That's why I was crying yesterday. But I'm going to get better. I'm not going to do that anymore."

"How?"

"How what?"

"How are you going to get better and not worry anymore?"

"Oh, well—"

"You can trust Jesus, right?" Her eyebrows rise. "I'll pray for you to trust Jesus more, Mommy." Then she leans back against me as though the problem is solved.

As though it's just that simple.

After leaving Gaby to her book and getting the twins settled with a few toys—well, as settled as they ever get—I find myself unsettled and wishing for a friend. Someone to talk to about life. Maybe Marcos is right: I should call Valerie. After our meeting the other night, I vowed I'd avoid her—I vowed I'd never let her see my craziness in action again. But isn't talking to Valerie preferable to calling a stranger? A therapist? I have to call one or the other—it's no longer an option. Marcos wouldn't give me an ultimatum—that isn't his style—but if I love and respect him, and I do, then I have no choice but to follow through this time.

For many reasons, I know getting help is no longer optional.

I pick up my phone and hesitate for a moment before punching in the number. The line rings on the other end. And rings. Calling her was silly. Just as I'm pulling the phone away from my ear to push END, I hear a breathy, "Hello."

"Melanie, you answered."

"A novelty, I know. I almost didn't, but I'm desperate. I can't stand looking at my computer screen for one more second. Plus, I like to think I'm above needing human contact, but good grief, it's quiet here. At least at home you interrupt me on occasion. Thank goodness you're still doing it even from afar."

"I just thought I'd check in." Melanie and I have fallen into an easy, and maybe even a safe, routine in our friendship. We talk about books, writing projects, the Deep Inkers, recipes, and decorating, and I tell her details about my kids because she feigns interest. Or maybe she really is interested. She does seem to relish her role as godmother. "So, how *is* the writing going?"

She sighs. "It's like scaling El Capitan in the summer, alone, without food. Or water."

"Wow, anything I can do to help?"

"You were supposed to laugh."

"Sorry, I missed my cue. Is it really that bad?"

"I've eked out a few words and finally chose a setting. figuring out Chloe's story, slowly. You're sure I need to stick brand?"

"At this late date, sticking to your brand will save every headache and a lot of marketing dollars. You're making right?" I pull out a chair from the kitchen table and sit do the boys are in my line of sight.

"I suppose, but I think I'm..." She sighs again. "Never n

"What were you going to say?"

She hesitates before responding. "Could you take off the for a minute and put on the friend hat?"

I smile. "Done."

"Okay, so I think I'm losing my mind."

My smile fades. That makes two of us.

"Or at least my ability to focus. My mind just wanders petulant toddler. One minute I'm staring at the screen and come up with a word, and the next minute I'm on a beach thin."

"You are thin."

"No, I mean like model thin. Or highfalutin interior des Strike that. I didn't really say that out loud, did I?"

This time I do laugh, but then I wonder if I should ha It's hard to know when you're being serious. Does the desig building for really bother you? Are you really concerned ab relationship with her?"

"No. I don't let my mind go there."

"You just let it go to the beach?"

"Exactly. I guess I do have a measure of control over Anyway, I've heard brain fog can be a symptom of menopa that's all it is. No longer ovulating equals no longer think Age is a bully."

"Listen, I'm younger than you, and I understand. My ders, too. And sometimes"—I hesitate—"it feels like I can' Like my thoughts have a mind of their own or something With the exception of Marcos, this is the most I've said about what goes on in my head.

"Really? Does it distract you from, you know, real life?"

It's my turn to sigh. "You have no idea. In fact, yesterday I got so acted that I. . .upset Gaby."

"Gaby? Don't you mess with the Gabster."

I smile. "It wasn't intentional. But, in answer to your question, yes, etimes the distractions become problematic."

"Huh. Well, maybe we both need to just get over it."

I laugh. "Let's do that, shall we?"

———————————◆———————————

be it was Gaby's childlike faith in God and in me. Or maybe it Melanie's moment of honesty. Or maybe it was the knowledge if I don't get help, I will wound my children in ways I likely can't imagine. Whatever it was, as I sit in the small coffee shop wait-for Valerie, a melee of conversations swarming, I am glad I'm here. to my stomach, but relieved in an odd sort of way.

I fold and refold a straw wrapper into a tiny square, my iced tea s sweating on the table.

"Jill, I am so sorry I'm late! I was writing and"—she throws her ds up—"I lost all track of time." She sinks into the seat across the e from me.

"It's okay. You're only a few minutes late. Do you want a drink? fee or something?"

"After a full morning of writing, I'm already coffee-logged, if there ch a thing. Let's just catch up. I was so glad when you called. You w me: as much as I love to write, I love people more. I needed to out."

Her expression, so warm and accepting, encourages. "Thank you coming. I really appreciate it."

"As I said, it's my pleasure. You said you had something specific to to me about? I'm all ears."

"Oh, well. . .yes." I pick up my glass and take a sip of the cold tea. Valerie watches me. "This is hard for you?"

I bite my lower lip and tears, unwelcome, fill my eyes.

"Oh, sweetie." She reaches over and puts one hand on top of mine. hatever it is, I admire your bravery. I'm just here to listen, not to e."

"Thank you." Although I've practiced this conversation in my head

a hundred times since calling Valerie, I struggle now to find the words. "I. . .I don't know where to start."

"There's no rush. Take your time."

I shift in my seat. "Okay, I. . .I think I need to see someone. A therapist, maybe? Or a doctor? I'm not sure. But something is wrong. With me." I look down at the table, unable to meet her gaze.

"Jill?" Her tone is gentle, just above a whisper, and requires that I look back at her.

"Whatever is going on, I assure you, there's nothing inherently wrong with you. You are a beautiful creation of God."

My eyes well again. "The other night? At our meeting? When I was. . .checking my phone?"

She nods.

"I do that a lot." I glance down at the table and then back to Valerie, who waits for me to continue. "And other things, too. The baby monitor. I switch it off and on. Four times. Always four times. And then there are the germs. . ." I shake my head. "I'm afraid everyone will get sick and. . .die, so I keep things clean. Very, very clean. I go through cases of paper towels."

Valerie nods again. "Sounds like some compulsive behaviors. What else?"

I swallow. "I'm. . .scared."

Her expression offers compassion. "What are you afraid of?"

"I'm afraid that if I talk to a. . .professional. . ."

She squeezes my hand. "You're doing great, Jill."

I take another deep breath. If I don't say it now, I never will.

"I'm afraid I'll lose my children. They'll be taken away. And I can't let that happen. Valerie, I can't let that happen. I can't. I can't let that—"

"Jill, are you hurting the kids?"

I shake my head, tears wetting my cheeks. "No. Never. I would never. But. . .I scared Gaby. I'm not hurting them physically, but I'm afraid I will hurt them emotionally if I don't get help."

"What happened with Gaby?"

I explain about the nightmare, the memories, the phone call to the cemetery, and Gaby's reaction. Marcos having to come home. I tell her everything. The information gushes out of me like a waterfall after a spring melt. And when I'm done, I'm parched—physically and emotionally. I reach for my tea and take several sips.

"You've told me and you're okay, aren't you? You've survived the biggest hurdle—telling someone the truth."

"But. . .now what?"

"Now you take the next step. Jill, it sounds to me like you're struggling with obsessive-compulsive disorder. It's like your mind is stuck in mud and spinning its wheels. Those obsessive thoughts just spin and spin and spin. The compulsive behaviors are your way of handling the obsessive thoughts, but it becomes a vicious cycle, doesn't it?"

I nod.

"OCD is often a condition that runs in families. Do either of your parents exhibit compulsive behaviors?"

"Not that I've noticed."

"It may stem from another source, but it's similar to depression in that there's a chemical imbalance in the brain. It's an illness, Jill."

I consider Valerie's words and then work hard to maintain eye contact. "Are there medications that can help?"

"There are medications, but behavioral therapy is also very helpful. In fact, I just read a study about how behavioral therapy can actually change the chemistry of the brain. It's fascinating, really. Let me call a colleague in the Bay Area who specializes in anxiety disorders and see who he recommends in this area. You'll likely want to see both a therapist and a psychiatrist."

A disorder? Psychiatrist? "Am I. . ." My face heats.

"Go ahead. You can ask me anything, Jill."

I swallow. "Am I. . .mentally ill?"

"If you're asking if obsessive-compulsive disorder is a mental illness, then yes. It's classified as a mental illness, but there's a wide spectrum for mental illness. Jill, if you had cancer, would you feel shamed by that diagnosis?"

"I don't think so."

"There's no shame in mental illness either, though people do attach a stigma to it. Mental illness is widely misunderstood. Sweetie, you're an intelligent, wise, loving young woman. Don't buy into the stigma. Don't let shame win. Work through this. Treat it as you would any other physical issue. And when shame threatens your mind and heart, you call me. Or you call someone else who loves you, and you talk it through. Promise me that, please?"

My eyes fill with tears again as I nod my head.

"One more thing. About the nightmares and memories. Those aren't typical OCD symptoms. So when you talk with a counselor, share those experiences with him or her and see if you can figure out the root of the nightmare and memories."

I wipe my eyes with a napkin then nod again. "Okay."

"How do you feel?"

"Overwhelmed."

"I'm sure. But know that you're doing the right thing—you've taken the first step. Each step will move you closer to health. And think how wonderful it will feel when those horrible thoughts cease their spinning."

"I can't even imagine. Honestly, I've had thoughts like that for almost as long as I can remember." And as those words leave my mouth, another memory accosts me. I'm standing next to my mother at the casket, and I begin to cry. I reach up to hold her hand, and as I do, I wail. *Daddy!* Then I bury my head in the skirt of my mother's dress.

"Jill?"

My mind struggles to process the odd memory. Or is it a memory at all?

My dad isn't in the nightmare nor a part of the other memories I've had.

It makes no sense.

————————◆◆————————

I wake with a start, heart pounding. I sit up, trying to orient myself.

Marcos shifts, rolling from his side to his back. His voice is thick with sleep. "What? What's wrong?"

"I. . .I don't know."

"The nightmare?"

"No. Yes. I'm not sure." I reach over and put my hand on Marcos's shoulder. "Sorry. . . Go back to sleep."

"You're okay?"

"I'm going to get up—get some. . .water."

He rolls back over as I ease myself out of bed, the images of the dream shadowed, fuzzy. Dread, like a viper, sinks its teeth into me and won't let go. I exhale, draining the air from my lungs. Inhaling requires energy I don't have. I only force myself to do so when I stumble in the darkened hallway on my way to the kitchen, my head spinning without oxygen. I take a slow, deep breath and hold it.

Only ceasing to breathe altogether will stop the turmoil writhing within.

But. . .how can I even think that?

I exhale as I drag myself into the kitchen, trying to re-create the dream, yet afraid to do so for fear of what I may remember. Standing in front of the sink, the only light coming from the digital clock on the microwave, I let the counter hold me up.

The images are blurred around the edges, shadowed. But then. . . I turn my head one way then the other, trying to dull the sound in my mind. The wailing. My own cries. I close my eyes and put my hands over my ears. "No. . .no, no, no, no, no, no. Stop. Make it stop. No, no, no. . ."

There's pressure on my arms, and my body rocks back and forth, back and forth. "No, no, no. . ."

Someone pulls my hands from my ears.

"Jill!"

I open my eyes as Marcos wraps his arms around me and holds me tight. I wet his shoulder with my tears.

There will come a time when you believe everything is finished.
Yet that will be the beginning.
Louis L'Amour

Chapter 23

CRAIG

A delta breeze stirs the leaves overhead, creating a shushing sound that seems to quiet the rest of nature.

But it doesn't still the voice in my head. Nothing seems to shut that down.

"How does your wife feel about us partnering on a project like this?"

"There's no reason for her to object."

"Isn't there?"

I sit on the bench, head bowed, eyes closed. But it isn't a stance of prayer. It's a stance of defeat. When Melanie called this morning, it jolted me back to reality. How could I think of telling her that I'd decided to form a business partnership with Serena after knowing she has concerns about my relationship with her? Women and that intuition thing. They're so often right on. I lift my head, open my eyes, and stare at the landscape lighting that illuminates the Stations of the Cross.

How did I get so far off track after setting my course with Marcos? Instead, I've worked it. Not just the proposal for Serena and the potential conversation with Mel, but every other possible financial alternative. I've considered every angle. Played out every scenario.

I've wrestled with God most of the night for several nights running.

But tonight, I know I have to let it go.

All of it.

The partnership with Serena, my business, the house, and whatever else God wants from me.

If I have to work it that hard, then it isn't meant to be. I've known that but haven't wanted to accept it.

I bend at the waist again, eyes closed. Head in my hands, I swallow back tears. "Why?" I hiss into the night. "Why are You letting this happen?"

But even as I stand ready to accuse God, I'm reminded of my own words to Marcos. *"My plan is to trust. One day—one dollar—at a time."*

I've done everything but trust.

I've figured. Calculated. Cajoled. I've taken things into my own hands, sure I could fix what was broken.

A partnership with Serena wasn't God's provision. It was my plan. And Serena knew that. Maybe it was something she sensed in me, or maybe God led her—I may never know, and it doesn't matter now.

But she was right: the partnership wouldn't be wise.

I sit up and breathe in the warm night air. Millions of stars cut a milky path across the dark sky. "So, now what? We lose it all?" I whisper.

This time I let the tears come. *What do You want from me? What do You want me to do? How can we sell the house? Where will we go? What will we do? What about my business? I've worked so hard. I feel like such a failure.*

I hear no answers to my questions. Get no sense of what's ahead. God leaves me in the dark. But He doesn't leave me alone. I wipe the tears from my eyes with the palms of my hands and then focus on the final station, where a replica of Jesus hangs on a cross.

This is my own Garden of Gethsemane moment. Not that I can really compare the two. But it's my moment to let go of my will.

To open my hands and just let go.

And then make the choice, again, to trust. Just as I told Marcos I would.

I can't see what's ahead. I can't see my way out of the mess. But I will trust that God is setting the course. Not only with the business and the house. But also, most importantly, with my wife.

What Jesus suffered for mankind, for me, makes what I'm going through look trivial at best. Yet the Spirit assures me that God feels my pain—it isn't trivial to Him.

I also know that the course God sets may not follow the path I'd choose. I may lose my business, my home, and. . .my wife. But I can trust—I do trust—that God will use whatever He allows for His good.

The tension in my neck and shoulders eases, and God's strength, like a steel beam, supports me for whatever lies ahead. "Thank You," I whisper.

The breeze has stilled and all is silent. But it's not just the absence of external noise—it's also silent inside my head. The constant jabber of my own thoughts—the figuring, calculating, worrying—all of it has stopped.

Surrender is a hard-won battle.

Fatigue weights my eyelids. Tonight, I will sleep. I stand up, reach for my cell phone to light the path back to the library parking lot, and then head in that direction.

"Pray."

I cross the bed of plants, careful not to crush any of the foliage, and then step onto the pathway that leads to the grove of trees.

"Pray for Melanie."

I slow then stop on the path. I turn back toward the bench and hesitate.

"Pray."

The sense that I need to go back to the bench, sit back down, and pray for my wife is so strong that, if I ignore it, I'll regret it. Every muscle in my body wants to go straight home to bed, but instead I stand, look at the bench, yawn, and then head back and sit down. This time I bow my head in prayer.

Something is going on that I don't know about. Melanie has slipped away. From me. From God. Is there something more? I only know that I'm supposed to pray. It's imperative that I pray. So I trust the Spirit to intercede.

For Melanie.

For my wife.

For the woman I love. And, yeah, have always loved.

———————◆——————

When I get out of my truck in the garage, the bays that house my woodshop and the one where the boat is parked catch my attention. The tools, specialty saws, drills—you name it, I've got it—sit ordered on the workbench or in their space in the garage. The boat is covered, unused the last couple of years.

When Melanie called about her declined debit card, I told her I'd see what I could do.

I flip the switch to turn the light on in that section of the garage, take my phone out of my pocket, and begin snapping photos of the most valuable tools, with the exception of those I know I'll need to make a few repairs on the house. As I take the pictures, I know I'm following a lead, but not my own this time.

Then I pull the cover off the boat.

Once I have the photos I think I'll need, I go into the house, grab my laptop out of my messenger bag, and sit at the kitchen table. I begin listing the tools for sale on Craigslist.

And the boat.

Selling things I worked hard for, we worked so hard for, and took pride in wasn't something I would have considered on my own.

Just as selling a house we designed and built wasn't part of my plan.

I rub my eyes, blink them a few times, and then finish listing the items. I close the lid of the laptop and lean back in the kitchen chair.

How'd things get this bad?

But even as that thought invades my mind, I know the truth: Everything belongs to God. Anything I've earned or worked for was really a gift from Him.

It's all Yours, Lord. . .

———————◆—————————

I drag myself up the stairs. On the way to the bathroom I throw back the comforter on the bed then brush my teeth and trade my jeans and shirt for a T-shirt and gym shorts.

I fall into bed, my mind and body done.

With eyes already closed, I pull the sheet up and over my shoulders, grateful I'd decided to take tomorrow off. The cabinets for Serena's house have been delayed—waiting for hardware she ordered from Europe. I'm not expected either on-site or at the office. My breathing slows and steadies.

"We were created to live life to the full, and we can only do that if we're willing to fully participate."

I roll over.

". . .fully participate."

146

I am only participating in sleep tonight. Nothing else.

"We were created to live life to the full, and we can only do that if we're willing to fully participate."

I open my eyes, push back the sheet, and sit up. *You've gotta give me a break, God. I can't do this every night.* I lie back down, flat on my back, my left arm stretched out where Melanie would normally be. If she were here, I could sleep. If she were here. . .

Nah, I push the thoughts away. Blame isn't the answer.

Fine. I sigh. I'll *participate.*

I adjust the pillow under my head. *Help me to understand, to see what You want me to see, because I really need to sleep.*

Though I surrendered earlier and let thoughts of Serena go, I let the conversation with her the evening we sat together at her house replay again. But this time I rewind to the beginning. What was it she'd said that evening?

"Grief is powerful. It will. . ." What?

There was something else.

"Either we own it and experience it, or it owns us."

Yeah, that was it. Eyes heavy, I close them again as sleep takes over. But just as I drift off, the screech of an owl sounds outside my open bedroom window. I startle, sit up on my elbows, and look toward the window.

All is quiet.

But the familiar ache—that void of loneliness that seems to plague me now—returns.

"Experience it."

Or is it grief? That's what Serena had talked about.

"Fully participate."

I'm willing, but what am I grieving?

I fall asleep with the question on a loop in my mind.

To love someone means to see him as God intended him.
Fyodor Dostoyevsky

Chapter 24

CRAIG

Shafts of light push through the open slats of the shutters I forgot to close last night, waking me. I squint against the sunlight to read the time on the digital clock on the nightstand. 9:48 a.m. Really? I roll over and stretch. Man, that felt good. I could sleep the rest of the day, but I pull myself out of bed anyway.

I splash some water on my face, brush my teeth, and then make my way downstairs to the coffeepot. Since Melanie left, I've avoided making coffee at home. Instead, I've popped a pod into the machine at my office. Easy. But this contraption requires more skill. I open the cabinet above the coffeemaker, pull out a bag of beans, and then look for a grinder. I know it's white. But that's all I know.

I open a few more cabinets, look in the pantry, and even search through the cabinets in the laundry room. Coffee isn't optional this morning, so I pick up the pair of flip-flops I keep by the back door, slip them on, and head for Jill and Marcos's house.

After ringing their doorbell, I run one hand over the stubble on my chin. I should have at least shaved.

Jill opens the door. "Hi there, neighbor." She grins. "You look like a man in need of. . .something?"

"I can't find our coffee grinder. Have one I can borrow?"

Jill laughs. "We do have one, but you don't need it. Your coffee-maker is also a grinder. Open the top and you'll see where the beans go. It grinds and brews."

"Are you sure? We had a white coffee grinder. . . ."

"I'm sure. Melanie gave me your grinder when she bought the new pot. But come on in, I just made the second pot of the morning. It's never as good as Melanie's, but I'm happy to share." She opens the door wide. "What are you doing home this time of day?"

"I'm taking the day off to get some things done around the house." As I step into the entry hall, the twins slide in like they're stealing third base. When they see me, they both squeal, get up, and run to tackle me. They can't take me down, but they try, each standing on one of my feet and hanging on to one of my legs.

"Boys, give Uncle Craig a break—he hasn't even had his coffee yet."

"Nah, you know I love it." I look down at the boys, give them my best snarl, and then lunge across the entry hall, Luis's arms wrapped around one of my legs and Thomas's arms wrapped around the other, both of them giggling. "Fee! Fie! Foe! Fum!"

When we get to the rug in the family room, I drop down, letting the boys think they've wrestled me to the floor. Then they climb all over me.

What am I grieving? The question from last night returns now. It's an odd question to consider amid the twins' laughter and my own. Then I know. I just know. The isn't about *my* grief. . . . Thomas climbs off me, gets to his feet, and then lands, spread eagle, on my chest. My laughter stops as I cough then fight for breath.

"Boys, enough." Jill pulls the twins off me, and I sit up, gasping.

Thomas's eyes are wide as he stares down at me. Then he looks up at his mother. "Uh-oh, he hurt?"

Concern registers in Jill's expression. "Are you hurt?"

I shake my head. Then I reach for the boys like I'm going to grab both of them. They run off, squealing all the way down the hallway.

I suck in a breath. "Got the wind knocked out of me."

"I'm so sorry." Jill puts out a hand to help me up.

I get to my feet. "No problem. They're getting bigger. And heavier."

She smiles. "That they are."

I follow her to the kitchen, where she pours me a mug of strong, hot coffee. I hold the mug to my nose, breathe in the rich scent, and then take a long draw of the brew.

"Have a seat." Jill points to the stools lined up at their kitchen bar. She stands near the coffeemaker, a roll of paper towels in her hand. She begins to rip a few towels from the roll then stops. She seems to hesitate and then puts the roll back on its holder on the kitchen counter. She puts her hands in the pockets of her shorts and crosses the kitchen to stand on the opposite side of the bar from where I claimed a stool.

I set my mug down. "Mind if I ask you something?"

It seems to take a moment for the question to register. "No, of course not." She pulls her hands out of her pockets and reaches for her own mug of coffee, which she'd left on the bar.

"I don't want you to divulge a confidence or anything—I just want your opinion."

"Okay."

"Do you think Melanie ever grieved our inability to have children?"

Jill sets her mug back down. "Wow. That's a big question. My opinion?"

I nod.

"Probably not. I'd guess she just moved on—or tried to. And honestly, my opinion is all I can give you. It isn't a topic we've really talked about. I knew the two of you had struggled with infertility issues, but that's about all I know. She's never seemed to want to talk about it." She comes around the bar and sits on the barstool at the end of the counter. "What about you? You're so good with the kids. I've always imagined you would have been a great father. How did you deal with that loss?"

"Huh, it was a loss, wasn't it?" I take a sip of my coffee, taking a moment to consider her question. "It was hard. Really hard. It's still hard sometimes. But at the time, and for a long time afterward, when I'd think about it I'd just sort of let myself feel it, you know?"

Jill doesn't respond, so I continue. "And every year about this time, I think about it, and I feel it again, though. . .the pain has eased with time. Anyway, someone told me recently that maybe that's my way of grieving, of acknowledging the pain—or the loss, as you put it. But now I wonder if Melanie ever really dealt with it."

"Maybe she's afraid. Afraid of the pain. Sometimes it's easier to deny our fears." She stares into her mug. "Facing them can be"—her tone drops to a whisper—"terrifying."

Is she still talking about Melanie, or is she talking about herself? It isn't my place to ask. It's several seconds before she looks back at me, and when she does, there's a haunted look in her eyes.

When I cross Jill and Marcos's driveway into our yard, I stop in front of the house. The black shutters on the exterior need a fresh coat of paint, as does the front door, and the landscaping needs sprucing up. Both will cost money. But both need to be done before we put the house on the market. The yard work I can do myself—just needs a good cleanup and a few new plants. That's the easy and inexpensive job. I can put a few plants on the credit card this afternoon and do the work early tomorrow before the heat sets in.

I'll also need to repair the back door, finally. And the damaged floor in the laundry room, of course. That will be the most costly repair.

I study the traditional architecture of the house—used brick, lap siding, fire-retardant shingles on the peaked roof. It looks like a Cape Cod saltbox from the front, but the backside of the house doesn't fit the typical rectangular saltbox footprint. The design was a melding of Melanie's love of the Cape Cod style and my desire for something a little more interesting.

The interior plantation shutters on the second-floor windows are closed against the sun's heat, making the rooms look like what they are: unused. Those are the rooms we'd assumed we'd fill with a couple of kids, at least. Now, one is a guest room and the other we use for storage.

Maybe selling the house will give us a fresh start. A new perspective. Maybe it's something we should have done years ago. Hard to say if it would have made any difference in how we felt.

How is Mel feeling about putting the house on the market?

Is she letting herself feel anything?

Of course not. She's run away from our financial issues, the house, me—

"Pray."

"Pray for Melanie."

The exhortation comes again just as it did last night—loud and clear. But I don't know what to pray or how to pray for Melanie. I walk across the lawn toward the front door, but I slow before I get there. What was it Jill said? *"Facing them can be terrifying."*

She was talking about facing fears. *Maybe she's afraid. Afraid of the pain.*

That's it.

The woman I married was vibrant, engaged, present...

Melanie, my emotional Houdini, ran from pain—the pain of giving up the dream of motherhood—because the pain was so great, she feared facing it. The longer she's denied that pain, the more afraid she's become. Now denial, escaping, running—whatever you want to call it—has become a habit.

I've known this on some level, but now I know it with a certainty I've rarely felt.

Unless you face pain, let yourself feel it, how do you know you'll get through it? Maybe she doesn't know what she can handle. Maybe she doesn't give herself enough credit. Maybe she doesn't know that God will walk with her through her pain.

And so will I.

"Pray for Melanie."

I stop in my tracks, my chest tight, because now I know exactly how the Spirit is leading me to pray.

But...

As the late morning sun crawls westward, the house casts a shadow over the yard where I stand.

How can I ask that?

How can I pray that she'll face pain, feel pain? How can I ask that she'll grieve?

That's like asking You to break my wife's heart wide open.

Yet that's exactly what I know I have to do.

And as her heart breaks, so will mine.

I sigh as I climb the steps to the front door.

If this is what participating is about, I understand why people run.

I'm an escapist kind of writer.
Maeve Binchy

Chapter 25

MELANIE

She'd rented a car—one of those small-budget rentals—and she'd rented an equally small condo on a month-to-month basis. She missed the views and the restaurants at the Buccaneer, but since she was also taking an unpaid leave of absence from work, practicality ruled. She had the inheritance her mother left her, which would allow her to live the rest of her life and then some at the Buccaneer, but she wanted to do this on her own.

She *needed* to know if she could do this on her own.

She would determine, at the end of the month, what came next. In the meantime, she had thirty days to figure out what she wanted.

And why she wanted it.

Marriage? Or not?

Maybe that wasn't the right question. Maybe the question was whether she wanted Chad or not. Because that's what it came down to, wasn't it? Asking if she wanted the marriage was too impersonal. And this was as personal as it got.

It wasn't just her life she was considering. It was also his.

She pulled into a space in the small lot of the cottage that housed Dr. Hammond's office near the medical center. She got out of the car, smoothed the new navy T-shirt dress she'd purchased—along with a few other necessities—over her hips, and then followed the path from the parking lot into the building. As she did, she considered her last conversation with Chad. Again.

"You're really not coming home? Is there. . .is there someone else, Chloe? Someone you work with? Someone you met there?" His tone wasn't accusatory; instead, she thought she'd heard fear. Or, again, maybe she was assigning the tone she hoped to hear.

"Of course there's no one else. I can't explain it. I don't know how to explain it. You deserve a straight answer, but I can't give you one. I'm sorry. I just have some things to. . .to figure out. I need some time. A month. Give me a month."

"A month is a long time." Then he'd whispered, *"I love you, Chloe."*

She'd lowered the phone from her ear for just a moment. What was she doing?

Now was the time to figure that out—that's why she'd made this appointment. What would she tell Dr. Hammond? What would she say? Could he really help her?

Could anyone?

What are you doing, Chloe? Chad seems like a nice enough fella. He obviously loves you. Or maybe it isn't obvious. Maybe there's more to a marriage than love? Who knows? I'm certainly not the expert. So why am I writing about this? Because I didn't have any better ideas than the one Valerie suggested.

My next scene will be Chloe's first appointment with Dr. Hammond. It will take some time for me to create his voice and further develop his character. Though I've spent hours considering Elliot Hammond, or at least staring at pictures of the man, I won't really know who he is until I begin writing. Such is the bane of the seat-of-the-pants writer. Or pantsers as those plotters call us. Why does one term sound derogatory and the other noble? We both get the job done.

At least, I hope I get the job done this time.

But first, I need sustenance.

I close the lid of my laptop then blink several times, trying to clear my vision. Staring at those little letters on the screen for so many hours has me seeing double. I get up out of the recliner where I've spent the last three hours, stretch my arms toward the ceiling, and then twist from side to side. I take a few stilted steps toward the kitchen until my demented muscles regain their memory.

With the door to the fridge swung wide, I consider my dinner options, none of which look appealing. What sounds appealing is that little Mexican restaurant I passed the evening I arrived. Tortilla chips and salsa, chicken enchiladas smothered in a verde sauce, and melted jack cheese—I salivate at the thought. "Careful, ol' girl. Soon you'll be drooling like a dog."

I close the refrigerator and go to the end of the counter, where Valerie said she keeps a stack of takeout menus in a drawer. I pull open a couple of drawers until I find what I'm looking for. I shuffle through the four or five paper menus, hoping to find one for the Mexican place. Sure enough. I peruse the menu, add up the cost of my choices, and then go in search of my purse, where I find a crumpled five-dollar bill and two ones in my wallet. Is that all? I dump the contents of the purse. Score! Six quarters, three dimes, a nickel, and several pennies land among a receipt from Safeway, a gum wrapper, and—"Hey, I've been looking for you"—one silver hoop earring.

Eight dollars and change. If I order the enchiladas à la carte, I've got dinner covered.

———◆———

I enter the restaurant, just five minutes from the house, through the bar. When I placed my order, they told me I could pick up my food here. The area is spacious, with a long bar facing windows that overlook the lake. It's quiet for a Friday night, but it's still early.

"*Hola.*" The bartender greets me. "How may I help you?"

"I'm picking up an order. I'm Melanie."

"*Si.* It will be a few more minutes. Have a seat. Would you like a drink?"

"No, thank you. I'll just wait." And I certainly don't need to sit any more than I already have today. A wall covered in photos beckons: a gallery of who's who that have, evidently, visited the restaurant. Why would so many stars make the trek all the way here? I turn back to the bartender and point at the photos. "Your food must be really good."

He smiles. "Si, but that's not why they come. They film movies here—in the vineyards. It's cheaper and less congested than the Napa Valley."

"Ah. . ." I turn back and walk the length of the wall. Many of the photos show an actor or actress with an older Hispanic man—the owner of the restaurant, I assume. When I reach the end of the photos, there's a bulletin board with flyers about events in the area, most of them wine related. Just as I'm about to turn away from the bulletin board, my heart does a somersault in my chest. *Elliot!* He smiles at me from a flyer tacked to the board.

I step closer to read the information. He'll be serving tastings at a local winery? From the photos posted, it looks like a beautiful setting right on the lake.

I turn back toward the bar. "Excuse me?"

"Si."

"Do you know if this actor"—I point to the flyer—"is shooting a film in the area?"

The bartender comes around the bar, wiping his hands on a towel, and walks over to stand next to me to look at the flyer. "No, ma'am, he the owner of that winery. Sometimes he comes. It's always an event when he in town. He grew up around here and owns much of the vineyard land." He smiles at me. "He a local."

How did I not know that? I glance back at the flyer to check the dates of the event—a week from this Saturday. I'll be in the same region, just a few miles away from him? What are the chances? "So are the events only open to wine club members?"

"No. When he in town to pour, it's a fund-raiser, open to the public."

A waitress rounds the corner with a bag in her hand, which she hands to the bartender.

"Ah, here your food, ma'am."

I take one more gander at the flyer so I'll remember the name of the winery. I can google the event once I'm back at the house. Then I go to the bar, pay my bill, and pick up my bag of food. "Thank you."

"You go to the winery—have fun."

I laugh. "Maybe." I wave to the bartender as I walk out the door. Go to the event? No. I'll just look it up online.

I'm curious. That's all.

Who am I kidding?

———————◆◆————————

The enchiladas are still steaming when I take the carryout box from the bag and open it. "Oh, look at all that luscious cheese." I'm tempted to eat them right out of the container, and why not? It's just me. I set the food, including the tortilla chips and the container of salsa, on the table and then grab my laptop and set it next to my feast.

I savor the first few bites of cheesy, tangy delight before opening my laptop and typing the name of the winery into the search bar. When the website appears, so does the same photo I'd seen on the flyer.

Elliot, dressed in worn jeans, a chambray shirt, and work boots, looks at home among the vines. This is one of the photos I'd seen earlier in the week—the one I'd thought was taken in Italy, France, or even Napa. Instead, it was taken just across the lake.

"Well, Dr. Hammond, from the Virgin Islands to Lake County, you do get around, don't you?" I pick up my water glass and hold it up. "To Chloe." I set the glass down and begin scrolling through the website.

By the time I've read every word and studied every photo, the remainder of my enchiladas are cold and the cheese rubbery.

———————◆◆————————

She sat in one of three upholstered chairs in the office, Dr. Hammond in another. She'd avoided the small sofa—it reminded her of psychiatrists' offices she'd seen on TV, and she wasn't here to lie on a sofa and bare her soul.

She just needed to figure out a few things.

Her muscles were pulled taut like a rubber band. She sat with one leg crossed over her knee, her sandaled foot bouncing. Her long blond hair cascaded in loose curls over her shoulders.

Dr. Hammond reached for a notepad and pen and

then stretched his long legs out in front of him. "So Chloe, tell me a little bit about yourself."

"What would you like to know?" She wasn't ready to divulge too much.

"Well, you mentioned on the phone that you're from California. You're a long way from home. What brought you to St. Croix?"

Small talk. Good—she could do small talk. She told him about her job as a meeting planner and her decision to stay on the island, though she didn't tell him why she wasn't going home.

"Sounds like satisfying work. What about your personal life? Married?"

She bit her bottom lip. Her wedding ring gave her away. "Yes. For almost a year."

He smiled. "Newlyweds. How's that going?"

She looked down at her lap then stole another glance at Dr. Hammond through her dark lashes. On the phone, he'd sounded fatherly. Safe. But in person, he was anything but. Old enough to be her father, possibly, yet not fatherly at all.

He was taller than she'd envisioned, and he was toned—a runner, maybe? His dark hair was graying at the temples, and his tanned, weathered complexion highlighted his bright smile.

She hesitated then looked back up at him. She may as well get to the point. "As I said, I came to St. Croix for work but then decided to stay. I'm not sure I want to go back to the marriage."

He scrawled something on the notepad. "You're not sure you want to go back to the marriage or to your husband?"

His question echoed her earlier thought. Coincidence? Maybe. But she bristled at the question nonetheless. "They're one in the same, aren't they?"

"Do you love your husband?"

It wasn't the response she'd expected. She shifted

in the chair. It wasn't a question she was prepared to answer. Her tone was tight. "Love isn't the issue."

Dr. Hammond leaned forward. "Love is always the issue, isn't it?"

It wasn't Dr. Hammond's good looks that disturbed Chloe. That wasn't it at all. It was his ability to perceive, to choose just the right question.

Safe? Not even close.

Safe? Not even close. I click the manuscript file closed so I can see the photo of Elliot on my desktop. I cock my head to one side and stare at him for a moment. The tanned skin around his hazel eyes crinkles with his smile, but there's gentleness in his expression, isn't there? Does that come through in the dialogue?

What's Chloe afraid of?

I stare at the screen a moment longer before getting up and going to the kitchen, where I left my purse. After pulling my wallet out, I find my business credit card, the card I almost never use. Craig wants to save the available balance on our personal card for emergencies, so I'll use this one instead.

Anyway, this will be a business expense.

I return to my laptop, open my browser, and click the HISTORY tab. I click on the website for the winery and then purchase a ticket for the fund-raiser.

It's time to meet Elliot in person. Well, my inspiration for Elliot, at least.

Not actually meet him. Just observe him.

Call it research.

*What's coming will come
and we'll just have to meet it when it does.*
J. K. Rowling

Chapter 26

JILL

I sit across from Cara—as she asked me to call her during our first appointment—not sure what to expect. She isn't what I expected. About my age, she looks like most of the moms I know. Photos of her children are displayed on her bookshelves. Her office is decorated in warm earth tones, and the lighting is soft. The cozy space relaxes me like a welcome embrace. As much as I've dreaded getting help and talking to someone, I'm ready. I have to talk, regardless of the outcome. The nightmares, the memories, the obsessions of my mind, and the compulsive behaviors—all of it has to stop.

I can't take much more.

Marcos can't take much more.

He was right: the time had come to get help. I only wish I'd had the courage earlier. But as Cara told me when I scheduled the appointment, I can't second-guess the timing.

I am here now because this is the right time.

We spent the first few minutes chatting but then dove right into the issues I'd shared with her on the phone, the issues Valerie suggested I discuss with her. I told her about the obsessive thoughts and the compulsions. Today, I need to talk about the nightmares.

Cara leans forward, her focus intent. "Do you remember what you said in the dream?"

I nod.

"Can you tell me?"

My eyes well as I open my mouth, but the words are lost to me.

"Breathe, Jill. Stay with me."

I take a deep breath.

"Good. Now exhale."

I do as she says. As I wipe a tear from my cheek, Cara leans forward and hands me a box of tissues. "You're doing fine. Take your time."

I wipe my eyes with a tissue. "It doesn't. . .make sense."

"That's okay; it doesn't have to make sense. But talking about it may release the power the dream has over you. There's no rush—we have plenty of time."

I take another breath. "Okay. . ." I try but falter again. "Why am I so. . .scared?" Maybe I wasn't as ready for this as I thought.

"I don't know. But you're safe here. I'll go through this with you."

I nod then start again. "I was. . .crying. Screaming, almost. My mother. . . She was there. I was little, like in the other nightmare I told you about. But it wasn't the same. It wasn't the cemetery. I don't know. . . . I don't know where we were. . ."

"You're doing great, Jill."

"I said the same thing over and over. . ."

"And what was that?"

"I was asking my mom. . ." I wipe my eyes again. "I was asking her why. . . I said. . ." I take a deep breath. "Why did. . . Why did my daddy. . .have to. . .die?" I bend and bury my face in my lap and let the tears flow.

I'm aware of movement and then Cara sitting next to me on the small sofa. She puts her hand on my back and soothes like a mother consoling a crying baby. When my tears are spent, I lift my head and, again, she hands me the box of tissues. I wipe my eyes and blow my nose as Cara returns to her seat across from the sofa.

"Why do I feel so much grief when it didn't even really happen?"

"You're very close to your father?"

I shrug. "I love him, but. . .I've never felt a strong connection to either of my parents. We're very different."

"Jill, was there any trauma in your childhood—something involving your dad?"

"I don't know. Nothing I remember, exactly. Just those memories of a funeral. But now I don't even know if those are. . .real. And my dad isn't in either the nightmare or the memories I've had." I look down at my lap. "I feel crazy."

"You're not crazy. We'll work through this, and even if you don't remember any more, I can help you work through the feelings you're dealing with now. You said you have an appointment scheduled with a psychiatrist?"

"Yes. I have my first appointment with him next week. Dr. Luchesse?"

"Good. He's wonderful." She writes something on a notepad and then tears the sheet off the pad. "When you meet with him, I want you to talk to him about both of these." She hands the note to me.

"PTSD/OCD? What does that mean?"

"PTSD is post-traumatic stress disorder. Your nightmares and memories—repressed memories, perhaps—are symptomatic of PTSD. I'd like you to tell Dr. Luchesse about the nightmares and memories when you talk to him about the OCD. The two aren't typically linked, but you're certainly experiencing symptoms of both."

I nod. "Okay." I don't really understand what Cara's suggesting, but I don't have the energy to question her further.

—————————◆◆——————————

On Saturday, Marcos and I both brace ourselves for a visit from my parents. My session with Cara yesterday exhausted me, and I'm not sure I'm ready to face my mother, especially after the recent dreams and memories. But they're coming through for business that my father has up north and will spend the night here. The date's been on the calendar for weeks.

As I finish the breakfast dishes, my mother's voice singsongs from the entry hall. She's never bothered ringing the doorbell or knocking. "Yoo-hoo. . . We're here!"

I dry my hands on a clean kitchen towel, hang it under the sink, and then go to greet them.

Marcos is shaking my father's hand as I come into the entry hall. "Hey, Diane, Tom. Good to see you."

They've set their overnight bag on the floor, and, any minute now, my mother will instruct Marcos to take it to the guest room.

"Hi, Mom." I lean in for her standard kiss on my cheek.

"Jillian, darling, remind me again why you live in the godforsaken valley. I'm positively melting. The heat is unbearable. You must move to the coast."

I raise my eyebrows at Marcos, who just smiles. His patience is seemingly endless.

"Marcos, be a dear and take our bag to the guest room." She pats Marcos on the shoulder then leaves us both standing in the entry as she goes down the hallway. "Gabriella? Boys? Nana's here." My father follows behind her as he always has.

"It's just one night," I remind Marcos.

"You're the one it's hard on. I'm just the help."

I swat him on the arm then give him a peck on the lips. "You're a saint," I whisper.

"Si, *lo se*." He picks up my parents' bag and follows them down the hallway to Gaby's room, which my mother refers to as the guest room. Gaby will sleep on an air mattress in our room tonight. When we remodel, adding a true guest room is on the top of my list of desires.

I go back to the kitchen, where I fill four glasses with ice, add sprigs of mint from the garden, and then pour tea over the ice. The tapping of my mother's heels on the hardwood as she heads for the kitchen lets me know my time alone will be brief.

"Gabriella is awfully quiet. Do you really think keeping her at home instead of sending her to a traditional school is healthy, Jill? Children need socialization. They need friends. You can't keep her cooped up with a pile of books all the time." She follows me to the table, where I set napkins and our glasses of tea.

"Mother, she has a lot of friends and is involved in social activities. But she is naturally quiet and does love to read. I see nothing wrong with either of those things."

"Well, she's just like you, I suppose. You were quiet, too. And, Lord knows, you loved your books."

"And that served me well, didn't it? It directed me to a career I love."

"Yes, but one that doesn't pay nearly enough."

I smile. "Money isn't everything."

"No, it certainly isn't. But it does add a lovely touch to life." She laughs. "So, what's new here?" She looks around the kitchen. "Still thinking of remodeling? I assume you'll add a proper guest suite when you redo the place."

"Yes, Mother. But we'll probably wait a few more years. I have my hands full at the moment."

She laughs. "I'll say you do."

From my mother, that's high praise.

My dad and Marcos appear with the boys in tow. I fix each of them a sippy cup of juice, and they run off to the family room to play. And though Gaby loves my mother, I know she hides from her. Her exuberance exhausts Gaby. And me.

"Have a seat." I point to the kitchen table. "Gaby made cookies." I set a plate of chocolate chip cookies on the table and then sit where I can see the twins.

Marcos pulls out a chair for my mother then joins us at the table.

My dad picks up his glass. "Jill, you're looking as beautiful as ever. The good Lord drew from the right gene pool when he created you. You look just like your mother did when she was your age."

How many times through the years has my dad used that same line about the gene pool? "Thanks, Dad. How's business?"

"Which one?"

"Whichever one you want to tell me about."

"Oh, they're all fine, especially now that, for the most part, someone else is running them."

Marcos reaches for a cookie. "Sounds like you're spending a lot of time on the boat."

My dad nods. "Yessiree, just as it should be. I'll never fully retire, but partial retirement suits me just fine."

My mother picks up a napkin and sets it in her lap. "Tom, partial retirement is all you're allowed. You'd drive yourself and, more importantly, me crazy if you didn't have something to fill your hours."

As the small talk continues around the table, a memory plays in my mind. I'm standing next to my mother at the open grave. I reach my hand up to hold her hand—her left hand. I know it's her left hand because her wedding ring is turned around and the small diamond presses against the palm of my hand. I reach up and twist the ring around her finger so the diamond faces the right way. The band of the ring is yellow gold, the small diamond a solitaire.

Across the table my mother reaches for a cookie. "I'll have just one, and only because Gabriella made them." The large diamonds in her wedding ring sparkle under the light fixture that hangs over the table. The bands—there are three of them—are white gold. The middle band holds a three-carat solitaire, while the surrounding bands have five marquise-cut diamonds, each forming a circle around the solitaire.

I reach across the table. "Let me look at your ring."

She holds out her hand, and I take it in mine.

"Still gorgeous, isn't it?" she purrs.

Her hands are older now, spotted with age, blue veins visible. "How long had you been married when dad gave you this ring? Do you still have your original wedding ring?"

My mother draws her hand back. "Original ring?"

"The smaller one—yellow gold."

"Smaller?" She laughs. "You don't know me very well, do you?" She glances at my father then back to me.

"I. . .I thought Dad gave you this one. . .later."

She looks at my father again.

"Yes, well. . . I added the third band as an anniversary gift one year. I'm sure that's what you're thinking of."

I look back at my mother, and when her gaze meets mine, there's something in her expression I can't read.

She gets up from the table. "I'm going to get Gaby. It isn't healthy for her to have her nose in a book all afternoon."

Is she. . .lying about the ring?

Borrow trouble for yourself, if that's your nature,
but don't lend it to your neighbours.
Rudyard Kipling

Chapter 27

CRAIG

I lift the laundry room door off its hinges, carry it out to the garage, and set it on the sawhorses I set up in the space where the boat was. Using a finishing saw, one of the tools I didn't sell, I cut about one-quarter inch off the bottom of the door to lift it off the floor. In the twenty years we've lived here, the house has settled, a natural occurrence, and the door has dropped just enough to make that gouge in the floor. If I had fixed it when it first began sagging, I wouldn't also have to replace the floor.

Maybe if I'd paid closer attention, things would be different now.

I make a clean cut, the scent of sawdust as familiar as freshly brewed coffee or one of Mel's pies baking. Then I take a sander to the bottom of the door and smooth the cut. A fresh coat of paint and it will look like new.

The floor will be more work.

As I pour the paint into the sprayer, I wonder what Melanie is doing this weekend? Writing, I know. But she can't work around the clock, can she? She'll need to get out at some point.

Maybe I'll suggest I join her for a night or two. I've heard the bass fishing is great at Clear Lake, and I wouldn't mind dropping a line. Marcos and Jill spent a weekend with Valerie and her husband at the place when Valerie's husband was still living. Marcos said he fished right off the end of their dock.

Maybe I'll surprise. . . No, forget that. Melanie hates surprises.

If I call and suggest visiting, would she welcome me? Or will she balk at the idea? Beats me. I'd like to think it'll depend on how the writing is going, but honestly, at this point, even if she's finished the manuscript, I don't know that she'd want to see me.

The cabinets for Serena's house have been delayed—still waiting for the specialty hardware she ordered. So I have a couple days ahead of me with little that needs doing.

Serena. . . I haven't seen her since the meeting in my office. I don't know if she's steered clear or if our paths just haven't crossed. At some point, I'll need to talk to her.

And not just about her house.

I lean the door against a wall in the garage I draped with plastic and then turn on the spray gun. It takes just a couple of minutes to fully cover the one side of the door with paint.

If only restoring a marriage was as easy.

Like the door, I wish I'd paid closer attention. Maybe I could have prevented some of the damage. I guess I thought that when we had children we'd become intentional about keeping the marriage fresh, working through issues, building something that would last.

But when children didn't come and our ideal of what comprised a family vanished, so did our idea of what marriage would look like—or at least my idea of what it would look like.

How will we handle the stress of selling the house, downsizing, finding a new place—all while also dealing with the daily financial stress? Can we—can the marriage—withstand that kind of stress?

Will Melanie weather it with me?

Can we salvage what's left?

I have neither answers nor assurances.

My cell phone vibrates in my back pocket just as I'm turning off the spray gun. I pull it out and see Marcos's name on the screen.

"Hey, neighbor. What's up?"

"You don't have plans for dinner, do you? Because you need to have dinner here tonight."

"You sound desperate."

He whispers now. "Si, *muy desperado.* Jill's parents are here for the night. Please come for dinner. We need a distraction."

I chuckle. "Is that all I am, a distraction?"

"A welcome distraction. You'll come, right?"

"What's for dinner?"

"I'm grilling steaks, and Jill's doing the rest."

"I'm in. I'm tired of frozen food. What time?"

"We'll eat at six, but come early. In fact, now is good."

I laugh again. "How about five thirty? I need to shower or Jill's mother will boot me before I cross the threshold."

"Five thirty. I'm counting on you, amigo."

"I'll be there."

We aren't the only couple facing challenges.

After I shower and dress, I still have about twenty minutes before I told Marcos I'd be at their place, so I pick up the phone by our bed and dial Melanie. The call goes to voice mail.

"Hey, Mel, just checking in. I'm heading over to Jill and Marcos's place for dinner. Hope the writing is going well. I was thinking. . . ." Just as I'm about to suggest I drive up for a night or two, something stops me. "Yeah, I was. . .thinking about you. That's all. I'll catch up with you soon. Love you."

I hang up the phone and then sit on the edge of the bed. *What was that about, Lord?* I have the same sense that I had yesterday, that I'm to pray for Melanie to feel. To grieve.

As I pray, understanding comes. . . .

God is working.

And I need to stay out of His way.

＊◆＊

The heavy scent of Diane's perfume precedes her as she crosses the kitchen and kisses my cheek. "Craig, you handsome man, so good to see you again."

"Hello, Diane."

"Where's that wife of yours? Jill said she's holed up somewhere. . ."

"Yes, Lake County, finishing a book."

Jill turns from where she's standing at the sink. "Hi, Craig. Help yourself to some lemonade." She gestures to a pitcher sitting on the counter. "I'm glad you could join us."

"Thank you for including me."

"Oh, let me get that for you, Craig. You shouldn't have to pour that yourself." Diane takes the glass I just picked up and fills it with ice and then lemonade.

Diane is like a fussy Victorian with all that gingerbread trim, whereas Jill is a traditional classic. They may share similar structural elements—or, as Tom says, the same gene pool—but beyond their physical similarities, they're exact opposites.

Marcos comes in through the French doors from the patio. "Good to see you!" He shakes my hand and then leans in. "You're saving me."

"You owe me."

Diane sidles up to us. "Didn't your mothers ever tell you it isn't polite to whisper?"

Marcos smiles. "You're right. Poor manners. I apologize."

"Me too." I give Diane my most charming smile, but she isn't buying it.

"I'm going to find Tom. We'll change for dinner."

"Mother, there's no need to change. We're casual." Jill comes around the bar to where we're standing.

Diane looks her up and down. "Yes, I know you're casual. We'll change nonetheless."

When she's left the kitchen, Jill whispers, "Thank you for coming, Craig. She adores you."

"I don't know about that, but I'm happy to be here."

"Pull up a barstool, amigo. Take a load off."

I pull out the end stool and take a seat.

Marcos reaches for the two monitors plugged in at the end of the bar. "Here, let me move those for you." He moves them from the bar down to the countertop. Just as he sets them down, a rustling sound followed by Diane's voice comes through one of the monitors. "I've been trying to get you alone all afternoon!" she hisses. "First she calls me and asks that question about the funeral. . . ."

Jill gasps. "I forgot to. . ."

Marcos moves to turn the monitor off, but Jill catches his arm. "Wait."

"Now she's asking about the ring. It's too much, I tell you, just too much."

Tom's voice is softer but still audible. "Diane, it was inevitable. I've told you from the beginning that she'd find out one day."

The three of us stare at each other.

Jill is the first to speak. "Find out what?" she whispers, tears glistening in her eyes.

Marcos reaches over and turns the monitor off. "*Mi amor...*" He wraps his arms around Jill.

I clear my throat. "Maybe I should go. It sounds like you may have some things to discuss with your folks."

Jill pulls away from Marcos. "No, Craig, please stay. Please. I...I don't know what to say to them. Not yet. I need...time."

For the rest of the evening, I work to carry the conversation with Diane and Tom.

Jill and Marcos are silent.

We're all grateful, I think, for the distraction the kids afford.

All we are asked to bear we can bear.
Elizabeth Goudge

Chapter 28

JILL

After a sleepless night, I sit on the edge of the bed, head throbbing. Marcos hands me a glass of water and two ibuprofen. "Are you going to talk to them?"

"I don't want to, but I have to. I can't let this go. I've felt crazy most of my life. And lately, with the nightmares, the memories. . .I need answers. At least now I know it isn't just me—it isn't just my mind. They've. . .kept something from me."

"It sounded that way. I'm proud of you."

"I. . .I haven't done anything yet."

"You will. And I'll be there to support you."

"What about the kids? Do you think Craig would watch them this morning?"

"I'll call him. I can walk them over there as soon as we've fed them breakfast."

I nod. "Okay, one step at a time."

"I'll get the boys up and call Craig. You rest a few more minutes."

"What would I do without you?"

He bends down and kisses my forehead.

When he's gone, I swallow the ibuprofen and then lie back down on the bed, knowing I won't sleep but grateful for a reprieve, if only for a few more minutes. But the monitors on the nightstand taunt me, disturbing any moments of peace I'd hoped for.

After overhearing my mom and dad last night, I didn't even want to look at the monitors, let alone check them to see if they were working. Maybe I should feel relieved that one compulsion has vanished, at least temporarily. Instead, I just feel sick at the thought of the conversation ahead.

What have my parents kept from me?

And why?

———————◆———————

When I walk into the kitchen, my mother is setting the table for breakfast—she has plates on the table for seven.

"Mom, Marcos already fed the kids and took them over to Craig's for a few hours. It's just the four of us for breakfast."

She stares at me a moment then begins taking plates off the table. "I certainly hope you and that husband of yours worked through whatever was bothering the two of you last night. Dinner was dismal."

My tone is curt, but I have no patience this morning. And I'm no longer willing to play games. "His name is Marcos. We've been married for over a decade. Please call him by his name and treat him with the respect he deserves. And there was nothing for us to work through—at least, not between the two of us."

"How dare you talk to me like that. I know his name."

Marcos will be back any minute, but I can't wait for him. I have to speak my mind now, or I may lose my courage. "Where's Dad?"

"He's packing our things. We'll leave after breakfast. It's still a three-hour drive, and your father has meetings early tomorrow morning. Why ever are the kids with Craig? We'll want to tell them good-bye."

My father comes into the kitchen carrying their overnight bag. "There's no rush, Diane. My first meeting isn't until ten tomorrow—we have the whole afternoon ahead of us." He sets the bag in a corner. "That coffee sure smells good, Jilly."

My mother goes to the coffeepot to pour a cup for my dad.

"I need to talk to both of you. Please, sit down."

My mother turns. "Whatever it is, I'm sure it can wait until we've eaten."

"It can't wait."

She comes to the table. "Your hostessing skills need some work," she mutters as she hands my dad his coffee then takes a seat at the table. My father joins her.

Just as I sit down across from them, Marcos walks in the front door and then into the kitchen. I motion for him to join us, but I begin talking before he's even had a chance to sit down. I address my mother, "Yesterday afternoon, when you went to find Dad to change for dinner, I overheard you talking in the bedroom. I heard what you said about my phone call and the question I asked about a funeral as well as my question yesterday about your ring."

Then I look at my dad. "And I heard what you said about knowing I'd find out someday."

My dad looks to my mother, choosing, I assume, to follow her lead as he always has.

My mother's expression is blank. "I have no idea what you're talking about, Jillian."

Confused, I look at Marcos.

He rests his arms on the table. "Listen, folks, we didn't mean to eavesdrop. The monitor was on, and before we could turn it off, we heard what you said. It's time for truth. What is it that you've kept from Jill?"

My mother's poise is unnerving as she responds to Marcos. "I've wondered how you've dealt with these issues, Marcos. I haven't said it often enough, but I am grateful for you—for the way you care for Jill. Living with someone with mental illness can't be easy."

It takes me a moment to find my voice, but in that moment, anger bubbles from my core and is evident in my tone. "What are you talking about? You can't deny what we heard. I know what you—"

She holds up one hand. "I am still your mother, and you will speak to me with respect. Yes, I mentioned the phone call and your question about the ring to your father. I was concerned—*am* concerned. Your struggle has become more evident in recent months. That question about a funeral was simply morbid. Jill, as I told you then, focusing on such things isn't healthy. And the ring? You're creating scenarios that have no basis in reality. There was never another ring. You've obsessed over nonsensical issues since you were a child. I hoped it was something that would work itself out, but obviously, it's only gotten worse."

"Mother, no, you. . .you can't turn this back on me. I heard—"

She interrupts me again and turns her focus to Marcos. "When Jill called last week, she mentioned a dream of some sort and memories. . . . What in the world is happening?"

Doubt flashes in Marcos's eyes.

No. He can't believe her. "Marcos...you heard her...." I turn to my dad. "You said you always knew I'd find out. Find out what? What are you keeping from me? Please, Dad..."

He glances at my mother again then looks back to me. "Jilly, it's clear you misunderstood what I said. Whatever you think you heard, you just misunderstood."

"I didn't misunderstand. I heard it. We heard it. Craig was here—he heard it." I look at Marcos again. "Marcos..."

My mother leans forward, a look of pleading in her eyes. "Marcos, please, she needs help. She needs professional help. Surely you know that?"

My dad reaches into his back pocket and pulls out his wallet. "If it's a matter of money"—he pulls several hundred-dollar bills out of the billfold—"you know we'll help."

I push the chair back and stand, bumping the table as I get up. My dad's coffee sloshes over the side of his cup. "No. No!" Hot tears wet my cheeks. "No! This is not happening! Noooooo!" I sob.

Marcos gets up from the table. "Jill..." His tone is gentle, and then he says something else, but I can't hear him.

I shake my head so he'll know I can't hear him.

A long wailing howl, like that of a wounded animal, pierces my eardrums. It's all I can hear.

He speaks again and I shake my head.

Then I realize...

The sound is coming from me.

*With each book I write, I become more and more convinced
that the books have a life of their own, quite apart from me.*
Madeleine L'Engle

Chapter 29

MELANIE

He tucked Chloe Knopff's file into his leather messenger bag, slung it over his shoulder, and turned off the lights in the office. He'd bought the small house he converted to offices near the medical center shortly after arriving on the island.

He hadn't known he was staying on St. Croix until he'd made the offer on the place.

Maybe he and Chloe shared some things in common. He understood the pull of the island, though he knew he and Chloe had chosen to stay for very different reasons. But maybe they shared similar reasons for coming in the first place. He sensed that, like himself, Chloe had run from something.

Converting the house to offices, the physical work of remodeling, had been his therapy. It seemed rebuilding, fixing what was broken, was in his DNA.

He'd divided the entry and living room into a reception area and main office. He'd added a half bath for clients and created another office out of the second bedroom. He'd hoped to lease the second office to another therapist, but as it turned out, he was the only licensed counselor on the island. Something he hoped would change soon.

He'd separated the rest of the house—a bedroom,

full bath, and kitchen—from the office spaces with a door he'd framed in the hallway.

He used the back of the house when he needed a respite.

As much as he loved going home to April, there were nights he preferred the quiet stability the house offered. He kept some clothes in the closet, toiletries in the bathroom, and a few nonperishables in the kitchen. Anything else he needed on the nights he chose to stay he could pick up at a local restaurant or market. He'd hired a contractor to create a small parking lot in the front and add the necessary features to make the entry and one bathroom ADA compliant. He'd handled the rest of the job himself.

Of course, it had taken longer than he'd anticipated. Everything here was done on island time. But for that season, island time had suited him just fine. He'd been in no condition to see clients anyway.

He'd had his own rebuilding to do.

Once the construction work was completed, he painted the straight lines of the house butter yellow in keeping with the Dutch-style architecture on much of the island.

He stepped out the front door and stood on the porch for a moment. The evening sky was mostly clear with the exception of a bank of pink-tinged clouds to the west, and the winds were mild. The sea wooed him, as it did most evenings, and tonight he was anxious to get on the water.

He turned the key in the lock, securing the office. It had been a long day. After a simple dinner on the deck, he'd call it a night. He looked forward to April lulling him to sleep.

As he made the drive home, he considered his new client again. She'd held her story close, which wasn't unusual during a first appointment. It took time to forge a relationship, to build trust.

Why had she stayed on the island? What had she run from? She'd learn soon enough that geographical distance didn't always solve the problem. He knew that firsthand. He'd hear her story before too long. She'd scheduled a second appointment for the end of the week. She indicated she'd see him twice a week for the next four weeks if he could fit her in.

It seemed she was in a hurry to get somewhere.

Write what you know, they say. So, Elliot, what'd you run from? At least you understand. But this means I have another plotline to figure out. Great. And what did you mean by *"Love is always the issue, isn't it?"* I don't think Chloe will agree with that. Or will she?

It's all a mystery to me.

Sometimes I think those plotters may have an advantage.

One more scene down, too many to go. I reward myself by playing a few hands of Spider Solitaire, one of which I actually win.

Chloe looked at her phone again. No messages. She'd asked Chad to give her space—not to call—and he was abiding by her request. But that's what he did, didn't he? Respected her requests. Respected her.

He was predictable.

"Love is always the issue, isn't it?" Dr. Hammond's statement still nagged at her. Love wasn't everything. There were other factors to consider, weren't there? Chad was a romantic, and, so it seemed, was Dr. Hammond. Where did practicality come in? You can't build a life on romance.

This time, as she pulled into the parking lot in front of the little yellow office, she was better prepared. The nervous stomach she woke with was gone now. She'd talked herself through the anxiety. She'd assessed Dr. Hammond during their first appointment and deemed him acceptable. Safe? Who knew? She didn't have time to find out. She decided she'd have to take a risk.

As she walked into the small reception area, he was there waiting for her, standing in the doorway to his office. "Good morning, Chloe. I was just stretching my legs."

"Hello."

"Come on in." He ushered her into his office and closed the door. She sat in the same place as last time and already thought of it as her chair.

"How's the island treating you?" He took the seat across from her again, his long legs stretched out in front of him.

She wished she felt as relaxed. "I could get used to it here."

He chuckled. "That's easy to do." He picked up his notepad. "So, how are you?"

"Fine." She was certain that wasn't the answer he was looking for, but as her stomach churned again, she decided she would have to ease into this.

He smiled. "Good. How did you feel after our session on Tuesday? Did anything from our conversation stand out?"

"Well. . ." She bit her bottom lip. "Your comment about love always being the issue stayed with me."

"I wasn't sure that resonated with you."

"It didn't. I don't agree."

"You certainly don't have to agree with me. I rarely use the terms *always* or *never*, but in the case of love, my personal beliefs slip in. Love always marks our lives one way or another. Whether we're extending love or withholding love—receiving love or rejecting love. Love is what life is all about. But enough of my philosophizing."

Is Elliot's belief about love my own belief? Is love what life is all about? That's what Jesus taught, and, as distant as Jesus seems these days, I do still believe. . . .

I stare at the blinds covering the windows, streaks of light peeking through the slats. What is it about writing that pulls things out of me that I didn't know I know?

Or didn't know I feel?

Although, it hasn't always worked that way, has it? What happened to burying my pain under a pile of words? That's what I used to do, isn't it?

No...that isn't quite right. I buried my failure under a pile of words so I wouldn't have to feel the pain of having failed.

—————————————◆◆—————————————

Dr. Hammond picked up his notepad and pen. "Where would you like to start today?"

She'd thought she was prepared when she walked in, but now, she faltered. Where did she want to start? She hadn't talked about her relationship with Chad with anyone. Her girlfriends, the few she had, weren't in the same place she was, at least not emotionally. Either they were still maneuvering through the dating scene or they were already having babies. She didn't fit in either category.

There were a couple of girls on her team who were both newly married and still pursuing their careers, but they weren't really friends—they were her employees. As their manager, she engaged on a friendly level, but she wouldn't share the intimate details of her life with them. That was the professional line she'd drawn. It was easier to write an objective review of an employee if she wasn't emotionally attached to them.

Maybe that's how she should have entered marriage—emotionally detached. It would make it so much easier.

"I'm sorry. I'm not accustomed to talking about my personal life. But. . .I'd like to talk about Chad. About marriage. And whether or not I'm going back. . . I know that sounds like I want to talk about love, but I don't think it's as simple as love."

"You're safe here, Chloe. There's no judgment. I'm

here to help you understand what you're feeling so you can decide on your next step."

She nodded. "Thank you."

* * *

Chloe's comment about the simplicity of love rattled around in his mind for several hours. As he prepared for his last client of the week, April's sleek beauty came to mind. She reminded him daily of the complications of love. It was paradoxical—precious and painful.

Simple? Almost never. At least, not in an imperfect world.

Chloe's resistance to the idea of love as something of import, something that marked every individual, may indicate that she's resistant to the pain involved in loving relationships.

Perhaps she's never let her heart go.

Maybe she's never braved diving into love's depths.

I pull my fingers back from the keyboard like I would from a hot stovetop. *Just keep at it, Melanie. Focus. Don't overthink it.* But I ignore my own advice and set the laptop aside. I get up and pace the length of the living room. Jill was right: writing off-brand wasn't a good idea. Why isn't Chloe out shopping? There's great shopping on St. Croix. After all, she has all that lovely inheritance money. What's wrong with her?

"Buy a bikini, Chloe. Go to the beach, for goodness' sake!"

I stop mid-stride. Chloe isn't the problem, is she?

It's Elliot. . . .

The air in the house is stale. The afternoon heat has crept in under the doorways and through the cracks and crevices. I'd turn on the air conditioner, if there was one. Instead, I walk over to the picture windows and pull the blinds open. I squint against the sunlight that streams into the room. The lake sparkles, and cattails sway at the water's edge.

There's a breeze.

I walk away from the window, away from my computer, and out

one of the French doors to the patio. Head down, I trudge across the expanse of grass to the dock. I climb the two steps up to the dock then walk its length to the end, where a large covered platform offers protection from the sun.

I pull a plastic chair off a stack, set it near the railing overlooking the water, and then sit. A breeze stirs just as Valerie said it would. I pull my hair up and hold it off my neck, and then I close my eyes as the air swirls and cools.

When I open my eyes, two Canadian geese swoop low and land on the water just off the dock. Mr. and Mrs. They mate for life, don't they?

That same sense of longing, still undefined, an ache in my chest, accosts me again. It's as though something within is splitting wide. The line I wrote for Chloe and almost deleted comes back to me now. *The cavern of her soul. . .*

There is a cavern, a chasm, an abyss, and I'm teetering on its jagged edge.

The edge of my own soul.

Will I let myself fall?

*The search for the truth is the most important work
in the whole world, and the most dangerous.*
James Clavell

Chapter 30

JILL

When I wake, the light in our room is dim and the house quiet. I roll over, but Marcos isn't next to me. What time is it? My phone is sitting next to the monitors on the nightstand, so I pick it up to check the time. 4:03 p.m. What? Then, like a freight train, the memories of what happened with my parents roll over me.

I drop back onto the bed and stare at the ceiling, gray in the afternoon light. But then I sit back up. Where are the kids? I reach for the monitors. The red light indicating they're on is steady on both monitors. But still, I have to know for sure. I turn the first one off, then on, then off, then back on. I do the same with the second.

No sound comes from either monitor.

Where is Marcos? Where are my children?

Are my parents gone? Please, let them be gone.

I pick up my cell phone again to check for texts, but Marcos hasn't texted. I push his number into the phone and listen to it ring once, twice. . . .

"Hey, you're awake?"

"Yeah, where are you?"

"We're in the backyard. I set up a sprinkler for the kids—it was too hot out here for them otherwise. They're soaked. But they're having a great time."

"Thank you," I whisper.

"Are you okay? You were pretty—"

"I know. I'm. . .sorry. I just. . ." I shake my head.

"It's okay. You rest. We'll come in soon and then we can talk."

"Okay." The kids' laughter sings through the line. "Marcos, wait!"

"What?"

"I...love you."

"*Te quiero pase lo que pase.*"

After he's hung up, I set the phone back on the nightstand, but the look of doubt I read in Marcos's eyes earlier as he considered what my mother said crushes me. Yes, I have a form of mental illness. I am beginning to accept that, but...what my mother claimed...

I roll over and bury my face in my pillow.

If Marcos can't see her lies, their lies, for what they are, how will we...survive? How will I survive? Marcos is my rock—my gift from God.

I roll back onto my side, tears filling my eyes again.

It's all too much.

———————◆◆———————

I sit in the sterile outer office, grateful, following the weekend, that I already had a Monday morning appointment scheduled with Dr. Luchesse.

"Jill Rodriguez?" His receptionist calls my name.

I get up and follow her to Dr. Luchesse's office. She taps on the large dark wood door then opens it and directs me to step inside. I'd envisioned Dr. Luchesse the same way I picture Melanie's character, Dr. Hammond. Tall, dark, and handsome. Melanie's male characters almost always look like Craig—at least, that's how her descriptions read—and I assume Dr. Hammond follows that pattern.

However, Dr. Luchesse, getting up from the imposing chrome and glass desk he's sitting behind, is a fireplug of a man. He's also balding and wearing steel-rimmed glasses.

"Mrs. Rodriquez? I'm Dr. Luchesse." He puts his hand out to shake mine. "Please, take a seat." He gestures to two contemporary-style black leather chairs situated across from one another. Each with a small chrome end table next to it. I choose the seat next to the table without the coffee cup on it.

Like the outer office, Dr. Luchesse's office is contemporary in style—grays, blacks, and chrome—sterile compared to the warm hues of Cara's cozy space.

Dr. Luchesse takes the seat opposite me. "So, tell me why you've honored me with your presence today." He pushes his glasses up on his nose.

Having faced my fear of speaking out about my issues—first with Valerie and then with Cara—I'd hoped I'd feel more confident with Dr. Luchesse, but after the altercation with my parents over the weekend, any confidence I had has disappeared.

I reach across the space between us and hand him the packet of information I filled out as I waited. Pages and pages of questions ranging from "Do you hear voices?" to "Do you have trouble differentiating between reality and fantasy?" No and maybe. I don't know.

I don't seem to know much of anything now.

"Thank you." He sets the packet next to his coffee cup. "Are you feeling some anxiety?"

I nod.

"Take a deep breath, please."

I do as I'm told, already knowing from my time with Cara that it will help.

"And another."

I exhale and then fill my lungs again.

"Better?"

I nod. "Why. . ."—I take one more breath—"does that help?"

"Much of the anxiety we experience is either related to past experiences or future concerns. Intentional breathing brings us back to the moment. Focus shifts to the act of breathing, which is taking place in the present. While this experience in the here and now may still induce some anxiety, breathing is typically a nonthreatening activity."

"Oh." I store the information away, knowing I'll want to consider it later.

"So, Mrs. Rodriguez, rather than go through the questionnaire you completed now, I'd prefer to hear directly from you. What brings you in today?"

"You may call me Jill."

He smiles. "Thank you, Jill."

His courteous manner eases some of my anxiety, and I explain about Valerie's referrals and that I'm seeing Cara. "My counselor. . . suggested I mention both OCD and PTSD—she believes I'm showing. . .symptoms of both. I signed a waiver so you can discuss my. . .case"—I avoid using the term *disorders*—"with her."

"Very good. Is there a family history of obsessive-compulsive disorder?"

It's the same question Cara asked. "No. At least, not that I'm aware of."

"All right. Describe, specifically, your struggles, beginning with obsessive thoughts, presuming that is one of the symptoms."

I spend the next twenty minutes describing what I've experienced—the fear that, unless I'm diligent in checking on the kids, checking the monitor and phone, cleaning, disinfecting, all of it, that I know, absolutely know, someone will die.

"Are you responsible for the well-being of everyone?"

"It feels that way."

"Is that logical?"

"Isn't my job as a mother to protect my children?"

"Yes, that is one of the responsibilities parents shoulder, but can you control their environment at all times?"

"I try. I only leave the kids with my husband or occasionally his parents. I even homeschool my daughter. Really, I rarely let them out of my sight."

"That must prove exhausting. What do you do to relax? Friendships? Time with your husband? Hobbies?"

"I. . .play with my children. Oh, and I work—I have a job I enjoy."

"You work outside the home?"

I shake my head. "No. I. . .work remotely, from home."

"Let me ask you again: Is it possible for you, or anyone, to completely control the circumstances surrounding another individual?"

You have to try. They're all going to die. You have to check; you have to watch. If you don't, they're all going to die. I reach for my purse sitting next to me on the floor. I have to check my phone for messages or texts. I have to make sure everyone is okay.

"Are the thoughts plaguing you now?"

My heart rate has accelerated, and my palms are damp. I set my purse on my lap. I need to get my phone.

"Jill, are you paying attention to the thoughts now?"

I nod as I reach into my purse.

"Please stop what you're doing. It will be difficult. But stop. Tell yourself: This thought is not true. It is the OCD causing the thought."

My phone is in my hand, but I've not yet pulled it out of the purse. I still my hand for a moment and stare at Dr. Luchesse. Then I whisper, "I. . .I have to. . . ." This is the same process Cara has used with me, but this morning the choice to ignore the thoughts feels impossible.

"You can stop. As I said, it will be difficult. Perhaps one of the most difficult choices you make, but it is possible and imperative. Remove your hand from the purse, and focus on the fact that the thought directing you is not true, that it is simply the OCD—the faulty chemistry of your brain."

I don't move.

"Take a deep breath, please. Then another."

No one will die. No one will die if I don't check. No one. . . I counteract the thought with intentional logic, as Cara has taught me, and then I loosen my grip on the phone and let it drop to the bottom of my purse.

I continue repeating the mantra in my head until I've removed my hand from my purse and set it back on the floor.

"Very good. Tell me what just occurred. What went through your mind?"

I explain the thoughts and how I counteracted them.

"Excellent. This is the first step in your behavioral therapy. The therapy can—and will, when practiced consistently—actually change the chemistry of your brain. The longer you employ counter-attacks, the easier the battle will become. There is hope, Jill."

"Okay." I can't say more than that now.

"Let's move on. Tell me, if you will, about the PTSD symptoms."

Already exhausted, I glance at a large chrome clock hanging on one of the office walls. I'm halfway through the appointment. I can do this. . . . "I have nightmares—or one nightmare that I have over and over. And also some"—I look down at my lap—"memories."

"You seemed hesitant to call them memories. Why is that?"

I look back at Dr. Luchesse. "Because. . .I'm the only one who remembers them."

"Tell me, Jill, how old would you say you are in both the dream and the memories?"

"I don't know exactly, but young. Very young. Three? Four?"

"I see. Detail the memories for me, if you would."

I describe the snippets of memory, including the recent incident with my mother's ring, the sense that she was lying, and the way my father seemed to support the lie. And then I tell him what we overheard on the monitor.

"I'm sorry. That must have been quite painful for you."

I nod as I wipe away a tear. "I feel. . .crazy."

Dr. Luchesse's smile offers compassion. "I am not prepared to make a diagnosis of *crazy* quite yet. All right?"

I can't help but smile through my tears. "All right." Then I grow serious again. "You. . .believe me? About the memories?"

"I have no reason not to believe you."

I stare at the floor for several moments then look back to Dr. Luchesse. "My parents—well, mostly my mother—suggested that I'm mentally ill and that my questions about the memories are part of the OCD."

"So you've discussed the OCD symptoms with your mother?"

"No, I haven't. Ever. I. . .I just assume she's noticed some of the compulsions, though. . .I thought I'd hidden them from her. But I guess I wonder if she's right. Are the thoughts that I think are memories actually just more of the same?"

Dr. Luchesse appears thoughtful for a moment, and then he pushes his glasses up on his nose again. "Jill, do the memories have the same recurring, suggestive nature as the obsessive thoughts? Do they compel you to do something to prevent something else from occurring?"

I consider his question a moment then shake my head. "No. Not at all. It's like recalling something that actually happened but that you haven't thought about in a long time. It feels like that, only like I'm recalling it for the first time. Am I just. . .imagining all of this?"

"It's possible but not probable. There are different schools of thought on Freud's theory regarding repressed memories, and we don't have time to cover them here, but I suspect that if you are indeed remembering an event that took place, the memories are fragmented due to your age at the time rather than repression or suppression. Perhaps these comprise some of your earliest memories. Through your continued work with your therapist, the memories may become more connected."

I'm not sure if I'm relieved or disappointed. Part of me wants to remember fully—to make sense of the fragments I've recalled so far. But another part of me doesn't want to remember at all.

"My role in this process is to discuss treatment options with you and suggest a course of treatment."

As Dr. Luchesse talks about medications, possible benefits and side effects, and more about behavioral therapy, for which he cites several studies, I work to remain focused by employing the breathing technique. But my mind is like a dog off leash following its nose.

But the wandering isn't without purpose.

By the time I climb into my car to drive home, I have not only a treatment plan in place but a compelling sense that I need to do some research—to follow up on the idea that presented itself as Dr. Luchesse spoke of treatment options.

It's time to take action.

To participate in my own recovery.

Everything that has existed, lingers in the Eternity.
Agatha Christie

Chapter 31

JILL

Long after Marcos and the kids are asleep, I stare at the screen of my laptop, the whirring of the refrigerator the only sound as I work sitting at the bar in the kitchen. I had an edit I needed to finish after my appointment with Dr. Luchesse, and the afternoon and evening got away from me. After finalizing my notes for the author, I move to shut the laptop down, but then hesitate. If I'm going to participate in my own healing, as I decided earlier, then I'd better use the time alone now to begin. I pick up the laptop and move to the den.

When I'm doing a copy edit, whether it's a fiction or nonfiction project, my mind is working on several levels as I read through the manuscript. One of the things I look for is consistency—in grammar, mechanics, and usage. I also look for consistency in presentation. Does an example used really fit the premise the author is trying to convey? And I look for consistency in facts. Are the facts presented accurate throughout the manuscript?

I spend a good deal of my time checking facts.

Researching facts.

I set the laptop on the desk, but before I sit down, I open the fire-proof file box we keep under the desk. I riffle through the files until I find what I'm looking for.

I hold the birth certificate under the light so I can read the small print:

NAME: JILLIAN ADAIRE WHEELEN
DATE OF BIRTH: APRIL 7, 1979

MOTHER: DIANE ADAIRE WHEELEN
FATHER: THOMAS ROBERT WHEELEN

I read through the rest of the information. All of it is exactly as I expected.

I sit down at the desk, open my laptop, and begin searching for verification of the facts, both those listed on my birth certificate, and a few others.

I am not crazy.

And it's time to prove it.

Not only to myself, but also to my husband.

My vision blurs as I stare at the small letters on the computer screen. I rub my eyes, yawn, and then look at the time posted on the corner of the screen: 1:37 a.m.

What am I doing?

I don't even know what I hope to find.

In the still of the morning hours, I let my mind wander back over the recent conversations with my mother. First over the phone, when I asked if we'd attended a funeral when I was a child. Then the question I asked about her wedding ring. During both conversations, my mother was. . .what? Impatient? Uncomfortable? Definitely anxious to end them.

But why?

I picture the ring on her finger—the thin yellow gold band, the small solitaire diamond. Confusion, tornado-like, spins through my mind, making it difficult to focus. I rest my elbows on the desk, close my eyes, and rub my temples. Why would my mother lie about the ring? That's the one thing that feels certain. She was lying when I asked about the ring.

I open my eyes, look back at the computer screen, and then type my mother's full name into the search bar. Because her middle name is unusual—it was her grandmother's maiden name, which she also used as my middle name—her name pops up on the screen without a long list of others with the same name.

There's a link to her Facebook profile.

A link to her Twitter profile. Twitter? Since when is she on Twitter?

Address information.

Property records.

And then there's a link to a site where, for a $23.99 subscription fee, I can request a report on my mother that includes personal information such as address, phone number, names of relatives, public records, and criminal and traffic records. In other words, they do all the work for you. The subscription allows me to request reports on as many people as I'd like during the course of one month. I've avoided these sites thus far, but now, I'm tired.

Physically and emotionally.

Mostly I'm tired of feeling like I'm losing my mind.

I click on the PayPal option and authorize payment of the requested fee. Then I wait as the report is compiled, knowing I've likely wasted the money spent.

What could it possibly reveal that I don't already know?

I fold my arms on the desk then rest my head atop my arms as I wait.

———◆———

"Mom. . .Mommy. . ."

"What?" I lift my head. "Ouch." I reach up and grab my neck. Gaby stands next to me, her little forehead creased. "Sorry, I must have. . .fallen asleep and gotten a kink in my neck. What time is it?"

"Morning. Did you sleep there all night?"

"I worked on something until early this morning, and then. . .I guess I fell asleep." I rub my neck. "Where's your dad?"

"Right here. I was just coming to find you." Marcos stands in the doorway of the den. "Long night?"

I nod, and then I smile at Gaby and ruffle her hair. "Thanks for waking me up. How about if you go brush your teeth and get dressed and I'll make some breakfast?"

"Pancakes?"

"Maybe."

As Gaby leaves, Marcos comes into the den and stands behind me, massaging my neck and shoulders. "What were you working on all night? An edit?"

I sigh. "No. I was, as my mother would say, following an obsession of my mind, most likely."

His hands still on my shoulders. "What do you mean?"

I swivel the desk chair to face him. "I was searching for information—facts of some sort—to prove to myself, and to you, that my parents are hiding something from me."

"What kind of facts?"

"I don't know. I. . .don't know what I was looking for. Maybe. . . maybe my mother is right about me."

Marcos is silent for a minute. Then he puts his hand under my chin and tilts my head up so I'll look at him. "No. Your mother is not right about you. Yes, you may have a chemical imbalance in your brain, but you are dealing with that. Your parents are hiding something from you, Jill. Remember, I overheard their conversation, too. I'll do whatever it takes to help you prove it."

Tears fill my eyes. "Thank you," I whisper.

He bends down and kisses my forehead. "I'm going to hop in the shower. You've got breakfast?"

I nod.

After Marcos has gone to take a shower, and before I head to the kitchen, I put my hand on the mouse, click on the link for the report I'd requested, and then take a quick look at the contents.

When I reach the section that shows court records, I glance at the information. What? I read it thoroughly.

That doesn't make sense.

I lean forward, squint at the screen, and read it one more time. "Marcos. . .Marcos!"

It is only with the heart that one can see rightly;
what is essential is invisible to the eye.
Antoine de Saint-Exupéry

Chapter 32

CRAIG

I stand on the curb in front of the house and take stock. I pulled out a few dead shrubs and planted the flowerbeds with marigolds, flowers that will last through the fall and, hopefully, through the sale of the house. The entire yard has been trimmed, mowed, and blown. And this morning, before the heat set in, I painted the shutters and the front door.

A car slows to a stop behind me, and I turn to see Marcos, window rolled down, staring at the house, too. "Looks good. Really good." Then he shakes his head. "I hate to say this, but it'll sell—and pronto."

"I don't know—the market's just beginning to recover."

"You're the one who told me that with interest rates as low as they are, it's a buyer's market."

"Yeah, but people are still hesitant. I have a Realtor friend coming by in the morning. He'll list it for us. We'll see what happens."

"You putting a sign up?"

"Yeah."

"I better tell Jill. I know you need to sell, but selfishly, I'm still asking God to provide through other means."

I walk up to the side of the car and clap Marcos on the shoulder. "I appreciate that, man."

"Hey, thanks again for watching the kids Sunday morning."

"Yeah, how's Jill doing?"

"Honestly, I don't know. I thought I was going to have to hospitalize her after that conversation with her parents on Sunday, but she rallied. She did see a doctor on Monday, a psychiatrist, and he was encouraging." Marcos leans back in his seat and stares out the front windshield for a few seconds and then looks back to me. "The hardest part of this is that I don't know what to think. Her parents are hiding something from her, right?"

"It sure sounded that way."

"But when she confronted her mom and Diane started talking about Jill's mind"—he shrugs—"I had to wonder. We heard what they said, but none of it adds up. Diane made some sense, too. Jill's mind. . ."—he shrugs—"but I don't want to doubt her."

"Nah, you're her support right now. Believe the best about her, buddy. Believe the best."

He nods. "Good words, amigo."

◆

The doorbell rings early Wednesday morning, tolling what I wish we could avoid. *Isn't there another way, Lord?* But so far God hasn't revealed another plan. I pull the front door open. "Hey, Brian, come on in."

"Craig, the place looks great outside. Nice curb appeal. But I'd expect nothing less from a home you built."

"Thanks, man. How are you doing? Selling anything?"

"Things have picked up in the last month, but it's still slow. Nothing like what we were doing a few years back."

"Yeah, those were the days, huh? Who knew? Well, you ready for the grand tour?"

"You bet. How many square feet?"

"Just under four thousand."

Brian pulls a notepad and pen out of his briefcase, sets the briefcase on the floor in the entry hall, and then jots down the square footage. His camera hangs over one shoulder. "I'll take some notes and photos as we go through the house."

I lead Brian from the entry hall through the entire house, room by room, and then out to the backyard, where the pool with its waterfalls spilling provides an inviting oasis.

Brian wanders around the yard and takes a few measurements, jots a few more notes, and snaps several pictures. Then he joins me at a table under an oak tree near the pool. I point to a chair. "Have a seat."

He pulls out a chair. "Beautiful place."

"Thanks. So what do you think we're looking at in terms of a listing price?"

Brian looks around the yard and then back at the notes he took as we went through the house. Then he gives me the number.

I lean back in the chair and shake my head. "Really? The last appraisal we had on the place was almost double that."

"I wish it were more, but I've checked the comps in the area, and if we list it higher than that, we'll price it out of the ballpark and won't get any traffic. I'm sorry to say, but it is what it is. If you wait six more months. . ." He shrugs.

We don't have six months, but I don't say that. "Yeah, I know. I'm not really surprised. I know how much prices have dropped. Guess I was just hoping for more."

"Are you ready to list it?"

I rake my hand through my hair. "Yeah, let's do it."

———————◆————————

When I pull up to the job site after my meeting with Brian, the cabinet guys are just beginning to unload the kitchen, bathroom, and laundry room cabinets from their rig. I hop out of my truck and follow them into the house, where a few cabinets are already sitting in the kitchen. I whistle. "Look at that hardware. Fan-ceee!"

One of the guys shakes his head. "The price of that hardware would pay my kid's tuition for the next four years. And that's just on this load. We still have a slew of built-ins back at the shop."

I run a hand over the satin surface of one of the cabinets. "Must be nice, huh?"

"You're tellin' me." He wipes his forehead on his sleeve. "We'll get the rest unloaded then start setting 'em."

"Find me when you're ready. I'm here to help."

As they unload the rest of the cabinets, I walk through the house making notes of things I need to take care of and subs I need to call. After inspecting each room, I go out to the veranda—rock is scheduled for early next week. I stare at the trees beyond the veranda, but my mind is stuck on the listing price Brian mentioned. There has to be another way. . . .

I turn at the sound of Serena's voice. "Hi, Craig."

"Serena."

She smiles and comes toward me. "The cabinet installers said you were around here somewhere."

"Yeah, I just did a walk-through and then came out here to check the progress. And the view."

She looks around. "Everything looks wonderful."

"Did you see the cabinets?"

"Yes, they're lovely. I'm very pleased."

"That's what I do—aim to please. Hey, do you have a minute?"

"Of course."

I gesture for her to follow me over to the balustrades surrounding the deck, out of earshot of anyone nearby. We stand for a moment, mesmerized by the view, as we did the evening we spent time out here together.

She looks up at one of the giant heritage oaks. "That breeze is such a relief, isn't it?"

"Our delta winds have come out of hiding." I know what I have to do, but it's like letting go of the last shred of hope. I clear my throat. "Listen"—I turn toward her—"I want to thank you. . . ."

"For?"

"For your wisdom and your honesty. For calling things as you saw them when we met last week."

"Ah. . . You're welcome, Craig."

"I appreciated your offer of a loan or the suggestion of possibly investing in my company. And while a partnership seemed like a good idea, it wasn't a wise idea. You know?"

She nods. "I do know."

"Serena, I love my wife very much. Our marriage isn't perfect, and things have been rough lately, which means we're likely pretty vulnerable. If I did anything to make you uncomfortable, or if there was anything inappropriate, I didn't mean—"

She holds up one hand. "Craig, I understand vulnerability, believe me. We're both, it seems, vulnerable right now. But there's no need to apologize. You've respected me in every way throughout this project. I am aware that others may have taken advantage of what they saw as an opportunity. You didn't. You've handled yourself with integrity."

"Thank you. And. . .thank you for considering Melanie when I didn't."

"She's a very fortunate woman." She smiles and then holds out her hand. "Friends?"

I give her hand a quick shake. "Friends."

She turns back and looks around the veranda. "So, rock next week?"

"You bet."

"Great. I can't wait to see it finished."

I have no desire to go home. No desire to see a FOR SALE sign staked in the front yard. But I have nowhere else to go.

Instead, I make the familiar fifteen-minute drive and pull into the library parking lot. It's only half past seven and still light as day, but the front gate is closed for the night. I cross the parking lot and make the trek in to the retreat grounds.

When I come through the grove of trees and reach the lawn, Father Ashcroft is standing by one of the benches, shaking the back of the thing, which is obviously loose.

I cross the lawn to where he stands. "Looks like the bolts need tightening. I have a wrench in the truck."

Father Ashcroft turns and looks me up and down. "Are you still trespassing, son?"

"I am."

He laughs then looks back at the bench. "A wrench would do the job."

"Consider it done."

"Thank you. It's a liability otherwise. How are you, Craig?"

"I'm. . ." I start to say I'm fine then decide to be honest. Father Ashcroft has been around for as long as I can remember. He was a young priest when my mother came here—he told me they knew one another. And a time or two, when I've asked, he's shared his wisdom or even some advice with me. He's a good man. "Actually, I've been better."

"Want to talk about it?" He points to the bench I've claimed as my own.

"You have time?"

"Sure. I'm done for the day and would enjoy the company."

I follow him to the bench, where we each take an end. I lean back and look up at the canopy of trees. "You ever wonder what God's doing?" I look back to Father Ashcroft.

"Yes. Frequently. Wondering is fine, but trying to figure it out is futile. I know because I've tried."

"Yeah, me too. And when I felt like He wasn't doing anything, I took things into my own hands."

He chuckles. "How'd that work out for you?"

"Got myself into some trouble."

"I'd imagine so. It seems to work that way. What is it that has you wondering what God is up to?"

I lean forward, resting my elbows on my knees. "A couple of things. The recession has hit us hard—hit my business hard. I had to put our house on the market today. Even if we get a full offer, we'll still be short about fifty grand to pay off the loan. Hopefully the bank will work with us. But it won't leave enough for a down payment on another home." I shrug. "There are a lot of people in worse circumstances, I know."

"Maybe so, but that doesn't make yours any easier. What else?"

I hesitate. "Marriage stuff, but specifically"—I sit up straight again—"and this might sound crazy—but I feel like God's asked me to pray for my wife's heart to. . .break."

Father Ashcroft is silent for a moment then nods his head. He doesn't say anything.

"Crazy?"

He reaches over and puts his hand on my shoulder. "Son, it isn't crazy at all. But it sounds like a prayer that'll cost you." He squeezes my shoulder then pulls his hand back. "Do you know the purpose? Why God would lead you in that way?"

"Not exactly, except I think it has something to do with grief—a wound she hasn't grieved. Instead, she just sort of escapes." I shrug. "She isn't present, doesn't live in the moment, the here and now, you know? Sometimes she does, of course, but whenever life gets hard, she seems to check out. Maybe it's too painful for her. I don't know."

"Does she have a relationship with our Lord?"

"She used to. She still believes, but. . ."

"Well, you have to be present to experience God. Although He is beyond time—is past, present, and future—we, as humans bound by time, experience Him in the *here and now*, as you say."

"Huh, I never thought of it that way."

"May I offer a word of advice related to both issues?"

"Please."

"The Holy Scriptures advise us to give thanks in all circumstances."

"I'm not feeling very thankful at the moment."

"It says give thanks, not feel thankful. I find that the act of giving thanks even when—*especially* when—I don't feel thankful is a discipline that changes my focus." He smiles. "And my heart." He claps me on the shoulder again and then gets up. "I'm going to leave you now, so you can give it a try."

"Thanks, Father."

I sit for a long time considering Father Ashcroft's words before finally taking his advice. I rest my elbows on my knees again and lean my forehead on my folded hands. *Lord, thank You. . . .* I'm not sure what else to pray, so I wait until something comes to me. *I'm grateful that You're in control and I'm not.* I wait again, and then Serena comes to mind. *Thank You for Your strength through my weakness. Thank You that the hardship I'm experiencing has drawn me closer to You. Thank You for Melanie, for giving me a wife I love. Thank You for the jobs You've provided for both of us. Thank You for the way You're working in Mel's life, even though I can't see it yet. Thank You for. . .*

I must pray for at least an hour. When I open my eyes, the sun has dropped behind the trees and the landscape lights have come on.

As I walk back to the truck for a wrench, the dread I've felt for weeks has been replaced with something else.

I reach the truck and click the key fob to unlock it. What is it I'm feeling? I open the driver's side door, reach behind my seat, and open the toolbox I keep there. I pull out a wrench and shut the box.

As I walk back toward the retreat center, I consider what lies ahead—selling the house, moving, finding a place to live, maybe even starting a new business of some sort.

Doing something new.

And doing all of it, I hope, with my wife. . . .

When things are really dismal, you can laugh,
or you can cave in completely.
Margaret Atwood

Chapter 33

CRAIG

When I back out of the garage early Thursday morning, something on the front lawn catches my eye and I slow the truck to a stop. I didn't notice the FOR SALE sign when I drove in last night—didn't even think to look for it. Huh.

The sign stands front and center on the lawn, announcing our plan to anyone interested.

Attached to the sign is a plexiglass pocket filled with brochures Brian must have made up yesterday. I hop out of the truck and go and pull a brochure out of the pocket. The photos of the interior of the house and backyard are good—appealing.

Maybe Marcos is right. Maybe it will sell fast.

It's a beautiful house. . . .

Whether it sells quickly or not isn't in my hands. *It's Yours, Lord. All Yours.*

I put the brochure back into the pocket, step away a few feet, and then pull my phone out of my back pocket. I snap a photo of the sign against the backdrop of the house.

When I get to the office a few minutes later, I send the photo to Melanie with a text: I GUESS THIS MEANS IT'S OFFICIAL.

Within moments Mel's name flashes on the screen of my ringing phone. I answer. "Hey, good morning."

"I'm not sure *good* is the word I'd have chosen for this morning, but let's just go with it. I was checking my e-mail on my phone when your text came through."

"Sorry to interrupt."

"No, I'm glad you did. So it's real? What did Brian say yesterday? Does he think it will sell?"

"He thinks there's a good chance, but not at the price I'd hoped for." I tell Melanie the amount the house is listed for.

"As you know, numbers are not my friends, but it seems the last time I glanced at a mortgage statement, we owed more than the listing figure."

"Yeah, we do. We could go to the bank and do what's called a short sale, where we basically just walk away from the loan and the bank gets what they can out of the house. It may come to that if it doesn't sell soon, but. . .I don't know, I just haven't felt like that's the route I want to take, you know? It makes sense, but. . ."

"I trust your judgment. So. . .are you okay? You designed that house—you built it."

"We designed it and built it, Mel. But yeah, I'm okay. Yesterday was hard, but God gave me a new perspective. I don't want to be owned by a house—or by anything else, for that matter. Right now, the stress of making that mortgage payment each month is my primary focus. I don't want to spend life focused on a payment. This feels like a new beginning. I don't know what that's going to look like, but it could be an adventure, at least as long as you're willing to take that adventure with me?"

"An adventure? It won't include jungles or reptiles, will it?"

I laugh. "I think I can promise you that."

"Okay, then I'm in. There's just one thing. . . ."

"What's that?"

She's quiet for a moment. "Can we take. . ." She sniffs. "Jill and Marcos and the kids with us?"

"I'm sorry, Mel. That is the hardest part of this, I know."

She says nothing more. The emotion I heard in her voice has thrown me, and I'm not sure what to say. "Well. . .I guess we'll just see what happens, right?"

"Right. I'm sorry I'm not there to help you with all of this, to support you. I should be there."

"That means a lot. Really. But you are supporting me—supporting us. You're working to bring in a paycheck. I guess one of us should have been a brain surgeon."

"That's messy work."

I laugh. "You've always kept me laughing, Mel."

"I do my best." Her tone is light again. "So how about one of us just inherits millions?"

"Good plan. I'll start looking for a benefactor."

"Perfect."

We both laugh. I stand in my office enjoying the moment. "Speaking of millions, I made the mortgage payment and deposited just over nine hundred into the checking account. Not quite a million, but it's a start. Get whatever you need at the grocery store."

"Where'd that come from?"

"I cleaned out the garage."

"And found cash in an old coffee can you'd stashed away?"

"Something like that." Then it occurs to me that I haven't spoken to Melanie since the weekend. "Hey, have you talked to Jill this week?"

"No, why?"

"Her parents visited over the weekend. I was there for dinner Saturday night. Things got pretty tense."

"Sounds like fun. What happened?"

"Jill, Marcos, and I overheard something her parents said, and it upset Jill. I don't really know all the details. But Marcos brought the kids over on Sunday morning so they could talk with Jill's folks. Doesn't sound like it went too well. Anyway, thought I'd let you know. You might say a prayer for them. Sounds like Jill's really struggling."

"Nice that you could help them out. I have to talk to her soon about the book, so I'll give her a call."

"Yeah, okay. So are the words stacking up?"

"*Stacking* is a strong word. But I've made some progress. I'm doing some research on Saturday that may help. I'm feeling a little more confident about meeting the deadline, but the story still isn't exactly what I'm contracted to write. Jill will read it and, hopefully, help me make it fit my brand. Or not. I'll see." She hesitates. "How's the custom coming along?"

"Good. Getting close. Cabinets were delivered today. Turns out Serena's pretty easy to work with." I sit down at my desk. "Mel, you know there's nothing there—nothing between me and Serena, right?"

"Of course." It's obvious the topic is not open for discussion.

"Okay. Well, hang in there. Keep me posted."

"You too. Let me know if anything happens with the house."

"Will do." I end the call and set the phone on my desk. That was the most relaxed conversation we've had since Mel left.

The prayer God's asked me to pray for Melanie flashes in my mind, casting a shadow over the ease of the moment. If God has asked me to pray for Melanie to break in some way, then God will be faithful to answer that prayer.

There has to be another way. . . .

But just as with the house, it seems this *is* God's way.

The writer works in a lonely way.
Irwin Shaw

Chapter 34

MELANIE

I stare at the blank page of my manuscript document, but all I can see is a FOR SALE sign sticking out of our lawn. I close the laptop, pick up my phone, and look, again, at the picture Craig sent this morning. Though why I bother—when it seems it's burned itself into my retinas—is beyond me.

I close the message app on my phone with the text and photo from Craig. I can't let the potential sale of the house disrupt my work. I have to focus. I put my fingers on the keyboard, hoping for words to magically come through my fingertips.

But. . .

I pull my hands back from the laptop.

It isn't the house that's bothering me. So what is it? Craig's words come back to me. *"That is the hardest part of all this, I know."*

How many times has Jill walked in our back door and poured herself a cup of coffee?

How many times have we stood in my kitchen and chatted about nothing as she's disinfected my countertops?

How many times have I walked next door, laptop in hand, to ask her why a scene I'm writing isn't working?

At least a hundred memories knock on the door of my mind, just like Gaby knocks on our front door when either Marcos or Jill walks her across our driveway.

I wipe tears from my cheeks.

Writing is a solitary endeavor, and I'm okay with that, even relishing the solitude most of the time. But when the silence becomes oppressive and I can't remember why I do what I do, Jill's always right next door.

Maybe we don't go deep. But we've gone where we've each needed to go. At least, I think that's true.

Sounds like Jill's really struggling. . . .

Would she call me if she needed a friend to talk to?

I don't wait to find out.

I pick up my phone and key in Jill's number. Surely she's seen the sign in our front yard by now. If she doesn't want to talk about whatever it is she's going through with her parents, we can certainly talk about the house.

"This is Jill. Leave a message and I'll return your call."

Disappointed, I start to hang up, but then remember that, unlike me, Jill *will* return my call, so I do leave a message. "It's me. Just checking in. How are you? The kids? Life? Thought I'd see what you think of our new yard decor. Not sure how to feel about it. Clueless. As usual. Give me a call when you have a few minutes. I'll turn up the volume on my phone so I can surprise you and actually answer. Although, I guess now that I've told you I'll answer, I've spoiled the surprise. Oh well. Talk to you later. . ."

I do as I've told Jill I would and turn the volume all the way up on the phone. Then I notice the battery is low, so I get up and go into the kitchen, where I've left my phone charger plugged in. Once I've connected the phone to the charger, I go in search of a box of tissues, which I find in the bathroom.

I wipe my eyes and blow my nose, getting myself in order.

It's time to put all thoughts of moving out of my mind.

It's time to focus.

Chloe kicked off her flip-flops, bent down and picked them up, and then walked down the beach, the surf lapping over her bare feet. The late morning sun, high in the sky, already burned her shoulders, and the balmy air encased her like a tomb.

The trade winds, almost ever present, had stilled. The cool water was her only escape.

Without work to fill her hours, her mind flipped

through an album of memories, images of her child-hood and vacations spent on beaches like this one building sand castles with her mother, running from the waves, yelling over their shoulders, "Catch me if you can," and, years later, lying side by side on beach towels sunning themselves, passing a tube of Ban de Soliel Orange Gelee Sunscreen between them.

When she'd opened a new tube of Ban de Soliel this morning, the scent nauseated her, the memories it evoked too much.

She wished her mother was here to confide in. To offer words of wisdom. To guide her.

Chloe walked the length of the beach then sat on the wet sand, the gentle waves breaking over her long, tanned legs.

Would her mother have liked Chad?

After her father had deserted them when Chloe was just a baby, her mother had never remarried. She hadn't needed a man, it seemed, financially or otherwise.

"You're all I need. You're my sun, my moon, and my stars," she'd told Chloe.

Would her mother have approved of her choice to marry?

She'd never know.

Tears welled in her eyes, as they had so often in the last several weeks. Her emotions had a will of their own these days.

She needed to make a decision about her marriage and get her emotions, and her life, under control.

* * *

The office was warm despite the portable air conditioner in the reception area that he had turned on when he arrived this morning. The air conditioner didn't provide much relief, but at least it stirred the warm, damp air, which was something.

Chloe sat in her usual seat.

"Do you mind if I leave this open?" He stood by the door that separated his office from the reception area. "I'll lock the front door so we're sure no one walks in, if you're comfortable with that."

"Sure. The air helps."

He came back in and claimed his seat. "So, Chloe, how did you spend your weekend in paradise?" He'd noticed her pink cheeks and nose.

"I spent most of it in the water—at the beach. The first time I came to St. Croix I was nine years old. My mother enjoyed vacationing here—we loved the beach." She looked away. "I spent some time remembering. . . ." Then she looked back to him. "How about you?"

"I spent most of the weekend on the water." He smiled. There was no wind, so he and April motored out several miles where the air was a little cooler, although he hadn't found the relief he'd hoped for—physically or emotionally. "I hear the trade winds will pick up again this evening and blow some of the heat and moisture out of here. So, where would you like to begin today?"

"I'm not really sure."

"Well, you mentioned your mother. Why don't we start there?"

She hesitated. "I'm not sure how that will help with the issue at hand—deciding what to do about my marriage."

"It may not, but oftentimes the past informs the present. You said you spent time remembering—were the memories enjoyable or painful?"

She looked at her lap. "Both. I was very close to my mother."

"Was?"

"She was killed in a car accident eighteen months ago. It was instant—no time to even. . .say good-bye." When she looked back at him, tears glistened on her lashes. "It was just the two of us. She raised me on her own."

When he was counseling, he kept his own wounds tucked away in a safe compartment where they wouldn't impact his client. But it wasn't always easy. "I'm so sorry, Chloe. Your grief is still fresh. How have you dealt with your loss?"

My fingers pause on the keyboard. Oh, this story is a barrel of laughs. Jill will have to work a miracle when she does the edit.

Who am I kidding? It isn't Jill's responsibility to fix this.

It was weeks ago that Jill advised me to talk to my agent about this story, but I kept hoping I could fix it—make it fit the story I was contracted to write. But. . .I open my e-mail app:

Subject: Houston, we have a problem. . . .

Maybe if I can make him laugh, the news will. . . But there's no way to wrap this package that's going to help its delivery.

Dave,

Actually, I do have a problem, one I should have alerted you to several weeks ago. I apologize for the delay. As you know, I'm contracted for a manuscript due 10/1. However, the story I proposed is not the story I'm writing. . . .

I go on to explain the brand issue and tell him I've attached a new partial synopsis for his review, along with a few sample chapters.

I spend the next hour writing a synopsis of what I know about the story thus far and then attach it to the e-mail.

I'd like to say I'll fix this and make the story fit the genre I'm contracted to write, but, for reasons I can't yet explain, I don't know if that's possible.

I'll appreciate your advice on the best way to present this issue to the publisher, short of breaking my contract and returning the

portion of the advance already paid.
Thank you.

I lift my finger to click SEND but hesitate. It isn't just my portion of the advance I'd have to repay. I would also owe the 15 percent my agent received. Repayment isn't an option. With the financial struggles we've had this year, we've already spent the advance and then some.

What am I doing?

After sixteen years, this is the year I choose for an author meltdown? But. . .did I really choose this?

I get up from my laptop and walk out one of the French doors into the heat of the day. The lawn, still damp from the sprinklers that soaked the property this morning, creates an unnatural humidity that rivals that of the Midwest. I tilt my head skyward. "I could use some help here. . . ," I whisper.

I hope for inspiration to descend on the wings of an eagle or any one of the seemingly hundreds of avifauna fluttering about. But the only message I receive isn't a message at all but more a sense—and a weak one at that.

"Keep writing."

Seriously? That's the best You can do?

I go back into the house, the screen door slamming behind me, and press SEND. The uninspired e-mail about my uninspired manuscript wings its way to my agent's inbox.

Then I get back to work.

Chloe lifted one shoulder then let it drop. "I just kept going, I guess. I got up each day. I worked. I met Chad. I got married. I did life."

"You've been married just about a year, you said?"

"One year next month."

"And you met Chad after your mother died?"

"Actually, I met him because she died. As executor of her estate, there were quite a few legal issues for me to deal with. She had a lot of real estate holdings, investments, business dealings. . . . Anyway, Chad worked, still works, in her attorney's office. He'd just passed the bar. He wasn't involved in my mother's dealings, but that's where we met."

I set the laptop on the little table next to the recliner and get up to think. I walk through the living room, into the kitchen, and then back through the laundry room and second bedroom which connect back to the living room. I do laps as an idea—or maybe, an *understanding*—of Chloe's problem begins to form.

I try to put myself in Chloe's circumstances. How would it feel to lose the person you're closest to? How would it impact the choices you make? What would it do to a marriage?

What does Chloe feel? Head down, I pass through the living room again. Who am I kidding? I don't have an emotionally astute bone in my body. How would I know what Chloe's feeling?

What am I doing? What made me think I could write a story like this?

As I round the corner back into the kitchen, something occurs to me and my pace slows. Valerie knows how Chloe would feel. She lost the person she was closest to—her husband.

I stop in the kitchen and put my hand over my heart as I recall the fear just hearing Valerie's story evoked. If I ever lost Craig. . .

But still something nags. . . .

I close my eyes as my mind searches through files of memories.

"It's like you died, too."

Craig was sitting on the edge of our bed. . . .

"I've lost you."

No.

I open my eyes.

No.

I won't. . . I can't. . .

No!

217

Most of the basic truths of life sound absurd at first hearing.
Elizabeth Goudge

Chapter 35

JILL

It isn't until after the kids are in bed again that I finally collapse onto the sofa in the den with my laptop. The information I read in the report this morning and then showed Marcos nagged at me as I made breakfast, showered, helped the twins get dressed, braided Gaby's hair, grocery shopped. It nagged through an entire day of mundane activities and a work deadline.

After dinner, while Gaby played a game with the twins, I had a few minutes alone in the kitchen with Marcos.

I handed him a plate I'd just rinsed and then turned off the faucet. "I'm afraid to follow that trail, to do more research. I'm. . .afraid of what I'll find."

He set the plate in the rack in the dishwasher and then looked at me. "You don't have to do anything with the information you found. You don't have to follow that trail, as you say. Maybe it's enough to know that you weren't imagining things."

"Is there any way it could be wrong?" But even as I asked Marcos, I sensed the answer.

He shrugged. "You won't know unless you search further or talk to your mom."

"Talking to her won't help. I've tried that. No. I. . .I have to do this. I have to figure it out. I have to know."

"Okay. You know I support you whatever you do. I'll give the twins their bath and get them to bed."

"Thank you. I'll finish cleaning up the kitchen and spend some time with Gaby before she goes to bed."

Marcos leaned over the dishwasher separating us and gave me a slow, tender kiss. "I love you."

I brushed my hand across his cheek. "You must. I. . .I'm not easy these days."

"Maybe not, but you are muy *interesante*."

He laughed as I swatted his arm.

Now, I sit with the laptop open and my heartbeat pounding in my ears. I open my browser, type in the URL of the site I accessed the report through, and then log in with the username and password I chose when I established the account early this morning.

Once I'm logged in, I click on the report link and then scroll down to the section that lists public records, including marriages.

There are two marriages listed:

DIANE A. O'SHEA
THOMAS R. WHEELEN
MARCH 19, 1983

DIANE A. FITZGERALD
JAMES H. O'SHEA
AUGUST 20, 1977

I set my laptop on the coffee table, get up, and go over to the desk where my birth certificate is still tucked into the corner of the blotter. I pull the certificate out.

NAME: JILLIAN ADAIRE WHEELEN
DATE OF BIRTH: APRIL 7, 1979
MOTHER: DIANE ADAIRE WHEELEN
FATHER: THOMAS ROBERT WHEELEN

It doesn't make sense. Surely the year of marriage listed for my parents is wrong. Or maybe they had me before they married and my mother, the rule follower, didn't want me to know? That, in my mind, is the most likely explanation.

But. . .who is James O'Shea? Was my mother married and divorced before she met my father? Was she embarrassed by that? Or ashamed?

Why wouldn't she have told me?

But. . .there's no divorce record listed.

I move the cursor over the unfamiliar name. The cursor hovers. . . .

It takes just one moment to divide time, to change a life forever.

The moment of impact in a fatal car accident.

The moment cancer is diagnosed.

The moment a lifelong lie is uncovered. . . .

I lift my hand off the trackpad, hesitate, and then lower it back and click on the name James H. O'Shea.

———————◆◆——————

I drag myself down the hallway and into our bedroom, where, without waking Marcos, I slip into bed still fully clothed. I turn my head on the pillow—the red lights on the monitors shine.

Someone is going to die. . . .

I stare at the lights but see a white flower dropping onto a casket. I turn and bury my face in the skirt of my mother's black dress.

They're all going to die. . . .

I reach my hand up to hold my mother's hand—the diamond on her ring presses into the palm of my hand. I let go of her hand and twist the band around. The ring is yellow gold. The diamond a small solitaire. Then I grasp her hand again.

It's going to happen. . . .

The wailing cry of a child echoes in the still bedroom. *Why did my daddy have to die?*

It isn't going to happen.

It has already happened.

Marcos stirs next to me then rolls over so he's facing me. "You okay?"

Tears wet my cheeks and pillow. "No," I whisper. "No. . .not at all."

Make a difference about something other than yourselves.
Toni Morrison

Chapter 36

MELANIE

There are too few things in life that can be counted on, and a returned phone call from Jill is a given. Always. So when she hasn't called me back by midday Friday, I pick up my phone and call her again. And again, the call goes to voice mail.

I hang up without leaving a message this time. But before I've even set the phone down, it rings and Jill's name appears on the screen. "Hi, stranger."

"Melanie, I'm sorry I didn't get back to you, I'm. . .it's. . .I can't—"

"Jill, it's okay. You sound. . . How do you sound?" I get up out of the chair and walk the length of the living room.

"At the. . .end of my rope? Exhausted? Overwhelmed?"

I have no idea how to respond. "Oh, okay, well. . . Wow." I turn and walk the other way.

"I'm sorry, Melanie. I shouldn't—"

"No. Actually, you should. Just spill it. That's what friends do, right? Say whatever you want to say. Tell me whatever you want to tell me. I'm listening."

"This is new territory. . . ."

I stop in front of the bookshelves. "New is good, I think. Let's do new."

"Okay, well. . .here's something new. . . ." She hesitates. "I discovered that my dad isn't. . .really my dad."

My mind can't process what she's said. "Wait. What?"

"My dad isn't—"

"No. I heard you. But. . .Tom isn't your father?" I shake my head.

Her tone is flat, void of emotion. "They've lied to me. All these years, they've lied to me."

"Oh, Jill. . . I don't know what to say. No wonder you're overwhelmed."

"Melanie. . .how would you. . .would it be an intrusion. . . I mean. . .I know you need to. . .but I. . .it's just so—"

"Jill, you're going to have to speak in sentences. They don't have to be compound sentences. Simple will do. But I need a subject and a verb."

Then a smile sounds in her voice. "Simple sentences—okay, I can do that. Ready?"

"Ready."

"I'm. . .seeing a counselor."

I nod. "Good. That's really good."

"The sentence or the counselor?"

I laugh. "You're perking up. The counselor, of course. Keep going."

"She suggested I get away."

I raise my eyebrows. "Leave the kids?"

She falters again. "Just for. . .a night or maybe. . .maybe two. Marcos. . ." She trails off again.

"You want me to come home to babysit so you and Marcos can get away?" Please say no. Those twins scare me to death.

"No. I want to. . . I thought maybe. . .could I come there?"

Here? "Yes. Absolutely yes. Do it. You need time and rest and the kids will be fine. I know you've never left them, but Marcos will take good care of them, you know he will. Just come. Come here. Is that what you asked? Yes, definitely. I'd love it. Really. I won't even talk to you. Or I will. Whatever you need. I'll make you coffee." As words spill from my mouth I realize that maybe I don't do *new* all that well.

"What about your deadline?"

"I need your input. If you're up to reading just a little, then that will help. And if not, if you just need to sleep or eat or whatever, then I'll just keep winging it. Okay? Please come."

"Okay, I'll come Sunday. Cara—my counselor—set an appointment to see me and Marcos tomorrow. She doesn't usually work on Saturdays, but. . .I called her. . .after. . . That's when she suggested I take some time for myself. Anyway, Craig's going to watch the kids again while we're at the appointment. What would we do. . .what will we do. . .without the two of you?"

"That's too big a topic for now. Let's take one thing at a time. So Sunday afternoon, okay? I'll see you then. Do you have the address?"

"Oh, no. I guess that would help."

"I'll text it to you."

"Thank you. And. . .thank you for, you know. . ."

"I know. I do. You're welcome."

After I end the call, I drop into the recliner but can't sit still, so I pop back up. Wow. Just wow. Why would her parents, her mother, do that? What's the backstory on *that*? I can't imagine what Jill must feel.

I walk over to the windows, push back a section of the blinds, and look out at the lake. "Please. . ." I pause. "I know I have no right to ask You anything, but please help her. Comfort her. Amen. I mean, thanks. Amen."

How long has it been since I've prayed?

I mean, really prayed?

I drop my hand from the blinds and let them fall closed again, and then I turn away from the window. As much as I want to be a good friend to Jill—and if I'm honest with myself, I have very little idea of how to do that—I'm glad she's coming for another reason. . . .

I need a distraction besides writing.

A distraction from myself.

And the feelings waking within. . .

Like a long dormant volcano.

You can give without loving, but you can never love without giving.
Robert Louis Stevenson

Chapter 37

CRAIG

*P*ray..."
I roll over, eyes closed.
"*Pray...*"
I open my eyes and sit up, my heart pounding like a hammer. What was that? The bedroom is dark, the plantation shutters closed against the rising sun. Was it a voice? The bedroom and the house beyond are silent.

"*Pray for Melanie...*"
The skin on my arms and the back of my neck prickles. Was the voice audible or did I dream it? I push back the sheet and swing my legs over the side of the bed. I couldn't go back to sleep now if I wanted to. I make my way to the bathroom then to our closet, where I grab a T-shirt and pull it over my head. I turned the air conditioner off before I went to bed last night and slept in just a pair of gym shorts. We have to save wherever we can. I slide my feet into a pair of flip-flops, and then I head downstairs.

I set the coffeepot to brew and watch as the beans grind and then the hot coffee begins dripping into the pot. *Is Melanie okay?* The clock on the coffeemaker reads 5:42 a.m. Too early to call and check on her. I push my hand through my uncombed hair.

"*Pray...*"
I grab a mug, pull the pot out from under the stream of hot liquid, which stops its flow, fill the mug, and then put the pot back. I carry the mug through the family room and head out the French doors to the backyard.

I set the mug on the table near the pool then turn toward the east, where the sun has cast a pink hue across the sky. The morning air is cool against my skin, and I breathe deep. "Thank You. . ." I whisper. *Thank You for waking me. Thank You for the privilege of seeking You. Thank You for Melanie.*

I turn back to the table, where I pull out the same chair I sat in on Thursday when I met with Brian. I brush oak leaves from the tabletop, pick up my mug, and slurp my first gulps of coffee. Then I look up at the twisted trunk and gnarled branches of the stately blue oak.

Melanie has always loved oak trees. . . .

I've always thought they were a bother.

But the oaks do thrive in the harsh summer heat, even tolerating extended drought conditions.

In fact, too much water will kill them.

I study the tree as words form in my mind. . . .

Lord, may Melanie. . .break, like an acorn. . .sending new roots into the soil of You. May she grow and thrive in harsh conditions—through the loss of her dreams, the loss of provision, the loss of our home. . . .

I look from the tree to the table, where I rest my elbows on its surface. I bow my head. *I pray her roots will travel deep, seeking You for sustenance and strength. May she drop her leaves of fear each season, making room for buds of new growth. May she stand tall, limbs outstretched in worship, present and attentive to You. . . .*

Tears wet my cheeks. *Father, thank You in advance for restoring the wife of my youth, that I might rejoice in her.*

My prayers continue until the sun is hot on my back. The words, I know, are not my own. Nothing I would ever have thought to say or pray on my own. Instead, the Spirit prays through me.

When my mind finally stills and no more words come, I lift my head and reach for my now cold mug of coffee. I take a sip then set it aside.

What's going on with Melanie today?

Or what will go on?

Why did God wake me to pray for her?

One can live in the shadow of an idea without grasping it.
Elizabeth Bowen

Chapter 38

MELANIE

As I dress for the fund-raiser, my choices are yoga pants and yoga pants—cropped yoga pants, long yoga pants, fitted yoga pants, and loose yoga pants. Mind you, I've never done yoga in my life. I shuffle through the piles of clothes I transferred from my suitcase to drawers when I arrived. Well, I also have a couple sets of pajamas and a nightgown to choose from.

I opt for a pair of wide-legged, black nylon and spandex yoga pants that, if no one looks too closely, will pass for real pants. I pair them with a cornflower blue V-neck T-shirt, black sandals, and the only necklace I threw into my suitcase when I packed—a chunky silver thing. When I thought I'd wear it, I have no idea, but pack it I did. I add my silver hoop earrings now that the prodigal has returned.

Standing in front of the full-length mirror on the back of the bedroom door, I decide the outfit has a casual-chic look to it. At least, that's what I tell myself. The T-shirt is one of Craig's favorites—he says it's the exact color of my eyes. The memory pricks like a thorn, and my breath catches.

I go into the bathroom, stand at the counter in front of the mirror, dab a bit of makeup on my eyes and lips, and layer on a couple coats of mascara. Though really, why bother? It's not like I'm attending the event to impress anyone. Just collecting fodder for the book.

The money goes to a good cause, too—to help the homeless population in both Lake County and St. Croix. In fact, by attending I'll learn more about Elliot's—I mean the actor's—foundation and how he's impacting homelessness. It's a great topic to discuss as I'm promoting the book, since part of the story is set in St. Croix.

Or. . .if we become homeless.

What will Craig and I do if the house sells?

Where will we live?

Anyway, the event promises to be just the distraction I'm looking for until Jill arrives tomorrow.

———————— ◆ ————————

From the road, the winery looks like a dozen others, but when I pull off the highway and through the gate, the long driveway is flanked on either side by fields of lavender, much of it still blooming even this late in the season. I crack the driver's side window and breathe deep of the sweet scent. In the distance a grove of olive trees sway in the breeze, and red-tile roofed buildings, Mediterranean-style, stand against the backdrop of the lake, sparkling in the afternoon sunlight.

Within moments I'm transported to another part of the world. I've spent so much time staring at a computer screen in a dark house that my senses are overwhelmed.

I park, get out of the car, and then follow terra-cotta pavers into a courtyard. From there I follow a throng of people into the winery. With my head up I take in the details of what look like Old World beams, maybe brought in from Europe, dark wood ceilings, and white plaster walls. I've learned a thing or two about design from Craig over the years and appreciate the attention to detail. I stop and do a slow turn. Craig would love the architecture and the quality of the finishes.

I stay back from the crowd of people surrounding what I assume is a tasting bar where my leading man is presumably serving drinks.

A jazz combo plays and the music, along with the sound of chatter from the duos, trios, and quartets clustered in the room, floats to the high ceiling, filling the space.

It appears I am the only solo.

Others wander, carrying glasses of wine purchased at another bar, or serve themselves appetizers at one of the food-laden tables set up around the room.

Craig is so good in this type of setting. The handsome extrovert with the ready smile who, as they say, never met a stranger. He takes social ease for granted, never giving it a second thought. Typically, he serves as my shield when we walk into a room of people. He's the armor that protects my introverted self, though I've never really thought of it that way until this moment. As I stand here alone.

"*Mel. . .I miss you.*"

I miss you, too.

More than I knew.

My anticipation of meeting, or at least observing, my inspiration for Elliot has faded like a pair of worn jeans. Why am I here? I turn to leave but then know I'll regret it later, so instead I adjust the shoulder strap of my purse, take a deep breath, and walk toward the crowd at the bar. I should at least get a glimpse of the man.

I shimmy past a few people until I can view the bar, where four servers are pouring tastings. In the middle of the four is a fifth. Elliot. His hazel eyes flash as he says something to the woman who holds out a wine glass. He pours a small amount of wine into her glass, and then they both laugh about something. She swirls the wine, lifts the glass to her nose to sniff the wine's bouquet, and then takes a sip. Attentive, he watches her and then seems to ask her something.

I try to skirt around a few more people to get closer—close enough to hear the timbre of his voice. But as I'm skirting, I get pushed and earn a few dirty looks. People have paid to get close to this man, and they aren't about to let anyone maneuver in front of them.

Having seen him, my doused sense of anticipation reignites, so I move to the left, toward one of the other servers, where there are fewer people. I scoot up to the bar, decline the wine with a wave of my hand, and slide into a space at the bar between the server and Elliot. I shift so my body is turned toward the other server so it isn't obvious I'm gawking at the actor. But from here I can hear every word he says.

"Oh man, really?" He says to the guy he's serving now. The tone of his voice is melted butter—warm and rich. My heart rate quickens. I turn slightly so I can see him. Up close, he looks as perfect as his photos. He isn't one of those actors who appear plastic—skin stretched like a trampoline, hair dyed an unnatural shade. Instead, he's a man who wears his age well.

As I listen to him and watch him, that same sense of familiarity I've felt before washes over me. But that's reasonable, isn't it? This is someone I've watched in movies and seen in a hundred photos, if not more.

Or is there something more about him. . . ?

He pours another tasting then glances up and looks right at me. He smiles and lifts up the bottle of wine. "Care for a taste, pretty lady?" He reaches under the bar, produces a wine glass, leans toward me, and hands it to me. I edge closer to where he stands behind the bar, ignoring the glare of the man he was serving.

He pours the garnet-colored liquid into my glass and then looks back up at me. I'm close enough now to see the flecks of color in his hazel eyes.

I've stared into those eyes so many times when looking at photos.

But—my breath catches—looking into his eyes in person is like looking into. . .

I swallow as memories flash through my mind, each striking like lightning. My hand begins to tremble, and the wine dances in the glass. I set the glass on the bar, the foot of it clattering against the wood bar top.

I take a step back.

"Steady, love. . ." He smiles, but I can't return the gesture. "Give it another go. This is one of Lake County's finest—our 2012 Syrah. An estate wine." He chuckles. "It'll take the edge off."

I take a deep breath, step back toward the bar, work to steady my shaking hands, and then—just as I dare to pick up the glass again—someone down the bar calls his name, and he turns away. With his back to me, I set the glass back down on the bar and turn to go. As I'm walking away, I hear his voice, but his words are lost amid the clamor.

I disappear into the crowd, threading my way through the crush of people, my vision blurring. I bump into a woman, causing her wine to slosh over the sides of her glass. "Excuse me. I'm sorry," I mumble as I push past her.

Once I clear the crowd, I take my first breath since looking into his eyes. I spot an exit and quicken my pace.

When I reach the courtyard, I swipe tears off my cheeks.

I keep my head down and follow the pavers back to the parking lot, where I jog the rest of the way to my car, fumbling for my car keys as I go.

I have to get out of here.

I have to get away.

As I close in on my car, I punch the key fob to unlock the doors. I grasp the door handle then yank my hand away, the metal branding my hand. Hot tears flow as I dig through my purse for some tissue. When I find a packet, I pull a few tissues out and place them between my hand and the door handle. I open the door and then slide into the car's oven-like interior, the leather seat scorching the backs of my legs. Sobs build, but as I cry, the searing heat of the car's interior deflates my lungs, making me gasp.

I turn the key in the ignition, flip on the air conditioner, and then roll down the windows before putting the car in REVERSE and pulling out of the parking space.

My tires spit gravel as I plow down the long driveway toward the highway.

I can escape him.

But I can't escape myself.

Nor can I extinguish the fire of emotion now raging within.

If I find in myself desires which nothing in this world can satisfy,
the only logical explanation is that I was made for another world.
C. S. Lewis

Chapter 39

MELANIE

I stand in front of the bathroom mirror where I coated my lashes with mascara just a couple of hours ago. Now that mascara runs in rivulets down my face. I grab a washcloth, run it under hot water, lather it with soap, and then scrub the makeup from my eyes and face.

The soap burns my eyes, but I accept the pain as something deserved.

I unclasp the silver necklace around my neck and unhook the earrings, dropping them on the bathroom counter.

I need to get busy. Get back to work.

I grab the laptop off the table near the recliner, where I left it this morning, and carry it into the kitchen. I set it on the kitchen table then go to the coffeepot, dump the grounds from this morning, and set a fresh pot to brew. While I wait for the coffee, I pull the drapes closed across the windows in the nook. I don't need the distraction the lake affords.

I intend to make some headway on this manuscript so I can get this story behind me.

Maybe I'll shoot for a ten-thousand-word day. I've seen other authors celebrating word-count achievements like that on social media. Why not me?

Who am I kidding? I'm only good for about a thousand words a day. But maybe today is a good day to change that.

I go to the refrigerator, open it, and slide the carton of half-and-half off a bare shelf. I need to shop before Jill comes tomorrow, which means another trip to Safeway. As I stand in front of the open fridge, tears well in my eyes again. I slam the door of the refrigerator closed.

I spend half my pathetic life at Safeway. And I haven't figured out the all-important nuances of the store here. But missing my home Safeway is not worth crying over.

I rip a paper towel off a roll hanging above the counter and wipe my eyes then blow my nose. I grab a mug, fill it with coffee, and then sit down at the table, opening the laptop and rereading the last scene I wrote. I blink back tears as the words blur on the screen.

Focus.

Just focus on Chloe.

I spend the remainder of the afternoon writing, deleting, rewriting, and deleting. I get nowhere. The only thing I know for sure about Chloe at the moment makes no sense, and I have no idea what to do about it.

I want to manipulate the story to go one way.

But it seems Chloe is intent on going another way.

I stare at the screen. "Who's in control here, anyway?"

Obviously, it isn't me. I close the laptop, get up from the table, and go to the sink and rinse my mug. I don't understand what Chloe's thinking.

Or feeling.

What's new?

Maybe it's time to run to Safeway. Or... Where's my purse? I walk back through the living room and find my purse sitting on the bench by the front door. I dig through it until I find my phone then search through my contacts for Valerie's home number.

As soon as she's said hello, words spew out of me like hot lava. "Chloe wants to go home. Desperately. But I don't know why. I mean, she took a leave from work, told Chad she was staying, and even rented a place on the island. Now she wants to go home? I can't figure out what she's feeling. I thought maybe you'd know. Do you know?" My voice cracks on the word *you*. I clear my throat as I wait for Valerie's response.

I hold the phone away from my ear for fear her laughter will split my eardrum.

"Melanie?" She laughs again.

"What?"

She seems to catch her breath. "I'm sorry. . . . It took me a minute before I recognized your voice and recalled who Chloe is. Oh, you have me in stitches. How long has it been since you've spoken to anyone?"

An image of Elliot, wine bottle in his hand, flashes through my mind. "I talked to Jill on the phone yesterday, and I talked to a Girl Scout who came to the door a couple of days ago. She was selling cookies."

"Did you buy any?"

The tension in my shoulders eases. Valerie's laughter, even at my expense, does me good. "Buy any what?"

"Girl Scout cookies."

"Oh, Thin Mints. Two boxes. The little girl was cute, and she said sales had dropped since last year, what with the recession and all. I think it was a pitch, but I fell for it. She was good."

"Things are always better in twos, as you well know."

"Right. What does my talking to people have to do with Chloe? Could we get back to the point? I mean, if you have a few minutes? I know it's my point, not your point. I get that. Life isn't all about me, I know. I just wondered. . . Why, psychologically speaking, would a woman who was desperate to leave home suddenly want to return home?"

"So, you're wondering about your character's motivation?"

"Yes. Hey, you're learning something about writing fiction."

"I've picked up a few things from the Deep Inkers." The smile is evident in Valerie's tone.

"So. . . ?"

"Well, maybe she's homesick."

I don't have to look into a mirror to know my brow has furrowed. "Isn't that what I said? Not exactly, I know. But I said she wants to go home."

"What I mean is that maybe she's experiencing the longing for home that each of us feels at one time or another—not home in the sense of a house we live in but that longing for something more, something beyond. It's a universal experience, don't you think?"

"Maybe? I guess I'm not sure what you mean by longing for home. If it's a universal experience, maybe I'm from a different universe."

"Bingo."

Maybe calling Valerie wasn't a good idea. "Okay..."

"You're calling from your cell phone, right?"

"No, actually I'm standing in a phone booth on Main Street."

Valerie giggles. "You're a hoot. Okay, since you're not tied to the landline at the house, go stand on the back patio."

"What? Why?"

"I want to show you something."

I head for the nearest French door that leads out to the patio. This seems pointless, but I'm stuck and I need answers, so why not play Valerie's game? I have nothing to lose. But minutes. Which are ticking away much too quickly. The screen door bangs behind me as I step onto the stone patio overlooking the expanse of grass and trees between the house and the lake.

"Okay, I'm on the patio. Now what?"

"What do you see?"

"Valerie, this is your house. You know what I see."

"Tell me."

"Grass, trees, water."

"What else?"

I bite my bottom lip to keep me from spouting something I'll regret. What else do I see? "Okay, hydrangeas surround the patio—white hydrangeas, some are still blooming. At least a dozen trees." For the first time since I arrived, I notice that the giant trees are several different varieties. "Wow... Have you ever noticed how many varieties of trees you have? Is that a sycamore?" I've always loved trees. I've forgotten...

"Yes. There are fruit trees along the side of the house, too."

I wander to one side of the patio and peek around the corner of the house. "That huge tree outside the kitchen window is a fig tree?"

"It is. My grandmother used to make fig jam every year."

I look from the fig tree to the vines hanging on a trellis overhead. Plump green grapes hang in clusters, and some of the leaves are beginning to change to hues of goldenrod and russet. "It's really beautiful here, Valerie." I walk down the stone steps out to the lawn and take a few steps toward the lake; then I stop and turn back to face the house. A giant heritage oak stands in front of the house towering over the roofline, its twisted branches silhouetted against a goldenrod sky. "The sun is setting. . . ."

"I thought it might be—it sets a bit earlier here than it does there. Why don't you walk out to the dock and enjoy the sunset from there."

"I. . .I don't have a lot of time." I don't want Valerie to know how little progress I've made on the book since I've been here. I don't want her to think I've wasted the opportunity she's given me. I don't want to think about it myself. With the phone still to my ear, I lean my head to one shoulder then the other, trying to relieve the tension that's settled there again. "Anyway, the sun sets in the west, in front of the house."

"Yes, but the colors are still nice over the lake. You'll see. It won't take long. And it might help you move forward on your manuscript. Give it a try."

"What does this have to do with Chloe?"

"Maybe nothing. Or maybe everything."

"Fine." I start out for the dock, my strides quick. "So, are you writing?" I ask to fill the space between the house and the dock.

"Yes, I just sent a new proposal to my agent."

"Wow, that's great. What's the topic?"

Her sigh soughs through the phone line like the breeze through the treetops—something else I hadn't noticed until now.

"It's about grief. The difference between letting go of someone you love and letting go of love altogether. That's the temptation, isn't it? To think we'll never love again. But really, every person we encounter, each relationship we're involved with presents an opportunity to love. I want to explore how letting go of romantic love may open up space in our souls to love others with agape love—the type of love God has for us."

I stop walking and stare out at the lake. "Wow. . ."

"It's a tough topic, and one I'm not sure I'm ready to write about, but at the same time, love is healing, so maybe writing about it now, while the grief is fresh, will be part of my own healing—something I can pass on to others in similar circumstances."

I recall Valerie's ready smile the morning I ran into her at Safeway and today her easy laughter as we've talked. It's easy to forget she's just lost her husband, a man she must have loved very much.

"I'm sorry, Valerie. You're so full of. . .joy"—is that it?—"that I forget you're grieving."

"Joy and grief aren't mutually exclusive."

They aren't? "Right." I pick up my pace again until I reach the few steps leading up to the dock.

"Almost there?"

I climb the steps. "Just walking the plank," I say in my best pirate brogue, which elicits the giggle from Valerie that I'd hoped for. Best to take her mind off her grief, right? I make my way to the end of the dock and stand looking over the water. "Okay, I'm here."

"What do you see? Tell me like you'd write it. Or close. Describe it."

"There's a breeze, warm—like Indian summer—which is causing the lake to ripple. Is that what you want to hear?"

"If that's what you want to tell me."

"This is your game, remember? I'm just playing along."

"Okay, then you're doing great. What else?"

Something cuts a line through the water close to shore and I smile. "Is that an otter?"

"Could be. There are freshwater otters in the lake."

The otter swims toward the dock belonging to the next property over and lifts itself onto the swim platform floating at the end of the dock. As it shakes the water from its fur, the droplets reflect the setting sun, and it looks as if the otter is shaking sparkling amber-colored gems from its coat. "Oh. . ." I put one hand on my chest, trying to quell something stirring within. "It's so. . ."

"What?"

"I can't. . .describe it."

"That's okay. Stay present. Enjoy it."

I'm quiet for a moment as I watch the otter. Then I lift my gaze to the mountain across the way. "The clouds are like cotton candy." I roll my eyes. "Strike the cliché."

"Describe what you see."

"They're. . ." I swallow a lump forming in my throat. "Trying to describe them will dilute their splendor."

"I understand."

"You know the mountain across the lake just south of your

property? Have you ever noticed that it looks like a woman? She's lying on her back, hair flowing behind her."

"Or is the mountain a profile of her face? People see her differently. That's Mount Konocti. Named by the Pomo Indians. Roughly translated, it means 'mountain woman.' The Indian legend goes that she was angered by her husband, so she left, telling him he'd never see her alive again. Days later, she was found on the peak of Konocti, her body having been crushed by a large snake."

I swipe my hand across my damp cheek.

"Melanie? You still there?"

"Yes," I whisper.

"What are you feeling?"

The shifting clouds reflect the sun in ever deepening hues: pinks, corals, lavenders, blues. "Does it matter? Aren't we talking about Chloe? How is this. . .helping me unravel her story?"

"Maybe Chloe feels what you're feeling?"

Or maybe I feel what Chloe feels. . . .

Again I put my hand on my chest to soothe the ache that's settled there—the same ache I've felt since arriving here. Before that even. Since as far back as my memory takes me. "Maybe."

"Let me ask you again. What are you feeling?"

"I don't know, exactly. I'm not very good at the whole feeling thing. But the beauty makes me. . . It stirs the same feeling I've always felt. Or, honestly, tried not to feel."

"Ah. . ."

"Maybe *longing* is the right word. Or *desire*. Or, I don't know, *loneliness*?"

"You know, Melanie, when I said the longing for home is a universal experience, I meant that we all experience it in some way. But we call it different things: nostalgia, romanticism, desire, loneliness. They're all similar, if not the same, at the core, aren't they? We feel misplaced, alone, and we long for a place to belong. We desire love in its purest form. When we're present, experiencing ourselves—emotions, relationships, beauty, music—we often feel that sense of longing or desire.

"One way to describe it is a longing for home, though that's not quite accurate. The Welsh have a word for it: *hiraeth*. It's difficult to translate in English, but I've heard it described as a homesickness for a home you can't return to. Or a place that never was. I've come to acknowledge it in myself as a longing for God. 'Eternity set in the hearts of men,' as Solomon so eloquently wrote."

When I don't respond, Valerie continues. "I'm not sure that's what's going on with Chloe, but maybe there's something there you can draw on."

"Do you think Chloe's. . .afraid? Afraid to stay present? To fully engage?"

"I don't know, is she?"

Swallows dart to and fro off the side of the dock. "It would explain a lot. . . . Thank you, Valerie. Really."

"My pleasure. I'm always up for a good conversation."

I stand on the end of the pier looking out over the water, small whitecaps roiling the middle of the lake now. A hundred varieties of birds, or so it seems, dot the sky or float lazily. Birdsong serenades. And laughter skips, like a smooth stone, across the surface of the water from a dock down the way.

I pull one of the chairs off the stack, move it to the edge of the dock, and sit witness to the spectacle, one phrase playing through my mind like a refrain: *stay present.* . . .

As twilight descends, the palette changes again, the lake now reflecting the midnight blue of the darkening sky. On one edge the water shimmers a wavering reflection of the rising moon.

As the birdsong fades, crickets pick up the chorus.

I let the song evoke what it will. . . .

Longing.

Loneliness.

And tears.

Good books, like good friends, are few and chosen;
the more select, the more enjoyable.
Louisa May Alcott

Chapter 40

JILL

Gaby stands in the entry hall holding my computer bag. "How long are you going for?" Her dark eyes look up at me through her bangs.

I take the bag from her and put my arm around her shoulders. I work to make my tone casual, assured. "Just two nights. I'll sleep there tonight and Monday night. On Tuesday morning, after breakfast, I'll get up and come home. In the meantime, Daddy is here, Uncle Craig is next door, and you can call me anytime. Okay?" I bend down and kiss the top of her head.

"Did you pack enough books?"

I smile at her and then ruffle her hair. "I'm going to read the one Aunt Melanie is writing—we're going to work on it together while I'm there. And while I drive, I'm going to listen to an audiobook."

Marcos comes down the hallway carrying my overnight bag. "Gaby, can you keep an eye on the twins while I walk Mommy out to the car?"

"Okay." She wraps her arms around my legs, gives me a tight squeeze, and then turns and runs down the hallway to the boys' bedroom.

As we walk out to the car parked in the driveway, my heart races. Marcos opens the trunk, sets my bag inside, and then closes it.

They're all going to die.

You're leaving them, and they're all going to die.

He comes around to the drivers' side where I'm standing. "I. . .I don't know if I can. . ."

"You can. You can do this, Jill. You're so much stronger than you know. The medication. The behavior therapy. You have resources now. You know what to do."

I nod.

"Going away is a healthy step. The kids and I will do great. There's nothing to worry about. Remember what Cara said? It's time for you to take care of yourself." He wraps his arms around me. *"Mi amor. . ."* he whispers. Then he pulls back. "Let me know when you get there, okay?"

"Okay. Thank you for everything you're doing."

"We're in this together. Always."

I nod and then turn and get into the driver's seat, wishing I felt as confident about this as Marcos seems to feel.

I close the car door, turn the key in the ignition, and then watch as Marcos walks back to the front porch. He turns and waves at me.

He's going to die.

They're all going to die.

I take a deep breath. *That's not true. That's the OCD talking. They'll be fine.* I counteract the thought as Cara and Dr. Luchesse are teaching me to do.

They're all—

"No. They'll do great," I whisper.

I reach for my phone, plug it into the MP3 port, and turn on the stereo.

Yesterday, at the end of our appointment with Cara, she talked me through this trip. *"The time alone in the car may be the biggest challenge. It's when the obsessive thoughts may intrude. It's important that you occupy your mind—keep it busy. You can download a book to your phone and listen to it while you drive. I've had clients who've found that helpful."*

As the voice of the narrator, her tone animated, fills the interior of the car and my mind, I put the car in gear and, looking over my shoulder, back out of the driveway.

As Melanie said, *"Let's do new."*

As I-5 leaves Sacramento, crossing over the river, the causeway, rice fields flanking either side, and then wending through miles and miles of agricultural land, my heart rate slows, my breathing steadies, and the obsessive thoughts still.

When I turn off at Williams, row after row of fruit trees flash past me. I crack the window and breathe deep, the scent of fruit fermenting in the orchards intoxicating.

When questions about my parents intrude, I turn the stereo volume higher and let the lyrical cadence of the novel I'm listening to fill my mind and the questions go the way of the obsessive thoughts.

As Cara said, I don't have to figure it all out now. *"Give yourself time, Jill."*

By the time my GPS tells me I've arrived, I am relaxed and looking forward to seeing Melanie.

After Melanie greets me with a warm hug—something else new—she leads me into the living room of the small house. The view of the trees and grass that rolls down to the lake is stunning, but out of the corner of my eye, shelves of books lure. I look from the view to the books and back again.

Melanie laughs. "I knew this room would confuse you. I suggest starting with the books, and then we can walk down to the lake. There are some great titles on those shelves."

I set my overnight bag down and go and stand in front of the shelves, where I peruse a plethora of classic titles. "How old are these?" Gingerly pulling a clothbound hardback off a shelf—*To Kill a Mockingbird* by Harper Lee—I open the cover and gasp. "Melanie, this is a first edition. Of *To Kill a Mockingbird*!" I turn to her. "Does Valerie know what she has here?"

Melanie shrugs.

I put the book back on the shelf and then turn back to Melanie. "I could spend months here."

She looks down at my overnight bag. "I don't think you packed enough." She picks up my bag. "I'll put this in the second bedroom, and then we can walk down to the dock. Sound good?"

"Yes. Thank you."

I wander over to the windows. The lawn, almost a football field in length, stretches to the lake and is shaded by at least a dozen giant trees—trees Valerie's parents must have planted when they built the house. A dock bridges the lawn over a cluster of tall cattails to the water.

Melanie joins me at the window.

"How do you get anything done here? I'd just want to stare at this all day."

"Easy. I keep the blinds closed."

"Oh, but that's such a shame."

"How about a glass of iced tea? I made a pitcher this afternoon. We can take it down to the dock and sit for a while."

"Perfect." I follow Melanie to the kitchen, where the view is equally lovely.

She hands me a glass of tea, pours one for herself, and then leads me out the back door, down a few steps to the lawn. When we're on level ground, she looks at me. "So, how are you? How are you handling your. . .discovery?"

"Oh. . ."

"I'm sorry. I don't mean to pry. If you don't want to talk about—"

"No. I do." I nod. "Thank you for. . .asking. It's just that each time I remember, I'm shocked all over again. I still can't. . .believe it." As we walk, I tell Melanie about the nightmare and then the memories. I don't go into detail. Instead, I tell her just enough to explain what led me to the Internet search.

When we reach the covered platform at the end of the dock, Melanie hands me her glass of tea to hold while she sets up two chairs with a small table in between. She takes our glasses from me and sets them on the table.

We both take a seat and are quiet for a moment. As I take in the deep blue of the lake and the surrounding golden hills, peace, lost to me for so long, returns in spite of the unresolved issue with my parents. Maybe it's the peace that passes understanding that I've heard others speak of. Two days ago I thought I'd never be okay again, but now. . . "Thank you for letting me intrude on your time." I look over at Melanie. "Don't feel like you need to entertain me. I know you need to work. I'll stay out of your way. I guess I just really needed a. . .break."

"Honestly, I was looking for an excuse to take a break myself. I'm stuck—I have no idea where the story goes next. Anyway"—she shrugs—"I might have missed you a little bit."

I smile. "I'd love to read what you've written so far. E-mail it to me when we're back at the house and I'll dig in. I need to keep my mind busy."

"Thanks, I'll do that. So, I keep thinking about Tom and his favorite gene-pool comment. . . ."

"Me too. He knew all along that my mother was the only gene pool in the equation."

"Have you talked to your mom since you found out?"

"No." I stare at the water. "I don't even want to think about it. But when I get back, I'll. . .deal with it." I look back to Melanie. "From what I could find online, my biological father—or at least I assume he was my father—died before my fourth birthday. My mother remarried soon after."

"Married Tom?"

I nod. "When I searched the records, it showed two marriage licenses for my mother. The first was dated 1977—two years before I was born. When I researched the name of the man she married—James O'Shea—I found a death certificate. The timing would coincide with the memories I've had of attending a funeral as a child. I remember my mother was wearing a black dress and a hat with a veil. Now it makes sense. She was the mourning widow. Or, at least, that's what I've put together in my mind."

"How did he die?"

"I don't know. The death certificate listed UNDETERMINED under CAUSE OF DEATH. Something else I'll have to ask my mother. But now. . .I don't even know if I can believe what she'll tell me."

"Maybe once she knows you've discovered the truth she'll no longer have a reason to lie."

"Maybe. It's just so. . .confusing. I don't understand. It's like. . .the mother I knew died, too, when I uncovered the lie. I don't know what to do with all the feelings."

"What does your counselor say?"

"That I'll grieve. . . She said there are five stages of grief, and I may bounce between the stages."

Melanie seems thoughtful for a moment. Then she looks at me, one eyebrow raised. "Sounds like good times."

"Right now, I'm just kind of numb. And honestly? I wish I could stay that way."

We eat dinner at the table on the back patio. The temperature has dropped and the evening is inviting. Melanie and I have never spent this much time alone together, but we've fallen into an easy compatibility. We talk or we're quiet. It doesn't seem to matter either way.

I savor a bite of the spicy chicken salad with toasted almonds and plump golden raisins. "Mmm. . . It's so good to eat something other than chicken fingers and macaroni and cheese. What's the spice in the salad?"

"Harissa paste. It's a new recipe."

"Mmm. . . Real food. Adult food."

"You're going to have to get away more often. How were the kids and Marcos doing when you called?"

"They were fine, just like you said they'd be. Marcos said Craig was coming over to grill hamburgers. Gaby was going to set the table while Marcos wrangled the twins." The question I asked Melanie on the phone when we spoke occurs to me again. "Melanie, what are we going to do without the two of you right next door? I know it isn't all about us, but if your house sells, we'll miss you so much. The kids will miss you so much."

"There's a simple solution."

"There is?"

"Yes. Just come with us."

"I'm being serious. . . ."

Her smile fades. "I know. I can't go there. I just. . .can't."

"How's Craig dealing with it?"

"We haven't talked about it much. But I think we were both more concerned about how the other would feel than we were about actually losing the house. I don't know—maybe it will hit me when it actually sells, but until then, I'm just not thinking about it."

It seems there's a lot we're each trying not to think about.

*Most things break, including hearts. The lessons of life amount
not to wisdom, but to scar tissue and callus.*
Wallace Stegner

Chapter 41

MELANIE

I stand at the kitchen sink washing our breakfast dishes in hot sudsy water. Why Valerie and her husband never had a dishwasher installed, I don't understand. Although, the process of washing, rinsing, and drying all by hand transports me to an earlier time when conversations were had and emotions mined over a sink of dirty dishes. Emotions mined? Clearly that was before my time.

Jill sits at the kitchen table, laptop open, reading the portion of the manuscript I e-mailed to her last night. When I glance her way, I can't read her expression. What does she think? Will she like it? More importantly, will my publisher like it? Will they accept it even though its off-brand? It isn't a humorous story which, if I'm honest with myself, is a novelty. There isn't much humor in me these days. I just can't pull it off.

"Mel"—Jill looks away from her computer to me—"this is some of your best writing. Really. What does your agent say?"

"Shoot! I e-mailed him a few days ago but forgot to check for a response." I grab my phone off the counter and open my e-mail, scrolling through until I find an e-mail from Dave. I open it and read his brief message:

Call me.

"I have to call him." I look at Jill. "Ugh."

She laughs. "Dave's had your back for over twenty years. He'll help you work through this. Tell him I'm happy to talk to the in-house editor if he thinks that will help."

"Thank you."

"Mel, I think you can make this work. Sure, the tone is a little more serious, but let's brainstorm and see what we can come up with. It's not that far off mark."

"That will take time I don't have."

"It just needs some tweaking here and there." Jill glances back at the screen. "You write a clean manuscript, so editing won't take a lot of time. There are some things to clean up, but overall it's great work."

"Things to clean up?"

"You know, just the usual. For instance, you have Chloe nauseated a lot. You'll need to come up with some other ways to show her anxiety. That kind of thing. Nothing major."

"She's nauseated a lot? Huh. Guess that's my go-to for showing stress. But you really think it just needs tweaking to fit the proposed genre? What about adding some humor?"

"You can inject some humor or at least levity. Look, Chloe's a twenty-something young woman, and you've left her friendless. Give the poor gal a friend—make her funny, sarcastic. Someone who helps keep Chloe afloat. Don't limit yourself. You can do this."

"Maybe, but I don't know if I can do it before the deadline."

"Well, God knows, right?"

I nod. If God has a plan, it's my only hope at this point. Jill goes back to reading as I pull a dish towel off a hook near the sink. I pick up a juice glass and wipe the inside with the towel. *Chloe's nauseated a lot.*

I wipe the towel around the outside of the glass and put it in the cupboard, and then I pick up another glass and begin drying it.

Nauseated?

I stop wiping the glass, and then it slips from my hands and crashes to the floor, where shards scatter.

"Oh, shoot." Jill gets up from the table. "Here, let me help you clean that up."

I don't move. I can't move.

"Melanie?"

I shake my head as tears brim.

"It's just a glass. What. . . ?" Jill watches me.

I turn away from her, unwilling to let her see me shatter just like the glass. I swallow a sob as I walk out of the kitchen, the sound of Jill's footsteps trailing me.

"Mel?"

With my back still to her, I hold up one hand, indicating, I hope, that I want her to leave me alone. I go through the living room and out the French door to the patio. The screen door bangs behind me then squeaks as it's opened again.

I keep walking, faster now.

"Melanie, wait. Please. I know you don't want to talk, but maybe"— she raises her voice the farther I get from the patio—"it will help."

I stop. Turn. And trudge back toward her, my breath catching as I fight sobs. "Help?" I gasp. "How will it help?" I glare at her as I swipe the tears from my face. When I reach her, I stop in front of her. "How? Tell me."

She shrugs. "I don't know. It just. . .does."

"Fine. You want to know? You want me to talk? Chloe's"—I sob—"pregnant. She's"—I will myself to stop crying, yet still the tears fall—"pregnant!" I gasp for a breath. "I. . .I didn't. . .know. I know that sounds so. . .stupid. It's not like she's real. But. . ." I shake my head then look from Jill to the grass beneath my feet as I wipe my eyes again. "I. . .I don't even know. . .why I'm crying. The whole thing is just stupid. Stupid!"

"Oh, honey. Oh, Melanie." She steps close and wraps me in a hug. That's when I stop trying to stem the flow of tears and just let them come. I lean against her, my head on her shoulder.

I cry.

And cry.

Then I pull away from her and turn toward the lake.

And I run. . . .

She lets me go.

When I reach the platform at the end of the dock, I don't even bother with a chair. I drop down onto the metal platform, hang my legs over the side, and rest my forehead on the rail. My tears drop into the lake below until they're finally spent.

I sit for a long time, the morning sun filtered through gray clouds, the air thick and moist, the lake still, reflecting the sky like glass.

There's nowhere to go.

No place left to run.

———————◆———————

Thunderheads hang over the lake, and the afternoon heat is thick and sticky. Lightning splits the sky across the lake from where we sit under cover on the dock, but no rain falls. "Dangerous weather."

Jill nods. "Fire weather."

"Good thing it isn't windy."

"Mm-hmm."

After the emotion of the morning, Jill and I are both spent. We sit in silence for a long time, each lost in our own thoughts as we watch the light show like it's the Fourth of July.

Finally, I turn to Jill and break the silence—not only the silence of the afternoon, but the silence that's marked our friendship all these years. "Will you tell me what it's like?"

She looks at me, her auburn eyebrows raised in question.

"What it feels like to be. . .pregnant."

"Oh. . ." She reaches over, her fingers lighting on my arm like a butterfly. "Are you sure?"

I nod, though I'm not sure at all. But I'll never know otherwise, and I've always wondered. . . .

She stares out at the lake for a moment as though she's trying to find the right words. Then she turns and looks at me. "It's like nothing else. This sounds so trite, but it's miraculous. And, at the same time, it's ordinary. The morning sickness, at least for me, lasted all day. I was nauseated all day, every day, for months. Especially with the twins. It was horrible. Well, you remember. How often did you watch Gaby for me because I couldn't pull myself out of bed except to rush to the bathroom? I couldn't keep anything down at first."

I nod. I do remember. "That was one of the few times I was grateful I was infertile."

"It's also like your worst case of PMS ever. Hormones on steroids." She laughs. "Why am I laughing? It isn't funny. It's horrible. I was so grumpy. I thought Marcos would walk out and leave me for good. Is menopause that way?"

I nod. "Yep. At least some days. And think, you still have that to look forward to." It's my turn to look out at the lake and the clouds reflected on its surface. "I have all these raging hormones, moods, hot flashes—the whole nine yards—yet I never got to experience the point of it all. The reason our bodies are made the way they are is so we can bear children. So all those years of monthly cycles, the cramps, the inconvenience, the mess of it all. . . I got the curse but never the blessing."

"Oh, Melanie. . .I never thought of it that way. I'm so sorry. You would have been a fantastic mother."

I shrug. "Maybe. Maybe not. But I would have liked the chance to try. I would have loved to give. . ." Tears fill my eyes. "I would have loved to have given Craig the chance to be a father. He's the one who would have excelled at parenting."

She nods. "Definitely. He's so good with the kids. But so are you. Gaby adores you."

"Ah, the Gabster. The feeling is mutual." Lightning crackles, followed by a low rumble of thunder. "What else?"

"For me, just when I thought I'd die from the nausea"—she puts one palm on her abdomen—"I felt that first flutter of life. Though at first I thought it might just be gas." She laughs again, her joy in the recollections so obvious. "But within a day or two, I knew I was feeling the baby move. With the twins, I knew right away what I was feeling. My cervix, and my bladder, felt like a trampoline with those two.

"Toward the end of the second trimester, Marcos and I would lie in bed at night and watch my belly move. Sometimes you could see a hand or knee or foot—whatever it was—pushing against the wall of my abdomen. It's odd. And thrilling. But. . ." She turns and looks back out at the gray water, rippled now by a slight breeze.

"But what?"

When Jill looks back at me, her earlier joy is replaced by something else, something dark. "That's about the time, toward the end of my second trimester with Gaby, that my thoughts. . .or fears. . .really took over."

"What do you mean?"

She glances back at me, and her cheeks are colored a deep peach, her neck splotched with color. "I. . .I've never told you, but. . .I'm sure you've noticed. I have. . ."—she looks down at the dock—"I've never said this out loud. I have"—she takes a deep breath—"obsessive-compulsive disorder. It was just diagnosed."

"Oh. . ." Images click in my mind. "The antibacterial wipes, the disinfectant, the cleaning?"

She nods. "Those are part of it. I'm trying a medication that seems to be helping, and I'm doing some behavioral therapy. That's why I sought a counselor in the first place."

"So even as you were experiencing the joy of pregnancy, you were struggling. . . ."

"The obsessive thoughts, at least for me, are very dark. Very frightening."

"I'm sorry, Jill."

We both stare at the lake a few moments. Then I look back at Jill. "Nothing is ever perfect for any of us, is it?"

"No. Not this side of heaven."

I leave Jill on the dock, pleading my word count as the reason I excuse myself. But few words will get written today. I don't have the emotional energy to even consider what happens next for Chloe.

Nor do I want to consider Elliot. . . .

When I reach the house, I go into the bedroom, close the door, and pull the blinds closed on the doors leading out to the patio. My head throbs from the tears shed this morning. I pull back the lightweight spread on the bed and climb under it.

"I got the curse but never the blessing." As the words I spoke to Jill earlier come back to me, hot tears fill my eyes again. *So why did You curse me? What did I ever do to You?* In my mind, I spit the words at God. But I don't dare speak them aloud—that would feel as dangerous as lightning on a dry California afternoon.

The windows and glass doors rattle as another clap of thunder rumbles.

Whether the words were spoken out loud or not, it seems they were heard and acknowledged.

A family is too frail a vessel to contain the risks of all the warring impulses expressed when such a group meets on common ground.
Pat Conroy

Chapter 42

JILL

I sink into the comfort of the sofa in Cara's office as she takes the wingback chair across from me.

"How was your time away?"

"Better than I expected. It was restful and. . .it felt purposeful."

"How so?"

"The friend I spent time with. . . We were able to deepen our friendship and talk about things we haven't shared before."

Cara smiles. "Were you able to leave the OCD at home?"

"Not entirely, but it was better. The medication and the therapy are helping. But honestly, finding out what I did about my mother. . . It's like that unlocked something. It made me realize that I can trust myself—my intuition."

"I'm so pleased for you. Did you give talking to your parents any thought?"

"A little bit. . . Part of me wants to confront them as soon as possible. But the other part of me wants to. . .hide. After what happened last time—the way my mother turned what we'd heard back on me. . . I. . .I don't know. She was so controlled. So believable. What if. . .she does that again? What if she twists everything again?"

"What's the difference between confronting her last time and confronting her now?"

"Now, I have proof. Or. . .I think I do. Can she deny the marriage licenses?"

"She—"

"Wait." I shake my head. "Wait a minute. . . . I just thought of something. My dad? His name is on my birth certificate. If he wasn't my real father, how. . ." I swallow. "Did I. . .did I connect the wrong dots? Maybe. . ." Confusion shadows my mind. "I was so sure. If I'm going to confront them, I have to be sure. . . ."

"Give me a minute. Let me check something." Cara gets up out of her chair, goes to her desk, and sits down. "I think birth certificates are changed following an adoption. But that may differ depending on the state."

"Adoption?"

She looks around the computer monitor on her desk. "It's possible your dad, the man who raised you, adopted you after marrying your mother."

"I. . .never thought of that."

I wait as Cara searches the Internet for the information she's looking for.

"Yes, here it is. In California, once an adoption is finalized, the birth record for the child is changed—the biological parent or parents' names are removed and replaced with the adoptive parents' names. It says the original birth record is sealed and filed confidentially. It's only released by a court order in rare circumstances."

"A court order?"

"Let me check something else."

Again I wait. Then I see Cara jot something on a notepad. She tears the note off the pad and comes back to sit across from me, first handing me the note.

"That's the website address for the Department of Social Services for California—they manage adoption records. If your mother's husband did adopt you, it's possible you could obtain the record through the Department of Social Services."

"But I don't know. . .anything for certain. Unless I ask my mother, how will I know? It could take months to obtain official records."

Cara leans forward. "Jill, you have a choice to make. Talk to your parents—tell them about the marriage records you discovered—and see what happens. You have enough information to warrant confronting them." She smiles. "You're not crazy."

I nod. "I know that now. Everything adds up—the nightmares, the memories. All of it supports the probability that my mother was married before and that my biological father died."

"You can confront them now and hope they'll tell you the truth. Or you can do your research, request records, and wait until you have proof. But as you say, it does all seem to add up."

"I. . .I don't want to wait. For my own mental health, I. . .need to know."

"Okay, so let's talk through a few possibilities. First, if you'd like to, you're welcome to invite your parents here. We could set an appointment, Marcos could join you, and we could all meet together. I could help guide the conversation."

"I'm. . .not sure they'd come. My mom's already defensive."

"That's just one option."

"Thank you." I hesitate. "I hope this doesn't sound terrible, but. . .I'd like to catch them off guard. I'd like to surprise them with the information. Maybe, if they don't have time to prepare, they'll tell the truth."

"What would catching them off guard look like?"

"I'm not sure. It may mean"—I take a deep breath—"that Marcos and I go to them. We'd have to. . .fly down and stay—driving would take too long. I can't leave. . ." I swallow. "I don't know if. . ."

The plane will crash.

You'll die.

"If you can leave your children?"

"What if. . . I mean, it was one thing to leave them with Marcos, but. . .what if. . ."

"Jill, take a few breaths. Inhale. . . ."

I do as Cara tells me.

"Now, exhale. . . . Good. Again, please."

I take one more deep breath and then slowly exhale.

"Better?"

I nod.

"It's natural, given the circumstances, that confronting your parents will cause you some anxiety. There's no need to do it in a way that will exacerbate that anxiety. If traveling and leaving the children will increase your stress, let's talk through other options. I'm confident you can handle this, Jill. Consider what works best for you."

By the time I leave Cara's office, I've come up with a plan.

———————◆◆———————

I open my calendar on the desk in the den and check the date, although I already know exactly when it is. I circle the note I've made on the calendar. I hate to wait that long, but after talking it through with Marcos, we both agreed it's the best time.

It allows me the comfort of home.

And it gives my parents their own space.

I pick up my phone, my palms damp, and key in my parents' number. I haven't talked to them since they were here last and my mother blamed my questions on my mental illness.

My mom is usually the one to answer, so my dad's "Hello" catches me off guard.

"Dad?"

"Hi, Jilly, this is a nice surprise." He doesn't seem at all fazed by our last conversation.

For the first time since discovering that my dad isn't really my dad, I realize what that means. Or maybe, what it doesn't mean. Regardless of the lies told and the reasons behind them, this is the man who raised me. He's the one who attended my ballet recitals and debate competitions, the one who helped me with my math homework all the way through elementary school, high school, and even the GE-required math classes in college. He's the one who worked hard and provided everything I ever needed or wanted, including an education from one of the most prestigious universities in the country. He even, much to my chagrin at the time, interviewed each boy I dated—whether we were going to prom or around the corner for ice cream. Whether or not we share the same gene pool, he is the father who raised me.

And. . .loved me.

"Did I lose you?"

I swallow. "No, I'm here. Sorry. I was. . .distracted." I take a deep breath. "I was just looking at my calendar, and when you were here last time, Mom said you were coming up again in a couple of weeks."

"That's right. I have a board meeting in Sacramento—but we're staying downtown."

"Right. You know you're welcome to stay here."

"We know it. But I have several meetings over the weekend, so it makes sense to be downtown."

"Okay, well, what about coming out here for dinner on Friday night? Mom said you were coming in on Friday afternoon and your meetings start on Saturday. We'd like to see you."

"Sure thing. That sounds great."

"Will it be okay with Mom?"

"Of course it will, Jilly." It's as though the last conversation never took place. How can he just ignore the things my mother said to me? He isn't willing to, or maybe he can't, stand up to my mother in support of me. Is that really love? It isn't black and white. Maybe he's loved me to the best of his ability.

We set a time, and he says he'll tell my mom. When I end the call and set the phone on the desk, the tears I held back as we talked flow. Cara was right: I've gone from depression to anger to denial and back again. And I sense this is just the beginning of the grief to come. . . .

You are wrong if you think that you can in any way take the vision
and tame it to the page. The page is jealous and tyrannical;
the page is made of time and matter; the page always wins.
Annie Dillard

Chapter 43

MELANIE

After Jill leaves on Tuesday morning, I muster my courage, or lack thereof, and finally pick up the phone and call Dave.

"You've written yourself into a corner, haven't you?" He chuckles. "You pantsers. But I'll give you this: it's the first time in the eighteen years I've represented you that you've had an issue, at least a major issue, with a manuscript. Your track record works in your favor."

"Did you read the chapters I sent?"

"I did. The writing is solid, as usual, and I think the story is workable. Who's doing the edit?"

"It's Jill again."

"Has she read any of it yet?"

"Yes, she said the same thing you did—she thinks I can make it work. She's willing to brainstorm with me. She suggested adding a character—a friend for my protagonist—who can add some levity. Maybe we can come up with some other ideas, too. But I'm cutting it close. My deadline is October 1, and I'm dead if I miss it."

He laughs again. "Well, don't tell anyone this, but that's not always true. Have you missed a deadline yet?"

"No."

"Okay, here's what you need to do. Draft an e-mail to your senior editor asking for an extension. No more than a month, okay? Before you send the e-mail, send it to me and let me look it over. If she has a problem with it, I'll go to bat for you. At this point, the book will

261

already be in their catalog—they've already spent marketing dollars—so they're going to want to work with you to get an acceptable manuscript submitted. So make it acceptable, Melanie. Deal?"

"Deal."

"Get that e-mail to me today."

"I will. And thank you. I appreciate you."

"As you should." He laughs.

With that done, determined to get to work, I pick up my laptop and sit down at the kitchen table. Once the computer powers up, Elliot's face appears on the screen. Only. . .I no longer see Elliot or even the actor I'd chosen to represent Elliot.

I stare at the photo for a moment then delete the picture from the computer and reset the desktop to its default setting. The printed photo I'd tucked into the picture frame is already gone—crumpled and thrown away after the event.

I open my e-mail app and draft a message to my in-house editor as Dave instructed. Without going into too much detail, I explain that personal circumstances have kept me from accomplishing what I'd hoped on the manuscript, and I request an extension on the deadline. I send the e-mail to Dave, who will review it and get back to me.

"Oh, Lord, please. . ." I need that extension approved. Lightening doesn't strike; thunder doesn't rumble. "Thank You."

Since the event at the winery on Saturday, I've only participated in the write-and-delete dance. I've added nothing to my word count.

For so long I buried my feelings under words.

Now, the words seem bent on unburying those feelings.

That has to change.

My phone, set on silent, vibrates across the table. I grab it as Craig's name appears on the screen. I stare at the phone as it rings again and again. Then I close my eyes, swallow, and open my eyes. I press IGNORE, sending the call to voice mail, and set the phone back on the table.

After the tone has dinged, alerting me that Craig has left a message, I pick the phone up again and press PLAY to listen to the message. I listen to every word.

———◆———

I open a blank document, put my fingers on the keyboard, and center a title on the page.

- Anxiety
- Wringing hands
- Fidgeting
- Foot bouncing

I list all of the ways I can think of to show a character is feeling anxious. After I've come up with about twenty actions, I'm satisfied. *Nauseated* does not appear on the list.

Chloe took the ticket from the valet and tucked it into a pocket in her purse. Then she strolled through the familiar grounds of the Buccaneer, its lush gardens bursting with tropical blooms and swaying palms. Her appointment with Dr. Hammond, in which she talked about her mother, led her back here, where they'd spent so much time together. She wound her way down to the beach, enjoying the breeze that stirred the closer she got to the water.

She'd honor her mother's memory today by having lunch at the Mermaid, where she would order her mother's favorite splurge: local conch fritters. Her mouth watered at the memory of the lightly seasoned delight that had also became her favorite.

My fingers pause on the keyboard. "Gee, someone seems to be feeling better. . . ." Ha! Take that, Chloe.

Once she was seated, she slipped her feet out of her sandals and buried her toes in the warm sand under the table. The surf rolled in and out, the rhythm hypnotic. Chad would love the vibe, as he'd call it, of the island. Maybe someday. . . She caught herself. Would there be a someday with Chad? She knew that was up to her, but she still didn't know how to make that decision.

Was it that she didn't know how to make the

decision? Or was it that she wasn't sure why she needed to make a decision at all?

Doubt plagued her, as it had since she'd said, "I do."

It was hard to honor her mother's memory without thinking about Chad. The two were inextricably intertwined in Chloe's mind even though they'd never met. It was equally hard to think about Chad without her mother coming to mind.

Maybe Dr. Hammond was right. Maybe the past did inform the present.

If so, what was the past telling her today?

The waiter brought the dish she'd ordered and set the artfully arranged plate in front of her. The delicate fritters sat atop a bed of crisp greens with a key lime aioli. She picked up her fork, anticipating the fritters she remembered so well, but when the scent of the fried conch wafted from the plate, her stomach churned.

As a new wave of nausea swept over her, she pushed the plate away.

What?

No. No. No.

I push the chair back and get up. The laptop sits on the table, jeering at me. I point my index finger at it. "I said, no!" I turn, go to the cupboard, pull out a glass, and go to the sink and fill it with water. I carry the glass to the bathroom, where I dig through my travel bag until I find the small bottle of ibuprofen I always pack. I wrestle with the childproof cap until it finally loosens, and then I throw back two tablets with a swallow of water.

As I turn to go back to the kitchen, I catch sight of my reflection in the mirror and pause. My eyes are red around the rims, and dark bags protrude under each eye. The crevice between my brows is deeper, I'm certain, than it was just a few weeks ago. The wrinkle cream I ordered isn't doing the job.

I have to finish this book.

I have to get this story over with.

And I know, after fifteen novels, regardless of what I want, there's only one way to finish this manuscript.

Let the story lead the way. . . .

I drop my gaze to the floor, rub my temples, and then slog my way back to the kitchen. I sit myself back down at the table, resolved. I will write the story presented to me, regardless of what it costs me emotionally.

I just want it over with.

"You win, Chloe."

So. . . If Chloe is grieving the loss of her mother, I need to know what that looks like and what impact it's having on her relationship with Chad. I recall something Jill said about grief, so I open my browser and google the phrase *five stages of grief.*

A long list of related articles appear. I click on one of the articles and peruse the five stages. Two of the five immediately catch my attention, but one, *anger*, pulls up a fresh memory. The words I mentally spit at God yesterday afternoon repeat in my mind. My reaction followed the emotion of discovering Chloe was pregnant and the conversation with Jill about pregnancy.

The reaction followed the emotion of discovery? Or the. . .grief of discovery?

Chloe's pregnancy triggered my own grief?

But I didn't grieve. . . .

That's when the second stage that caught my attention convicts me like a judge and jury.

Denial.

———◆◆———

"Hi, Valerie, me again. I'm sorry to keep bothering you, but I have a couple more questions. When you have a few minutes, give me a call." Phone between my shoulder and ear, I pull the blinds open partway. "By the way, it's hot and still here today—not a single leaf is fluttering. Even the cattails are standing at attention, not daring to breathe." I smile. "Thought I'd let you know. Talk to you soon."

I close the blinds again, hoping to keep the inside of the house from becoming warmer than it already is. Sitting on the dock won't even offer relief today.

I spend another hour or so doing research online until Valerie returns my call.

"Thank you for the Clear Lake weather update."

"Anytime. If it's this hot here, I hate to think what it's like there."

"It's a scorcher, but we have air conditioning. So enough about the weather, although it was fun to hear you'd noticed it. How's the writing coming?"

"I think I had a breakthrough, but I hoped you could answer a few questions for me about grief."

"It seems I'm an expert these days—both experientially and because of the research I'm doing for my own book. What do you want to know?"

"First, I'm sorry you're an expert."

"Thank you, Melanie. I may not embrace the circumstances that led to my grief, but I've accepted where God has me, and He's faithful to send those who offer His comfort. Honestly, there are sweet moments that come along with the grief."

"Really? That's. . .surprising."

"Things are rarely all or nothing. It seems we get a dash of this or that, too."

"So, I guess you're familiar with the five stages of grief?"

"Elizabeth Kübler-Ross's work on the emotions experienced by those who grieve. You bet I'm familiar with it."

"Do people ever get stuck in one of the stages?" I walk over and switch on the fan I've set on an end table in the living room. Then I sit in the recliner, a notepad and pen ready.

"Sure. I've seen it happen with clients."

"So, what would it look like if, say, someone was stuck in denial? And why might they get stuck in that stage?"

As Valerie talks, I scribble notes so I can consider what she's said after we hang up.

And so I won't forget anything.

Even though so much of what she says feels so familiar.

The worst guilt is to accept an unearned guilt.
Ayn Rand

Chapter 44

MELANIE

With my notes spread out on the kitchen table—those I took when I talked to Valerie and others I've jotted as I've done my own research—I open my laptop and a new document. As a proud pantser, I'll never admit it to the plotters I know, but I proceed to outline the next few scenes I want to write, incorporating some of what I've learned, including an additional stage of grief many psychologists agree is common.

But I know, even as I think through the outline, I'll hold it loosely, letting Chloe and Dr. Hammond lead.

Elliot. . .

The ache that's resided in my chest for so long, the one I've worked so hard to ignore, reveals itself again. It is the ache, I understand now, of a heart broken by loss.

I'm tempted to reach for my phone, as I have been so many times since Saturday, but now isn't the time to call.

Not yet.

I still have some things to work through.

———◆———

After Chloe was seated, Dr. Hammond took his seat and crossed one ankle over his knee, the crease of his khaki slacks bending with his leg. "So, Chloe, we meet again." He smiled. "What did you do with yourself between Tuesday and this morning?"

Chloe had come to like the small talk Dr. Hammond began each session with. It put her at ease, and even though he directed his questions to her, the snippets of conversation felt reciprocal.

"When I left here on Tuesday, I went to the Buccaneer for lunch."

"The Mermaid, by chance?"

"Yes. It was one of my mother's favorites—she loved having lunch on the beach."

Dr. Hammond seemed to look through Chloe for a moment as though he was remembering something. Then he cleared his throat. "The Mermaid is a special place."

"Do you go there often?"

He hesitated. "No, not anymore. So, where would you like to start today?"

"Well, I've wanted to talk to you about something you said on Tuesday."

"All right."

"You said that sometimes the past informs the present?"

"Yes."

"When I was having lunch on Tuesday, I realized that whenever I think about Chad, I think about my mother, and vice versa. The two are connected in my mind, but when I remember my mother"—tears filled Chloe's eyes— "it's so painful. I. . .I miss her so much."

Dr. Hammond uncrossed his leg and leaned forward. "I'm sorry, Chloe. I'm sure it is painful. And each time you think of Chad, it leads to grief over the loss of your mother?"

Chloe nodded. "I asked myself on Tuesday what the past was telling me."

"And did you come up with an answer?"

"I think it's telling me I'm stuck. I can't seem to get over losing my mom. But I don't know what that has to do with Chad."

"Chloe, during our first session I asked you a question that you seemed to react to forcefully. I'd like to ask you that same question again, and I want you to give it some thought before you respond."

She wiped a tear from her cheek. "Okay."

"Do you love your husband? Do you love Chad?"

Her eyes filled with tears again. She wished she could get control over her emotions.

Dr. Hammond reached for a box of tissues and handed it across the coffee table that sat between them.

She took the box, pulled out a tissue and wiped her eyes, and then crumpled the tissue and held it tight. She looked at her lap for several moments then looked back at Dr. Hammond and nodded. "I do love him. Very much. But. . ."

"But what?"

Chloe reached for another tissue, her tears flowing now. "But. . ." She choked back a sob. "How. . ." She wiped her eyes and nose. "I'm. . .sorry."

"There's nothing to apologize for. What you're feeling is real. It's okay to cry."

Chloe wrapped her arms around her waist, no longer able to contain her sobs.

I wipe a tear from my cheek then move my hand on the track-pad to close the document and open Facebook, losing myself in status updates. Or instead of Facebook, maybe I'll play a hand or two hundred of Spider Solitaire. But before I click, I pause. A few more tears slip from my eyes. *Stay with it. Just stay with the emotion. Feel it.* I leave my manuscript document open and get up and tear a paper towel off the roll hanging above the counter. Valerie really needs to keep a box of tissues in the kitchen.

I pull the key to the outside storage closet off a hook in the laundry room and then open the back door. As I step outside, the sweltering heat blisters. I quickly open the door to the storage closet and search the shelves for extra tissues. I find a box behind a flat of soda cans. I grab it and walk back into the house, which, as hot as it felt while I worked, is still much cooler than the outside temperature.

I set the box of tissues next to my computer and then pace the length of the kitchen and back.

I'm still not exactly sure what Chloe's feeling, but I'm close. I've reached for the brass ring and just missed. Next time around, I'll get it.

Next time around?

My heart weighs in my chest.

I'd rather get off the merry-go-round and, I don't know, get a chocolate-dipped cone, maybe? I stop in front of the refrigerator and open the door—a rush of cold air a welcome respite. I reach for the pitcher of tea.

I have to go around again.

I have to finish this ride.

I pull an ice tray and bin out of the freezer, crack the cubes into the bin, and drop a few of the already-melting chunks into a glass. The ice crackles as I pour tea over it. I pick up the glass, push my bangs aside, and press the cold glass of tea to my forehead.

Dr. Hammond let Chloe cry—it was the first real emotion she'd expressed since she'd begun seeing him. As painful as he knew this was for her, it meant she was allowing herself to experience the grief of her mother's death.

After a few moments, Chloe's sobs ebbed. She reached for several more tissues and wiped her eyes and nose.

"Grief is a powerful force. Unless we experience the feelings, we don't move through it. It stays with us, coloring everything we do and every relationship we're involved in."

Chloe shook her head. "I. . .don't want to feel *this*. It's too much."

Though he was careful to keep his own feelings compartmentalized when he counseled, there were times when sharing his experience proved helpful. He ran his hand over his chin as he made his decision. "I'm familiar with the pain you're experiencing—with the depth of pain a loss like that can cause."

Chloe's eyes widened. "You are?" she whispered.

He nodded. "Several months before I came to the island, I lost my wife to cancer. She was"—he smiled—"everything I'd ever dreamed of. Sounds trite, I know, but it's true. She was my best friend. When she died, I didn't know if I could go on. I didn't know if I wanted to go on."

"How. . .did you?"

"One minute at a time." He shook his head. "I won't pretend it was easy. It wasn't. I shifted between depression, denial, anger, and guilt. Lots of guilt.

"When I slipped into denial—when I refused to accept that she was gone—I bought a plane ticket, packed a bag, and came here. We'd spent our honeymoon here. I thought I'd feel closer to her on the island." He shrugged. "At first, I saw her everywhere, including on the beach"—he looked away from Chloe for a moment as though he was seeing something that wasn't there—"laughing over drinks at the Mermaid." He looked back to Chloe and shrugged.

"Oh. . ."

"But she wasn't really there, and I could either accept that and move on—or not. In the end, the pain of those memories helped me move through that denial. That's when the pain, the heartache of losing her, was the worst. But, as I said, unless we allow ourselves to feel that pain, to experience the depth of our grief, we get stuck."

"I'm so sorry. . . ."

"Thank you, Chloe."

She shifted in her seat and reached for another tissue. "This is the first time I've really cried since she. . .died."

"I hope it won't be the last. That may sound odd, but your tears are a natural, healthy response to the loss you've experienced. They'll help you move forward, if you let them."

She dabbed at the corners of her eyes again. "You mentioned guilt. Can you explain that?"

"Guilt, in a sense, became my default setting. At first, I felt guilty that I wasn't the one who got sick. Then I felt guilty that I wasn't the one who died. Then after she died and I came here, once I began healing, I felt guilty that I was starting to live again. Maybe I didn't love her enough if I could actually begin enjoying life without her."

Chloe nodded. "Exactly."

"Sound familiar?"

Her tears fell again as she spoke. "I kept asking myself how I could fall in love just months after my mother died. How could I be so callous, so unfeeling? If I'd really loved her, I wouldn't. . .I couldn't. . ." She looked at her lap again.

"Chloe. . ."

She hesitated before lifting her gaze to Dr. Hammond again.

"Don't believe shame's lies. My guess is that meeting and falling in love with Chad when you did was a gift. But it's one you haven't fully accepted because of the guilt you've claimed as your own. Your mother's death wasn't your responsibility. She'd want you to live, wouldn't she? Push the guilt aside."

"How? How do I let it go?"

———————◆———————

I ponder Chloe's question until the sun has passed over the house and is dropping in the western sky. The heat of the day is waning, so I open up the blinds in the living room and kitchen and open the windows and French doors. If a breeze stirs, I want it to flow through the warm, stagnant rooms.

Standing at the picture window in the living room, the lake, its surface still except for the ever-present birds diving into its depths and floating atop the water, invites me. I go to the kitchen and throw together a salad—cold, crisp iceberg with a sprinkling of blue cheese and crumbled bacon leftover from the breakfast I made for Jill before she left. I drizzle the wedge of lettuce with a vinaigrette dressing.

I carry the salad down to the dock and set it on the small table still between the two chairs Jill and I occupied. I pull a small citronella candle and a box of matches out of the pocket of my shorts and set the candle on the table, too. I light it as much for the ambiance it provides as for its protection against mosquitos.

The throaty rumble of an engine breaks the silence as a bass boat heading in for the night passes off the end of the dock. A heron swoops low and lands on the next dock over, its spindly legs splayed at awkward angles.

Watchful, I eat the salad as nature, in all her grace, pirouettes across the ever changing stage before me. Fiery hues splash across the sky as the sun sets. Soon all will be doused by the cool hues of twilight.

I set the salad plate on the table and watch the show until the curtain of darkness descends. The candle's flame flickers with the cool breeze off the lake—evening's gift.

"How do I let it go?" Chloe's question lifts and falls on the drafts.

Along with my own memories.

Craig sitting on the edge of our bed...

I want to lean over, blow out the candle, and let darkness envelop me. Instead, I sit still and let the flame cast shadows as the memory unfolds.

"Mel, it's been two years since we found out we couldn't get pregnant."

"We? You mean me. I couldn't get pregnant. I'm the one who failed."

"You didn't fail. It isn't something you didn't do well—something you could control. It was something God allowed."

"Why?" It was a question I hadn't dared ask until that moment.

"I don't know why. But we need to trust even when—especially when— we don't understand."

I turned and walked away.

"Stop. Please, just listen to me."

I stopped at our bedroom door, turned, and saw the tears in Craig's eyes. Tears I knew I'd caused.

"Our dream died, but it feels like you died, too."

He stared at me a moment, his features etched with what I know now was grief. *"I've lost you,"* he whispered.

"No. I'm here. I'm right here." I stood at the door of our bedroom, my

husband's face wet with tears. I didn't know what else to say. What else to do. I didn't know how to bridge the fissure separating us.

My breath catches as the memory stabs. I swipe at the tears on my cheeks.

It's so clear that Chloe has embraced guilt that isn't hers to own.

But...can I say the same about myself?

If I hadn't let guilt, or the shame of failure, nest in my soul, things might be so different now. Maybe we would have adopted. . . . Maybe Craig and I wouldn't have grown apart. . . . Maybe. . .

Even now, as I try to let go of guilt, I pick up more and hold it tight.

How do I let it go?

The answer eludes me.

By the time I make my way back to the house, the moon has risen over the lake and a multitude of stars twinkle overhead. I rinse my salad plate and set it in the sink then begin shutting up the house, closing the windows I'd opened earlier. If Craig were here, we'd leave them open all night long.

When I've closed the windows in the living room and locked the French doors, I go back to the kitchen to close the windows there. My phone sits on the table next to my laptop, where I left it hours before.

I pick up the phone and hold it against my chest.

Maybe now is the time to make that call.

But...

I have no idea what to say.

Instead, I plug the phone into the charger on the kitchen counter and turn off the kitchen light.

Life is not a matter of holding good cards,
but of playing a poor hand well.
Robert Louis Stevenson

Chapter 45

CRAIG

When I walk into the kitchen Wednesday after work, there are several business cards scattered on the countertop that weren't there when I left this morning. I pick up a couple of the cards. Realtors.

Once the house hit the MLS, Brian scheduled a tour for Realtors in the area.

I drop the cards back on the countertop then go to the entry hall and out the front door. A lockbox hangs from the outside door handle—Brian said he'd leave it after the tour. I walk back inside and try to see the house through the eyes of Realtors and potential buyers, but it's hard to see anything beyond our lives here.

I pull my phone out of my pocket and punch in Brian's number. He answers after the first ring.

"Hey, Craig. I was just going to call you. Wanted to let you get through your business day first."

"Yeah, thanks. I saw the cards on the counter. How'd the tour go?"

"Good. Positive feedback. Several Realtors mentioned clients they thought would like to see the house. I've had a few callbacks already—two Realtors are bringing clients through tomorrow."

"Anyone comment on the price?"

"Yep. Most agreed it's priced right. One or two thought we're a little high. But as I said, based on the comps, I think we're on target."

"Yeah, okay."

"Let's give it a week and see what happens. I know you're motivated to sell. If nothing happens, I want to schedule an open house for the following weekend. That work?"

"That works. Thanks for your help, man."

"You bet."

After I end the call, I walk through the entire house room by room, turning off lights. Brian wanted the place lit like a Christmas tree for the tour every day it's on the market in case Realtors bring clients through. Since I'm at work all day, I'll turn the lights on before I leave in the morning. I get it. I know a house shows better when lit up. When we built the place, I added specialty lighting throughout the house. But our electricity bill will break the bank this month and next if we don't get an offer soon.

Who are you kidding? The bank's already broke. I can hear Mel now. . . .

Still holding my phone, I give her a call, but the call goes to voice mail again.

"Hey, just checking in again. The house looks good. Realtors came through today. Hope you're making your word count. Talk to you later."

I shove the phone back into my pocket.

The bank is definitely broke, that is for sure.

I never had to choose a subject—my subject rather chose me.
Ernest Hemingway

Chapter 46

MELANIE

After spending the early morning hours at my computer, I carry my phone out to the dock with a reheated cup of coffee. For a woman who dislikes the phone, I'm spending way too much time talking on the thing.

The lake woos and I pause before pulling a chair off the stack and sitting down. The breeze carries the marshy, organic scent of the lake on its drafts, and a mother duck—quacking instructions, it seems—paddles off the murky shore, her brood of ducklings in tow.

How many children would Craig and I have had, given the choice?

The raft of ducks disappears under the dock.

I sit in the chair, stretch out my legs, and key Jill's number into the phone and then listen as her line rings.

She answers, her tone welcoming. "Hello, there. How's the lake?"

"Lovely. I'm sitting on the dock. I'm glad I caught you. You called?"

"And you're calling me back?" She exaggerates her surprise.

"No need to sound quite so shocked."

She laughs. "Yes, I called. How's it going?"

"Okay. I've made some progress. I even came up with a working title."

"Good. What is it?"

"*Home.* Simple. Easy to remember. And, in the end, I think it will fit."

"I like it. And speaking of home, when do you think you're coming back? Do you know yet?"

"Soon, maybe. Why?"

She sighs. "My parents are coming. . . ."

I straighten in the chair. "What does that mean? Are you going to talk to them? Confront them?"

"Yes. I thought if you were home we could have the kids stay with you for the evening. Craig told Marcos he'd watch them again, but it's good to have a two-to-two ratio with the twins. One adult per toddler. For the adults' sake—not the boys' sake. Actually four-to-two is better." She laughs. She sounds better than she has in a long time, even with the unresolved issues with her parents. "If you're not here, we can ask Marcos's folks, but his dad was just diagnosed with dementia, and they're working on figuring out medications. I'm not sure. . . . The boys are a lot to handle."

"Sorry about Marcos's dad—that's rough."

"Thanks."

"So what's the date? When are they coming?"

Jill tells me the date, and I make a mental note of it. "So not this coming weekend, but the next?"

"That's it."

"Just plan that Craig and I will watch them. That gives me a goal—a date to shoot for. It's just over a week before my deadline and, though I can't imagine it happening, maybe I'll wrap this thing up before then."

"Really?"

"No, not really, but a girl can dream, right? Actually, I asked for an extension on the deadline. I'm waiting to hear back. Dave doesn't think it will be an issue, but I still hated asking. It's such a failure, you know?"

"Melanie, you've worked hard. It's going to be a great book."

"Whatever you say. Anyway, plan on leaving the kids with us. I'm happy to help out." Who knows how much longer they'll be able to walk the kids over. . . .

"Thank you. I invited my parents to come for dinner—they're staying downtown. I have no idea how long the evening will go. They could walk out as soon as I open my mouth."

"Oh, I hope not. I'm hoping for the best possible outcome for you, whatever that looks like."

"It's funny, but I don't know what that would look like. I can't imagine a positive scenario."

"Maybe you'll be surprised."

After we end our call, I stand up and walk to the railing as the duck family floats out from under the platform.

As much as I dread the next few scenes I need to write, it's time. I'm ready to go home.

Wherever, or whatever, that means.

Chloe wandered the aisles of the small market by the condo, dropping a few things into the basket she carried over her arm. She knew she needed to eat, but nothing appealed to her. She picked up a mango and gently pressed her fingers against its thick skin. It was almost ripe. Chad loved mangoes. She laid it in the basket, careful not to bruise it. Maybe it would sound good to her in the morning.

She added a few more items to the basket, the thought of eating each one more nauseating to her than the last.

What was wrong with her?

And why was she still here when all she wanted was to go home?

If she loved Chad, wasn't that all that mattered?

Dr. Hammond was right—her mother would want her to live, to be happy. But she still wasn't clear on how to let go of the guilt that plagued her. And that's exactly what it was, though she hadn't recognized it until Dr. Hammond told her his story.

Of course, she hadn't caused her mother's accident any more than Dr. Hammond had caused his wife to succumb to cancer. Logically, she knew that, but still her mind accused. *If you'd really loved her. . .*

She paid for the items then carried the bag out of the store. Though the condo was only two blocks away, it felt like a mile. The bag was heavy, the air heavier. Her hair stuck to the back of her neck, and the skirt she'd put on this morning dug into her waist.

By the time she climbed the stairs to the second-floor unit, she wanted to sit down and cry. Instead, she set the bag on the kitchen counter and made herself drink a glass of iced water. Each sip nauseated her more until she finally darted down the hall to the bathroom, where she hung her head over the toilet bowl.

When she was sure there was nothing left to come up, she curled up on the bathroom floor, her hot cheek pressed against the cool tile, her tears puddling beneath her.

Her mother would have helped her up, pressed a warm washcloth to her face, and stood close as she'd have Chloe rinse with mouthwash. She would have led her to bed where she'd have sat next to her, her cool hand on Chloe's forehead until she'd fallen asleep.

But. . .her mother was gone.

Her tears spilled again.

She eventually pulled herself up, blew her nose, and washed her own face. The thought of mouthwash brought on another wave of nausea, so she swished water in her mouth instead.

She made her way back to the kitchen, dug her phone out of her purse, and then landed on the sofa, where she lay very still until her stomach settled.

After a while, she picked up the phone and called Chad. . . .

"Chloe?"

"Hi. . ." Her chin quivered.

"Are you okay?"

The concern she heard in his tone evoked another round of tears. She caught her breath as she tried to answer, "No. . .I'm not okay. I miss. . .you." She cried.

"Oh, baby. I miss you, too. What are you doing

there? Come home, please. If we have things to work out, we need to do it together. But I don't even know what's wrong. . . ."

She sat up and willed the tears to stop. She took a deep breath. "I can't come home. Not yet. I have to. . . stay. I have to work through some things."

"What things? Can't you at least explain it to me? Can't you tell me what's wrong?"

"It's. . .my mom." She sobbed.

"Your mom?"

"She died, Chad. She. . .died." She got up and went back to the bathroom for a box of tissues.

"Babe, I know. . . ." She heard the confusion in his voice.

"If she hadn't died, we'd have never met. She had to die for us to meet. I. . ." She wiped her nose. "I. . . don't know what to do with that. I don't know. . .how to handle. . .that." The sound of her sobs filled the small condo.

"*Shh*. . . Babe, it's okay. Don't cry. Chloe, honey, please don't cry."

She knew he felt helpless, but so did she. "I'm. . . sorry."

"You don't have to be sorry. I just wish I were there. What can I do?"

Chloe curled up on the sofa again. "Just talk to me. Just keep talking to me."

"Okay, what do you want to talk about?"

"Nothing. I just want to hear your voice."

"Oh, well. . . Have you heard who's in the play-offs?"

She fell asleep to the comfort of his voice and dreamed of dugouts and diamonds.

* * *

When she woke in the morning, she was in bed, the fan above her bed doing a slow spin and the sheet pulled up to her chin. Her skirt was on the floor.

Sometime during the night, she'd gotten herself to bed, though she didn't remember doing so.

She rolled onto her side, bunched the pillow under her head, and then remembered Chad. . . . Where was her phone? She threw the sheet back, got out of bed, and padded out to the living room, finding her phone on the sofa, the battery dead.

She would charge the battery and call Chad back. But first, coffee.

She went to the kitchen, dipped a scoop into the canister of dark Colombian beans, ground them, and then set the pot. As it brewed, she went back to the bedroom, put on a pair of shorts, plugged in her phone, and pulled a comb through her hair. After coffee, a shower sounded heavenly.

Whatever made her sick yesterday had passed, and her energy had returned. Even the coffee smelled good this morning—lately, even that aroma had bothered her.

When she heard the coffeepot gurgle as it pulled the last of the water through the grounds, she went back to the kitchen and filled her mug.

Her mother had loved coffee—especially the rich, dark blends. Chloe lifted the mug to her lips but then turned her head away and lowered the mug. Her stomach roiled.

"The only time I couldn't drink coffee"—her mother held a pottery mug in her hand, lifted it to her lips, and took a sip—*"was when I was pregnant with you."*

Chloe, hand trembling, set the full mug on the kitchen counter.

Was she. . .

Was it possible?

I stare at the screen for a long time. How would I have discovered I was pregnant, if. . . ? I was so watchful, so expectant, I'd have likely known the first day after a missed cycle.

How would I have told Craig?

How would he have responded?

A tear slides down my cheek.

I close my eyes and let my mind wander.

For the first time, I let myself imagine what never was. . . .

*The writer operates at a peculiar crossroads where
time and place and eternity somehow meet.
His problem is to find that location.*
Flannery O'Connor

Chapter 47

MELANIE

Chloe went back to the bedroom, picked up her phone, and opened the calendar. When was her last cycle? She counted back. When she'd counted back forty-seven days and still hadn't found the spot she marked on her calendar each month, she stopped counting.

How had she not realized?

She set the phone back down, went into the bathroom, brushed her teeth, and then grabbed her purse and took a quick walk back to the market. She scoured the aisles until she found what she was looking for. She took the test to the register, where the clerk, a woman, smiled. She held up the test. "Good luck."

Chloe clutched the bag and nearly ran back to the condo. She followed the instructions included with the test and then paced as she waited the number of minutes specified before viewing the results. When she picked up the stick, the result was clear.

She dashed back to the bedroom, where she'd left her phone. *Mom won't believe*—but then she remembered all over again.

Her mother was gone.

* * *

Though the morning sickness had grown worse over the last few days, now at least the nausea was a reminder of the secret she held. She wanted to tell Chad, but not over the phone. She'd wait until she was home.

She slipped a sundress over her head, pulled her long hair into a loose knot at the nape of her neck, and applied a bit of makeup.

Then she went to the kitchen, pulled up the airlines on her laptop, and booked her flight.

After her appointment with Dr. Hammond this morning, she'd come back and handle the rest of the details.

* * *

He closed the office door and then went to the calendar on his desk. He flipped it open to check his schedule for the day. Chloe was his first appointment of the morning.

He went to the small kitchen, heated a mug of water in the microwave, and then dropped a teabag in to steep. He wandered back to his office and glanced at the clock on the wall. Chloe was a few minutes late. He filed some paperwork until he heard the door to the reception area open and close.

"Come on in, Chloe." He stood from his desk and turned to greet her.

She smiled as she came in and took her seat.

He closed the door, grabbed his notepad and pen off his desk, and took his seat across from her, her expression making him smile.

"Go ahead. Ask me how I am," she teased.

He laughed. "All right. So, Chloe, how are you?"

"Pregnant." She threw back her head and laughed. "You're the only one I've told. I don't know anyone here. And I didn't want to tell anyone else before I tell Chad."

"You seem thrilled." He'd dreamed of having children, but it wasn't to be. . . .

"I am pleased. Surprised, but happy."

"When will you tell Chad? And how does this impact your decision about the marriage?"

Her expression softened, though the joy remained in her eyes. "I'm going home. The day after tomorrow. But I'd already decided before I found out. . . ." She rested her hand on her abdomen. "I still have work to do, but now I know what I need to work through."

"What's that?" He knew, but he wanted her to voice it aloud. To speak the words herself.

"I need to let myself grieve. . . ." Tears glistened in her eyes. "When the feelings come, instead of pushing them away, I need to let myself feel them—let the pain move me forward."

He nodded.

Her brow furrowed. "But I also need to figure out how to let go of those feelings of guilt. I called Chad and explained. . . . I wouldn't have met him if my mother hadn't died. I'd never said that to him. He didn't know I was struggling. How do I. . .get over that? How do I let that go?"

He leaned forward. "It isn't easy, but it's possible. The guilt you feel, Chloe, is condemning. It's accusatory. It's telling you that you did something wrong in a circumstance you had no control over.

"You didn't control your mother's accident. Nor did you control the timing of meeting Chad. You did nothing wrong in either situation."

"I understand that, logically, but I can't seem to get my heart to accept it."

"I want you to practice something until it becomes routine. Each time a condemning thought enters your mind, I want you to replace it with truth. Say it out loud, if you need to." He leaned forward. "Give me an example of a thought that triggers guilt."

She looked at her lap. "I only married Chad because I didn't want to be alone."

"Is that true?"

She looked back at Dr. Hammond. "No. I married him because he is kind, thoughtful, loving, and"—she smiles—"funny. I married him because I loved him deeply. I do love him deeply."

"Perfect. Let's try another one."

She took a deep breath. "If I really loved my mother, I wouldn't have fallen in love with Chad so soon after she died."

"What's the truth?"

Tears filled her eyes again. "I'm. . .not sure."

"Did you love your mother, Chloe?"

She wiped a tear from her check. "Yes, very much."

"So the truth you might tell yourself is, 'I loved my mother very much, and I love Chad very much.' It's both/and, not either/or."

"Oh. . ."

He reached for the tissue box and handed it across the coffee table to her. She took a tissue and wiped the tears from her eyes. "It was okay to love them both."

He nodded. "It *is* okay to love them both. Your love for your mother will never die. It will always be with you—she will always be with you. In fact, I suspect now that you're a mother"—Chloe's smile bloomed through her tears—"you'll think of your mom even more often. And you'll miss her terribly, I'm sure."

Chloe nodded. "She was the first one I thought to call when I found out, but then. . .I remembered."

"As you give yourself permission to grieve, that pain will lessen, I promise you. But it will never go away completely, not as long as you carry your mother's memory with you."

"Thank you. . ." she whispered.

"Remember the truth, Chloe."

* * *

After he closed up the office following his last client, he got into his car, its interior still hot from the heat of the day. He turned on the ignition, opened the sunroof, and then pulled out of his parking spot and pointed the car toward home.

But it wasn't April he thought of as he drove.

It was Beth. . . .

His conversation with Chloe during her appointment this morning brought Beth close again. If he let himself, he could still feel her breath on his cheek the last time he bent over the hospital bed to kiss her.

She was so thin. So frail.

By the next day, she was gone.

But she hadn't wanted him to remember her as she was at the end. She made that clear. *"Think of me with the sun on my shoulders and sand beneath my feet, swaying to the rhythm of steel drums."*

In his mind, he could still see her bare shoulders burnished by the sun, her blond hair hanging loose, blowing in the wind. Her eyes were the color of the Caribbean Sea, and in her gaze he found all he'd ever wanted. Her laughter was the melody of the only song he ever cared to hear.

"When the time comes," she'd whispered to him, her voice weak, *"let me go."*

"Let me go. . . ."

But after her death, he'd clung to her like a life preserver, fearing he'd drown in his sorrow.

But bit by bit, one minute at a time—as he'd told Chloe—he loosened his grip.

Instead of turning into the harbor, he drove on, knowing the time had finally come. He pulled into the resort, but rather than taking the time to walk through the grounds, he followed the road around to the small parking lot behind the Mermaid.

It was time to share one last drink.

It was time to say good-bye.

Time to finally let her go. . .

* * *

The sun was setting as he drove into Christiansted Harbor. He parked in his space, closed the sunroof, locked the car, and then made the long walk across the parking lot and through the maze of slips.

As he approached the boat, her teak deck polished to a sheen, her hull low and sleek, he paused on the dock and watched the sun as it dipped into the sea.

How many nights had he sat on her deck and watched the sun until it disappeared on the horizon, each time wishing Beth sat next to him?

This had been their dream, not his alone.

Before he boarded, he ran his hand along the smooth fiberglass hull. "Hello, *April*." He whispered. "It's good to be home."

Beth was born during the month of April.

And she died during the month of April.

Although the time had come to let her go, Elliot knew he'd carry Beth with him for the rest of his days. She was woven into the fabric of his soul.

But tonight, maybe for the first time since Beth's death, he'd sit on *April*'s deck.

Alone.

And let himself dream again.

Dream a new dream.

I pull my hands away from the keyboard, get up, and bend at the waist and then side to side. I go and stand in front of the living room windows. The blinds are open, as are the French doors. A breeze wafts through the screens, carrying a hint of fall into the living room. The lake beyond is hidden by the dark of night.

Somewhere near the patio a lone bird sings a lilting melody.
Is it possible to dream a new dream?
I turn from the window and go in search of my phone.
The time has come....

Women are made to be loved, not understood.
Oscar Wilde

Chapter 48

CRAIG

I switch off the light on the nightstand. Just as I climb into bed, my cell phone, which I had just plugged into the charger on my nightstand, rings. Who would call this late? I reach for the phone, see Melanie's name, and answer it. "Mel? Are you okay?"

"I am okay. Did I wake you?"

"No, I worked late. I just climbed into bed and was about to reach for the remote."

"Ah, the mouse will play while the cat is away."

"Well, I know the volume keeps you awake."

"So when I'm there you no longer fall asleep to the sound of the television like you used to."

"A minor sacrifice."

"It's one of many you've made for me."

I comb my fingers through my hair. "Are you sure you're okay? What are you doing up so late? You sound tired."

"I am tired. I wanted to call you earlier. Actually, I've wanted to call you every day since Saturday, but I guess I wasn't quite ready. I'm still not sure I'm ready."

I unplug the phone from the charger and stand up. I walk through the dark room over to the window. A reflection of the moon shines on the pool below. "Ready? For what?"

"I want to tell you something."

"Mel, you don't sound like yourself. . . ."

"C'mon, who are you kidding? We both know that might be a good thing."

I chuckle. "There. That's better." But she doesn't laugh with me.

"I realized something on Saturday."

"What's that?"

"I realized just how much I. . .love you."

A lump forms in my throat, making it hard to speak, but she continues.

"Do you know that I've written you into every one of my books? You're always the hero—never the bad guy. I didn't realize that until Saturday. Not only are you my reality, you're also my alternate reality."

"Mel—"

"In this book, you're wise and tender and"—her voice breaks—"you're a hunk. Although Elliot, my character, may be an inch or so taller than you are, but again, I didn't realize that until Saturday and it wasn't intentional."

"Melanie—"

"I almost packed it up and came home on Saturday afternoon. I wanted to. . .more than you know, but I have a job to finish and a few more things to still work out. But I miss you. I want you to know just how much I miss you. I've missed you for a long time. Too long. For far too many years. I just. . .didn't know it."

"Mel—"

"I hope. . ." Her tears are evident in her voice now. "I hope it isn't too late. I hope I'm not. . .too late."

I rub the palm of my hand across my eyes. "Melanie, I love you. I have always loved you. I will always love you."

As I stand at the window, something stirs in the oak just beyond our bedroom. A branch bounces and then something takes flight. Its wings spread wide. It turns its head back, as though to look at me, its yellow eyes shining in the moonlight.

And then it's gone.

"Mel, it isn't too late. It will never be too late. We're just beginning. . . ."

You're braver than you believe,
and stronger than you seem, and smarter than you think.
A. A. Milne

Chapter 49

Jill

Marcos walks into the kitchen after taking the kids next door. "What can I do?"

I pull the stuffed pork roast out of the refrigerator and set it on the counter. "You can sit and talk to me. Please?" I set the oven to heat.

"You don't want me to grill that?"

I turn from the oven. "No. I don't want you outside. I don't want to be left alone with. . .them."

Marcos pulls out one of the barstools and sits down. "This is going to be okay. Really, Jill."

Mouth dry, I fill a glass with water and take a sip. "I'm expecting the worst for tonight so I'm not the one caught off guard. I. . .can't see how this can have anything but a negative outcome. Are we. . .am I. . . doing the right thing? What if. . ." I shake my head. "I can't even think of all the what-ifs."

He gets up, comes around the counter, and puts his hands on my shoulders. "You're doing the right thing and the courageous thing. You've taken all the right steps. You've done your research, you've talked this through with Cara, and I'm here to support you. Most importantly, you're taking care of yourself—this whole evening, whatever happens, is another step toward emotional health." He pulls me into his embrace.

I linger there, in the safety of his arms.

"I'm so proud of you, *mi amor*," he whispers. "And I am with you and for you. Always. Don't ever forget that." He leans back and kisses my forehead then pulls me tight again.

When the doorbell rings, I look at Marcos. "Who is that? My parents always just walk in."

Marcos smiles. "I locked the front door. This is our house—I would like your mother to respect that." He gets up and I follow him to the entry hall, where he opens the door. "Diane, Tom. Please, come in."

"Who locked the door?" But my mother doesn't wait for a response. She walks past Marcos and, without looking at me, gives me a kiss on the cheek. "Jillian, dear. You're looking well." Then she looks past me down the hallway. "Where are the children?"

My dad shakes Marcos's hand and then comes to me. "Hi there, Jilly." He gives me a hug.

My mother has gone down the hallway and opened the kids' bedroom doors. Then she turns and comes back.

"Where—"

Marcos is quick to respond this time. "They're next door with Craig and Melanie. We thought it would be nice to have some adult time. More relaxed."

"Well, no offense to either of you, but they are the main reason we visit." My mother laughs, but her tone is tight. It seems evident *she* has not forgotten our last conversation.

"Mom, they'll be back after dinner. Come into the kitchen—Marcos will fix you a drink. I made an appetizer."

My mother looks at her diamond-studded watch. "After dinner? That's hours from now, at least. If Marcos is grilling again, it will be even longer."

"Mom..."

"I'm just saying that grilling always takes longer."

Marcos, who is always gracious with my mother despite her barbs, gestures toward the kitchen. "Folks, iced tea? Lemonade?"

My mother raises one eyebrow. "Tell me you have something stronger, please. If it's an adult evening, let's at least enjoy an adult beverage."

"A glass of wine?"

"That will do. Jill, how can I help? I assume the table still needs setting? She goes to the dining room then returns. "Well, I see you're organized."

Is that a jab or a compliment? "Mom, everything's taken care of. Just relax." I wish I could do the same. Although I'm grateful—as I pull the bubbling artichoke and spinach dip out of the oven—that I have something to occupy myself with.

Marcos pours my parents each a glass of wine then holds the bottle up. "Jill?"

"No, thank you." I need my mind perfectly clear. Plus I don't dare mix the alcohol with the medication I'm taking.

Marcos sets the bottle aside and pours himself a glass of lemonade. When we talked about this evening, we agreed I would lead the conversation when I felt ready.

Now, my nerves taut, I just want it over with.

"Let's sit in the family room." I carry the dip and a basket of crackers and set them on the coffee table.

Marcos follows with plates and napkins. "Help yourselves."

My mother serves herself some of the hot dip and crackers and settles on the sofa, my dad next to her. She nibbles on a cracker then sets it back on her plate and places the plate on the coffee table. Her wine sits untouched. She fidgets with the napkin in her lap, the large diamond on her wedding ring catching the light.

Marcos and I sit in the wingback chairs across from my parents. I don't bother with the pretense of eating.

My mother crosses one slim leg over the other then uncrosses it. She runs her hand along the crease of her perfectly tailored slacks. Her timeless beauty is marred only by the tight slash of her mouth and the deep lines in her brow.

Instead of the woman sitting across from me, I see a young mother dressed in black, standing at an open grave. Her face awash in tears. Her hand firmly holding mine.

"Mom...Dad...I—"

My mother holds up one hand. "Wait..." She glances at my father, the man who raised me, and then back to me. "Jill, please..." Her hand shakes. "I have something I want to say. Need to...say."

My father reaches over and puts his hand on her knee—offering what? Encouragement? Strength?

She takes a deep breath. "When we were here last, I...behaved badly. I said things, Jill, that were unkind and...unnecessary. I am sorry. I would like to"—she glances at my dad again—"*we* would like to explain."

I look at Marcos then back to my mom. Of all the scenarios that played out in my mind over the last few weeks, this wasn't something I'd imagined. My mother apologizing? Explaining. . .what? Can I believe whatever it is she'll say?

She grasps my dad's hand and then looks at me. "I wasn't honest with you." Her tone is breathy. "The questions you. . .asked. I wasn't. . . honest." Tears fill her eyes.

"Mom. . ." My voice trembles. I'm suddenly afraid of what she's about to say. I was prepared to confront her. I was not prepared for. . . I look down at my lap and shake my head.

Marcos reaches over and clasps my hand in his. "Go ahead, Diane."

"Jillian. . . ," she whispers.

I look back to her.

"I wanted to, I hoped to. . .protect you. But. . ."

In that moment, images flash in my mind of the mother I grew up with—extroverted, socially involved, reveling in the niceties my father provided. But I understand now that I've never known her. I've never known who she was, who she is, beneath the facade. A facade I readily accepted.

"By protecting you, or trying to, I. . .may have done more damage."

"Mom, what are you saying?"

"There was a funeral. . . . You were so young. I didn't think you'd remember. I hoped you wouldn't remember. I prayed you wouldn't remember." She looks at her hands in her lap.

"It was my. . .father. He was my father. James O'Shea." My tone is flat. I no longer know what to feel.

Her head snaps up, and I read the surprise in her eyes.

"Jilly, he was ill. He suffered a great deal."

"Ill?" I whisper.

"Mentally ill." My dad leans forward. "He took his own life."

My mother buries her face in her hands.

Marcos's grip on my hand tightens. "Mentally ill? Tom. . . What. . . ?" There is fear in Marcos's tone.

My dad pulls a handkerchief out of his pocket and hands it to my mother.

She wipes her eyes and then clings to the square of fabric. "We didn't fully understand it at the time—the illness wasn't fully understood. But I was told, at the time, that it ran in families. . . ."

Cara and Dr. Luchesse's questions about my family history replay.

"And I thought by not telling you about your biological father, I could somehow protect you from the disorder. Protect you from his. . . fate." She wipes her eyes again.

Mouth dry, I try to swallow. "Obsessive-compulsive disorder?"

My mother nods. "He was so tormented." Fresh tears fill my mother's eyes. "It got worse and worse. Finally, he. . ." She shakes her head.

Marcos whispers, "He committed suicide."

My dad looks at the floor. "Jim was a good friend. We went to school together and then went into business together. He was like a brother to me. I could see him spiraling, but I felt powerless to help him. He was under psychiatric care, but the meds weren't working." He looks back at us. "I couldn't. . .help him."

"It was a horrible, horrible time." The anguish in my mother's expression is genuine. "I'm so. . .sorry, Jillian. So, so sorry. I never wanted you to have to know. I wanted to protect you from the stigma of the illness, from the stigma of suicide. Things were different then. It was a different time." She looks at my dad again. "After we married, we moved. Left the area. I thought I could leave all that behind. Later, when I began seeing signs of the illness in you, I wanted to deny it. Pretend it didn't exist. I just closed my eyes to. . .all of it."

No longer able to sit still, I let go of Marcos's hand and stand up. I pace the living room through a blur of tears.

I don't know what to say.

What to do.

What to feel.

———◆◆———

I cover the roast, uneaten, with foil and put it in the refrigerator. Marcos rinses the glasses and puts them in the dishwasher. We're both silent. My parents left without eating—none of us were hungry.

Marcos closes the dishwasher. "I'll go get the kids."

"I'll come with you."

"You sure?"

I nod.

I follow Marcos out of the kitchen to the front door. He holds it open for me, and I step into the cool night—a touch of fall in the air. Marcos and I walk down our front steps and across the driveway. He grasps my hand and holds it tight. When we reach Craig and Melanie's driveway, he slows then stops. I turn and look at him.

He comes close, puts his hands on either side of my face, leans in, and puts his lips on mine. His kiss is warm, tender. Then he wraps me in his arms and whispers in my ear, "Thank you for getting help. Thank you for taking care of yourself. I. . .don't ever want to lose you. Not ever."

Tears brim in my eyes and I hold him tight. I can't imagine what he must feel. I can't imagine what my mother must have felt. . . .

When my parents left, all of us exhausted, I gave them both a hug and told them I loved them. It was not how I'd anticipated the evening ending. I couldn't have anticipated any of this.

Did they make the right choices so many years ago? I don't know. There's still so much to process—so much to unravel in my mind and heart.

"I love you," I whisper. "I couldn't do this without you. You are my gift."

We make our way to the front door and knock lightly, knowing the kids are likely asleep.

Craig's footsteps sound in their entry hall. As he opens the door, Melanie comes up behind him. He flips on the light in the hall and gestures for us to come in.

Melanie comes around Craig. "How'd it go?"

Marcos and I look at one another, words hard to come by. But he speaks for both of us. "It wasn't what we expected."

Craig puts his arm around my shoulders, and we all walk into the family room—the warm scent of cinnamon a welcome greeting.

"I baked a pie—apple. Will you eat a piece?" Melanie asks. "À la mode?"

Marcos smiles. "Actually, that sounds really good."

"It does sound good. May I help you?"

Melanie waves me away. "Sit. Relax. You've had a long evening."

As she fixes the pie, we settle on the love seats in their family room.

Craig sits across from us. "The kids did great. They're all three sound asleep."

I smile, though even that small act takes effort. "Thanks so much for having them—and letting them stay so late."

"I'm surprised you're still standing, amigo."

Craig laughs. "Me too. I don't know how you two do it."

We chat about the kids until Melanie returns with the pie. She serves Marcos and me first then goes back to the kitchen for pieces for herself and Craig. She hands a plate to Craig and sits down next to him. "So, are you up to talking about it?"

Marcos looks at me.

"I. . .I don't even know what to say." I look at Melanie. "Remember when you said you were hoping for the best outcome and that maybe I'd be surprised?"

She nods.

"That may be what happened, but. . .I'm still trying to make sense of it all. It will take time. It was painful and hard. So hard. Yet, I think my relationship with my parents—our relationship with them—will be stronger."

Melanie sets her fork on her plate. "They told you the truth, then?"

Marcos wipes his mouth with his napkin. "Yes. Absolutely." He looks at me, eyebrows raised, and I nod my agreement.

"That's what you needed." Craig cuts into his piece of pie.

As the tension of the evening begins to wane, the warmth of friendship enwraps me like a warm blanket, and fatigue sets in. I finish my pie, set the plate aside, and yawn. Then I scoot closer to Marcos, occasionally leaning my head on his shoulder.

It's there, next to the man who has loved me through so much, who continues to love me, and with friends whom we've grown with, that I tell Craig and Melanie the details of my parents' story.

My story.

It's there that healing begins. . . .

Faith given back to us after a night of doubt is a stronger thing,
and far more valuable to us than faith that has never been tested.
Elizabeth Goudge

Chapter 50

MELANIE

I wake early, unaccustomed to my own bed. I slip out, not wanting to wake Craig. There's a chill in the air, so I grab my bathrobe out of the closet, slide my feet into my slippers, and tiptoe out of the bedroom, closing the door behind me. I flip on the hall light, throw the robe over my shoulders, and make my way downstairs to see if I remember where we keep the coffee.

It feels like I was gone forever.

How can so much change in a month's time?

There's a FOR SALE sign in the front yard. Brian's holding an open house today. Anything that resembled clutter in the house is now boxed and labeled and sitting on shelves in the empty bay of the garage that once housed our boat.

And that's just the beginning. . . .

The other changes run so much deeper.

I scoop coffee beans into the coffeemaker then fill it with water and turn it on. I stand and watch as the beans grind and the brew begins to drip into the pot. The aroma intoxicates rather than nauseates. "Sorry, Chloe."

I rinse our dessert plates from last night and set them in the dishwasher as Jill's story replays in my mind.

When the coffee is ready, I fill a mug and then wander from room to room. I switch on lights, fluff pillows, and run a dustcloth over the furniture.

When I've gone through all the downstairs rooms, I venture back upstairs. I stand in the hallway in front of the first of two unoccupied bedrooms.

I haven't entered either room in years.

To do so would have required I be present.

And I wasn't.

I turn the knob on the door, step inside, and flip the switch, casting light on the pale yellow walls. Sometime in the last month, I assume, Craig, or maybe Brian, has staged the room with a few pieces of furniture, a lamp, and other accessories.

The last time I was in here, I'd thrown our dreams into a few boxes. Sealed them tight. And left them in a corner. Stuffed animals. A handmade baby blanket from a craft fair. Children's books collected from all over the country, including a few we picked up in St. Croix.

I walk to the closet and open the door. An antique bassinet still hides in the shadows. I step into the walk-in closet and run my hand over the aged wicker. The boxes I'd packed are now stacked on the floor in the back of the closet.

A wave of grief washes over me, but rather than run, I stand still. I let it come, let it cleanse, knowing it will soon ebb.

Elliot was right: the pain lessens with time.

"Mel?"

I turn and walk out of the closet. Craig stands in the open doorway of the room, his hair still mussed from sleep, his bathrobe open over his shorts and T-shirt.

"You okay?"

I swallow the ache in my throat. "I will be." I close the closet door, and Craig meets me in the middle of the room. He puts his arms around me, and I lean into his warmth, the scent of him more intoxicating than the coffee—and just as familiar.

We stand in the middle of that room, a lost dream threading us together into a tight seam instead of fraying us as we allowed it to do for so long. I pull away from Craig and give the room one more look. Then I turn back to him. "We'd better get going. Brian will be here before we know it."

Craig sighs. "Yeah. . ."

I follow him out of the room, but linger in the doorway as he goes downstairs. I turn off the light switch and then notice the shutters on the window are still closed. I cross the room and push the slats open, and the room fills with shafts of sunlight.

"Thank you," I whisper.

Though I may never understand God's allowance, I am making peace with His ways.

————◆—————

The murmur of conversation, the clatter of dishes, and the scent of coffee, bacon, and grease surround us. I push the plate away, half a biscuit left uneaten. "I'm stuffed."

Craig chuckles. "Me too."

"So, now what do we do? How long did Brian say we need to be out of the house?"

"Until four." Craig pulls his wallet out of his pocket and counts out the bills for our tab, plus a tip. "We certainly can't eat anything else, at least for a few hours."

"A few hours? Try a few days. That was the largest biscuit I've ever seen. And the best. No wonder you and Marcos like this place."

Craig leans back in the booth, stretching his long legs under the table. "Whaddaya say we drive around and try and figure out what to do if the house sells? We could look at some rentals."

"You really need to work on your salesmanship."

He chuckles. "Rentals are a hard sell."

"You aren't kidding. But okay, I'm game. Let's do it."

We walk out of the café hand in hand and through the parking lot to Craig's truck. He opens the passenger door for me, and I climb in. He closes the door then comes around and gets behind the wheel. "Want to look up listings on your phone and tell me where to go?"

"What area? I don't even know what you're thinking. We haven't talked about this at all."

"I haven't really thought about it at all."

We both stare out the front windshield. Then he turns and looks at me. "Roseville? Say, nothing more than a five-mile radius from Marcos and Jill?"

I bite my lower lip and nod.

"Forget listings for now. Let's just drive around." He turns the key in the ignition and backs out of the parking space.

"I still can't believe this is happening...."

"I know."

We ride in silence for a long time, each of us lost in our own thoughts. I stare out the window, scenery flashing by unnoticed.

"Mel. . ."

"Hmm?"

"I'm glad you're home." He reaches over and takes my hand in his.

I squeeze his hand. "Me too." We pass a few familiar landmarks and then a few that are unfamiliar. "Craig, this isn't Roseville."

"I know. I want to show you something." He pulls up to a stoplight, and when the light turns green he makes a wide U-turn, the bed of the truck barely clearing the intersection. Then he makes a hard right into a parking lot.

"A library? You want to show me a library?"

"It's free."

I laugh. "True. Free books. How could we go wrong?"

But instead of parking in the spaces up front, he pulls around to the back and parks under a streetlight. Then he turns to me. "We're not going to the library—it's something else." He shrugs, his expression sheepish or shy or something I don't recognize. "C'mon." He hops out of the truck, so I do the same.

I follow him across the parking lot to a gate locked with a chain and padlock. He pulls the gate as far as the chain allows and then shimmies through. He holds the gate for me. "Your turn."

"What are you doing? We're going to get arrested for trespassing."

"Have I ever given you reason to distrust me?"

It's the same question he asked the night I probed about where he'd gone instead of attending the BIA reception.

I hesitate. "No, you haven't. But. . ." I smile. "There's a first time for everything."

He chuckles. "C'mon. I have permission."

I slip through the gate and under Craig's arm, and then he lets the gate close. I follow him into a grove of trees and my steps slow. Blue oaks, heritage oaks, redwoods, pines. "Wait." I whisper. We stop and I tilt my head up. Blue sky peeks through the thick canopy as a million leaves and needles rustle overhead. I reach out and run my hand over the rough bark of an oak then breathe deep of the scent of mulching leaves, dry grass, oaks, and pines.

When I look back to Craig, he's watching me. "I should have brought you here years ago."

"Where's here? What is this place?"

"You'll see."

We traipse through the rest of the grove until it gives way to rolling lawn and landscaped beds. Craig takes my hand and leads me along a pathway until I begin to see buildings, benches, and people milling about, including what looks like a priest and. . .a nun?

Craig stops on the path and laughs. "I forgot it's Saturday. They're probably holding a retreat this weekend. We could have driven in the front gate."

"A retreat?"

"It's a Catholic retreat center."

"Did we convert?" I whisper.

He laughs. "Mel, I've missed you." He leans down and plants a quick kiss on my lips. "It looks like my bench is free."

I follow him to the bench, which, by the looks of the way he plops himself down, you'd think he owned. He pats the space next to him. "Sit."

But just as I'm ready to join him, a small brass plate, just to the right of Craig's shoulder, catches my eye. There's something inscribed on the plate. I lean in to read the inscription. "Craig. . ." I step back and look at him. "That's your mother's name."

He turns and rubs his thumb over the plate. "Yeah."

I cock my head and stare at him for a moment. "She wasn't Catholic either."

"Nah, but she loved this place. After she died, I"—he shrugs—"donated the bench in her name. I never told you. I'm sorry."

The brass plate glistens in the late morning sun. I shake my head then sit down next to Craig. But then I lean away from him so I can see his face. "There's a whole side of you I don't know?"

"Not a whole side—maybe just an eighth of a side or one-sixteenth of a side." He chuckles.

I look into his hazel eyes and my heart flutters. I shake my head then lean back against the bench, in the crook of my husband's arm. We sit, enjoying the peace for a few minutes, and I take in our surroundings. Then I point. "The Stations of the Cross."

"Yeah, you know about those?"

"I researched them for a book once."

"Huh. . ."

"So do you come here often, or. . . ?"

"Lately, I've come once, twice, sometimes three times a week. Usually at night, after work, or when I can't sleep. I come here to pray."

I lean away from him again to see his face. "What do you pray for?"

"It depends. Sometimes I pray for wisdom, other times I lash out at God—those probably aren't my best moments, but. . . The last time I was here, I prayed for you."

"Oh. . ." I lean back, emotion welling within, though I can't name the feeling. "Thank you," I whisper.

"When I was a kid, just after I got my driver's license, I followed my mom here. She'd always disappear a couple times a week, and I wanted to know where she went. I found her here. I've felt like this was her legacy to me, you know?"

I don't respond. Instead, I just listen.

"At first, I felt like it was our secret, though I'm not sure she knew I'd followed her. Later, it became my. . .sanctuary. The place I meet with God. It was personal, is personal, just between the two of us. But. . ." He looks at me, his expression serious. "I want to include you; I should have included you. I haven't. . .shared this part of my life with you. I'm sorry. No matter what happens, no matter where we end up, this, our relationship with God, is our foundation. It's our stability. It's all that really matters."

I grip his hand and squeeze it tight. All I can do is nod.

And whisper again, "Thank you."

———————◆———————

When we pull into the driveway a little after four, Brian's car is still parked in front of the house. We go into the house and find him in the kitchen, talking on his phone and jotting notes on a pad.

He holds up one finger indicating he'll just be a minute or so longer. Nine or ten business cards are spread across the counter, those of various Realtors who came through with clients, I assume.

When Brian ends his call, he looks at us and shakes his head. "You're not going to believe this, but that was an offer."

My heart skips a beat. An offer? As in, someone wants *our* house?

"Was it a decent offer?" Craig asks.

Brian shakes his head again. "More than decent. It was the second offer of the day, and now they're bidding against one another. Bro, I haven't had that happen in at least three years. That offer was twenty thousand above your list price. Since June, we've been on an upswing, but interest rates are still low. What can I say? You're selling at the right time."

Craig looks at me, and I read the conflicting emotions in his eyes.

"It's okay. It's going to be okay." I smile, though I know the effort is weak.

Brian gathers his things. "I gotta run."

We follow him out to his car.

"I'll call the other Realtor and let you know where we land, but it looks like you'll have a solid offer within a day or two. Both parties are prequalified. No contingencies. Either way, it'll be a quick close."

Craig holds out his hand to shake Brian's hand. "Thanks, man."

"Yes, thank you, Brian."

We watch as he drives away, and then we stand on the curb and look at the house. Neither of us says a word.

There's no place like home.
L. Frank Baum

Epilogue

MELANIE

Boxes surround my desk, which, along with the desk chair, are the only pieces of furniture left in the room. Two long trucks and trailers are parked in front of the house. Movers swarm, loading the trucks with our belongings.

I told them the office was the last to go.

Tomorrow, November 1, a month after my original deadline, my manuscript is due. Not only have I spent the last month packing up the house, but I've worked with Jill to make the manuscript both authentic to the story I was given and fitting for my brand.

I lift my fingers from the keyboard. . . .

"Home is the imprint on our heart, the song of our soul, the memory we've yet to live. . . ."

I lean back in my chair and read the final snippet of dialogue again. Though I assign the phrase to Chloe, the truth is my own. One I've learned over the last two months as I've discovered my own *home.*

"Melanie?" Jill's voice sounds down the hallway.

"In here."

She skirts around a guy carrying a load of boxes out of the office. "This is crazy. Are you done?"

I look back to the screen and nod. "I'm done. I just read through the epilogue, made a couple of corrections, and it's"—I look up at her—"done. I thought I'd never say that."

"Honestly? Me too."

"What? You kept telling me this was possible. 'It just needs a little tweaking,' you said."

"I lied, but it was for a good cause."

We both laugh, and then. . .we don't.

Jill's eyes are wide, tears brimming.

"No, don't. You promised." I swipe at the corners of my eyes.

"I just. . .I hate this. It hurts too much."

I get up from the desk and put my arms around her. "If it didn't hurt, then it would mean it didn't matter." I hug her tight and then pull back and look at her. "And this"—I gesture between us—"matters."

She nods, and we both wipe our eyes again.

She points at my laptop. "Send it. Now."

"Thank you for all your help."

"Anytime."

"And you won't miss me too much. We still have a whole edit to do."

She smiles. "Right."

"Plus, we're only two and a half miles down the road. Just a brisk walk away."

"With the twins?"

"A quick drive in the minivan."

She hugs me again. "Send it. And call me when you two are back from Clear Lake. I'll come over and help you get settled."

"I will. Thank you." I watch her leave, walk out my office door—at least this office—for the last time.

I sit back down, type a quick e-mail to my editor, cc my agent, and then attach the manuscript document to the e-mail. I lift my finger to click SEND then pause. . . .

"Take it where You will. . . ," I whisper. "It's Yours. . . ."

I drop my finger on the trackpad and click, letting go of the story I was given. A story written on my heart and soul.

I close the laptop and unplug it then drop it into my bookbag just as my phone rings. I pick it up and see Valerie's name on the screen. "Hey, you."

"How's the move going?"

"Crazy, of course."

"I think that's normal. Although, what's normal? Listen, while you're at the house, would you mind having Craig check the faucet in the bathroom? It's leaking."

"Sure, he'll take a look. Valerie, thank you again for letting us stay there until the condo is ready. I can't tell you how much that helps us. Plus, I'm anxious for Craig to see your place—my home away from home."

"I'm so glad it worked out. Enjoy it. You two deserve a break. We'll get together when you're back."

"I'd love to. See you soon."

I end the call and drop the phone into my bag. I pick up the bag, sling it over my shoulder, and then look around the room. I wrote most of my sixteen novels here, in this space.

But today, a new chapter begins. . . .

———————————◆◆————————————

It was dark by the time we arrived last night. Craig carried in our overnight bag, and we both dropped into bed, beyond exhausted. "That was the longest day of my life," I mumbled. "I'm never moving again."

"It was the longest month of our lives. And I'm never moving again, even if you do." He rolled over and was snoring before I'd even turned out the light.

Now gray light washes the small bedroom, and the patter of rain sounds on the rooftop.

I lift my head off the pillow. The lake, a palette of grays, beckons out the French doors. We were too tired to even pull the blinds last night. I glance at Craig, still asleep, and gently pull the sheet and blanket off and slide out of the bed. I stop in the bathroom, find my slippers, and then sneak out one of the doors in the living room.

Large sycamore leaves in hues of goldenrod skip across the lawn. The surface of the lake ripples in the distance. I fill my lungs with the damp air, and then I step out from under the eave of the house, walk down the steps, and join the leaves in their pilgrimage toward the lake.

I follow the leaves' trail to the water's edge, where cool rain pelts my bare shoulders. I hood my eyes with one hand and lift my face to the sky, where a pregnant cloud births its gift. I let my hand drop, close my eyes, and stretch my arms in welcome, twirling a slow choreography to the song of my soul.

I throw my head back, eyes closed, as laughter bubbles from my core. My thin nightgown, soaked through, clings to my curves. I let my arms drop to my sides.

His voice sounds from the patio. "What're you laughing at, silly girl?"

I open my eyes, the smile still playing on my lips—the lips of a woman, not a girl. How long has it been since he's called me that?

His long strides cover the distance between us.

"I'm laughing because I'm happy. You, this"—I do one more slow turn—"all of this makes me happy." I yell over the sound of the rain pounding the lake now.

His lips curve into a slow smile as he moves close, his cotton T-shirt soaked through, clinging to his chest. He puts his arms around me and pulls me to himself. "You're the one I've always wanted."

His whisper tickles my ear, and I close my eyes as I fold into his embrace.

Overhead the sky rumbles, deep and resonant.

The sound of grace.

I look into his eyes, so familiar. "And you're my every dream."

We both laugh as the rain pelts us.

He pulls me close and holds me tight. "Welcome home, Mel. . . ."

The longing stirs then stills.

He is my home.

Until I reach my true home, the memory I've yet to live. . . .

About the Author

Ginny L. Yttrup is the award-winning author of *Words, Lost and Found, Invisible,* and *Flames.* She writes contemporary women's fiction and enjoys exploring the issues everyday women face. *Publishers Weekly* dubbed Ginny's work "as inspiring as it is entertaining." When not writing, Ginny coaches writers, critiques manuscripts, and makes vintage-style jewelry for her Etsy shop, Storied Jewelry (etsy.com/shop /StoriedJewelry). She loves dining with friends, hanging out with her adult sons, or spending a day in her pajamas reading a great novel. Ginny lives in Northern California with Bear, her entitled Pomeranian. To learn more about Ginny and her work, visit ginnyyttrup.com.

Dear Reader,

It's odd how some memories spin in our minds, round and round. . . .

The idea for *Home* was spun from such a memory.

I navigated the winding road to Mendocino, where I planned to spend a month finishing the novel I was writing at the time, *Invisible*. My dear friend Sharol sat in the passenger seat, along for the first few days of my adventure. In her gentle way, she asked me a pointed question. "Do you have any desire yet to meet someone?"

I knew what she meant—we'd traveled this way before.

I glanced at her and read both curiosity and compassion in her expression. "No." Then I, like my characters so often do, probably shrugged. "But I did figure something out. I write my dream man into every novel." Then I most likely laughed.

The memory is blurred at the edges, but Sharol's question and my response remain sharply focused.

A year or so later, the question each novelist poses came to me: *What if. . . ?*

What if a novelist did write her dream man into a novel?

What if she became infatuated with the character?

Those questions were all I had, but it felt like enough. So I conjured up a synopsis and a few sample chapters and sent them off to my agent. And because these things take time—sometimes lots of time—it was two years before the idea sold and I began writing *Home*.

But Sharol's question still spun.

And my answer was still the same.

Is still the same.

No.

I have no desire to meet a man. To date. Or marry again.

Honestly, I set out to write an easy story. A story that wouldn't require hours upon hours of research. Something fun. Something that might make both myself and you, my readers, smile. I didn't know how it would all play out—like Melanie, I'm a seat-of-the-pants writer. But I trusted my characters would lead the way. And they did.

But they led somewhere I didn't want to go.

They led me to grief.

And grief isn't easy to write about, especially when you've worked so hard to avoid grieving. . . .

When you've escaped.

When you've even committed to living an alternate reality—an easy commitment for a novelist to make.

As I wrote, I had to make a choice: follow my characters and let the story go where they led—where God led—or. . . what?

With a deadline looming, I couldn't come up with a viable option.

So, reluctantly, I followed. . . .

As Melanie and Craig grieved the loss of their dream, I grieved the loss of my dream. The loss of my twenty-nine-year marriage to divorce. But Melanie and Craig taught me something important: in order for God to begin healing our pain, we need to allow ourselves to *feel* the pain. And in order to experience God in the midst of our pain, we must remain present through the pain. Because, as Father Ashcroft told Craig, we experience God in the moment. In the here and now.

Not only did my characters lead me to grief, they also led me to healing.

Then they led me home. . . .

To the arms of my Bridegroom—Jesus Christ.

And in the end, this story *did* make me smile.

I hope it does the same for you. . . .

Discussion Questions

1. Are you aware of times when you try to avoid or escape pain? What are some things you use to escape?

2. Sometimes avoidance is a coping mechanism that is helpful for a time. Can you think of times it might prove beneficial for the short-term?

3. Melanie and Jill seem like extreme opposites—one avoiding pain, the other obsessed with pain in the form of anxiety. But they shared a core issue—neither lived in the moment. What distracts you from being present in the moment?

4. Do you, like Melanie and Craig, have something unresolved in your life? Something perhaps God is asking you to process with Him? Perhaps even something you haven't allowed yourself to grieve?

5. How did Jill's story impact you? Have you struggled with anxiety? Along with medical science that God has allowed, what provisions do the Bible offer for those suffering with mental illnesses, such as obsessive-compulsive disorder?

6. Did you learn anything about marriage through Melanie and Craig's marriage and Jill and Marcos's marriage?

7. 1 Corinthians 10:13 assures us that God will not allow us to be tempted beyond what we can bear and that He will also provide a way out so that we can endure temptation. Craig's relationship with Serena seems to exemplify that promise, yet we often fall to temptation. Why?

8. What do you believe the author of *Home* meant when she wrote, "Home is the memory we've yet to live"?

9. Do you have the assurance of spending eternity with Jesus Christ?

10. What message is God speaking into your life through this story?

Acknowledgments

Though it's the author's name on the cover of a book, it is never the work of the author alone that brings a story to life. As always, I am grateful for my agent, Steve Laube, who champions my work, encourages me, and answers my many questions, including a few specific questions I e-mailed him regarding this story. He also allowed me to quote him: "Why do you think the word 'dead' is in deadline?" I appreciate and ~~fear~~ respect you, Mr. Laube.

Special thanks to Annie Tipton with Barbour Publishing, who believed in this story from the beginning and ultimately acquired it for Barbour. Thank you, Annie! And thank you to the publishing team at Barbour Publishing for all your behind-the-scenes efforts. Also, thank you to JoAnne Simmons, whose insightful observations and comments during the copy edit made this book better.

Thank you to my dear friends and writers' group, the Deep Inkers. You've followed my journey to publication from the beginning—encouraging me, laughing with me, and even crying with me. Thank you for allowing me to use the name of our group in *Home*. And though we don't meet on a regular basis any longer, you each still inspire me.

I am especially grateful to my critique partners extraordinaire: Susan Basham and Laurie Breining. You are honest (I think), encouraging, discerning, and perceptive. I am so grateful for both of you and your enduring friendship. I also appreciate, greatly, that you're willing to read for me right up to the moments before my deadline. Oh my. . .

To my incredible sons, and my circle of dear friends who love and support me (you know who you are), thank you. Always.

Looking for More Inspirational Fiction? Check Out. . .

The Captive Heart by **Michelle Griep**

Proper English governess Eleanor Morgan flees to the colonies to escape the wrath of a brute of an employer. When the Charles Town family she's to work for never arrives to collect her from the dock, she is forced to settle for the only reputable choice remaining to her— marriage to a man she's never met. Trapper and tracker Samuel Heath is a hardened survivor used to getting his own way by brain or by brawn, and he's determined to find a mother for his young daughter. But finding a wife proves to be impossible. No upstanding woman wants to marry a murderer.
Paperback / 978-1-63409-783-3 / 320 pages / $14.99

Stars in the Grass by **Ann Marie Stewart**

The idyllic world of nine-year-old Abby McAndrews is transformed when a tragedy tears her family apart. Before the accident her dad had all the answers, but now his questions and guilt threaten to destroy his family. Abby's fifteen-year-old brother, Matt, begins an angry descent as he acts out in dangerous ways. Her mother tries to hold her grieving family together, but when Abby's dad refuses to move on, the family is at a crossroads. Set in a small Midwestern town in 1970, Abby's heartbreaking remembrances are balanced by humor and nostalgia as her family struggles with—and ultimately celebrates—an authentic story of faith and life after loss.
Paperback / 978-1-63409-950-9 / 320 pages / $14.99